I0615385

SATIN & Stone II

BETWEEN A ROCK & A SOFT PLACE

Tequilla'Chanté

SATIN & STONE II

SATIN & STONE II

11Seven Productions LLC
239 Fourth Ave, Ste 1401 #4702
Pittsburgh, PA 15222
11SevenProductions@gmail.com

ISBN 13-digit 979-8-218-67761-9
(Paperback)

Book Cover & Layout by Tequilla'Chante´
(Images AI Generated & Edited/Modified)

SATIN & STONE II

<u>*Dedication*</u>

To my mother *Juanita*, thank you for always supporting my dreams, your many sacrifices and speaking my name in rooms I'm not in.

To my father *Michael*, (May you continue to rest in peace), I chose my release date, May 4th, to honor you! Happy Heavenly Birthday!

To my Grandmother *Clair* thank you for rushing to grab you a book, reading it faster than everyone and giving me your lovely feedback!

To my Aunt *Linda* aka Der! Thank you for your giving and kind heart, may every blessing return ten-fold.

To my Aunt *Rhonda* (I know you're STILL bragging in heaven) thank you for always speaking highly of me and making me feel like I was the BEST to EVER do it!

To my sister *Michelle aka P-Chelle*, thank you for your constant encouragement as well as lending me your eyes and ears this year to affirm my work.

To my brothers *Michael & 'Meat'*, thank you for always showing up and having me back.

To my 'Chante´twin' *Alexis*, thank you for always reminding me to "get on my zoom" and for your willingness to always discuss my future casting plans ('cause it will be a show!)

To my BFF *Ayanna* (more like sister) you've been reading my work since it only available in black & white position books. Thank you for that no matter time or distance your love and support never change!

To my sister-cousin *Takeira*. Thank you for being my sister in Christ and my cackle partner. May continue to H.U.S.H. together til He comes riding on a cloud, shining like the sun!

To *ALL OF MY FAMILY & FRIENDS*, whether your support was big or small, constant or when the Lord laid my name on your heart. I am grateful for the color you add to my life! Thank you! Your support means the world to me. I LOVE YOU!

SATIN & STONE II

Acknowledgement

First & foremost, I must give honor and praise to GOD. It is through him that I was able to create this work. The gift of storytelling and creativity comes solely from GOD, and it is his Grace that has carried me along this journey. This book has been a 12-year labor of love that life has done it's darndest to get in the way of...BUT GOD! Can I get an Amen? Thank you, Jesus!

My unofficial editors and Arc readers: *Ayanna, Takeira & Alexis.* Thank you for reading my work and giving me honest feedback this past year and a half. Having your varied perspectives helped unburden me of my anxieties while writing.

Lastly, as always, I would like to thank *ME*! Thank you to ME for my unwavering YES to God and the use of my Gifts in the earth for his Glory and the uplifting of his people. Thank ME for the push of discipline that was HARD but beyond worth it! Coupling my hopeful passion and vivid imagination with this newfound discipline is a recipe for unsurmountable success! I am able to create even bigger worlds and deeper nuance in my characters because of the brilliant, resilient and fearless mind and spirit God has placed in me. I pray I'm making God and the ME of yesterday and the future proud, because TODAY I am proud of myself! To GOD be the Glory!

Tequilla'Chanté

SATIN & STONE II

Chapter One

"Oh fuuuuck...X!" Maleah moaned in a mix of pleasure and pain. Her eyes were rolled to the back of her head as Xavier stroked slow and deep, while her legs were hoisted over his shoulders.

"Uhn, uhn... move your hand." He whispered in her ear, in a commanding tone.

"Xavier." Maleah gasped as he pressed her legs back, above her head, and went deeper.

"What?" He whispered, falling deeper into a trance as her walls swallowed him.

"It's...ugh, it's too much." She moaned in exasperation.

"Too much?" Xavier leaned forward and stared down at her, her eyes were shut, and bottom lip was quivering. He kissed sweetly from her lips to her neck then her collarbone, "I love you." He whispered in her ear.

Maleah sniffled, "I love you too."

Overwhelmed with emotions she couldn't describe; she noticed his pace slowed to a halt and when she opened her eyes Xavier was staring down at her. The meeting of their gaze, in the dimly lit room, made her even more emotional and the tears began to fall. One after another, running down the sides of her face, they wet the pillow beneath her.

"Why're you crying?" He asked sincerely.

A faint smile crept over her face as more tears fell, "Because...I love you."

"So... happy tears?" He asked.

Maleah shook her head, "Yea...very happy."

Xavier leaned in and kissed her with as much passion as he could muster and she returned his intensity, sliding her fingers over his beard

1

and pulling his face closer. In the heat of their passionate kiss, Xavier threw her legs back over his shoulder and plunged in as deep as he could go.

"Baby..." Maleah moaned, digging her nails into his back.

"Fuck." Xavier swiftly pulled her arms from around him and placed them around her calves, "Hold them for me." He instructed, leaning up and position himself on his knees. He then used his hands to spread her as far as he could and slow stroked, digging into her G-spot with a steady force.

It took less than ten strokes before Maleah's legs were shaking again and her once soft moans became hollers of ecstasy. She released her calves, placing her hands on his stomach, overwhelmed by the orgasm she was experiencing but Xavier caught her legs and held them in place, stroking even faster and with more force against her spot.

"Oh, my fuck...Ughhhh! X! Baby!" She could barely articulate.

"Mhmm...gimme that!" He commanded, never breaking pace.

"Fuuuuck!" Maleah screamed as the orgasm took over her entire body, causing her to convulse. But Xavier kept going, holding her thighs firmly and just as he intended, she started to convulse uncontrollably.

"Baby!" Maleah cried out, panting, and convulsing as more tears fell from her eyes.

Xavier pulled out and leaned his body against hers, planting firm kisses all over her face. He then slid his arms under her and pulled her on top of him. Maleah laid like a quivering rag doll on his chest as he caressed her and her body slowly calmed, and breathing slowed.

"You good? Cause we ain't done." He whispered.

Maleah inhaled then exhaled deeply, "Yes we are."

Xavier slapped her ass, "You're not going to let me get mine?"

"Nope."

He smirked, "That's fucked up. I gave your ass a body shaking orgasm and you're going to leave me hanging?"

Maleah shrugged, never moving from his embrace.

"I feel so loved." He chuckled.

Maleah didn't respond and they laid in silence for a moment before she leaned up and looked at Xavier, who was wearing his signature smirk. She poked him in his dimple and giggled.

"God knows I love you...because I was two seconds from really falling asleep on you."

"After one round?" He smirked.

She slapped his chest, "Don't do that...you know I've been celibate for a while."

"I know...just sayin', that excuse ain't gonna work much longer."

"It's not an excuse, it's the truth. And aside from that, let's not act like your dick is some average sized thing. You try having a hole the size of a quarter stretched that wide and tell me how many rounds you go." She huffed.

"Ay! C'mon, that ain't an image I want in my head. You're really trying to put me on soft."

"No, I'm just being honest. But shit, if you're turned off..." Maleah giggled, moving to climb off of him.

Xavier slapped her ass and pulled her back, "Nice try. My dick gets hard just thinking about you, you really think laying on me, naked, won't keep me bricked up?" He began kissing her breast.

"Mmm...Baby I don't know if I have another round in me."

"Then give me half a round." He spoke between kisses.

Maleah sighed, "It's going to be ragdoll, pillow princess sex. I'm exhausted."

"Nah, I need you to ride it for me."

"Of course, you do."

"C'mon, show me what them Megan knees do." He grinned.

"You are so lucky I love you." Maleah chuckled to herself as she sat up and squatted over his hard member. She took it into her hands and stroked it slowly, causing him to moan.

Xavier was even more turned on at the sight of her naked body crouched over him, legs spread, and her fingers wrapped around his shaft. Maleah released him and turned around to position herself in reverse cowgirl.

"Reverse cowgirl? I was definitely enjoying the show I was getting from the front but it's your world, I'm just living in it." He commentated as he watched her use his legs to stabilize herself, "Mmm..." Xavier grunted as she lowered herself down onto him slowly.

Maleah slowly worked her waist in a figure eight, trying to ease down onto him, shuttering with every inch. Xavier leaned up and reached around her and massaged her clit as he met her rhythm with slow strokes.

"Uhn, uhn, this is about you." Maleah gently moved his hand and pushed him backward then she leaned forward, placing her hands on his legs and began throwing her ass back.

"Mmm, fuck…throw that shit." Xavier grunted with his eyes closed, massaging her ass.

"Mhmm…you're not talkin' shit now, huh?" Maleah moaned seductively as she picked up her pace a little and began to Kegel, flexing her *muscles* open and closed, in sync with every thrust of her hips.

"Mother-fuck! Ugh…" Xavier grunted.

"What were you saying…about…excuses?" Maleah teased, while trying to maintain her focus and not succumb to her own pleasure.

Xavier chuckled to himself maniacally, then swiftly leaned forward and lifted her enough to slide from beneath her.

"Xavier!" She whined.

"What?" He pushed her forward onto her stomach and put her legs together, only spreading her ass and thighs enough to see her pussy and slid back inside her.

"Oh, fuck…" Maleah gasped.

Xavier took her arms and gently pinned them behind her back and began stroking deep and hard in the *'froggy-style'* position. In that position, the g-spot was impossible to miss, and the clutch of her thick thighs being pressed together made her already tight walls a thousand times tighter. To say he was in bliss would be an understatement.

"Oh fuuuuck. Baby please! If I cum again I'm going to pass out." Maleah whined, feeling the orgasm creeping.

Xavier leaned down and slid his arms under hers, grabbing onto her shoulders. He stroked slowly against her G-spot until he felt her walls contract and legs began to shake.

"Fuuuuuck!" Maleah exclaimed as she came hard.

Feeling the wet warmth of her juices drip down his shaft, combined with her walls sucking him in, Xavier grunted and growled like a bear.

"Fuck!" He shouted, overwhelmed by the orgasm, "Shit, girl…"

Maleah panted, trying to catch her breath, "I love you."

"I…I love you too…" Xavier exhaled heavily, resting all his body weight on her.

VRRRRRRBBBB! Xavier's phone vibrated on the bedside table, but he ignored it rolling off of Maleah and pulling her into his arms. They'd both drifted off to sleep at the foot of the bed, cuddled up in each other's arms.

VRRRRRRBBBB! His phone proceeded to vibrate and did so repeatedly for a few minutes and then Maleah's phone started playing *Around the way girl* by *LL Cool j;* Sky's ringtone. Once it stopped it started again immediately after and began to play in sync with the vibration of Xavier's phone.

"What the fuck, man…" He huffed, reluctantly releasing Maleah, and stood up from the bed. Walking over to his side of the bed, he grabbed his phone as it stopped vibrating and Maleah's phone started ringing again.

"Who the hell is calling like that?" Maleah grumbled, leaning up in the bed.

"It's Isaiah. Something must be wrong because he doesn't usually call this late, and definitely not back-to-back." Xavier shared, re-dialing Isaiah.

"But who the hell is calling me?" She crawled toward the top of the bed and snatched her phone off the side table and saw it was Skylar, "Sky? What the hell…" Maleah stared at the phone confused and took it with her into the bathroom.

"Yo! What's up, why're you calling me non-stop? What's wrong?" Xavier asked, stepping into a pair of sweatpants, "Ok, but why're you calling *me* though?" He quizzed, putting the phone on speaker, and tossing it onto the bed.

"Because he's your brother and he need you. This nigga is up in here losing it, threatening the nurses and CNA's!" Isaiah's voice bellowed through the phone.

"Again, why're you calling me? He's a grown ass man. What the fuck am I supposed to do about him throwing a tantrum?" Xavier shrugged.

"X… come on man. I know y'all had some stuff between y'all, he told me bits and pieces, but it can't be so bad that you'd desert your brother when he needs you." Isaiah reasoned.

"Yo, Zay don't hit me with that bullshit! I ain't desert that nigga. He chose his loyalty to that grimy ass broad, so now I just remain cordial because we have a business to run. All that brother shit is dead, and he's the one that killed it."

"C'mon X…"

"Nah, fuck all that *'my brother's keeper'* shit. The nigga made his choice, so stop trying to save him from the consequences."

"Aye X, you on your period, nigga? Cause you're sounding like a real bitch right now!" Chris shouted into the phone.

"Nigga you got me on speaker phone?" Xavier huffed.

"No…you're on the car phone. Me and Chris are sitting outside the hospital." Isaiah explained.

"Man, whatever and fuck you Chris, I ain't no bitch. I just don't understand why y'all are calling me. Y'all are there… y'all are his brothers. Go help him." Xavier shrugged.

"Whatever nigga, stay couped up in your little love nest with bae and paint your fuckin' nails. But remember, this the same nigga who's literally risked his life for you on several occasions. Without hesitation." Chris spat.

Xavier sucked his teeth and sighed heavily, snatching the phone off the bed as he sat down, "Text me which fuckin' hospital it is." He huffed.

"Alright." Isaiah interjected.

Xavier hung up the phone and looked up to see Maleah standing in the doorway of the bathroom in a pink satin robe, looking concerned.

"So, was it an emergency?" She inquired.

"Uh, nah…not exactly. Why was your girl calling?"

"I don't know, I called back a few times but no answer. Called Lisa too but she didn't answer either…but I guess that makes sense, since it's almost 2AM. When I checked Sky's location, it showed it was last updated an hour ago, like she's somewhere without service or her phone is off." Maleah rambled.

"I'm sure she's okay." Xavier attempted to assure her but was too annoyed with his own issues to be his usual encouraging self.

"I don't know…I think I should go by her house."

"At 2AM? You don't need to be out in the streets this late." He rebutted.

"I can't just go to sleep, thinking something's happened to her." She felt herself growing anxious expecting the worst as she walked into her closet and pulled on a sports bra and the matching underwear then a pair of sweatpants.

"I'm not about to let you go out here searching the streets for your friend at 2AM." Xavier walked over to her and stood directly in front of her as she zipped her hoodie.

"I'm not asking you." She retorted, moving to step around him.

He caught her by the arm, and they stared at each other for a moment. Reading the offense on his face she sighed and turned around to fully face him.

"Look, I didn't mean that how it came out. I know you're just trying to protect me, and I love you for that, but Sky is my sister, and she would do the same for me." Maleah caressed his arm sincerely.

"Alright…how about this. I'll take you to go by her house and if she's not there we can check wherever you like, I just need to make a quick stop while we're out." Xavier bargained.

"A quick stop? At 2AM?" She twisted her lips and arched her eyebrow.

He sighed, "Yea…I just need to check on Khalil really quick. I'll be in and out."

"Check on him? Where? And why? Is he okay?" Maleah quizzed.

"He's fine, I just need to stop by the…the hospital." Xavier reluctantly divulged.

"If he's okay then why's he in the hospital?"

"I…I don't know. That's what I'm going to find out."

Maleah looked him over, searching for answers because his words were not matching his energy. He was hiding something and once she sorted things out regarding Sky, she'd press the matter further.

"Hmm…okay. Well, let's get out of here so we can check on both of our friends."

∞◌◌◌∞

It was unusually quiet on the wing of the ICU floor that was cynically nicknamed *"The farm"*; a reference to its inhabitants being unresponsive "vegetables" and a few comatose patients on ventilators.

The nurse at the station sat hunched over, half asleep as the clock above her head shifted from 1:59AM to 2:00AM.

"Hey, girl. You good?"

The nurse at the station was startled awake, "Oh, hey. Yea, I'm good. These damn doubles are wearing me thin. But my grandkids tuition isn't going to pay itself nor will their mother." She rambled.

"If you want to go grab a coffee and take a break, you can. When you get back, I'll do my patient check-ins." The other woman giggled.

"Yea…I think I'll do that. Thanks." The nurse got up from the station and stretched, "What's your name again? I'm sorry, we get so many travel nurses I forget names."

"Candice. But you can call me Candy."

"That'll be easy to remember. I love me some candy if you couldn't tell." The nurse pinched at her belly fat, "I'm Dorinda."

The two women shook hands and shared a laugh as they switched spots, Candy sitting behind the desk and Dorinda making her way down the hall.

"Alright…now let's see what room you're in." Candy typed away on the computer, "There you are, girlfriend." She smiled maniacally beneath her N95 mask.

She checked her surroundings and quickly made her way down the hall, making note of the camera's and doing her best not to look suspicious in case security was monitoring. When she arrived at the room she was looking for, she made her way inside and noticed a man sleeping in a chair beside the patient. She moved swiftly making sure to avoid making any noise and pulled a syringe out of the front pocket of her scrubs. As she positioned the syringe to puncture the IV the woman's eyes shot open.

The woman stared her directly in the eyes, it was like she was staring into her soul. She quickly inserted the syringe and pushed the clear fluid into the woman's IV and rushed out of the room. As she made her way down the hall toward the elevators, she heard the monitors beeping at the nurses' station. She quickly slipped behind the desk, hitting the mute button for the vitals monitor and then proceeded to the elevator.

Just as the elevator doors opened, she could hear a man yelling down the hall, "Nurse! Nurse! Help! She's awake but something's wrong!"

When she exited the elevator, she quickly made her way out the front entrance, toward a blacked-out Chevy Tahoe.

"Damn, Chi! What the fuck took you so long?" Mook fussed, pulling out the hospital parking lot.

China snatched off the N95 mask and scrub cap she wore, followed by the braided wig she was wearing, "Shut up nigga! You can't rush skill."

Mook sucked his teeth, "You ain't got no fuckin' skills. All you do is play dress up and scam niggas."

China stopped in the middle of undressing, wearing only scrub pants and a pink lace bra, "It really eats you up inside that I won't let you fuck me, huh?"

"Man, go 'head with that bullshit." Mook waved her off.

China chuckled as she changed into a pair of grey sweatpants and pulled on the matching hoodie, "Aw Mookie Bookie...I only fuck the niggas giving orders, not the niggas taking them."

Mook chose to ignore her taunting, driving in silence as she stuffed her feet in a pair of Nikes and unraveled the two braids her hair was in. She fluffed out her hair and finger combed it into a low bun, throwing on a red New York baseball cap.

"Where am I dropping you?" Mook huffed.

"Now Mookie, we both know, you know where." China grinned.

He shook his head and proceeded to drive in silence as she gathered the scrubs and medical paraphernalia into a hazardous materials bag.

"You'll put this in the incinerator for me, won't you?" China grinned like a mischievous child as Mook pulled in front of a Luxury high rise.

"Yea, whatever nigga. Get out."

"Thanks Mookie, love ya'!" She grabbed his face and planted a kiss on his right temple.

"Come on man, go 'head!"

"Later!" China winked, giggling her way from the truck into the lobby of the apartment complex.

SATIN & STONE II

∞∞∞∞

Monique Moore pushed through the side door of 'Lou's Bar & Billiards', capturing the attention of several of the patrons, men and women alike. Lou's was a local speak-easy and unofficial after-hour spot that she'd occasionally grace with her presence. Although it wasn't her favorite place to patronize, it was close to home, drinks were cheap and every now and then she liked to do her late-night drinking in a social setting. Not to mention the self-esteem boost she got from flaunting her age defying beauty and well-maintained figure, after four children.

Slowly, she sauntered toward the bar, dressed in all black, wearing her favorite knee-length mink coat, ass-hugging leather pants and off-the-shoulder top. Stepping up to the bar top, she nodded at the barmaid, who was serving a portly looking, older gentleman. The woman, who looked to be in her late 40's, waved back as she poured bottom shelf gin into a plastic cup.

Monique smirked as she glanced around at the sea of "well-seasoned" people, proud of the fact that though she was only a few years shy of 50, she didn't look a day over 35.

"Hey, Mo! I ain't seen you in a hot minute. I thought you said Lou couldn't get another dime out of you?" Theresa the bartender smiled, flashing a gold side tooth that matched her long gold acrylic nails, which curved in true 90's fashion. And as if her nails weren't enough of a time capsule, her finger wave mullet and multiple gold finger rings were a dead giveaway that she was definitely stuck in yester-year.

"Don't start your shit, T! Here, put my coat back there with yours." Monique took off her fur coat and passed it across the bar to Theresa, "Let me get an amoretto sour and put it on Lou's tab…baldhead bastard." She quipped, turning her back to the bar and scanning the room once more.

"Here you go." Theresa slid her drink across the bar.

Monique grabbed the glass and proceeded to people-watch as she sipped.

"Girl, I don't know why you're scanning the room, ain't nothing in here but empty pockets, bald spots, fake chains, and spray on hairlines. Half of them will be sippin' the same beer all night."

10

Monique burst out laughing so loud she caught the attention of a fat, bald man wearing a too small Pelle-Pelle Jacket that'd definitely seen it's best days in the 80's. He smiled a gap-toothed smile at Monique causing her to spit out her drink as she doubled over, laughing harder. She spun around to face the bar and when she locked eyes with Theresa the two women cackled uncontrollably. The man was so embarrassed he quickly squeezed his way through the crowd and left through the side door.

"Aw damn! Look what you done did! Made my best tipper leave...now what am I supposed to do without that dollar-fifty tip?" Theresa teased, causing them both to laugh harder.

"Theresa!" The owner of '*Lou's Bar & Billiards*' walked up behind Monique, causing her to cease laughing and roll her eyes.

"What you need, Lou?" Theresa tried to stifle her laugh.

"If you're done cackling, can you do your job and make my partner a drink?" Lou sneered.

Theresa sucked her teeth and rolled her eyes, "What does he want?"

"I'll take a double shot of Uncle Nearest, neat." A tall, handsome man who looked to be in his 50's stepped from behind Lou, toward the bar. The smell of his cologne caught Monique's attention, so she turned around and was met by the surprise of a familiar face.

"Paul?" Monique tilted her head to get a better look.

"MoMo...damn...it's been a minute." Paul looked her over, absolutely mesmerized by how she hadn't aged a bit since he'd last seen her. And the weight she gained around her hips made her even more appealing to him.

"Here you go." Theresa flashed her gold adorned smile, holding out his drink.

"Thank you." Paul took the drink and returned his attention to Monique.

"Y'all know each other?" Lou interjected.

"Yea...MoMo was my first love. But she chose her movie star dreams over me and skipped town for LA. Broke my heart." Paul explained, never breaking eye contact with Monique.

"Don't revise history, you know I asked you to come." She rebutted.

"And you know I couldn't leave my sickly mother."

"Ay, let me show you the rest of the place, I just upgraded the kitchen." Lou interrupted their stare down.

"Nigga can't you see we're talking? Scram! Go fry some chicken or something." Monique waved him off.

"Who the fuck are you talking to? You're lucky my regular security ain't here tonight or your trifling ass would've been thrown out, the second I saw you!" Lou bucked.

"Nigga, you and that snaggle-tooth mothafucka can kiss my ass. I go wherever I want!" Monique poked him in the forehead with her red stiletto nail.

Lou swatted her hand away, "Bitch, I'll break that finger. Keep playing with me!"

"Try it!" Monique taunted.

"Ay, chill out!" Paul interjected, sticking his arm between Lou and Monique.

"Naw, fuck that! I'm tired of her coming in here, testing me like I'm some sucka."

"This ain't how you handle shit with no woman!" Paul shouted.

"Maybe not a woman, but definitely this bitch!" Lou barked, pointing his finger in Monique's face.

Before she could even react, Paul yoked Lou up by his collar and slammed him against the bar, bumping an older man from his stool.

"Apologize." Paul demanded.

"Get your fuckin' hands off me!" Lou struggled to free himself from Paul's grip.

"Not until you calm down and apologize to her."

"Fuck no!" Lou continued trying to get free but had no success, so he felt around on the bar top until he grabbed a beer bottle.

Noticing out of the corner of his eye, Paul's entire demeanor shifted, "Nigga, don't be stupid. You know who the fuck I am...I've put niggas down for less."

Lou released the bottle and put his hands up in a surrender.

Paul yanked him to his feet, "Now apologize!"

"Man fuck that and fuck her."

Monique hauled back and slapped the shit out of Lou, turning the entire left side of his face red.

"I'm sick of you disrespecting me, nigga! All because I won't suck that soggy ass, cocktail frank you call a dick!" She shouted.

Lou lunged toward her, but Paul snatched him back, putting him into a headlock.

"Let me...go" Lou coughed, struggling to breathe.

"Nigga, you must've lost your fuckin' mind!" Paul tightened his arm around his throat, causing Lou to tap rapidly on his forearm.

"I can't...br-breathe!" He struggled to speak.

"Apologize! Now, nigga!"

Lou coughed, "Oh-kay!"

Paul released his grip, pushing him forward and Lou stumbled into the high-top tables across from them, which were vacant due to their altercation.

"Now, nigga! Or you and me are going to have a real problem." Paul gritted.

Lou struggled to catch his breath, "I...I'm sorry." He huffed reluctantly.

"Whatever." Monique rolled her eyes, "T, hand me my coat."

"Here you go girl." Theresa passed it over the bar, laughing to herself at the sight of Lou getting his ass handed to him.

"Wait, don't leave before giving me your number." Paul grabbed Monique's arm.

"I'll meet you at the door..." She looked over at Lou, "You're lucky my son's still upstate."

Monique tied the belt to her black fur coat and tucked her purse under her arm, then walked toward the exit.

"Whatever...ain't nobody scared of her son." Lou retorted, barely believing himself.

"Yes, you are..." Theresa muttered under her breath.

"Get the fuck back to work and mind your business before I fire your country ass." Lou threatened.

"And replace me with who? Who else gonna serve these broke, non-tipping niggas watered down liquor? Hell, I'm only here cause we're family."

"No, you're here because you can't work nowhere else looking like a broke down, Sheneneh reject!" Lou quipped.

"Ay nigga, did you learn nothing?" Paul interjected.

13

"Man, fuck this shit…you know what. I resend my offer; the deal is off. You and me ain't got no business." Lou huffed.

Paul walked up close on Lou, "Nigga, last I checked the money I gave you, to help save this shit hole, was cashed at the bank and judging by the renovations and that gaudy ass chain around your fuckin' neck, the money's been spent."

"Fuck it, I'll return this shit and have your money first thing Monday morning."

Paul whispered through gritted teeth, "Don't make me park your ass next to Ms. Ethel over at Evergreen cemetery. Cause I'll gladly go from partner to full owner."

Lou looked Paul in his eyes and saw no trace of bluffing and to add to his terror he felt the pressure of something cold and metal in his side.

"Alright…alright man. But she ain't allowed in here anymore." Lou stammered.

"Says who?" Paul smirked.

Lou huffed and sucked his teeth, "Man fuck this shit…" He stormed toward the kitchen.

"You coming?" Monique shouted over the music.

Paul nodded and made his way toward her.

Chapter Two

Xavier pulled into the visitor's parking lot of the hospital and found a parking space not too far from the front entrance. Once he put the car in park, he closed his eyes and took a deep breath.

"Alright, I'll be right back. I shouldn't be more than 10 minutes." He informed Maleah, who was dialing Sky's number for the 50th time.

"Shit, it's still going straight to voicemail."

"Babe."

"Huh? My bad…that's fine. Go handle your business."

Xavier stared at her concerned, as she frantically swiped through her phone opening the location sharing app.

"What the fuck?" Maleah blurted.

"What? What happened?"

"Her location just came back up…"

"Where does it say she is?" Xavier leaned over to see her phone.

"It says…it says she's here."

"Here? At the hospital?"

"Yes…what the hell. I knew something happened. Oh my god, I need to call Lisa." Maleah started to grow more anxious.

Xavier placed his hand on her phone, "Hey, look at me…Maleah."

She sighed and turned to face him.

"Let's go in and check things out before calling and alarming people…we don't know for sure something's happened." He suggested.

"Something's clearly happened. She was blowing up my phone and after a 2AM manhunt, her location shows up at the hospital! Something is wrong."

"Calling Lisa now, versus in a few minutes won't make a difference if something has happened. But if she's okay and you call Lisa now, you will have worked her up for nothing." Xavier reasoned.

Maleah sighed heavily, "Fine…let's go."

"Ay!" He scolded, as she started opening her door.

She released the handle and threw her hands up, "My bad, I forgot."

Xavier shut off the engine and got out, walking around to her side of the car, and helping her out.

"You don't get tired of the whole chivalry thing?" Maleah asked as they walked hand in hand toward the hospital entrance.

"No. Because it's not a thing. It's how I was raised, so it's a part of me." Xavier shared.

"Took you long enough nigga!" Chris shouted from behind them.

"Nigga, I wasn't rushing." Xavier quipped.

"Yea, whatever." Chris shook his head, as they all walked through the entrance and up to the security desk where a young, brownskin girl sat watching a movie on her phone.

"Hey, Tracey. They're with me." Chris informed the security woman.

"Okay." Tracey blushed, handing visitor badges to Xavier and Maleah. Chris had obviously been working his charm on the young woman.

"Actually, I'm looking for Skylar Michaels. I haven't been able to reach her, but her phone's location shows she's here." Maleah interjected.

"Uh…let me check." Tracey searched records on her computer, "I don't have anyone by that name in my system."

"Can you try just typing Sky?" Maleah pressed.

"I actually did, and nothing came up…I have patients with similar last name but not that first name." Tracey explained.

"Maybe she's here because of her mom or dad…do you have a Yolanda or Dan Michaels?" Maleah asked.

Tracey typed away and checked her records, "I do have a Daniel, but I doubt this is who you're looking for."

"Why? What does it say?" Maleah asked growing impatient.

"He's a newborn."

16

Maleah huffed, "Okay…try these last three: Penelope Shields, Tyra Michaels, and if not them, try Jared Parks."

"What's going on?" Chris whispered to Xavier.

"Man…something going on with one of her homegirls. I'll explain later." He explained.

"I don't have any of them showing up in the system." Tracey sighed.

"Okay, okay…last one. Try Lisa Martinez-Shaw, please."

Tracey typed away then pressed enter, after a moment she sighed letting Maleah know it was another unfruitful search.

"I'm sorry ma'am, but none of the names you gave me are in the system. You think maybe somebody stole her phone?" Tracey shrugged, looking from a distressed Maleah to Chris and Xavier.

"Thank you so much for checking." Xavier walked up, sliding his hand around Maleah's waist.

"No problem." Tracey smiled.

"Come on, baby. You can ask around at the nurse's station. Maybe they saw her." Xavier suggested.

Maleah nodded, refreshing Sky's location on her phone. It showed active and reporting in the hospital. Chris led the way as they followed him to the elevators.

∞∞∞∞

Room 720 was at the farthest end of the hospital hallway and that section of the floor was empty, except for Isaiah, who sat in the hallway in one of the two chairs facing the room. He was leaned over, elbows resting on his knees, in deep prayer when a nurse came out of the room and Khalil came storming out shortly after.

"Yo, I can't do this shit." Khalil gritted, leaning against the window ledge beside Isaiah, staring out at the dark sky in frustration.

"Amen." Isaiah ended his prayer and sighed, "What's going on man? She alright?"

"Yea man, she's fine…for now." Khalil sighed.

"What about the baby?"

"You know, she knew she was pregnant? For over a month, she's known and ain't say shit!" Khalil gritted.

17

"Damn…"

"After that shit went down with her homegirl, she started taking on more work, to distract herself and I ain't say shit because I knew she was hurting and I ain't know how to help her… the nurse said all the stress almost caused her to lose the baby." Khalil rambled.

"Ay, man, it's not on you. You didn't know." Isaiah reassured.

"You're fuckin' right! Cause had I known, I would've sat her stubborn ass down!" Khalil barked, "She really almost lost my fuckin' kid?"

"I get it, bro…finding out you're about to be a father can be scary enough on its own and you found out through some less-than-ideal circumstances. But GOD has them both in his hands, you've just got to pray and trust him." Isaiah encouraged.

"Hey man, no disrespect but you can save all that GOD shit for that lil' men's menstruation ministry you run." Khalil sneered.

"How're you gonna say 'no disrespect' then proceed to be disrespectful?" Isaiah shook his head.

"Nigga, you're the one who's always pushing that religion shit even though I've made it super clear that I ain't interested." Khalil rebutted.

Isaiah shook his head in disbelief and leaned forward again, clasping his hands and began to silently pray.

"Ask that nigga for a couple tax free millions, for me, while you're at it." Khalil teased.

"Yo, I know you're going through it right now, but you really need to chill." Isaiah sighed.

"Nigga shut your sensitive ass up! Are you the one who's girl and baby could've died?" Khalil rebutted.

Before Isaiah could respond, his phone started to ring.

"Hello?" He answered with a sigh, losing patience for Khalil's rageful projections, "Yea, we're still here…okay."

"Who that?" Khalil quizzed.

"My wife…she's just checking in." Isaiah responded, hanging up the phone and placing it back into the side pocket of his cargo pants.

Khalil turned around and stared exhaustedly at the closed door of the hospital room, "Let me get back in there and check on her."

As soon as Khalil entered the room, Chris came walking down the hallway followed by Xavier and a woman Isaiah recognized from pictures he'd seen on social media.

"He still trippin?" Chris asked, as they walked up.

Isaiah exhaled deeply, "Trippin is an understatement."

"You know that angry, yellow nigga can't help himself." Chris smirked.

Isaiah stood up and reached out to dap Xavier up. The men shook hands and gave a brief embrace.

"Nice to meet you." Isaiah extended his hand to Maleah who was so caught up on her phone that she didn't notice.

Xavier grabbed her hand, "Leah."

"Huh? I'm sorry, what's up?" She looked up at him.

"This is my homie Isaiah, I told you about." Xavier introduced them, "Zay, this is Maleah."

Isaiah reached out his hand again and this time she shook it, giving a forced smile.

"Nice to meet you…babe, I think the nurse's station was down that other hall. I'm going to go check and see if they can help me." Maleah informed.

Xavier, still holding her hand, pulled her into a kiss and then release her, "Breathe." He instructed.

"Okay…" She exhaled heavily, "I'll be back."

"Alright. I'll be right here." He assured.

Maleah made her way back down the hall and turned left down the side hallway toward the nurse's station and Xavier stood frozen staring toward the hospital room.

"Don't get scared now, nigga." Chris teased.

"Ain't nobody scared."

"Yea, whatever." Chris laughed, "Look, I've got to go make a few calls. Zay don't let them two niggas tare up these white people's hospital."

Chris pulled out his phone and proceeded to dial someone as he made his way down the hall and around the corner. Isaiah returned to his seat and Xavier sat down in the chair beside him.

"How've you been man?" Isaiah inquired.

"I'm good man…can't complain." Xavier leaned back in his chair, dreading the inevitable confrontation.

"That's good…you should bring your girl by the house. Keira and I would love to have y'all over for dinner. And the boys miss their uncle X."

"Damn man, how old are they now? Seven or eight?"

"Eight, about to be Nine in a couple of weeks. We're giving them a gaming party at the house if you've got time to stop by." Isaiah informed.

"Absolutely, send me the details. Damn…nine years old? Where the hell has the time gone? In a minute they'll be old enough to babysit my kids…whenever I finally have some."

Isaiah chuckled, "I don't know bro…looks to me like it won't be too long. Your attentiveness with her…I think that's your wife, man."

Xavier smiled, looking down the hall toward where Maleah disappeared, "She is."

"Hot damn! I knew it. Man, I'm so happy for you. You've been waiting for this for so long!" Isaiah giddily shook Xavier by the shoulders. And the two men laughed heartily with joy.

"Thanks man, I appreciate it. You're actually the first person I told." Xavier admitted.

"Aw man… I'm honored." Isaiah smiled sincerely, placing his hand over his heart.

Xavier laughed, "Alright nigga, don't go getting all emotional on me."

Isaiah sucked his teeth, "Now you sound like Khalil."

The mention of his name shifted Xavier's mood and brought him back to the reality of why he was there.

"So, what the fuck is going on with him?" Xavier quizzed.

"Apparently, his girl woke up in the middle of the night and realized she'd been bleeding vaginally." Isaiah informed.

"Oh shit…but she's okay, right?" Xavier asked.

"Yea…she's okay but the baby almost didn't make it."

"Baby? I ain't know she was pregnant."

"Neither did Khalil, apparently…and to make matters worse she's known for over a month and hadn't told him." Isaiah shared.

"Damn…no wonder he's pissed. Did the doctors say what caused the bleeding?"

20

"Yea...they said it was caused by emotional and physical stress...Khalil said she'd been taking on more work at her job to distract herself from the fallout between her and your girl."

Xavier sighed, unable to find a suitable response. On one hand, he still felt Korena was foul for what she did, but on the other hand he didn't feel she nor Khalil deserved to possibly lose a child because of it. He knew first-hand the pain of having the promise of fatherhood snatched away.

"He's been lashing out on everyone in his path since they got here. Threatening to put his hands on people." Isaiah sighed, "I know it's just his fear disguised as anger, but he's got to chill."

Xavier shrugged, "That's his go-to...he's been that way since we were kids."

"I get it...I know growing up in group homes taught him the only way to protect himself is by fighting, but he's got to talk to someone. This ain't healthy."

"Yea...that shit with his mom left him with some serious trust issues. But unfortunately, the chances of him talking to a therapist are slim to none." Xavier added.

"You're right, but I'm going to keep praying on it...it still trips me out to think of what he survived. Who leaves a two-year-old in an abandoned house?" Isaiah sighed.

"A Junkie." Xavier shook his head.

"Life for him definitely ain't been no 'crystal stair'...and that's why he needs us now more than ever. The thought of losing their baby has definitely triggered some deep, unresolved trauma." Isaiah sighed.

"I know..." Xavier leaned back and closed his eyes, rubbing his hands over his face.

"Hey, have you seen the nurse?" A woman's voice whispered.

"Uh, not since she left out the room almost an hour ago." Isaiah responded.

Xavier sat up and was shocked to see who Isaiah was talking to.

"Sky!" Maleah's voice echoed down the empty hall as she power-walked toward them, "What the hell Skylar! I've been looking everywhere for you. You had me stressed the fuck out! You called my phone a million times and then don't answer when I call back. I thought something happened to you!"

"I'm fine. Breathe." Sky rubbed her shoulder.

"What the hell is going on with your phone? It started going straight to voicemail and your location wouldn't show. I called Lisa and drove by your place. Shit, I started to call your mother!" Maleah rambled.

"Well thank GOD you didn't do that; Lord knows I don't need Yolanda getting worked up over nothing."

Maleah sighed, "So, you're, okay?"

"Yes. I'm fine. My phone died while I was trying to get ahold of you and when Jared dropped me off, I forgot to grab my charger. One of the nurses agreed to let me use her charger but I had to leave my phone at the nurse's station, and I haven't been over there to check it. I honestly started to call you from Korena's phone, but I figured you might have her number blocked."

"I just came from the nurse's station, and no one said anything about a phone ringing, and I've been calling non-stop since I saw your location showed up here." Maleah rebutted.

Sky sighed, "Oh shoot, you know what…it's probably on 'Do Not Disturb'. It turns on automatically after 11pm."

"Wait, did you say Korena?" Maleah took a step back.

"Yea…she's in the room. She's okay though."

"That's why you were calling me?"

"Well…yea, I mean I know things got ugly, but the two of you were the closest out of the four of us, so I thought you'd want to know."

"If she's okay, then I don't need to be here."

"What the fuck are you doing here?" Khalil sneered, stepping out of the hospital room, behind Sky.

"Aye nigga, you better calm that shit down!" Xavier barked walking toward them.

Khalil stepped back with a look of shock. Caught off guard by Xavier, he postured like a cornered animal, prepared to fight, "I know ain't nobody responsible for this pussy ass kumbaya shit but you!" He pointed his finger in Isaiah's face.

"Yo, get your hand out my face." Isaiah stood up.

"Oh, so you're tough now?" Khalil chuckled maniacally, stepping closer to Isaiah.

"Ay, ay! What the fuck is going on? I thought I told you to keep these niggas from fighting." Chris shouted, walking up the hall.

"You knew about this shit?" Khalil questioned.

"Yup. What, you're mad? What else is new?" Chris shrugged.

"You, this soft ass nigga and them two mothafuckas can go. I don't need y'all here." Khalil gritted.

"Yes, you do nigga. You're spiraling and someone needs to talk some sense into you." Chris rebutted.

"I don't want to hear shit none of y'all got to say at this point, especially not either of these two pussy niggas." Khalil pointed his finger in Isaiah's face again.

"Yo, Khalil...I'm not going to tell you again." Isaiah sighed hard.

"And what the fuck are you going to do? Huh? You've been bitch-made since high school. Or did you forget it was me keeping niggas from robbing and beating your ass every day?" Khalil laughed cynically.

"Yo, chill out." Chris interjected.

"Nigga, we ain't kids no more." Isaiah spoke stoically.

"You put on some weight and some muscles now I'm supposed to be scared? Nigga I'll still beat yo ass."

Chris moved in between the two men and Xavier scooted Maleah behind him, away from the potential fight.

"Don't worry, I ain't gonna put my hands on this nigga. Last thing I need is his prissy bitch sending the law my way for beating his ass." Khalil taunted.

WHAM! The sound of Isaiah's fist slamming into Khalil's jaw was the prelude to an all-out brawl. Chris managed to slip from in between them as the two men threw blows and tussled, falling through the doorway, into Korena's hospital room.

"Oh my GOD! What the fuck is going on!" Korena screamed.

"Chill the fuck out!" Chris shouted as he attempted to pull the men apart but was having no luck.

Sky rushed in trying to keep Korena from getting out of bed.

"Get the fuck off of him!" Korena shouted hysterically.

"Korena, please! You're going to disconnect your IV." Sky pleaded.

"Nigga grab him!" Chris shouted at Xavier.

Xavier moved to grab Isaiah and the sight of him caused Khalil to become even more enraged. Khalil lifted his foot and kicked Isaiah in the stomach causing him and Xavier to fall backward into a chair on the other side of the room.

"Khalil! Chill the fuck out!" Chris shouted, trying to hold him back.

"Khalil stop, please!" Korena cried out.

"Get the fuck off of me!" Khalil barked.

Chris used all his force and swung Khalil around then skillfully put him in a full-nelson hold.

"Calm down nigga!" Chris shouted.

Korena cried in Sky's arms as Isaiah slouched in the hospital chair beside her bed, trying to catch his breath. Xavier stood shaking his head in pity, watching Khalil continue to struggle in pain to get free from Chris's hold.

"Fuck y'all niggas." Khalil gritted.

Isaiah stood up and slowly walked toward the door.

"Bitch nigga, I should put a bullet in you." Khalil sneered.

"I still love you, bro…GOD does too." Isaiah spoke over his shoulder, shaking his head as he left the room.

Chris waited a moment more before releasing Khalil. Angrily rubbing his shoulder, Khalil turned to charge out the room, but Chris stepped in the doorway.

"Move nigga." Khalil gritted.

The two men were locked in an icy stare down. Jaws flexing and shoulders stiffened.

"You really wanna do this…with me? Cause we both know I ain't Zay." Chris spoke calmly.

"Khalil…please." Korena pleaded exhaustedly.

He closed his eyes and sighed deeply then turned to face Xavier, "What the fuck you still doin' here?"

"Say less." Xavier responded coldly, walking past him into the hallway.

Maleah walked up, concern all over her face and locked eyes with Korena but neither of them said anything. She quickly diverted her attention to Xavier.

"Are you okay?" She asked.

"Yea, I'm good. Let's go."

"Ay, X don't leave…I'm serious. And tell Zay's ass not to leave either. I'll meet y'all niggas out front." Chris instructed.

"Alright man, I'll be in the lobby." Xavier responded reluctantly. He grabbed Maleah's hand and led her away from the room.

"Leah!" Korena shouted weakly.

Maleah stopped in her tracks but didn't respond.

"You good?" Xavier asked, squeezing her hand gently.

Maleah nodded *'Yes'*, eyes fixed forward.

"Leah, please!" Korena pleaded.

"Stop stressing yourself out about that girl before you lose my fuckin' baby!" Khalil barked.

"She's pregnant?" She looked up at Xavier for confirmation. In all the commotion, she hadn't even thought to ask why Korena was in the hospital.

"Yea…" He nodded.

Maleah stared blankly in thought, trying to process the new piece of information.

"You want to go talk to her?" Xavier asked.

She looked up at him as if she was searching for the right response.

He pulled her close and rubbed her chin, "Baby, it's okay to still care. Go talk. Bare minimum, you'll get some closure."

Maleah took a deep breath, "Okay…"

"I'll be downstairs." He leaned in and kissed her.

"Okay."

Maleah slowly walked back into the room and Xavier headed down the hall, through the exit doors to the elevator.

∞◇◇∞

Xavier stood in the vestibule between the automatic doors of the main entrance. It was too cold to stand outside but he couldn't sit in the lobby and listen to Tracey the security guard cackle for another second. He stepped directly under the vent blowing heat and checked the time on his phone. It was almost 3AM.

"You'd better not have left, nigga." Chris smirked, walking through the automatic doors followed by Khalil and as soon as they stepped outside, Isaiah pulled up in Chris' blacked out Tahoe truck.

"Get in." Chris instructed.

"Get in?" Xavier quizzed.

"Yes! Both y'all niggas, get in the truck." Chris barked.

Xavier shook his head and obliged, too tired to fight. He went around to the driver side and got in the backseat. Khalil reluctantly followed suit and climbed in the backseat on the passenger side.

"Where're we going?" Isaiah asked.

"Just make a left out the lot and drive." Chris instructed.

Isaiah put the truck in drive and followed Chris' instructions.

"On some real shit, I don't have time for this. My woman is up there sick, and I don't feel right leaving her alone with his girl." Khalil added.

"Nigga, you weren't concerned about her wellbeing when y'all were tearing up her fuckin room, scrappin' like two niggas on the prison yard. Had all of them fuckin monitors beeping and shit. Y'all are lucky nobody called security." Chris ranted.

"Alright nigga. You made your point." Khalil huffed.

"Nah, I ain't made my point yet. But I'm about to." Chris turned around in the passenger seat to face him and Xavier, "What the fuck is going on with y'all niggas? Huh? Y'all two grew up like brothers and yet y'all treating each other like the Ops."

"Man, I ain't the one who started this shit; questioning niggas loyalty over some bullshit!" Khalil spat.

"I wouldn't exactly call that grimy shit your girl pulled, 'bullshit'." Xavier rebutted.

"Nigga fuck you, that shit was over a decade ago and had nothing to do with us. Why the fuck would I tell you some shit that doesn't affect either of us? What, you gossip now, nigga?" Khalil sneered.

"Nigga ain't nobody talking about gossip. I'm talking about keeping me in the loop, especially when shit involves my woman, which does affect me!"

"What? Nigga, she wasn't even your woman at the time! I had no reason to tell you shit."

"Man whatever, I don't have time for this shit. Just drop me back at my car." Xavier huffed.

"Not til we squash this shit." Chris spoke sternly, "From what I'm hearing it sounds like you two niggas fell in some cat and came up smelling and acting like a bunch of pussy."

"I ain't pussy." Khalil rebutted.

"Nigga, bullshit! You're over here beefing with your brother over a woman, aka Pussy! This is a big reason why I don't do that domestic shit. You and I used to be on the same page with this shit, but I knew one day you'd fall in the trap...cause unlike you, I chose to avoid commitment for logical and practical reasons: I like fast money and women and children are liabilities. But you on the other hand, only avoided love because you were afraid of it."

"Man, I ain't scared of shit." Khalil interjected.

"You can save all that tough shit, Kha. You ain't talkin' to your Ops. We're your brothers and that nigga right there knows you better than any of us..." Chris pointed to Xavier.

"Y'all don't know shit." Khalil spat, staring out the window.

"Really nigga? So, your fucked up childhood ain't got you scared of love and now that you're in it, you don't know what the fuck to do with your emotions?" Chris interrogated.

Khalil ignored his inquisition, keeping his gaze fixed out the window.

"Ignore me all you want but you know it's the truth. Almost losing your girl and y'all baby shook you and got you acting like a fuckin' dirtbag toward the only mothafuckas who care about you."

"So, you're just gonna air all my shit out and not say nothing to this nigga?" Khalil retorted.

"I'll get to him, but you really need to deal with your shit. The issue between them women, from what I've learned, is fucked up but it should've never come between y'all." Chris scolded.

"Tell that to this nigga..." Khalil huffed.

"I'm talking to both of y'all..." Chris turned toward Xavier, "Honestly, I ain't even shocked cause you and this nigga Zay been *'captain save a hoe'* since high school. Always taking on the problems of your woman. Beefing with niggas, they ended up leaving you for. Just dumb!"

Xavier sucked his teeth, "That's a stretch."

"No, it ain't, it's the fuckin' truth. That's the other reason I can't do commitment. Them emotionally unstable creatures will have you on dummy missions. Mad one day then forget why the next…X, you need to stay out of that shit. As long as she's safe, let them women work their shit out. You hear me, man?"

Xavier sighed, "Yea, alright…"

"I'm serious… you are your brother's keeper. Shit, like Kha used to say: '*Right or Wrong, I'm riding*'. If we don't have each other's backs in this grimy ass world, who we got?"

Chris turned back around, facing forward and they rode in silence down an almost empty street.

"Chris is right." Isaiah broke the silence, "Y'all are the closest thing to siblings for me. I need my brothers. All of y'all."

"Close? Nigga, we *are* your brothers. Blood couldn't make us any closer." Chris rebutted, "Pull into that empty lot over there, next to the church." He pointed.

Isaiah pulled into the vacant lot and put the truck in park.

"Alright, get out." Chris instructed.

"Get out?" Xavier blurted.

"Yes."

"Nigga it's brick outside! I don't even have the right coat on for that." Khalil complained.

"Yea man, it's like 20 something degrees." Isaiah added.

Chris reached over, turning off the engine and Isaiah looked at him in confusion.

"Now, we can sit here until it gets just as cold in the truck as it is outside, or we can hop out really quick and then come back to some heat." Chris smiled maniacally.

Khalil sucked his teeth and opened his car door, "Come on, man. Fuck!"

Xavier reluctantly followed suit as Chris and Isaiah also exited the truck.

"Alright, what the fuck are we out here for?" Khalil quizzed, shoving his hands into his pockets to keep warm.

"Apologize and hug your brother." Chris instructed, pointing to Isaiah.

"Nigga, what? You must be smoking. You got us out here to hug? You sound like this nigga. What next? We gonna pray and ask GOD for forgiveness?" Khalil ranted.

"Ay man, stop disrespecting GOD." Isaiah warned.

"He's right, you've got to stop disrespecting his GOD, man. That's foul, even for you." Chris interjected.

"He's all of our GOD." Isaiah corrected.

Chris sucked his teeth, "You know what I meant, nigga."

Khalil huffed, "Fine. My bad. Can we get back in the truck now."

"No, I said apologize, like you mean it, and hug your brother." Chris reiterated.

Khalil clenched his jaw, and a strong, cold gust of wind blew through the four of them.

"Jesus! Whew." Isaiah exclaimed, "Alright I'll go first...I apologize for putting my hands on you. It wasn't cool, I just...when it comes to my wife, I can't let disrespect slide."

"Fuck! It's cold as shit." Khalil hugged himself to keep warm, "I uh...apologize for putting my hands on you too and disrespecting Keira."

"And?" Chris chimed in.

Khalil looked at him confused and Chris made a gesture like he was pulling the trigger of a gun.

Khalil huffed, "And...for saying I'd put a bullet in you."

"Now hug." Chris instructed, tightening the lapel of his wool trench coat.

Isaiah reached out his hand and Khalil reluctantly shook it and then two men gave a quick embrace then released one another.

"Now y'all two." Chris pointed from Khalil to Xavier.

"I apologize...for questioning your loyalty. Chris is right, we should've never gotten in the middle of our women's shit." Xavier spoke up first.

Khalil nodded in acknowledgement.

"Alright, go-ahead Kha, it's your turn again nigga... it ain't gettin' no warmer out here." Chris instructed.

Khalil sighed hard and threw his head back trying to fight back his anger and tears started to form in his eyes, "Fuck! I hate this pussy ass shit..." He gritted.

"Nigga it's okay to cry. You're a human being, not a fuckin robot. And we ain't you, so ain't nobody about to clown you for it." Chris interjected.

Khalil violently swiped the tears from his eyes, "You know how hard shit been for me; how hard it is for me to let a mothafucka in. You been down with me the longest. But instead of recognizing that I finally found love and was just trying to protect it, you pulled some sucka shit and treated me like some bum ass nigga off the street." He barked at Xavier.

"That's a fuckin' stretch." Xavier rebutted.

"Let him get his shit off, X." Chris interrupted.

"I've always had your fuckin back, since we were kids! Half the bodies I've caught were to protect you and the one time I really needed my brother, I couldn't fuckin call him. Because of some bullshit. I almost lost my fuckin baby! Probably still could. And now Korena's talkin crazy, sounding suicidal and shit, talking about this is karma for what she did." Khalil fought back tears, but a few fell before he could swipe them away.

Xavier sighed, "I fucked up. I'll own that...I should've never let their shit come between us."

"My loyalty to Korena wasn't me betraying you...it was me trying to protect her. I know what it's like to be abandoned, being thrown between group homes and foster homes as a lil nigga, because I couldn't control my anger. So, I promised myself that no matter what, the people I love would never feel that way." Khalil shared sincerely.

"You're right. You've had my back since day one and I abandoned our brotherhood over some shit that didn't even have to involve us. For that, I'm sorry." Xavier admitted sincerely.

"Me too...especially for disrespecting your woman. She ain't deserve that." Khalil returned the gesture, reaching out his hand.

Xavier took hold of his hand and pulled him into a hug.

"I love you man." Xavier whispered.

"Love you too, nigga. Now unhand me before I grow a vagina." Khalil pushed back from the hug.

"Don't you just love a happy ending?" Chris teased.

"Whatever nigga, unlock the fucking truck. It's cold as shit out here!" Khalil laughed.

Chris unlocked the truck, and they all climbed back in, as Isaiah started the engine, then cranked the heat up to full blast.

Chapter Three

Detective Brenda Hanson sat on the edge of her cold, metal bunk, which had been her resting place for many sleepless nights while awaiting her next court date. It was by the grace of God and the merit of Mia's relationships, that she'd secured one of the best criminal defense attorneys in the Tri-state: Brynn James, Esq.

When Brenda's case came across his desk, it was an easy *'Yes'*, partly because of his respect and not-so-subtle attraction to Mia but mainly because of the notoriety he'd receive if he won. Brynn was a young risktaker, renowned for his 80/20 success rate and he considered the 20% a reasonable collateral in his zealous pursuits of high stakes cases.

Though many called him an egotist and overzealous, Brynn self-proclaimed to be the Kanye of Law; a genius, boundary pusher who did anything for the win, with very little regard for consequences. And his win to loss ratio of high-profile cases made his claims hard to dispute.

Brenda's case was Brynn's favorite flavor of litigation; it encompassed corruption, bribe taking, evidence planting/tampering across several cases, officers murdering one another, and black officers being used as scape goats to evade responsibility.

Winning her case against one of the most notorious gangs to ever exist, the **NYPD**, would undoubtedly set a legal precedent for all police related litigation going forward. It could potentially render the protections of the *'thin blue line'* almost obsolete and place Brynn in the law hall of fame. Forget a chapter, there'd be books written about him; where people once referenced Johnnie Cochran, they'd now mention Brynn James, *Esq*.

"Hanson! On your feet." The guard shouted.

"My lawyer's here?" Brenda inquired.

"Do I look like your fuckin' secretary?"

Brenda inhaled deep and exhaled the frustration that'd begun to swell in her chest, as she stepped toward the door and C.O. Dixon roughly placed cuffs onto her wrists. He yanked her out of the cell by her arm, then down the corridor. As they walked, Brenda partook in one of her new favorite past times: fantasizing about the day she'd regain her freedom and everything she'd do to the officer who put her fiancé in a coma.

But this particular fantasy included a trip to C.O. Dixon's home, which she imagined being a shithole, four by four efficiency in the grimiest part of Staten Island. And although the methods and means of vindication varied from one daydream to the next, it always ended the same: their faces under her boot as she stomped repeatedly until their skull popped like a water balloon.

In the few months she'd been locked up, she'd been starved, abused, and treated worse than the actual criminals in lock up, all while her fiancé clung to life. Brenda had quickly become someone she didn't recognize; she was so consumed by anger that she held little to no regard for the consequences of her murderous meditations.

"In here." C.O. Dixon stopped abruptly yanking her toward a private room reserved for inmates meeting with legal counsel.

"Brenda!" Brynn James beamed joyfully as they entered, "Can we get the cuffs off my client? She's not a danger to anyone here."

"That's above my paygrade." C.O. Dixon stated dryly, securing Brenda's cuffs to the table.

"Is that really necessary?" Brynn pressed.

C.O. Dixon stared at him blankly, "I'll be right outside the door."

Brynn sighed in irritation then recomposed himself.

"How are you? How are they treating you?" He asked, fully aware that she'd been being mistreated. If Dixon's behavior wasn't evidence enough, the bruises on her neck and visible weight loss were clear indicators.

"I'm good. What's the update on my hearing?" Brenda brushed past his inquisitions.

"Straight to the point, I respect that." Brynn nodded, pulling a folder from his brief case, "So, the court date is set for next month on the 23rd and I'm not going to sugar coat it, they're trying to throw the book at you. The main charges being two counts of felony murder in the first degree, followed by a conspiracy charge; they're clearly trying to make an example out of you and more importantly shift attention from the corruption allegations surrounding officer Shaw's crime scene tampering and alleged bribe taking."

"First degree! Conspiracy?" Brenda repeated in confusion.

"Yea…Shaw's overdose is now being considered a deliberate poisoning and they're claiming premeditation for both murders. But it's all bullshit, especially Johnson's death which was involuntary manslaughter at best. Although some would call it karma." Brynn smirked.

"Ex-partners who hated each other, one being investigated for tampering, planting, and taking bribes while the other was clearly into some shady shit. If anyone had reason and motive to kill Shaw, it was Johnson and vice versa. Shaw was probably going to implicate Johnson, so he killed him; case closed. Hell, he tried to kill me for asking about his old C.I. The mothafucka was dirty!" Brenda ranted.

"Trust me, I'm with you. There's absolutely no plausible motive for you to be implicated in Shaw's murder, we just need to provide evidence that proves your being there, that day, was just coincidence. Or better yet, it was a part of a larger plot put together by Johnson to kill two birds with one stone."

"Kill two birds…" Brenda repeated as vivid memories of Johnson's dead body flooded her mind.

"Yea, kill two birds…Johnson gets rid of Shaw and then implicates you in the murder, to cover his ass and prevent you from digging further into his shady history." Brynn explained.

"No, no…I know what you meant. It's just…that's what Johnson's C.I. Percy said that day. Right before shit got chaotic, he asked him '*is this what you meant by killing two birds?*'…you just triggered some memories, but I'm good." She assured.

"My apologies…look, I get it, this is a lot, but on the bright side I got them to drop Charles Campbell's murder, since you and Mia were being arrested at the time. Plus, all they had was speculation, based on your recent search history."

"Bright side?" Brenda scoffed, "Should I be thanking God or you that they're only charging me with two murders instead of three?"

"My apologies for how that came across, I just mean it's one less battle to fight." Brynn explained remorsefully.

"It's fine…so, what evidence do they have against me, besides me being at the scene of both murders?"

"My sources say they've got a neighbor confirming they saw you leaving Shaw's house. I've sent my investigator to check it out and with any luck we can find a doorbell camera with time stamps that conflict with the time of death."

"Okay and what's the plan for Johnson's murder?" Brenda quizzed.

"Right now, that's going to be our toughest battle…the only working street camera was two blocks away and not one doorbell camera, which is to be expected since most of the homes on that block were abandoned or being rehabbed. So, as of right now, there's nothing to corroborate your story or place anyone but you at Johnson's murder." Brynn shared.

"Fuck!" Brenda shouted, "That dirty mothafucka is still fucking with me from the grave! I'm a good cop…I do shit by the book and honor my oath to the badge…all I wanted to do was get justice for some young black boys. You know, make the system work for us for a change. It's why I joined the force!" Brenda fought back tears.

Brynn placed his hand on her cuffed wrists, "We're not going down without a fight. I will do everything in my power to get you free from these shackles."

Brenda adjusted her hands, in attempt to remove his and Brynn caught the hint, retracting his hand.

"How?" She recomposed herself.

"Well…with Charles being dead, that leaves us without a viable witness to testify to Johnson's misconduct. But I still have investigators looking for Percy and I've also got some details on an old associate of Charles who might've also dealt with Johnson."

"You think you can get them to snitch? And on a cop, to help another cop?" Brenda questioned.

"That's the hope and right now our best chance at clearing your name. The guy is in jail and has filed for an appeal, since Shaw was one of the arresting officers on his case. I looked into his case and, bad for him but lucky for us, his lawyer is basically a recruiter for private prisons.

He makes sure his clients find permanent residence upstate for a sizeable kickback."

Brenda shook her head in disgust, "That's so fuckin' sick."

"That's the prison industrial system working how it was intended...but lucky for this guy, I'm aware of his counsels' conflict of interest and will be offering my services pro-bono in exchange for his cooperation." Brynn smiled cockily.

"Hmm…if you manage to swing that, you might be as good as Mia said."

"Oh no, I'm better." Brynn winked.

"I'll believe that when I'm free." Brenda rebutted sarcastically.

"Soon enough. In the meantime, I need you to list every infringement of your rights and list the names of all who have participated." Brynn slid a pad toward Brenda, "Because when we win this thing, we won't just clear your name and expose the corruption but also collect reparations from every single person involved. When I'm done, everyone down to C.O. Dickhead out there will see garnishments on their wages." He boasted.

Brenda completed her list and slid the pad back, "Yea...I honestly don't give a fuck about the money...I just want to see my fiancé. And to make the mothafucka responsible for her suffering, suffer ten times worse."

"I understand…and I know I said it before, but I am really sorry about Mia. She's a great woman and even better lawyer; one I'm happy to work with and not against, because she'd probably win. But don't tell her I said that." Brynn chuckled, in attempt to lighten the mood.

Brenda stared at him, unamused and aware of the not-so-subtle attraction he had toward Mia, "Have you made any progress with her excessive force lawsuit?"

He sighed, "I did everything I could to pursue justice for Mia, but with her being in a coma and her parents having legal proxy, they had final say. And they decided not to press charges and just take the *'pain and suffering'* settlement."

"Of course…" Brenda gritted, filling herself growing angrier by the second.

"They're scared. And I do understand their apprehension. Most people fear going head-to-head with major organizations and agencies, especially law enforcement. The rumors of retaliation are enough to make the toughest people reconsider."

"They're fuckin' cowards! Don't make excuses for them. That's their fuckin' daughter, their only fuckin' child! I'd go to war with the devil in the lowest parts of hell for her, but they'd just as easily pretend she doesn't even exist, for simply…loving me." Brenda ranted; eyes blood shot with tears of rage.

A tense silence filled the space, it was sharp to the touch. Like a thousand cuts to the skin, Brynn could feel her agony but with every fiber of his well-tailored demeanor he maintained his professionalism and emotional boundaries. By doling out pleasantries and providing generic gestures of assurance and support, he avoided genuine emotional connection. It was the secret to his success; emotional detachment and desperation for his desired outcome, no matter the desolation that lay in the wake of his pursuit to win.

"I'll see you on the 23rd." He extended his hand.

Brenda raised her hand as high as the cuffs would allow and Brynn awkwardly shook her hand, nodding in salutation. He grabbed his things, headed for the door and as he exited, C.O. Dixon entered.

"Dearly beloved, we are gathered here today to sendoff one of God's mightiest soldiers, Reverend Maria Adelaida Ramirez. A true force to be reckoned with but a tender heart all the same. Gracious and kind to all who knew her while admonishing those she loved and always calling them to heights she truly believed they had potential to reach. While it is with deep sorrow that we say goodbye, it is also with full hearts that we shall return to our lives. Forever impacted by sister Maria's ministry and faithful servitude. She was a true treasure, lent to us by God for but a moment but never meant to be ours forever. So, with that we say: Earth to earth, ashes to ashes and from dust to dust. Receive your servant, Jesus. Amen." Bishop Benson, the lead parishioner of Maria's church, closed out the prayer and everyone said *Amen.*

Officer Sean Ramirez and his wife Amber stood somberly with their 7-yearold daughter Addie, the namesake of her grandmother. They were surrounded by family, close friends, members of the church and clergy.

As instructed by the minister, one by one, they each placed a flower onto the casket before it was slowly lowered into the ground.

"Where's your brother?" Amber asked Sean, as the crowd of mourners dispersed from the burial plot to their cars.

He shrugged, "I don't know. He said he was riding here with Fabian, because he needed to smoke, and I told him he couldn't do it in the limo."

Amber shook her head in disgust, "What the hell? He couldn't wait until after your mother was in the ground? Such a degenerate."

"Hey, that's still my brother."

"I know, I know… I'm just saying. Even during bureavement for his own mother, he refuses to get his shit together. Forgive me father for cussin'." Amber huffed in her heavy Cuban accent, while crossing her body in respect to God.

"Come on." Sean shook his head, leading his wife and daughter toward the limo.

Once all the cars were dispersed and the cemetery workers had completely filled in the burial plot, a car came driving up the pathway blasting *Big Pun's* song "*100%*".

The passenger side door opened, and the chorus filled the air, breaking the silence of the gloomy afternoon, *"Pronto llegara, el dia de mi suerte, Te lo juro por mi gente, Te juro que un dia llegara."*

Brandon Ramirez stepped out of the car, swaying and singing with a lit blunt in one hand and a bottle of *Don Julio* in the other.

"And we won't stop, we always knew we'd make it. Even though you playa hated. We still made it to the top!", He staggered over to his mother's burial plot, where workers were carrying away the tent and took a seat in front of the heap of fresh dirt.

"Ma…" He tearfully whined, sniffling and wiping his face roughly with the back of his hand, "Te qiero mucho, mama… lo siento por todo! I'm sorry you didn't get to see me do better, like you wanted…and I'm sorry didn't protect you, like you always did for me…baby when papi used to beat my ass for lil stupid shit like spilling juice in the kitchen, you stood up for me and took the hits. El un cagón! May he never find rest."

Brandon spit over his shoulder before taking a long drag from his blunt and then a swig from the bottle of tequila.

"Um, excuse me sir. But we need to load the chairs now." One of the workers walked over cautiously.

Brandon looked up at him like he'd lost his mind, "Nigga, don't you see I'm grieving?"

"I, uh, I understand sir. And you can stay as long as you like, we just need the chair."

"Mothafucka, if you don't get the fuck away from me before I put you in one of these plots!" Brandon gritted, flashing the silver 9mm Beretta in his waist.

The guy threw his hands up in surrender and backed away quickly. He whispered something to the other two men, and they packed up and left in their work truck.

"Sorry for your loss."

Brandon jumped up and spun around, pulling the gun from his waist band, "Who the fuck are you?"

The woman threw her hands up in surrender, "Be easy, cuteness. I come in peace."

"What, you're a cop or something?" Brandon questioned, looking over toward the car where his cousin Fabian watched intently.

She chuckled, "Not at all. I'm Niecy."

"What the fuck do you want, *Niecy*?"

"To solicit your help."

"Why the fuck would I help you? I don't even know you." Brandon sneered.

Niecy folded her arms, "Because you and I both lost someone dear to us, at the hands of the same person."

"What you know?" Brandon pressed, walking closer to her.

"I know who's responsible for your mother's death."

Brandon took a large swallow of tequila, "Name."

"I'll tell you…under one condition."

"Condition?" Brandon sneered, "How about I shoot you right here, toss you in with mi madré and then find out for myself."

"You could, but you won't. You're what, just shy of 4 months free after a 7-year bid? So, most of your contacts are either dead, in jail or went ghost. Which means you've definitely had a tough time navigating the new landscape, otherwise, the person responsible would already be dead. But they're very much alive, so you need me."

Brandon sighed heavily, annoyed with her arrogance, "What the fuck you want from me?"

"I simply want your assistance. You be the muscle and I'll be the brains. Let me work my network of information and set things up properly, then you can execute."

"What's to stop me from just handling shit myself once you tell me who the nigga is?" Brandon quizzed.

"The person responsible isn't some small time criminal. They're connected to very ruthless and powerful people. So, without careful planning, knocking them off could cause a shitload of dominoes to fall, landing on us." Niecy explained matter-of-factly.

"Ain't no *us*. And I don't give a fuck who the nigga is or what connections he got. I'll put the fear of God in all of'em. Lo juro por dios!" Brandon consumed the remainder of the tequila then flung the bottle at a tree, causing glass to shatter everywhere.

"Yea, well good luck finding *who* to put that fear in." Niecy quipped, as she turned to leave.

Brandon huffed, "Wait!"

She stopped in her tracks and turned wearing a *cheshire cat* grin, "Changed your mind?"

"If you try anything funny, I won't hesitate to put you down." Brandon threatened, walking up closely on her.

"Honey, that goes both ways. Don't let the pretty face fool you, fuck with me and I'll have la familia lighting candles in your name down at St. Anthony's. Tú entiendes?" She grinned, pressing a blade against his throat.

The two stood in a silent stare down.

"So, what's your plan?" Brandon puffed his blunt, unfazed.

Niecy frowned up her face at the smell of tequila and weed on his breath, "Sober up and… shower. We'll talk soon."

"How am I supposed to reach you?"

"I'll light a candle for tu madré on Saturday. You should too." Niecy winked before walking away and disappearing outside the cemetery gates.

"Qué cojones." Brandon huffed and headed back to his cousin's car, puffing on the remainder of his blunt then flicking it.

"Who was that?" Fabian inquired, putting the car in drive.

"Un bellaco."

"Ten cuidado." Fabian warned.

"Always." Brandon reclined in his seat, as they pulled out of the cemetery.

∞◇◇◇∞

Myeesha closed the oven door and adjusted the timer on the stove to add ten more minutes when the doorbell rang. She turned down the fire under her pot of collard greens and took the lid off the pot of rice that was almost done. When she turned to head out of the kitchen she was startled by Khalil.

"What's up, sis?" He reached out to hug her.

"How'd you get in?" She asked, hugging him back.

"I let him in." Korena stated.

"What part of bedrest don't you understand?" Myeesha fussed.

"The doctor said I can get up to walk around a few times a day." Korena retorted, carefully taking a seat on the couch.

"No, she said to the bathroom and maybe to the kitchen if it's not too far or up and down too many stairs. Which is why we decided you should stay with me until you're cleared from bedrest. But your ass has been everywhere beside the bed since you got here."

Khalil walked over to Korena, "Are you trying to lose this baby?"

"What? No! Why would you say that?"

"Cause you're still doing the same shit that put y'all at risk in the first place…I swear to GOD Korena, I will chain your ass to that fuckin' bed if you keep fuckin' around with my child's life."

"Khalil, I'm going fuckin' crazy in that room…I need fresh air and sunlight."

"Crack a fuckin' window!" Khalil barked.

Myeesha walked over and placed her hand on his shoulder, "Look, Ree I get it. I can see about getting you a wheelchair so we can go to the park. But you really need to follow the doctors' instructions. It's only for another weeks. Once you go in for your follow up, you'll hopefully be cleared and can resume your life."

"That ain't happening." Khalil interjected, "Won't be no resuming shit. Even after she's off bedrest, she's not going back to work or doing anything that could cause stress, not until she has the baby."

41

"That's almost 6 months from now!" Korena leapt up from the couch and immediately became woozy, "If the doctor says I'm cleared… I'm going back…to work."

Khalil grabbed her, "Look at you, barely able to stand too fast without getting fuckin' dizzy." He swung her up into his arms and carried her to the bedroom.

"You can't keep me locked up Khalil!" She cried, exasperated.

Myeesha just shook her head and returned to the kitchen to check on her pot of rice and the seabass baking in the oven.

DING DONG!

The bell rang, interrupting Myeesha's flow again. She turned off her pot of greens and headed to the door.

"Whaaaat? Your ass is early?" Myeesha exclaimed.

"Mommy changed her mind and decided to come, and I wasn't trying to hear her mouth the whole way here about being late." Tyson shared, stepping into the doorway and hugging his sister.

"Ma is with you? Where's she at?" Myeesha inquired.

"Parking the car. She said I wasn't close enough to the curb, so she told me to get out and let her do it." He shrugged.

Myeesha stepped out, onto the stoop and watched as her mother parked Tyson's car then got out, slamming the car door with an attitude.

"This is going to be a long night." She sighed.

"No it ain't, cause I gotta get back to my baby and fiancé."

"Fiancé? Since when and why you ain't tell nobody? Did you tell your mother?" Myeesha questioned.

"Tell me what?" Monique interjected as she stepped through the front door.

"I planned on telling y'all during dinner." Tyson informed.

"Telling us what?" Monique pressed, taking off her coat and handing it to Myeesha.

"Don't look at me…I know nothing." Myeesha hung her mother's coat in the closet by the front door then made her way back to the kitchen.

"Um, hello. Tell me what, Tyson?" Monique persisted.

Tyson sighed heavily, "Can we wait til Ree is out here? I'd rather do this all at once."

"Do what? Boy if you don't just say the shit, before you piss me off." Monique fussed.

"Ma, can we just wait?" He pleaded.

"Hell no. Tell me now." Monique demanded.

"Ty, go knock on the bedroom door and tell Ree and Khalil dinner is ready." Myeesha interceded.

Grateful for the save, he quickly made his way toward the bedroom. Monique sauntered her way into the kitchen, the heels of her boots clicking against the hard wood, then onto the kitchen tiles.

"What'd I tell you about trying to parent my kids? I'm the mother. Remember that." Monique sneered, standing so close that her chest was pressed against Myeesha's arm.

Myeesha sighed, never breaking her rhythm as she transferred food into serving bowls, "Excuse me." She paused, waiting for Monique to move, but she didn't budge.

"You think you're too grown for me to buss yo ass?" Monique whispered.

"Ma, I'm not trying to beef with you. You're right, those are your kids, and so am I. Remember?" She retorted sarcastically.

"Who're you talking to?"

"Ma, I just want to take this fish out of the oven before it overcooks." Myeesha tried to maintain her calm.

Monique slowly stepped away, "Mhmm…whatever."

"Hey Ma." Korena's voice broke the tension filled silence.

"Hey poo." Monique turned around with a smile stretched across her face and pulled Korena into a hug.

Khalil stepped out of the way of their embrace and noticed Myeesha wiping tears from her eyes. When she noticed him looking, she quickly turned, grabbing oven mitts off the counter, and removing the seabass from the oven.

"I should kick your ass for not calling me as soon as you got to the hospital." Monique pointed her finger in Korena's face.

"I know, I'm sorry…I was overwhelmed, but I did call you once I was admitted for the night. I called you and Eesha, twice. Sky's the only one who answered." Korena pleaded her case.

"Doesn't matter if your sister didn't answer…you should've kept calling *me* til I answered. I shouldn't have had to hear that shit on a damn voicemail." Monique fussed.

"Ma…I'm sorry, it wasn't my intention. It was just…a lot going on." Korena apologized, feeling herself getting lightheaded.

"Come have a seat." Khalil took Korena by the arm and guided her over to the sofa beside Tyson.

"You must be the baby daddy." Monique asserted.

Khalil stared at her for a moment, "Something like that."

"Ma, this is Khalil. He's not just the father of your grandchild, we're together." Korena explained.

"Together? Like, in a relationship? Hmph, never thought I'd see the day." Monique chuckled.

Korena sucked her teeth, "Really Ma?"

Monique waved her off, "Girl, please. You change men like the seasons and that's being nice because it used to be like drawls." She chuckled, pulling a flask from her purse and taking a long swig.

"Ma, that's not funny." Korena sighed.

"Dinner is ready. Tyson, can you help me take the food to the table?" Myeesha interrupted.

"Yea, I got you." He leapt up and took the serving dishes from her then took them to the dining room table.

"Ma, can you grab the pitcher of tea?" Myeesha asked.

"Mhmm…" Monique reluctantly went and grabbed the pitcher from the kitchen, and they all reconvened at the dining room table.

Myeesha connected her phone to the Bluetooth speakers and pressed play on her R&B playlist. After adjusting the volume, she took her seat at the head of the table, facing Monique who sat at the other end of the table taking the occasional swig of her flask.

Tyson sat across from Korena and Khalil, oblivious to the awkward silence at the table because he was busy texting.

"Alright, we're all at the table. Say what you had to say Ty." Monique broke the silence.

"Actually, Ma, can we pray over the food first?" Myeesha interrupted.

"Why? The food ain't goin' nowhere." Monique quipped.

"I know it's not…but I'd prefer we eat before discussing family matters."

"I don't care what you'd prefer." Monique spat.

"Family matter? What's goin' on? Tyson, you good?" Korena interjected.

"Yea, I'm good. I just had something I wanted to share while we're all together." Tyson explained.

"Is it bad?" Korena asked concerned.

"Don't go getting your pressure up, Ree. It's nothing like that." Myeesha inserted.

"Wait…you already know what it is?" Monique asked growing aggravated.

"No, nobody said that Ma. Please relax." Myeesha sighed.

"Bullshit! You clearly know something. How else would you know it's nothing serious?" Monique pressed.

"Y'all please don't start." Tyson pleaded.

"I ain't starting shit! Your sister doesn't know how to stay in her fuckin' place. She thinks she y'all mama but if she wants kids so damn bad, she should've kept one of the ones she got rid of."

Tyson gasped, "Ma, chill!"

"Don't tell me what to do! I'm the mother, I tell you what to do. Not the other way around." Monique shouted.

"Ma, please." Korena sighed in exasperation.

Khalil looked from Myeesha to Monique, then over at Korena who looked visibly overwhelmed with emotion. The expression on Tyson's face let him know that this was a typical occurrence for them. He sighed, frustrated by his own agreement to having dinner with Korena's family. Here he was trying to prevent her from stressing, and now they were sitting in the middle of a ticking time bomb of stress.

"Maybe I'd have the desire to have kids of my own if I hadn't spent my life raising *your* fuckin' kids while you ran the streets and drank yourself stupid trying to forget daddy!" Myeesha spat.

"Bitch!" Monique jumped up, slamming her flask down on the table, "Who the fuck do you think you're talking to?"

"You!" Myeesha screamed.

Korena began breathing rapidly as tears fell from her eyes and Khalil immediately stood up from the table.

"Come on." He pulled her up from her seat.

"Where the fuck are you taking my daughter?" Monique questioned.

Khalil ignored her and proceeded to walk Korena toward the front door. As he pulled her jacket from the closet and helped put it on Monique walked over.

"I don't know you like that to be leaving my daughter with you while she's in this condition." Monique snapped.

Khalil paused in the middle of helping Korena into her sneakers and inhaled deeply before standing up, towering over Monique.

"Ma, I'm fine. Khalil and Myeesha have been taking good care of me." Korena tried to intervene.

Monique glared at Khalil and Korena then looked over her shoulder at Myeesha who was leaned over at the table, her face resting in her hands.

"Tyson, let's go!" Monique shouted then pushed past Khalil to get her coat from the closet and headed out of the house.

Tyson walked over and pulled Myeesha into a tight hug, "I love you, Eesh." He held her for a moment then released her and headed to the door.

"I love you, Ree." He hugged Korena then turned to Khalil, "Take care of my sister."

Khalil nodded, not in the mood but respecting of his brotherly posturing.

"Give me a minute to talk to my sister." Korena requested.

Khalil sighed, "Alright, I'm going to grab your phone and pack your bag."

She walked over and sat in the chair beside Myeesha.

"Eesh."

Myeesha broke down into tears, "I'm done...I can't do this anymore."

"I know she's a lot, but she's still our mom. She just ain't been right since daddy died."

"It's been over 20 fuckin' years of her not being *right*."

"I know...but we can't just give up on her. She's the only mother we've got."

"I don't want to hear it…you do whatever you want, but I'm done. As far as I'm concerned, she's deader than daddy to me." Myeesha stood up from the table, gathering the untouched bowls of food, "But I won't miss her like I do him."

"Don't say that…" Korena sighed sorrowfully.

Myeesha ignored her as she took the bowls into the kitchen then returned for the rest.

"You ready?" Khalil walked out of the bedroom.

Korena fought back tears, "I guess so…"

"Okay."

He helped her up and they headed to the front door, "Wait here, while I pull the car up to the door."

Korena stood in the doorway, watching as Khalil walked toward the car, and Myeesha walked up beside her. Korena turned and threw her arms around her sister's neck.

"I can't lose you too." She whimpered.

"Ree, I'm not going anywhere. Just because I'm not fuckin' with Monique doesn't mean you're losing me too." Myeesha assured.

"You promise?" Korena stared into her sisters equally tear-filled eyes.

"Yes." Myeesha pulled her into a tighter hug, "You're stuck with me for life. You and my new niece or nephew."

They lingered in the embrace a moment, then released as Khalil came walking up the steps.

"I'll call and check on you in the morning." Myeesha informed.

"Okay."

Khalil took Korena by the hand, and they walked to the car. Myeesha watched until they were out of sight before closing and locking her front door. Turning to face her empty home, filled with loving melodies and the aroma of uneaten cuisine, she couldn't help but let the tears fall.

Her heart was broken.

Chapter Four

"I listened; I did…but after she said what she had to say. I realized that nothing had changed for me. Did I understand? Yes. Do I forgive her? I mean…yea, but do I desire to continue a relationship with her…honestly, I don't know. And you said it yourself, confusion leans closer to a *No* than a *Yes.*" Maleah shared as she laid back on the leather lounge chair in her therapist's office.

"Yes, I did say that but let's keep that framed in the correct context. That was several years ago, in reference to you feeling unsure in a relationship where you didn't feel like you and a prospective partner wanted the same thing." Dr. Cheri rebutted.

Maleah leaned up, "Okay, but how isn't this the same? I am not sure that I want the same thing she wants. She wants to start over and move on like nothing's happened and I don't know if I can or want to."

"It is similar, however in this scenario neither of you have been evasive about what you want going forward. You're not faced with confusion; you're faced with a choice: remain friends or don't. There is no ambiguity here. She's bared it all and so have you. Where there is full transparency, there is no confusion." Dr. Cheri expounded.

Maleah sat in silence, staring at the decorative wall art, trying to process Dr. Cheri's words. Like a swift kick to the chest, she found herself overwhelmed with emotions and short of breath as she began to cry.

Dr. Cheri reached over and slid the box of tissue beside her, "It's okay…let it flow. You've been holding on to too much, for too long. Whatever you are feeling, whatever you decide…it's okay. You will be okay."

"I'm so fuckin' angry!" Maleah sobbed, "We've planned so much of our lives around each other, since we were kids. She was supposed to be my maid of honor, godmother to my babies; we said we'd raise our kids like siblings...she ruined everything."

"The more life we live, inevitably leads to mourning what we thought would be." Dr. Cheri offered softly.

Maleah wiped her nose as she sniffled, "That's all poetic and what not, but this isn't just mourning what I thought my life would be. This is the painful realization that a major part of my life was a lie."

Dr. Cheri paused in contemplation and Maleah caught the vibe. Although it'd been close to a year since their last session, she was still very familiar with her mannerisms.

"You disagree?" Maleah challenged defensively.

"Was every single part of your relationship a lie? Or...was it built on the foundation of a lie, but thrived despite it?" Dr. Cheri offered gently.

Maleah twisted and pulled at her fingers anxiously, frustrated with the challenge of Dr. Cheri's words, "I'm tired...frankly exhausted. The people I love the most always hurt me and I'm over it. I'm getting up from the table; I refuse to ingest any more abuse. No more."

"Yes, people that you've loved have hurt you...but remember, we don't claim *always*. You've still got two healthy friendships with Sky and Lisa, a grandmother who loves you deeply and you're currently experiencing a healthy romantic relationship. If you weigh it all out, you're currently having more positive experiences with love than negative." Dr. Cheri encouraged.

"For now..." Maleah laid back, staring up at the ceiling.

"Uhn, uhn. No ma'am...we will not fall into self-defeating talk. What's your mantra? I am love..."

Maleah sighed, "I deserve love... I am loved."

"Again. Like you mean it."

Tears began to fill Maleah's eyes, "How can I mean it, when I'm struggling to even believe it?"

"The truth remains the truth, no matter who believes it. So, say it until you believe it, because *it is* the truth." Dr. Cheri gently instructed.

Maleah wept, struggling to utter words that felt so foreign in that moment. It was as if she was teleported back to her childhood, where the terror of uncertainty and aching hallow of abandonment left her in a perpetual cycle of *fight or flight*. What was wrong with her that no one could love her well and those that did, didn't stay? She felt a hopelessness that crept into her joints, leaving her physically and emotionally immobile.

"Maleah…" Dr. Cheri's voice brought her back to the present, "Instead of rehearsing the lie, recite the truth."

Maleah shook her head in acknowledgement, "I am love…I deserve love…I am loved." She spoke just above a whisper.

"Once more. Like you believe it."

"I am love." Maleah's voice trembled as tears fell, "I deserve love!" She shouted in exasperation, slamming her fist against the couch, "I am…loved. I am loved…I have people in my life, who love me…"

Maleah placed her hands over her heart and wept, but this time the tears weren't bitter. They were tears of sweet rebellion, forged against the intrusive thoughts that told her, her life and everything in it was a sham. The narrative that she was still that same little girl, scared and alone, abandoned forever to daydream of a life and love that would never be. But it was a lie. She was living in her wildest dreams, standing in answered prayers and recipient of blessings she hadn't even prayed for. So, despite the pain she'd experienced, she couldn't deny the fact that she indeed was *Loved*.

"That's gonna be our session for today. You did great work. I'm going to challenge you to recite your truth mantra any time you feel yourself sinking into self-defeating thoughts. Write it on your mirrors at home, set daily reminders on your phone, whatever it takes to retrain the way you see yourself, and by extension, your life. You are worthy of love and are blessed to have it. Don't let anything sabotage that truth." Dr. Cheri closed her note pad and stood up.

Maleah stood up and slid her feet into her blue snake-skin mules, smoothing out her canary yellow charmeuse skirt. She adjusted the straps on her white bodysuit, then slid her denim cropped jacket over her shoulders and shared a quick hug with Dr. Cheri before heading to the door. As she walked out into the lobby, she secured her blue suede fedora on her head and tucked her ceramic mosaic purse under her arm.

On the elevator ride down to the main lobby, she examined her face where tears had stained her cheeks and thanked God for waterproof mascara and *One Size* setting spray. She pulled the electric fan from her purse and dried her face, so by the time she exited through the main doors of the building her make-up returned to its original flawless state.

Maleah strutted down the street, looking photoshoot ready, and received compliments every step of the way, to support that truth. She was a real-life embodiment of the saying: *'Thank God, I don't look like what I've been through'*.

∞∞∞∞

Tyson adjusted the shopping bags in his hand as he reached to swipe his card at the pretzel stand. Brielle was already two bites into her pretzel and sipping her lemonade, unaware of his struggle.

"Babe, grab the little bag before it falls." Tyson requested.

Brielle sighed in a bratty fashion and took the mini bag of make-up from him as he concluded his transaction and grabbed his own pretzel and drink.

"I don't know what you're huffing for. I'm the one carrying damn near twelve bags. That one ain't gonna kill you." Tyson chastised.

Brielle rolled her eyes, "You're my fiancé, that's your job. It's called chivalry."

"Fiancé, not chauffer. Don't piss me off Bri, I'll take all this shit back." Tyson huffed.

"Alright, alright! You're so testy. Ruining our first kid free day."

"I'm not testy, I'm exhausted. We were supposed to spend today relaxing at the crib, but I let you finesse me into thinking we were just coming to do a return and then grab something to eat." Tyson ranted.

"I know…but you know TJ really changed my body, so I needed new clothes, and I can't shop online because I don't know my sizes anymore." Brielle plead for sympathy.

Tyson sighed, "I hear you and I understand…but I told you yesterday that I wanted to rest. We were supposed to just chill, eat good food and maybe watch a movie. Not walk around the mall carrying bags for 5 hours."

"You're right…and that's my bad. You've been doing a great job taking care of me and TJ, while working hard." Brielle cooed, caressing his chin, "Let's go home, so I can make it up to you."

Tyson stared at her for a moment, a smile creeping over his face, as he read between the lines. In an instant he was no longer upset and the bags on his arm felt light as a feather. Brielle was long past the 6 weeks the doctor advised, but the weight gain and postpartum changes had her feeling insecure about her body, so he was left to *handle things* himself.

Brielle reached and grabbed a few of the bags, freeing up his hand to eat his pretzel and they walked toward the exit.

"Elle!"

Tyson and Brielle both turned to see who was calling her name, as they stepped through the first set of exit doors.

"Cousin!" Brielle exclaimed, rushing over.

"Oh my God, I was just thinking about you. I've been meaning to call and come see the baby! How is he?"

"Oh, my goodness, you have to see him. He's so stinking cute and I'm not just saying that cause he's mine!" Brielle beamed.

Tyson walked over as Brielle showed pictures in her phone of the baby.

"Baby, this is my cousin Porsha. I don't know if you remember her from the baby shower." Brielle introduced them.

"Nah, sorry. How're you doin?" Tyson nodded.

Porsha smiled, "Hey. It's cool."

"So, what you been up to? How's Chelle?" Brielle pried.

"I've been…okay. It's been rough though." Porsha choked back tears.

"Oh my God, what happened?" Brielle rubbed Porsha's shoulder.

Tyson sighed and though he thought it was internal, it was very much audible. Brielle looked over at him like he'd lost his mind, as Porsha looked away, wiping tears.

"Here, give me those, I'mma take the bags to the car. Call me when you're ready and I'll pull around." Tyson took the shopping bags from Brielle and left out the exit avoiding eye contact.

Brielle took Porsha by the arm and walked her over to the bench inside the entrance, between the exit doors and they sat down.

"What's going on?"

Porsha breathed deep and then exhaled, "I haven't seen my sister since the end of October, last year."

"What? Why, did something happen between y'all? I know Chelle can be a little moody."

"No, no it's nothing like that…I think, no I *know* something happened to her."

"Something like what?" Brielle asked fearfully.

"I think she's…dead" Porsha broke at the utterance of the words.

Brielle gasped and pulled her into a hug, "Oh my God, No! Don't say that…have you called the police and reported her missing?"

"I did. But they've been no help. It took til January for someone to start taking my missing persons claims serious. They said since she took an extended leave of absence from her job and her apartment was basically empty, there was no evidence of foul play. Selling me some bullshit about how people go no contact from their families all the time and that maybe she decided to start over somewhere else." Porsha ranted sorrowfully.

"That's fucked up. They're at least supposed to do a basic investigation, not just dismiss your claims." Brielle fussed.

"Exactly. But something told me to try again and one of the officers saw me crying in the sitting area and felt bad. So, he agreed to at least try, but I would need to get some concrete evidence to back-up my claims."

"Okay, so do you have anything? Anyone who you think wanted to hurt her? How about any footage from her apartment? Anyone shady coming by?" Brielle pried like a detective.

Porsha sighed, "The fucked-up part is…I know who did it. I just…"

"Just what? If you know, why haven't you told the police?"

"It's complicated…"

Brielle sucked her teeth, "What's complicated? Your sister is missing, possibly fuckin dead and you know who's responsible. Sounds pretty simple to me."

"It's the *who* that's complicated. I honestly just want answers, so I can lay her to rest and get closure. As messy as she was, she was the closest thing I had to a mother." Porsha sighed, tears falling from her eyes.

"So, what's complicating things? Help me understand." Brielle pleaded.

Porsha opened her bubble coat and revealed her small baby bump, protruding through her bodysuit.

Brielle gasped, "Oh my goodness! You're pregnant? Oh my…cousin!"

She pulled Porsha into her arms as she wept into her shoulder. After a moment, they released and Brielle pulled a tissue from her purse and handed it to Porsha to wipe her face, as she wiped her own.

"Are you afraid the person might come for you, risking your baby's life?" Brielle inquired.

Yes and no…I'm mostly afraid of my baby ending up like me, no father or mother…no family at all."

Brielle tried to process what she was hearing, "Wait, who's the father and where is he?"

Porsha began to weep again, rubbing her belly gently and Brielle stared at her cousin, sorting through the details in her mind. Then, like the road runner smashing headfirst into a brick wall, she crashed into the omitted truth of her cousin's dilemma.

"Is that who you think killed Chelle?" Brielle whispered, tears forming in her eyes.

Porsha slowly nodded as the tears streamed down her face.

"Damn…" Brielle pulled her into her arms, and they rocked side to side.

Mall patrons walked in and out the doors, some with concerned looks on their faces and others quickly entering or exiting with awkward, uncomfortable expressions.

VRRRRRRBBBB!

Brielle pulled her phone from her jacket pocket and sucked her teeth, "Give me a second, Ty! Damn."

"No, no it's okay Bri. You go ahead. I'll be fine. I'm actually going to head out too, I'm starting to feel nauseous. Let me call my *UBER*." Porsha zipped her coat and wiped her face, pulling out her cellphone.

"Uhn, uhn we'll take you home." Brielle dialed Tyson, "Hey. Yea, you can come around. We're gonna have to make a stop though…to take my cousin home, if that's alright with you!"

Brielle hung up the phone and looked over at Porsha who was staring down at her phone, scrolling aimlessly on social media. She gently grabbed her hand and squeezed it.

After a few minutes, Tyson pulled up to the mall doors and honked.

"Niggas…" Brielle sighed, shaking her head.

She took Porsha by the hand and helped her up and they walked out the exit, toward the car.

"Where you stay?" Tyson asked, as he pulled out of the mall parking lot.

"My new place is over on Flushing and Bushwick." Porsha informed.

"Oh, that's not even far from us. That's like 10 or 15 minutes from where we stay." Brielle looked in the backseat.

They drove for about 45-50 minutes before pulling up to Porsha's apartment. Just as Tyson put the car in park, his phone that was mounted on the dash started to ring. Porsha looked up and saw a picture of him and Korena from the baby shower pop up on the screen.

"Yo, can I call you right back Ree?" Tyson answered.

Korena sucked her teeth, "Yea, I guess that's fine."

The call ended and Tyson hit the locks on the car and looked over at Brielle who was staring at him with her lips twisted.

"You can't talk to your sister while I'm in the car?" She quizzed.

Tyson sighed, "Don't start."

"Whatever. I'm going to hang here for a bit. Come back and get me later." Brielle rolled her eyes.

"What? I thought we was…" Tyson huffed.

"You thought wrong. Come on, cousin."

Porsha awkwardly smiled and exited the car.

"Brielle." Tyson grabbed her arm as she leaned out the car.

She snatched away, "Get ya' hands off me and go use it like you've been doing."

Tyson gritted his teeth as he watched Brielle get out the car.

"And take my bags in the house! I don't need niggas breaking the windows out and stealing my shit." She commanded.

Tyson didn't respond, he just shook his head and put the car in park, watching the two women enter the apartment building.

∞∞∞∞

VRRRRRRBBBB! Chris's cellphone vibrated against his nightstand, waking him from the first few hours of good sleep he'd gotten in the last five days.

55

"Yo." He answered half asleep.

"Wake yo ass up nigga. Streets don't sleep."

Chris huffed, recognizing the voice, "Nigga, your ass is supposed to be a ghost. Please don't tell me you're back in the city."

"Not yet." Tone's hefty, bass filled chuckle echoed through the phone.

Chris shot up in the bed, staring at his phone in irritation, "What the fuck you mean *not yet*? Your ass is supposed to be tucked away playing family man on that island. What reason do you have to come back, nigga?"

Tone chuckled, "Relax, nigga. I'm not on no bullshit. I don't know if you've seen the news, but there's a hurricane headed this way and the islands being evacuated. So, I'm bringing Jay and the girls home for a few weeks."

"You really think that's safe?" Chris quizzed.

"Why wouldn't it be?"

Chris sighed, "You got a secure line?"

"Nigga, I'm calling you on it. Ain't no number come up, did it?"

"Alright. Look…the big man called his soldier home to rest and let's just say, that shepherd has some sheep that won't just lay down beside still waters." Chris spoke in code, still desiring to be as careful as possible.

"Damn…" Tone sighed, feeling the persistent burden of guilt creeping in, "How big are the sheep and how many are there?"

"Nigga, that doesn't matter. What matters is you finding somewhere else to take your family, because if dots get to connecting, things could potentially go left." Chris warned.

"Nah. I'm not running again. When I came back here, it was because we'd already started a life but not to hide out again. I closed out that last *account* so we could move freely." Tone protested.

"Yea, well closing out one account opened several others. The owner of that account you *closed* is back. Sobered up and buying his way into local businesses, making it very clear that he has no intentions of leaving. And all though it may be coincidence or nostalgia, my gut says he's looking for more than investment opportunities."

Tone exhaled heavily, "Fuck…it's too late. We fly in tomorrow morning."

"Change the flight, nigga. You can afford it. Shit, I'll pay for it if you need me to. Go see the big mouse and ride some rollercoasters or hop on a cruise."

Tone quietly mulled over what Chris said, "Fine. I'll talk to Jay and tell her the change of plans. I'll have her find a cruise leaving out of the city or something."

Chris sighed with relief, "Good shit. I thought I was gonna have to threaten your ass."

"Don't get too excited. I'm still coming. I'm sending *them* away, so I can tie up these loose ends. Like I said, I'm done running." Tone stated brazenly.

"Fuck it. You're a grown ass man and clearly you love learning shit the hard way." Chris huffed.

"I'll hit you once I get them squared away."

"Please don't."

"Yea, ok. Don't make me have to come looking for you, nigga." Tone scolded before ending the call.

Chris looked down at the phone in bewilderment, "Did this nigga just? Who the fuck does he think I am, his runner? This nigga gonna make me pull rank on him."

He dropped his phone back onto the nightstand and collapsed back against his king size bed. Closing his eyes, he attempted to resume his slumber but frustrated by the new turn of events, he sat back up and grabbed his phone.

"Pick me up in 30 minutes." He instructed before disconnecting the call and then dialing someone else, "Yea. We're about to have a problem. Meet me at the brownstone."

Chris hung up and tossed his phone on the nightstand then begrudgingly made his way into his ensuite bathroom.

"What's up?"

The sight of China in the mirror behind him, slightly startled him, "What the fuck, Chi. I thought your ass left already."

"Uh, uhn. I was in the living room watching my shows. What's up? Why were you shouting?"

"Don't worry about it. Get dressed, the car will be here in 30 minutes." Chris instructed, stepping out of his boxers and into the standing shower.

China watched lustfully as he stepped under the cascading pour of the rain showerhead above him. The way the water rippled off of his muscular shoulder and chest, down to his perfectly sculpted glutes.

"Chi, hand me the soap from in the linen closet." He shouted; eyes closed under the water but still very aware of her lingering presence.

China reached and grabbed a bottle of body wash from the linen closet inside the bathroom and walked it over to the shower as she slipped out of her robe. Completely naked, she opened the shower door and stepped inside behind him pressing her chest against his back.

"Chi, we don't have time. The car will be here soon." Chris smirked.

"I'll be quick." China grinned, placing the bodywash on the shower ledge and sliding down to her knees.

China pulled at his waist, turning him to face her and grinned up at him as the water showered over her face. Before he knew it, she'd taken all of him into her mouth and his eyes met with the back of his head.

∞∞∞∞

"Lisa!" Maleah shouted, waving her over to the table she and Sky were sitting at.

The ladies had decided to meet up for lunch at *Legacy Lounge,* a black history themed restaurant that paid homage to the impact black people have had on every industry across the country and around the world. The upscale bespoke vibes were complimented by gold framed images of cultural icons and heroes of history adorning the walls; everyone from the likes of *Nelson Mandela* to *Maya Angelou.* And the mood was set by the mellow sounds of *Samara Joy's* song *"Guess who I saw today".*

"Ugh! Traffic was disgusting! I swear if I didn't have to take your niece to school this morning, I would've taken the train." Lisa huffed, as she plopped down at the end of the round, tufted booth.

"I thought you guys hired an *Au Pair.*" Sky scooted over in the booth.

Lisa sighed heavily, "I don't even want to talk about it…"

"Sounds like you need a drink." Maleah nudged her Lemon drop across the table.

"I can't." Lisa pushed it back, "I told you; I'm driving. Plus, I don't want to be the mom who shows up to pick up smelling like vodka. It's bad enough they already think I'm the worst mother ever."

"What? You're a great mother!" Maleah asserted.

"Did they say that to you?" Sky inquired.

Lisa sighed, "No...but I could just tell, when I dropped her off this morning...I forgot to pack a change of clothes, in case she has an accident, and they stared at me like I dropped her off already soiled."

"Can I start you ladies with an appetizer? The fried king crab bites are my fav at the moment." The young server interrupted.

"Uh, Hi, yes. I'll have the..." Lisa scanned the menu, "You know what, y'all go ahead and order, I need a few more minutes."

"Okay...I'll have the Caesar wedge salad and French onion soup." Sky ordered.

"Okay, and for you ma'am?"

"I'll try those king crab bites." Maleah responded, still looking over the menu, "And...let me get the fried calamari as well."

"Alrighty." The server scribbled on her note pad, "You ready ma'am or you need a few more minutes?"

"I'm ready. I'll try the Southern style Bruschetta, but can I have extra jalapeños on the side?"

"Absolutely. And what can I get you to drink?"

"The Lavender Lemonade and the cucumber mint water with lime."

"Got you. Alright, I'll go put in for your appetizers while you ladies decide on entrées, and I'll be right back with your drinks." The server smiled and headed toward the kitchen.

"So, back to what you were saying. Did someone say something or were they just looking at you funny?" Maleah resumed.

"No, no one actually said anything. And I'm glad, because I was already on edge after juggling a phone conference with one of my clients in South Africa and my current morning routine of toddler tantrums and bargaining to get her to wear close toed shoes in the winter." Lisa vented.

"I need a drink just listening to that." Maleah took a sip of her martini.

"It'll get better." Sky reached over and rubbed Lisa's arm, "They're definitely called *'Terrible twos'* for a reason. But you've got this...and I can send you some tricks to helping her self-soothe."

"Thank you, I know it will. It's just tough right now with Victor traveling so much for work. I really could use his help." Lisa sighed.

"Have you expressed this to him?" Sky inquired gently.

"I have, but...it's like he refuses to hear me. I don't want some stranger raising my child, that's not how I was raised. In my family, *we* take care of each other; La familia es la basé de todo!" Lisa huffed, "And when I agreed to starting a family, it was because he promised he'd lighten his workload to be an active partner in raising Mya. Especially with most of my family being in Florida and DR. But instead, he takes on more work at the label, while his parents enjoy their retirement, leaving me and mi madré, who's getting sicker by the day, to manage things."

Maleah and Sky stared at Lisa, making room for her to release what'd clearly been pent up for too long. Tears began welling in her eyes and Sky reached over, squeezing her hand as Maleah walked over to her side of the booth and sat down beside her, pulling her into a hug.

Lisa dabbed her eyes with a napkin, "Anyway, enough about me. We've only got an hour for lunch, and you did not come here to listen to me rant about motherhood. What's the tea on you and Korena?"

"Don't do that. Don't skip past your pain for our comfort. You don't have to have it all together to have value in this space." Sky gently scolded.

"Right. You don't have to always be the strong friend, Lis. It's okay, not to be okay. And what better place to come undone, than with your girls?"

"Yes, lean on us. We can handle it." Sky added.

Lisa instantly broke down in tears, "I'm just...so tired. I'm trying to juggle so much, and I feel like I'm losing myself in the process. I don't know whether I'm coming or going from one day to the next. But all anyone sees is how successful I am, and they just assume I'm okay; that I don't need help. But I do...I really do."

Overwhelmed with compassion for her sister-friend, Maleah also began to cry, "You're right...and that's partly on us for not checking on you. You shouldn't always have to ask for help. And I promise, going forward, I'll do better."

"Yea, me too." Sky chimed in, "We definitely need to be more intentional about checking in and supporting one another. No matter what, we must make it a priority."

Lisa grabbed them both by the hand, "Thank you…I appreciate that, more than you know. And I will hold myself accountable to that as well."

"You're our sister, you don't have to thank us." Sky placed her free hand atop Lisa's.

"Yea. We love you." Maleah sniffled, "You deserve to feel loved, by more than just our words. So, give me 48 hours to work out my schedule with my assistant Brittany and Auntie Leah will be reporting for duty. And don't even think about turning my offer down."

Lisa hugged Maleah tightly, "Thank you. I love you too."

"And I know your mom doesn't live far from Jared and I, so I can pop by a few times during the week and even take her grocery shopping with me when I go, if she needs."

Overwhelmed beyond words, the tears began to flow again from Lisa's eyes and all she could do is lean back, placing her hand over her heart, "Dios es bueno."

The women sat in silence for a moment as Lisa breathed through her feelings. The server walked close but sensed the vibe and walked over to another table, checking in with other patrons. After some time had passed, Lisa composed herself, dabbing her eyes and smiling to herself.

"Alright, now that I feel a hundred pounds lighter, we can commence the Korena debrief." Lisa laughed lightly.

Maleah sighed, rolling her eyes and took another sip of her drink.

Sky shook her head, "She explained everything, apologized sincerely and asked if they could start over."

"Hmph…where was all this transparency and apologetic energy when Charles was trying to coerce Leah into doing a bid for him?" Lisa huffed.

"Exactly!" Maleah blurted, catching the attention of the table behind them.

"Not to justify her actions…"

"Says the woman about to justify them." Maleah interjected sarcastically.

"No. I'm just looking at things from an empathetic perspective. A choice she made in her youth, terrible no doubt, has birthed some of the worst consequences imaginable. And she's still paying for it 15 years later."

"It didn't have to be that way though. She could've told Leah years ago. Saved herself the endless guilt and Leah the emotional trauma of being with Charles' toxic ass. May he rest…however GOD decides." Lisa rolled her eyes.

"I'm not disagreeing, I'm just offering some nuance. Korena's apparent need to feel accepted by her brother, in the absence of her father, led her to do something she couldn't possibly foresee the consequences of. A byproduct of abandonment and people pleasing." Sky expounded.

Maleah sighed, "I hear you… but, like I told my therapist, I don't know if I'm willing or even want to reconcile. I forgave her, for my own peace of mind, but resuming or restarting things isn't on my bingo card."

Lisa shrugged, "And there's nothing wrong with that. Your choice was originally taken, by way of omission *and* manipulation but now you have the ability and right to choose. If the choice is to move on, I support you 100%."

"So sorry for the delay. Kitchen got backed up and I had to help another server. Here's your Lavender lemonade and your cucumber mint water." The server walked over, placed down the two beverages in front of Lisa with two straws.

"Thank you. Can I also get lime?"

"Right! My apologies, I'll grab that now."

They watched as the overwhelmed server rushed to grab the lime from the bar area and hurriedly brought a saucer of limes back to the table.

"Alright, you ladies ready to order?"

"Yes."

"Absolutely."

VRRRRRRBBBB!

The ladies each checked their phones; it was Lisa's cell.

"Hello? What? Oh my gosh…" Lisa sighed heavily, "I told you guys she can't have real ice cream. No dairy. She's lactose intolerant! Yes, I'm on my way. I'll be there in like 30 minutes, depending on traffic."

Lisa hung up and abruptly slammed her phone down on the table as she violently snatched her coat from behind her and stood to put it on.

"Uh, can you come back in a few minutes?" Sky asked the server.

"Uh, yea, sure. No problem. Take your time." The server smiled awkwardly and quickly stepped away.

"Is everything okay?" Maleah asked Lisa, concerned.

"No…apparently one of the little kids at the daycare had a birthday party and one of the teacher's aids let Mya have ice cream cake, and of course because she can't have fuckin' dairy, she pooped on herself and has no change of clothes. Ellas sacas mi quicio!" Lisa fussed as she roughly secured her purse on her shoulder.

"Damn…" Sky grimaced, empathizing with her frustration.

"Why the hell would they let her have it, if you told them she can't? What if she had a severe allergy?" Maleah huffed.

"Exactly!" Lisa sighed, "Look, let me get out of here. Just text me what I owe, and I'll send it."

"No, no, you're fine. Go handle that, we've got you covered." Maleah assured.

"Yea, we've got it." Sky chimed in.

Lisa exhaled heavily, "Okay. Thank you. I'll text you later."

"Okay, I'll also call you tomorrow to coordinate our schedules."

She nodded and quickly made her way toward the exit without another word, just as the server walked up to the table with their appetizers.

"I'm really worried about her." Maleah admitted.

Sky nodded in agreement, "Same. But we're aware now and going to be intentional about checking in and supporting her through this."

"Yea… I'm also going to see if I can get my grandmother to watch Mya overnight, so we can have a decompress-girl's night soon."

"That'd be nice, I'm down. I'll also reach out to my friend Stephen. He's a great marriage counselor and I think he'd be a great resource for her and Victor."

"Hopefully he'll be open to it."

Chapter Five

The sun crept through the window and was shining so bright, Korena grabbed a pillow and plopped it over her head. Releasing a heavy sigh, she grunted and moaned in frustration, feeling the sudden urge to pee but wanting nothing more than to drift back to sleep.

"What? Man, get the fuck out of here with that!"

She leaned up and looked toward the bathroom and saw the door was closed. Carefully sliding out of the bed, she made her way over to the bathroom, stopping at the door to listen.

"That's bullshit!" Khalil gritted, sounding as if he was trying to whisper but failing terribly.

Korena slowly pushed the door open, and Khalil looked up; the expression on his face shifted from irritation to a subtle look of shock. He immediately ended the call and shoved the phone into his sweatpants pocket.

"You good?"

"I should be asking you that." Korena stared at him skeptically as his cell vibrated and the illumination from the screen shined through his pocket.

"What're you talkin' about? I'm good." Khalil rebutted.

Korena looked him up and down, "Mhmm…"

She shuffled her way to the toilet, too exhausted to argue but making a mental note to resume her inquisitions when she had the strength.

Khalil leaned back against the sink, staring at her, in deep thought. Korena sat with her eyes closed, still half asleep. When she was finished, she shuffled over to the sink and reach past him to wash her hands, then went back into the bedroom.

"You still feel up to it, to come with me today?" Khalil asked, standing in the bathroom doorway.

Korena adjusted in the bed, getting comfortable under the covers, "Mhmm...what time does the party start?"

"2 o'clock."

"Mhmm...wake me up like around 12:30." Korena spoke from beneath the covers.

In an instant, Korena drifted off to sleep, snoring lightly and Khalil made his way out of the bedroom, closing the door behind himself.

Stepping into a pair of Timbs he had at the front door, he grabbed his coat and keys, leaving out. Once he was in his car, he hit the redial on the unsaved number in his call log. After a few rings, the call connected to the car's Bluetooth.

"Hanging up on me won't change the truth, Khalil!" A woman's voice blared through the car's speakers.

Khalil adjusted the volume as he pulled off, "And you wanting that shit to be true, don't make it the truth."

"Nigga what? You're the last person on this fuckin' earth I'd want to have a kid with! Your ass is the reason my sister is missing."

"La'Porsha, I ain't gonna tell you again to stop saying that shit." Khalil gritted.

"Nigga, what, you think calling my government name is supposed to scare me? What, you gonna get rid of me and your unborn son, too?" Porsha spat.

Khalil drove in silence, ruminating on all the ways this could potentially fuck up his currently peaceful relationship. While he didn't believe her one bit, the mention of a possible baby would send Korena into a rage, and he couldn't handle another hospital stent.

"Don't worry...if you won't take me serious, maybe your new bitch will." Porsha taunted.

"You go anywhere near Korena-"

"And what? What nigga? Say it, so I can record it and give it to the detective looking into my sister's disappearance." Porsha barked.

Khalil sighed, clenching his jaw in frustration, "Look, don't call my fuckin' phone again. That ain't my baby, so check me off the list and continue your search for who is."

"Fuck you! I wasn't with nobody but your grimy ass!" Porsha shouted, offended by his accusations.

"Yea, whatever. You heard what I said. Get the fuck off my phone, Porsha."

"Fuck you Khalil! I hate you!"

Khalil ended the call and released an audible sigh that turned into a growl.

"What the fuck…it's always something!" He slammed his fist against the steering wheel, then reached to press play on the car's touch screen.

DMX's "Slippin" started to play and he turn the volume up as loud as he could.

∞◇◇∞

"No offense Your Honor, but I feel it's absolutely absurd to expect us to trust the testimony of some nameless, faceless character who could be nothing more than a tool of propaganda to further the agenda to destroy law and order." Leonard Eisenschmitt, Legal counsel to the Police department, argued.

Brynn James, Esq stood on the opposite side of him wearing a slight smirk at how worked up Leonard was. The pale skinned; middle-aged Jewish man was red as a beet.

Not only had Brynn successfully convinced a former associate of Det. Johnson to testify of his misdeeds, for early release, but to his welcomed surprise, they provided addresses. Some of which were police safe houses that Johnson used to hide drugs and money.

"I don't see how you can make that argument. I mean, did they or did they not find bags of pills and stacks of money in a police safe house? Money and drugs, might I add, that were not accounted for in any police report or related to any ongoing case. So, I'd say my witness is very much credible." Brynn argued.

"He's right Counselor. I understand that you feel knowing the identity of the witness would allow you to better assess their credibility. However, that's *my* job. In-camera testimony is at my discretion and given the nature of this case it was best for the witness's safety." Judge Alana St. Claire informed, unmoved by the two men's theatrics and peacocking.

"And I thank you for agreeing to it. We've all seen what tends to happen to people who go against his client. They end up paid off or…" Brynn shrugged suggestively.

"That's a brazen accusation! But I shouldn't expect any less of a spectacle from a clown in a shiny monkey suit." Leonard scoffed.

"Monkey what? Mothafucka I'll…" Brynn caught himself before the words left his mouth.

"Counselors! If you can't conduct yourself with decorum, I'll have you physically removed from the building." Judge St. Claire threatened.

"Let him go ahead and say it Your Honor. Show who he really is under all those big words and showboating for the media." Leonard taunted.

Brynn walked up on Leonard, towering over him, "You don't want to see what's up under here."

Judge St. Claire looked at the two men in annoyance, "Both of you shut up! Leonard, cut the taunting. You're not getting details on the witness and that's final."

"Again, no offense Your Honor but given the nature of the allegations, I feel it's only fair and justified for us to know who this person is. For all we know, they're some begrudged ex-cop who used all their free time to plant those drugs and the money. But how can we properly investigate without at least a name?" Leonard reasoned.

Judge St. Claire leaned back in her chair and folded her arms, "Let me get this straight, Counselor. You're not questioning the credibility of the witness's testimony; you're questioning *my* integrity? Or is it my competence that you're not too sure of? Huh? Maybe you're thinking I got this far on my looks and don't know how to determine a viable witness or testimony? But last I checked, I was a Harvard Law grad, top 10% in my class, 10 years as a state prosecutor with a flawless conviction rate and am entering my 7th year on the bench, with not so much as a mishandled DNA sample."

"Your Honor, I uh…that wasn't what I was implying." Leonard stammered and stumbled over his word, going from beet to fire engine red.

She leaned forward and resumed reading through documents on her desk, "I've heard enough. Testimony stands and will be considered, along with all other evidence procured during search and seizure. See yourselves out of my chambers."

Brynn left out without another word, frustrated that he'd let the old man get him out of character. Leonard however made one last attempt to apologize, and Judge St. Claire responded once more with threats to have him removed forcibly from her chambers and the building.

"We're in the clear…yup, his testimony helped us more than I hoped." He whispered into his cellphone, as he walked out of the courthouse, "Go ahead and submit the final documents for his release. I've got a meeting with his judge this afternoon."

"Attorney James! Tim Huan, freelance reporter. Can I get a statement from you on the current status of Detective Brenda Hanson's case?" The young Asian reporter walked up dressed like a high school student, wearing a crisp white button down, khaki pants and a black backpack. He pressed the record button on his cellphone and extended it toward Brynn's face.

Brynn pushed Tim's phone back a little, "Not much I can share at the moment, given the sensitivity of the case. But I will say, it's looking like justice may actually fall in favor of the oppressed for a change."

"So, Detective Hanson isn't guilty of killing two fellow officers?" Tim pressed.

"My client has dedicated her entire adult life to protecting and serving, the *right* way. And it is my hope that this city and country will rally behind one of its beloved black heroes, whose only crime is seeking justice in a broken system." Brynn professed boldly.

Tim nodded, "One last question, less serious but a persistent inquiry on social media. Are you single and who's your tailor?"

Brynn smirked, "That's actually two questions. But I'll let it slide this time… yes, and Yeboah Bespoke."

"Thank you for your time." Tim nodded and awkwardly walked away.

∞∞∞∞

It was 2pm at '*Lou's Bar & Billiards*' and aside from the regular derelicts who came in to blow their two-dollar drink budget for the warmth and shelter, only Theresa the bar maid was present.

69

"Y'all hiring for bartenders or servers?" A woman walked up to the bar.

"We don't get the kind of crowd that'd requires more than one barmaid, and the cooks serve from the same window they take orders out of." Theresa responded over her shoulder, never breaking her focus on the solitaire game she was playing on her phone.

"So…is that a yes, or no?" The woman asked with an attitude.

Turning only her head toward the woman, Theresa looked her up and down, "Lil girl, go on somewhere." She warned.

"I'm a grown ass woman." The woman rebutted.

"Well take your grown ass somewhere, because if I put this phone down, you're gonna wish you had." Theresa threatened calmly.

"Where's the manager or the owner? I don't even know why I'm asking your old, bitter ass. You're probably just worried that I'll take all your tips." The woman spat.

Theresa sighed then tucked her phone into her bra. She then reached to pull out the switch blade tucked tightly between her breast and turned around slowly when Paul came walking through the side door.

"Hey T!" He nodded, walking over to the bar, "You good?" Paul asked, sensing the tension between the two women.

"Yea, we're good. She was just leaving." Theresa glared at the woman.

"No, I wasn't. I want to speak to the owner or manager, cause it for damn sure ain't you." She rebutted.

"You know what bitch!" Theresa pointed the blade.

"Ay, ay! Chill out. T, tuck that shit back wherever you pulled it from. It's too early for that shit." Paul intervened, "I'm the manager. What can I do for you?"

"Thank you, I don't know why she's trippin'. I'm just trying to see if y'all are hiring." The woman walked toward Paul.

"Well, not necessarily. We're restructuring and don't really have the crowd to require more staff, yet." Paul explained.

"I just told her simple ass that!" Theresa chimed in.

The woman rolled her eyes, "That's not a problem. I actually can help with that. I have a loyal following of regulars who go wherever I go.

All I've got to do is post that I'm bartending here now, and the crowd will come."

"Yea and I'm sure the ratchet shit will follow. Ain't nobody got time for that!" Theresa asserted.

"T, relax. I got this." Paul held up his hand in a gesture for her to hush.

"Do you have an office or somewhere private we can talk?" The woman asked side eyeing Theresa.

"Yea, come on." Paul headed to the back office.

"These young bitches think shit sweet...I'll knock her ass out them plastic ass shoes." Theresa huffed to herself as she resumed the game on her phone.

Inside the office, the woman took a seat as Paul sat on the edge of the desk.

"So...you say you have a loyal following? What are we talking...10-15 people?" He inquired.

"Try 50 to 100. I pack out bars and make enough money off tips that my hourly rate is my pocket change, most nights. I bring out all the bad bitches and ballers." She gloated.

"Oh really?" Paul smirked.

"Really. The niggas wanna fuck me and the women wanna *be* me. What can I say, I just have an allure about me that most can't resist." She pursed her lips and shrugged, "Plus, my mixology is second to none."

"Why here? If you got it like that you can set up shop at any spot in the city." Paul quizzed.

"I could, but my regulars don't like traveling too far and I've burnt-out at most of the local spots. Once the owners and managers see how much I make, they get jealous and start doing weird shit like refusing to pay me hourly because of what I made in tips or mandating that I split tips with the other bartenders and cooks, even though I was the one packing the bar out and the food at most of those spots was trash." She explained.

"So, you figured you'd pick a small spot with no crowd, fill it with your people and at best you'd only have to share your tips with one other bartender?" Paul pried.

"Honestly...I scoped y'all out a week ago and figured you could just fire *Sheneneh* and let me run the mothafuckin bar myself. I'll negotiate

71

a tip-out percentage with the cooks, if the food is quality, cause my people won't eat bullshit. And I'll take whatever hourly you offer upfront, but we must renegotiate my rate after 30 days and you see your profit tripled."

Paul rubbed his chin in thought, "Hmm...if you collect the kind of tips that make your hourly rate look like pocket change, why not just take that and we knock down the cooks tip-out to 5%?"

"Because I'm damned good at what I do, but I ain't a magician. There will be days where people don't pour in: Snowstorms, torrential rain, some celebrity party in the city taking half my crowd. Shit happens and I need to be protected. Put me on payroll as salary, paid on the 15th of every month, so I'm protected regardless. You'll still make more than enough profit."

"How about a trial run. You come in Saturday night, work the bar with Theresa..."

"Uhn, uhn, hell no." She interrupted, "I will fuck that old bitch up."

"Relax, I'll handle T. You worry about showing me you ain't all talk. Make me a believer and we've got a deal." He offered.

She huffed, "And then you'll fire that old bitch?"

"No...I can't do that, she's good people. But I will consider giving you Thursday through Sunday solo from 8pm to 3am. She'll take day shift and the lighter nights of the week." Paul explained.

"Okay...but I want to work-day shift during major football and NCAA games. Once I get this place packed a few nights, you can upgrade them TV's and start drawing a regular sports crowd; then add wing and drink specials and your profits will be in the black." She added.

"I appreciate the suggestions, however tv's have already been ordered and there's already a fifty-cent wing and two-dollar beer special. As far as working day shift, that can be worked out. But you'll have to share the bar with Theresa unless, for whatever reason, she takes the day off." Paul informed.

She sighed, "Fine...you keep her on a leash, and I'll do what I do."

Paul reached out his hand, "I'll see you Saturday...Miss..."

"De'Shaye, but I go by DeeDee" She grabbed his hand and stood up, staring into his eyes sultrily.

"Paul."

"I look forward to working together…Paul."

Paul smiled, amused, and entertained by her boldness. Her natural sex appeal and ability to make him feel like steak on a plate, assured him that she could absolutely charm pennies from a pauper. Back in his youth, he would have used a woman like her to set niggas up and fish information from the opposition.

∞∞∞∞

"Daddy! Look!" Kameron shouted from inside the bounce house which was filled from wall to wall with kids.

The backyard of Isaiah and Keira's Secaucus, New Jersey home had been completely transformed into a mini gamer amusement paradise, all for their twins Kameron & Khaleb's 9th birthday.

Unwilling to let the frigid February weather disrupt the festivities, Isaiah had their huge yard custom fitted with a tent and heaters that made it feel like they were stepping through a portal, going from Artic tundra to summer getaway, whenever they stepped beneath it.

In addition to the bounce house, there was a mini track for racing remote controlled cars, and a pop-up gaming station outfitted with a PS5 and multiple controllers. Across the large yard was a Virtual Reality station equipped with a VR-treadmill and scattered throughout the yard were tables the children periodically visited, stuffing their faces before quickly returning to their games.

Just below the elevated deck, attached to the house, was a buffet featuring all the boy's favorites. On the right: a full nacho bar and customizable *savory or sweet* empanada station for Khaleb. To the left, for Kameron, an elaborate *Five Guys* display, outfitted with burgers, fries, hotdogs and a milkshake machine.

There was also someone serving popcorn in novelty containers that displayed a picture of the boys and another person making cotton candy shaped as various characters. And to add to the children's sugar high, there was a soda fountain that only served root beer, the boys favorite.

For the parents and more mature guests, there were refreshments atop the enclosed deck, which was also heated. There was smoked brisket, a salad bar, fruit salad shooters, charcuterie flights, and wine & beer.

"Ayyy! Y'all made it!" Isaiah exclaimed.

Xavier dapped him up and the two embraced, "Of course."

"Hey, Maleah." Isaiah smiled.

"Hey." She reached out her hand and he pulled her into a hug.

"You know, you're the *one*, right? You've got my boy's nose wide open." Isaiah whispered during their embrace.

"Ay, ay! That's enough. Back up off my woman." Xavier playfully pulled his shoulder.

"Yea! Back up off his lady, babe and let me get a look at the woman who's got lover boy all googly eyed." Keira came waddling up.

"Kiki?" Xavier gasped in shock.

She grinned, rubbing her large belly, "Hey, X."

"You're pregnant?" He pulled her into a hug, then turned to Isaiah and playfully punched him in the chest, "Nigga, why didn't you say anything?"

"Because man...it felt too insensitive, given the circumstances. You know, with Khalil's girl and the baby."

Xavier shook his head, "You're right. But you could've called me any time after that and told me! Especially since you promised to make me godfather of your next kid."

Isaiah smiled awkwardly as Keira rubbed his back, looking away.

"What?" Xavier looked from Keira to Isaiah confused by the energy shift.

"Hey! I'm sorry, how rude of me. I didn't get your name." Keira interjected, stretching out her hand.

"Maleah."

The two women shook hands.

"I'm Keira. Most people call me Kiki, but you can call me either one. You like wine, Maleah?"

Maleah nodded, "Yea, as long as it's sweet."

"Great! I've got a new bottle I plan to try after I drop this little nugget, and I'd love your opinion on it."

"Um...okay." Maleah looked over at Xavier.

"Go ahead babe. Enjoy yourself." He nodded.

Keira took her by the hand and the two women made their way up the deck stairs and then into the house.

"So, what...you chose somebody else to be the godfather?" Xavier questioned.

Isaiah sighed, shoving his hands into his pockets, "Look, it's not that I wouldn't love for you to be the godfather, it's just...your current lifestyle didn't seem set up for that kind of responsibility. And although godparents are a long-term contingency, the recent years have shown us we need to plan for the immediate unexpected."

"What? But Khalil is the godfather of the twins."

"Come on, X. I thought we moved passed this. You know why he's, their godfather." Isaiah rebutted.

"Yea, I know. It's because he was there when Keira went into labor. But I'm still confused as to why he's godfather of *both* the boys."

Isaiah sighed, "Because, while I was in Delaware for training and you and Chris were both out of town on business, Khalil was there, in the middle of a snowstorm, rushing my wife to the hospital. You do remember the doctors said that, if she'd delivered at home, Kameron might not have survived?"

"Yes...I remember. I just don't understand how my *lifestyle* makes me unfit but he's suitable for the boys. I mean, no offense, but we both know he's not the most stable."

"Really, nigga?"

Xavier turned to see Khalil and Korena walking up.

He sighed, "I ain't mean it like that, man. I'm just saying, we both know I'm more responsible."

"Nigga, what? Are you still on this? It's literally been 9 years. Let it go! I'm their godfather, not you." Khalil shook his head.

"Um, sorry to interrupt but where's your bathroom." Korena interjected.

"Oh, no it's okay. I'll show you where it is." Isaiah offered, "Y'all can put the boy's gifts over on the gift table."

Isaiah pointed toward an overflowing table of presents and then gently took Korena by the arm and led her toward the deck stairs. He silently thanked GOD for the opportunity to escape what was becoming an increasingly awkward situation. The last thing he needed was for it to turn into an all-out dispute, in the middle of his kid's birthday party.

Xavier and Khalil stood silently watching them disappear into the house and then simultaneously walked over to the gift table, placing down their gifts.

"For the record, that wasn't about you; I'm over not being the twin's godfather. That was about Zay basically saying he didn't think my lifestyle was suitable for being godfather to their...new baby." Xavier shared.

"Kiki's pregnant, again?"

Xavier nodded, "Yup...and judging by the size of her stomach and the waddle, it looks like she could drop any day."

"Hmm...so, who did he pick to be godfather? Because I know for damn sure, it ain't Chris."

"You're damn right." Chris walked up, placing a professionally wrapped gift box onto the table.

"Not Mr. Anti-kids showing up to a kids birthday party." Xavier laughed, dapping up Chris.

Chris shrugged, "Y'all my brothers, remember? That means doing a lot of shit I'd rather not do, for y'all."

"Ay, man. Even I know not to be cussing around the kids." Khalil chastised, dapping up Chris.

"My bad. See, this is why I don't do kids. Can't even speak freely." Chris huffed, "Where's the liquor at?"

They both just stared at Chris, amused at how physically uncomfortable he looked. He frowned up his face, watching the sugar-crazed children run around, screaming with sticky faces and hands.

Xavier and Khalil looked at each other and burst out laughing, causing Chris to laugh as well.

"It's making you itch, ain't it, nigga?" Khalil teased.

"Man, fu- *eff* you." Chris laughed.

"Come on, let's get you out of here before you melt." Xavier joked, leading the way to the deck stairs.

"I'll meet you up there, I'm gonna make me a plate first." Chris informed as he headed toward the burger station.

"I'mma grab something too. Knowing Keira, there's probably only charcuterie and *crudité* on the deck." Khalil quipped.

Chris laughed, "You better hope Zay don't hear you. You remember what happened last time."

"Nigga, what? Ain't nobody scared of Zay."

"Yea, whatever. You better keep his wife's name out your fuckin' mouth." Chris teased.

"Nigga, stop cussing around the kids!" Khalil shook his head.

Chris huffed, "I'm leaving as soon as I finish my burger. I can't do this censored shit."

Khalil just shook his head and grabbed a plate.

As Xavier stepped onto the deck, Keira came stepping through the glass sliding doors followed by Maleah, who was sipping a glass of red wine.

"Let me taste." Xavier slid his arms around Maleah's waist, and she tipped the glass toward his mouth.

"Mmm...I like that. What's it called?"

"I forgot the name, but Kiki said it's from a vineyard in Maryland. And she said they do a really nice Caribbean Winefest in the Summer. She said they take a group every year and it's really fun. I think we should go." Maleah gleefully rambled.

Xavier just smiled at the joy on her face, "Sounds like you and *Kiki* got really acquainted in there."

Maleah giggled, "We did. I really like her. You should plan some double dates."

"Oh, I should? Huh?"

"Mhmm." She smiled, sipping her wine.

"Dad! Kam keeps cheating on the game!" Khaleb came storming up the deck stairs, capturing the attention of everyone.

"No, I didn't! He's just mad, he's trash!" Kameron shouted, rushing closely behind his brother.

"Hey! Language." Keira chastised, "Apologize."

Kameron sucked his teeth.

"Boy!" Isaiah barked, stepping out onto the deck.

"Fine...sorry." Kameron sighed.

"Now, go play. I don't wanna hear this nonsense. You're supposed to be celebrating with each other, not fighting." Keira instructed.

"But mom!" Khaleb whined.

"Khaleb, you heard your mother. Go play, unless y'all want the party to be over." Isaiah asserted.

"No! Come on bro." Kameron pleaded.

Khaleb huffed, "Fine..."

The boys ran back down the steps, rejoining the joyful chaos and the adults returned to their card games and eating.

Keira placed a Bluetooth speaker on the table and turned the volume up a little. *"Can't get enough"* by *Tamia* started to play and a few of the women began doing the line dance at the front of the deck. Xavier and Maleah stood watching for a moment, then made their way over to the table and took a seat.

All smiles, Maleah placed her glass on the table, looking around at the array of joyful black people. It was a sight she'd always yearned for, daydreaming as a child about multi-generational gatherings: family reunions, thanksgiving dinners and summertime cookouts etc.

Khalil walked over to Isaiah, holding a plate of empanadas, "Korena still in the bathroom?"

"Oh, nah. She said she was feeling nauseous and wanted to stay inside, close to the bathroom." Isaiah shared discreetly.

"Alright, thanks man. Let me go check on her." He nodded and made his way into the house.

Chris stepped onto the deck carrying a plate overflowing with nachos, empanadas, a burger and fries. He placed the plate down on the table and grabbed a beer from the cooler before taking a seat across from Xavier and Maleah.

"Damn, that looks good." Xavier blurted, "Baby, I'm going to go get a burger. What you want?"

"Um...I don't want anything yet. I might get some fruit salad though."

"Alright."

He kissed her on the forehead then made his way toward the stairs. Maleah sipped her wine and swayed to the music as she watched him until she could no longer see him.

"You really love that fool, huh?" Chris interrupted her thoughts.

"Huh?"

Chris smirked, "Yea, you love him."

"Yea...I do." She blushed, "It's that obvious?"

"Mhmm...but don't worry, he's got it just as bad as you."

Maleah smiled proudly, "I know."

"What're y'all over here talkin' about?" Keira interrupted, as she and Isaiah walked over.

Isaiah pulled out a chair and sat down, pulling Keira onto his lap.

"Yea, what's he over here telling you? Hopefully he hasn't been terrorizing you with his theories on monogamy and it being *a poor man's paradise*." Isaiah added.

"Funny. But that's not what I said, I said only poor men consider monogamy paradise."

"Same thing." Isaiah rebutted.

"Not really."

Keira shook her head, rubbing her belly, "I thought you would've outgrown this mindset by now."

"What's there to outgrow? I just believe and know from experience that wealth comes with a vast array of luxuries. So, as much as I love women, being locked down to just one isn't the *jackpot*. It's not even close; at least not to *me*." Chris explained further.

"Well, I for one am glad X doesn't share your sentiments." Maleah quipped.

Chris raised his beer, "I'm in a league of my own."

"Nigga, you're on your soapbox already? We ain't even been here 20 minutes." Xavier interjected, walking back over to the table.

"Man, whatever. I was minding my business, eating my burger and drinking my beer. This nigga came over here starting with me." Chris rebutted.

"Yo, X! Can you pass me a beer?" Khalil leaned out the glass sliding doors.

"There's some inside, in the fridge." Isaiah shouted back.

Khalil nodded and went back inside the house.

Xavier chuckled, "Good looking out. I really didn't feel like getting up."

"When did he get here?" Maleah whispered.

"He got here a few minutes before Chris. You didn't see him come up?"

"No. I must not have been paying attention…um, is he alone?" Maleah pried.

"Yes, she's here." Xavier cut to the chase.

Maleah immediately felt uncomfortable, adjusting in her chair as she tried to stealthily peek through the glass doors, into the house.

"I'm surprised y'all didn't see each other when Zay walked her to the bathroom."

Maleah shrugged, "They must've come in while we were in the wine cellar."

"Wine cellar? Damn...Zay's really doing well. I've got to come back and get the full tour." Xavier smiled.

"This is your first time here?"

"Yea. I've only been to their house in Jersey City, which was much smaller than this one."

"Kiki, is there anymore fruit salad?" An older woman asked.

"Yea, there's another bowl in the fridge. I'll go grab it." Keira carefully tried to get up from the table.

"No, Kiki you relax. I know you've been running all day. Leah can go grab it for you." Xavier asserted.

Maleah almost choked on her wine, "I can?"

"Yea, you can. Didn't you say you wanted fruit salad?"

"So does that lady. Why can't she go get it." She tried her best to whisper.

"Babe, she's like 70. You're gonna make her go get the bowl and carry it out?"

"Then why don't you go be chivalrous and get the fruit salad yourself." Maleah huffed in frustration, trying to keep her voice down.

"It's okay, I can go get it. It's really no problem." Keira stood up.

"No, no...you sit. I'll go get it." Maleah forced a smile.

"Thank you." Keira smiled.

"No problem." Maleah nodded as she stood and made her way around the table.

Before stepping through the sliding doors of the house she turned around, wearing an annoyed look and flared her nostrils at Xavier.

"She's gonna cuss yo ass out later." Chris laughed.

Xavier laughed and shrugged, "I know...but she can't keep avoiding the inevitable. They're going to be around each other at some point."

When Maleah stepped into the house, she walked by the living room and caught a glimpse of Khalil and Korena on the couch. Hoping

80

they didn't notice her, since they were watching something on the tv, she hurried into the kitchen and retrieved the bowl of fruit salad from the refrigerator.

"Hey.", Korena's voice stopped her in her tracks as she tried to covertly exit the kitchen.

Maleah exhaled and then turned, giving a faint smile, "Hey."

"You just got here?"

"No. Been here a while." Maleah replied with brevity.

"Oh…um…it's good to see you." Korena nodded, sensing her lack of desire to converse.

Maleah smiled and nodded, "Okay…I'm gonna go take this outside."

"Wait." Korena blurted.

Maleah sighed, biting her bottom lip.

The tension filled silence was beginning to make Khalil feel uncomfortable, so he stood up and walked over to Maleah.

"I'll take it out for you." He took the bowl from her before she could respond and went outside.

"Can we please talk?" Korena pleaded.

"We've already talked."

"I know, but that was about the past. I want to talk about the future." Korena spoke sincerely, gently rubbing her belly.

Maleah massaged her temples and released an exasperated sigh.

"This isn't the appropriate time or place."

"When and where else can I talk to you? You have me blocked on everything and I'm not allowed at your office." Korena ranted.

"Whose fault is that?"

"I'm not saying I don't deserve it. I'm just asking for you to at least try to forgive me. 15 years of friendship can't just be erased, Leah. You're still my sister." Korena proclaimed.

Maleah stood frozen, fighting to regulate her emotions. On one hand, she missed her sister/friend like crazy. But on the other hand, she couldn't suppress her overwhelming feelings of distrust. Although she was working toward forgiveness in therapy, for her own sanity, she was still unsure if reconciliation was possible. Especially when the sight of Korena and sound of her voice brought the memories of her betrayal rushing to the front of her mind.

"I can't."

She walked away without another word, leaving Korena sitting on the sofa, with tears forming in her eyes.

Chapter Six

"Boss man, I wanna run something by you. You got a sec?" Ashley, Soulidified Records Brand Manager, walked into Xavier's office.

"Can you do it while I walk, I've got to meet someone in the lobby." Xavier asked as he checked his phone and headed for the door.

Ashley followed behind him, "Yup! So, elevator pitch: I want to rebrand Typhoon's image starting with his clothing. Get him taken more seriously and get him some brand partnerships with major designers."

"Okay. So, what do you need from me? Mr. Anderson's head of marketing, this should be a conversation for him." Xavier quizzed, stepping out into the elevator lobby.

"Right, right, I know. I've actually pushed this up the chain of command and they told me if I could convince Ty to stop letting his girlfriend's shop for him and to accept a real stylist, I'd have their full support." Ashley continued, following him onto the elevator.

Xavier sighed, pressing the button for the lobby, "Okay, so...again what do you need from me Ash? 'Cause this has now turned into a literal elevator pitch."

"Okay, sorry, I'm a little long winded. Definitely working on that. So, what I need from you is a really big, sort of personal favor." Ashley expounded awkwardly.

"Personal?"

"Yes...so, I heard through the social media streets that the creator of Yeboah Bespoke is in the city. He's partnered with J.M. Styling before, in London and I was hoping...that you could ask your girlfriend- I mean Ms. Smith if she'd be willing to convince him to make a few suits for Typhoon. I know J.M. strictly deals with clients under contract and I haven't gotten Typhoon 100% on board with adding a stylist to his team, but he did agree to wearing a suit to the *NAACP Image Awards* after I showed him *Kofi Seriboe* rocking Yeboah Bespoke. So, if you could help, I'd owe you big time!" Ashley spoke a mile a minute, finally taking a breath as the elevator doors opened to the lobby.

"I'll see what I can do." Xavier nodded and smiled at the anxious young woman.

"Okay, thank you so so so much!" Ashley exclaimed as two women stepped onto the elevator and the doors closed behind them.

"Hey, beautiful." Xavier walked up to Maleah, sliding his arms around her waist.

"Hi, baby."

"I missed you." He kissed her.

Maleah blushed, "I was only in LA for 3 days."

"Three long ass days." He pressed his forehead against hers and slid his hands over her booty.

She giggled, slapping his hand, "Cut it out. People are staring at us."

"So." He shrugged.

"Turn me loose, sir and come on." She laughed.

Xavier waited a moment, staring down at her lustfully before letting her go and taking her by the hand. He led her toward the elevator and pressed the *Up* button.

"I ordered breakfast. The app says it should be here shortly." Xavier informed, as he ushered her onto the elevator then stepped in behind her.

"Mmm...I was just thinking about them grits we had." Maleah moaned.

"With the eggs scrambled lightly, beef bacon and wheat toast, lightly buttered?" Xavier smirked knowingly.

"Did you?" Maleah looked up at him, mouth open in delighted surprise.

"I know, I know...you love me." He lovingly teased.

Maleah walked up to him, rubbing her hand across his broad chest, "I really do..."

DING! The elevator doors opened to J.M. Styling's floor and Brittany, one of Maleah's assistants was standing in the lobby.

"Ms. Smith, I wanted to catch you before you were caught off guard. I know you said no meetings and hold your calls until 12pm, but you have a guest and he's insistent that you'll be okay with seeing him." Brittany spoke quickly as Maleah and Xavier stepped off the elevator.

"Who is it?" Maleah quizzed.

"Eric Yeboah, of Yeboah Bespoke. He said you two worked together closely in London and were good friends." Brittany shrugged nervously.

"Eric?" Maleah felt like she'd gotten the wind knocked out of her, "He never comes to New York, he hates it. He has all his clients come to him in London or LA."

"So…is it okay that he's here or should I tell him you'll need to meet with him another time?" Brittany questioned.

"That's the guy Ashley wanted me to ask you about." Xavier inserted.

"Ashley?" Maleah asked, still trying to process.

"Yea, our new brand manager. She wants to connect with your guy, to get some suits made for Typhoon."

"My guy? He's not my guy. We worked together in London, but that was a while ago." Maleah rebutted defensively.

Xavier and Brittany both looked at her with confused and concerned expressions.

"So…what do you want me to do?" Brittany broke the awkward silence.

"Where is he?" Maleah tried to see through the frosted entry doors.

"I put him in the small conference room, since there's no meetings in there until 2pm." Brittany shared.

Maleah sighed in relief, "Okay…so, it's a *No* for today. I'm going to be in my office, just tell him I got called to supervise a location shoot and I won't be in today as expected."

"Uh, okay…" Brittany nodded awkwardly.

She turned and headed for the office, followed by Maleah and Xavier. When he opened the frosted glass door, Brittany quickly walked through and stopped in her tracks, halted by the sight of a man in a finely tailored suit. She turned on her heels and mouthed *"Sorry"* to Maleah.

"Mal." Eric grinned.

Maleah smiled awkwardly.

Eric Yeboah leaned against the reception desk, as the receptionist blushed, enamored by his charm. Standing a solid 5 foot 11 and built like a running back, he donned one of his original creations: A blue bespoke daishiki suit, with a cross-body lapel, Kente print trim, Ghana shaped cufflinks and matching blue suede loafers. His skin was deep and rich, indeed kissed by the sun and smile twinkled brighter than the diamond in his ear. As a first generation British-Ghanaian, his swagger and charismatic appeal was complimented by a South London accent and deep, base-filled voice.

"Mal?" Xavier mimicked.

"Yea. It's what I call her. A way of distinguishing myself from those who took the easy route of calling her *Leah*. No offense."

Xavier, caught off guard by Eric's statement, clenched his jaw in attempt to stifle the offense he'd indeed taken.

Sensing the tension, Maleah gently rubbed his back.

"Eric, this is Xavier; Head of Soulidified Records."

"Soulidified? That's Daleesha's label, right? My little cousin loves her." Eric smiled, never taking his eyes off Maleah.

"X, this is-"

"Eric Yeboah." He cut her off, reaching out his hand, "Of Yeboah Bespoke. But I'm sure you already know that."

Xavier paused for a second then grasped his hand and squeezed it.

"Firm grip you got there. What do you lift, about two-fifty? Three hundred?" Eric chuckled.

"Three-fifty." Xavier responded, unamused.

"Nice…I know Mal definitely appreciates a man who can lift her." Eric winked.

"What?" Xavier's jaw flexed.

Eric threw his hands up in a faux surrender, "No offense, bruv."

Maleah gently squeezed Xavier's arm, "Eric, what are you doing in New York? You hate this city."

Eric smiled, "Hate's such a strong word."

"And yet it's the one you always used."

"This is true…let's just say, I've had a change of heart. Finally decided to go beyond the façade of Manhattan and found a rare, inimitable vibrance." He expounded.

"Hmm…how Christopher Columbus of you to *discover* what's always been." Maleah snarked.

"Now, now Mal… sarcasm never suited you. You're far too beautiful for such pettiness."

BRRRRRING! The reception phone rang, disrupting the escalating tension of the moment.

"Okay…yes, that's fine." The receptionist hung up the phone, "Ms. Jones, there's a food delivery on its way up for Mr. Smith."

"Alright, thank you." She nodded, then turned her attention back to Eric, "Well, I'm sure you've got plenty to attend to, with your work being in such high demand. So, it was nice seeing you."

"Actually, I have a lot of free time. I flew in to hand-deliver some custom suits to a high-profile client but the rest of my time here, is set aside to see family and get reacquainted with…the city." Eric smirked suggestively.

"Well, I hope you enjoy the city." Maleah gave a sarcastic smile.

"Same." Eric winked.

Xavier cleared his throat, growing irritated with Eric's blatant disregard for his presence.

Eric nodded, "Nice meeting you, Zair."

"Xavier." He corrected.

"Right, right, Xavier. You know, you should get my info from Mal. The head of a label should look like royalty and Yeboah Bespoke can transform any pauper into a King."

"I have an order for Mr. Smith." The security guard announced, as he leaned through the frosted doors of the reception area.

Xavier released a subtle, frustrated sigh and walked over to take the bag from the man, "You ready?"

"Yea, just give me a sec. I'll meet you in my office." Maleah rubbed his arm.

Xavier stared into her eyes, trying to read her. Although it was more than obvious that the London Loverboy had a thing for Maleah, he couldn't quite gage Maleah's feelings toward him. There was definitely an underlying hostility that alluded to history that went far beyond a working relationship.

"Alright." Xavier kissed her sweetly.

Once he was out of sight, Maleah turned her attention to Eric, "Let me walk you to the elevator."

Eric smiled menacingly as he followed behind, checking her out lustfully. Once they got in front of the elevators, Maleah walked up close on him.

"I don't know what your game is but make this the last time you show up here." She scolded.

"Well, that's gonna be kind of hard since I'm in talks with Juanita Michaels about joining the J.M. Styling family."

"What?"

"Yup...turns out I'm good at more than just designing custom suits. And the credit's all yours; watching you run J.M. London inspired me to push my creative limits. What's it you used to say? *If all you can style is your own stuff, you're not as creative as you think.*"

"You're lying."

"Nope. I've been back and forth to the states the past few months working on brick-and-mortar locations for *Yeboah Bespoke* in Harlem and Beverly Hills. You're looking at J.M. Stylings new resident international tailor and stylist."

"This cannot be happening."

"Aw Mal, I missed you too."

Maleah exhaled hard, "Look, I really don't care where you work. Just cut all the flirtatious inuendoes because as you can see, I've moved on and am very happy."

"Very happy, eh?"

"Very."

Eric smiled his famous mischievous, grinch-like grin, "Okay."

"I'm not playing, Eric. Don't come here starting shit. Because I can't save you from the consequences." Maleah warned.

"I knew you still loved me."

She gasped, "I what? Tuh- you know what, bye Eric!"

Maleah huffed, turning immediately on her heels and stormed through the doors of the office leaving Eric grinning as he tapped the elevator button.

DING!

The elevator doors opened, and he stepped on, grinning menacingly to himself as the doors closed in front of him.

When Maleah returned to her office, Xavier was sitting on the sofa checking emails on his phone. She huffed and mumbled as she walked over to her desk, plopping down behind it and opening her laptop.

"Sorry you had to deal with that, he's...."

"Your ex."

Maleah froze in place, looking up from her computer to see Xavier staring intensely.

She sighed, "Was it that obvious?"

"Not at all." He retorted in a dry sarcastic tone.

"Well, trust me when I say, you have nothing to worry about. Eric is just full of himself, and as you can see, thrives on getting a rise out of people. One of the many reasons we didn't work out."

"What did you need to talk to him about, without me present?" Xavier's tone was as intense as his stare.

Maleah arched her eyebrow, thrown off by his energy. Although Eric was clearly out of line, she'd never known Xavier to be so easily upset.

"I pulled him aside to check him about the disrespect and showing up to my place of work uninvited." Maleah explained.

"And, you couldn't have done that with me there?" He pressed.

"Well, yes, but I was trying to avoid things escalating. And I could tell he was starting to get under your skin. The last thing I needed was for him to make one more smart remark and you try to put him through the glass doors."

"He didn't get under my skin, *you* did."

"What? Me? What did I do?"

"*This is Xavier Smith, Head of Soulidified records.*" He mocked.

"What did I say wrong?"

"It's what you *didn't* say. Did it slip your mind or was it intentional that you didn't tell him I'm your man?"

Maleah leaned back in her chair, "Really? That's what you're mad about?"

"Yes! And don't dismiss the shit like I'm overreacting. Because if the shoe were on the other foot, you'd be cussin' me out right now." Xavier huffed.

Realizing that he was genuinely upset, Maleah stood up from her desk and walked over to him. As she went to sit on his lap, he stopped her, moving her to sit beside him.

"You're that mad?"

He stared ahead, shaking his head, "I'm not mad."

"Could've fooled me."

Xavier stood up from the sofa, "I've got a busy day today. I'll see you later."

She leapt up and followed him to the door, "What? I thought we were having breakfast. What happened to you missing me?"

"I did. And I'm not hungry anymore." He leaned over and kissed her on the forehead then left out the office.

"What the hell?" Maleah belted so loud she startled one of the styling assistants passing by.

She grabbed the door and pushed it with as much force as she could, attempting to slam it, but the soft-close hinges prevented the impact. Frustrated by the sight of the slowly closing door, she stormed over to her desk and plopped down once more.

"Eric-fuckin-Yeboah!" She shouted, swatting a container of pens off her desk.

After a moment of sitting with her eyes closed and deep breathing she reached for her phone and contemplated who to dial. The only person who knew the full story about Eric was Korena, and there was no way she was calling her. And Sky's phone stayed on *do not disturb* during the workday, so, she decided to call Lisa. She could just fill her in on the missing details.

After several rings Lisa finally answered, "Hello?"

"Hey, girl. You busy?"

"Um, not at this second but I do have a meeting in fifteen minutes. What's up? Is everything alright?" Lisa sounded as if she was moving quickly.

"Oh okay, no I'm good. Well, sort of, if you don't count the fact that Eric Yeboah just showed up to my damn office and managed to disrupt my happy, drama-free relationship in a matter of ten minutes!" Maleah ranted.

"Eric who? Am I supposed to know who that is?" Lisa quizzed, sounding a bit preoccupied.

"Yes! You remember, the guy I sort of dated back in London?"

"Oh…okay, so what about him?"

Maleah sighed, "Never mind. You sound busy, I'll just talk to you later."

"Okay, that's fine. I need to take this time between meetings to grab breakfast anyway. I've been intermittent fasting all week."

"Alright, well you go ahead."

The call ended and Maleah slouched in her chair, staring at her phone screen which displayed a picture of her and Xavier. In an instant, she felt the sharp pain of undesired truth: She missed Korena. And it made her feel really small and silly because it took something as simple as just wanting to vent to someone, to realize it.

Korena was always willing to talk shit with her and laugh at the things other people thought were childish. She was a safe space to be all of herself: anxious, silly, mean, sensitive, unsure and wrong… she for sure would've been the first to tell her she was dead wrong for not telling Eric that Xavier was her man. And she would've probably even encouraged rubbing his face in it, to show him what he'd lost. But Maleah's inability to move beyond her feelings of betrayal kept her isolated, trapped in a silo of memories and daydreams of what could've been had things not happened the way they did.

∞◇◇∞

Monique stood at the kitchen sink, swaying her hips to the sound of *Marvin Gaye's "I want you"*, as she washed dishes.

"But I want you to want me too…" Paul sang seductively in her ear as he walked up behind her, sliding his hands around her waist.

The two swayed and sang gleefully, like two lovestruck teenagers, when the doorbell rang. Neither of them ceased their melodic utterances or stepped away.

DING DONG! DING DONG! The person at the front door began to press the doorbell more profusely.

Monique huffed, "Ugh! Who the hell is it?"

"You want me to get it?" Paul inquired, still holding her tight.

"No, hand me my phone. Let me check the doorbell camera and see if I feel like answering." Monique quipped.

Paul grabbed her phone off the counter and passed it to her. Drying off her sudsy, wet hands she opened the app and let out a scream.

"What? Who is it?" Paul asked concerned by the tears now forming in her eyes.

"It...it's..." She struggled to release the words.

"Who?"

Monique removed his arms from around her waist and sped out of the kitchen, toward the front door. Paul followed behind her, watching from the dining room as she opened the door and fell to her knees.

A man, dressed in a dark blue Dickie's set stepped inside and helped Monique off the floor, "Come on, Ma. Get up."

"T.Y.?" Monique exclaimed, wrapping her arms around her son and collapsing into his embrace.

"I'm home, Ma." Tyree spoke calmly as he walked his mother over to the sofa.

"Wha...when did you...why didn't you tell me you came home today?"

"My lawyer didn't know the exact day the judge was going to release me and I ain't want y'all all excited if he decided to play with my release date. They was already pissed they had to free a nigga." Tyree explained.

"Welcome home."

Tyree's head turned so fast, his neck could've snapped if it wasn't for the fact that he'd bulked up in prison and now had a neck like a tree trunk.

"Who the fuck is this?" Tyree pointed toward Paul, while staring directly into his mother's eyes.

She smiled nervously, "Oh, uh this is-"

"Paul." Paul interjected, walking into the living room.

As he walked closer, Tyree squinted trying to recall the familiar face.

"Where I know you from?" He quizzed.

"Nowhere. Your mother and I went to school together. But I've been on the west coast the past fifteen plus years." Paul shared, unfazed by Tyree's demeanor.

"Hmm..." Tyree sized him up, looking back to his mother to gauge her energy, "Well, I appreciate you looking out for my moms, but I'm home now. So, you can head out."

Monique gasped, "Tyree."

"Nah, it's cool baby. He's just being protective of his mother. I can respect that. I was the same way." Paul smiled, "But I'm not going anywhere unless your mother asks me to."

Tyree clasped his hands together and squared his shoulders in a defensive stance, "Oh really?"

Monique stood up and stepped between the two men, placing her hand onto Tyree's chest, "You know what we need to do? Celebrate. Paul is part owner over at *Lou's* and he's really revived it. It's nice. I'mma call your brother and sisters and tell them to meet us there."

She stared back and forth between the two men waiting for a response.

Paul nodded, "Yea, baby, that sounds good. Y'all come drink, on me, and there will be plenty of beautiful women in the place. My new barmaid works tonight, and she brings in a good crowd. You'll have your pick of the litter."

"What you think, T.Y.? You can hit up your homies and tell them to come out too." Monique stared up at him, but his focus was still on Paul.

She rubbed his chest, drawing his attention back to her. He placed his hand over hers and looked down into her pleading eyes.

"Alright."

"Alright?" Monique asked relieved.

"Yea."

"Alright, well you go upstairs and take you a hot shower. All of your clothes and sneakers are still in the closet in the back room. Not sure what you can fit but I'm sure some of those sweatsuits should still fit you."

Tyree nodded and picked up his bag of personal belongings he'd brought home from jail. Without another word he looked at Paul once more, then made his way upstairs.

Once he was out of sight Monique turned to Paul, "Thank you for not..."

"Baby...relax. He ain't the first nigga to get out and try to press me. I'm not scared nor worried. He'll figure out sooner than later that I'm his ally and not his enemy." Paul spoke soothingly.

"You're a good man." Monique caressed his chin.

"And you're a damned good woman."

They shared a brief but passionate kiss and then he tapped her on the hip, "Alright, let me get out of here. You spend some time with your son, and I'll see you tonight."

"Alright."

They kissed once more then Paul grabbed his coat off the banister and put it on as he walked toward the front door.

"See you later, Mo-Mo." He winked, stepping out the front door.

She smiled as she watched him walk to his car, leaning against the door frame.

"You love that nigga?"

Monique jumped, clutching her chest, startled by Tyree's presence behind her.

"I thought you were getting in the shower." She turned around, closing the door behind her.

"Not yet. So...you love him or what, y'all just fuckin?" He pressed.

"Um, excuse me. I know you've been locked away with animals, but you better talk to me like I'm your mother and not one of those bitches in the street." Monique pointed her finger in his face.

Tyree moved her hand, "Why are you avoiding the question?"

Monique huffed, "Boy...you know what. You just came home, so I'mma let you live but don't push it."

She walked past him to head back into the kitchen and he followed behind her, grabbing her arm.

"Nigga! Now I know you 'done lost yo mind." She snatched her arm away.

"Answer the question." He spoke unfazed.

"He's, my man!" Monique shouted.

"That's not what I asked."

"Nigga, I'm *your* mother. I don't have to spell out my love life to you." Monique rebutted, storming into the kitchen.

"So, you do love the nigga."

"Yes! I do. And he loves me. *And* we be fuckin! Anything else you would like to know?" Monique spat, roughly rinsing dishes and tossing them onto the drying rack.

Tyree chuckled, "Okay…"

Without another word, he turned and walked out of the kitchen. Monique watched him walk through the living room and upstairs, feeling like an involuntary participant in a twisted mind game. But that was Tyree. He seldom shared his intentions but always had very pointed questions, as if he was always gathering intel.

Monique pulled her phone out of her back pocket and dialed Korena. After getting no answer, she dialed Tyson and was left again without an answer. Finally, she huffed and reluctantly dialed Myeesha. The phone rang several times and just as she was about to hang up, convinced that she wouldn't get an answer, Myeesha picked up.

"Yes." She answered sounding irritated.

Monique sighed, "I just called to tell you that your brother came home from jail today and to let you know we'll be celebrating down at *Lou's* tonight."

"Wait, what? Why didn't he call me? His lawyer didn't even tell me!" Myeesha ranted.

"Look, I don't know all that. But he's here, has been for a little while. So, I need you to get ahold of your brother and sister and y'all come celebrate with your brother."

"You don't want to call them yourself?" Myeesha asked, confused by Monique's request, since she was hellbent on making it clear *she* was the mother.

Monique sucked her teeth, "I did, but they ain't answer. And I'm not about to keep calling. Maybe they'll answer for you."

"Umm, okay."

"Alright. I'll see y'all later."

Monique hung up the phone and walked over to the kitchen table, taking a seat. She closed her eyes and exhaled hard, rubbing her temples.

∞◇◇◇∞

"Cap, you got a sec?" Sean jogged toward Captain Dave Howard, as he headed out of his office to leave.

95

"Not really, can it wait until the morning Ramirez? I've got a charity fundraiser to attend and if I'm late my wife is going to nag me until my ears bleed. Do I look like I'm in the mood for that?" Capt. Howard rambled, headed for the side exit.

"No, not at all, sir. I just wanted to see if you'd finally decided whether or not I could assist in my mother's case. It's been three months of dead ends and no real answers. Now she's gone and we have no way of finding out from her."

Capt. Howard sighed and stopped in his tracks, turning to face Sean, "I'm truly sorry for your loss, Ramirez, truly. But I still think you should take the recommended leave of absence to grieve and let the detectives handle this. I know it's not happening as fast as we'd all like, but they're good at their jobs."

"At least let me see what they have so far. I really think I can help with finding who did this." Sean pleaded.

"I don't know…" Capt. Howard shook his head, as he walked up to the exit doors.

"I promise my relationship won't get in the way; I can put my emotions aside. Plus, there's no one with a deeper desire to bring her murderer to justice. I will eat, sleep and breathe this until I find who did it." Sean professed.

Capt. Howard stepped through the side door, into the parking lot and paused. He took a deep breath then turned to face Sean, whose face was eager with anticipation.

"If I let you consult on your mother's case, that's all you'll be doing. Consulting. You will report whatever you find to the detectives on the case and abide by whatever parameters they specify. If you hinder this investigation or commit any insubordination, I'll personally see to it that your ass is parked behind a desk until I retire next spring."

Sean nodded, "Understood.

Capt. Howard stared at him for a moment then shook his head as he turned and walked toward his car.

Sean watched until he was in his car and then pulled out his cellphone, "Hey. Yea, I finally got the greenlight. You can now look into the activity log, just notate that I asked you to as part of the investigation. Thanks, I appreciate your help."

He hung up and made his way to the detective division, receiving uncomfortable stares from a few people as he entered.

"Look, Sean. I'm sorry about everything but my hands are tied. You can't be anywhere near this without the Howards' approval." Detective Lydia Vance walked over to meet him.

"That's what I'm actually here about. He just gave me the clear to join the investigation." Sean informed.

"Join?" Detective Aaron Abrams walked over, "In what capacity?"

"As a consultant. Just offering a fresh pair of eyes to the case and seeing what I can do to help bring my mother's killer to justice."

"Uhn, uhn…I don't like this. You're too close to this. I'm going to talk to Cap." Det. Abrams walked away.

"He's gone for the day, and I wouldn't recommend calling him. He's preparing for some charity thing with his wife." Sean shrugged.

"Fine, but you get in my way, and you'll wish you left this investigation to us, Beat cop." Det. Abrams sneered, walking over to his desk and plopping down in the chair.

"He's right. You better be a help and not a hinderance, Ramirez." Det. Vance warned.

Sean threw his hands up in surrender, "I'm just here to help."

"Mhmm…so what've you got so far? Because if you're like every other rookie I know, you've definitely been doing your own digging." Det. Vance questioned, taking a seat at her desk.

Sean sat in the chair beside her desk, "Well, actually I haven't made a ton of headway, yet. Most of the files related to the case, I don't have clearance for, but I did stumble across something that could be a potential lead."

"Spit it out."

"So, you know the arrest I was part of a few months ago?" Sean spoke just above a whisper.

"The one where you helped that redneck in blue put an innocent woman into a coma?" Det. Vance stated bluntly, annoyed by his attempt to be discrete and how it reinforced her perception of him being a coward.

Detective Lydia Vance, a bi-racial black Italian woman, didn't take shit from anyone so she had little respect for cowardice. Lydia made a name for herself early in her career, due to challenging her superior officers; not taking their hazing quietly and it left her riding alone once she'd advanced from rookie status. But to her peer's surprise and leadership's behest she handled herself flawlessly, even when back-up was *coincidently* delayed or didn't come at all. Her partnership with Det. Abrams only came as a means of further hazing. The previous captain, a surly old Irish man, who felt women had no place in policing, thought their similar attitudes would cause them to tare each other apart. But yet again, she shocked them. She and Abrams became the best of friends and remained so for over ten years.

"Yea…well, I was sent back to the scene to recover any evidence that might be useful to Shaw or Johnson's murder case, and I found a notebook with most of the pages torn out." Sean expounded.

"Did you report what you found to the detectives assigned to the case?" Det. Vance questioned.

"I did. I followed protocol, by the book. But they said it was useless and that the most we'd probably get was a few fingerprints confirming the book had been handled by Hanson or her fiancé."

"Ok, so…get to the point, Ramirez. We're losing daylight." Det. Vance huffed.

"So, I suggested this technique I saw on…a show, where the person laid paper on top of something and shaded with a pencil to pick-up indentations from previous writings." Sean continued.

"And let me guess, they laughed in your face?" Det. Vance asked with a blank stare.

"Basically. So, I grabbed a pencil and proceeded to demonstrate but all that came up was… a grocery list."

Det. Vance leaned forward onto her desk, laughing.

"But, but…when I flipped the book closed, I notice the sun glare from the window showing indents on the back cover. So, I tried the technique again and saw a name."

"What name?" Det. Abrams asked, now standing beside Vance who'd recomposed herself.

"Anthony Waters."

Chapter Seven

The sounds of *"TGIF"* by *Glorilla* blasted through the speakers at *'Lou's Bar & Billiards'* as girls rapped word for word, twerking with bottles of top shelf tequila in their hand. After seeing the increase in crowd and revenue, Paul had booths installed along the back wall and arranged for a DJ to play on the weekends when DeeDee bartended. Theresa also noticed the significant influx of patrons and complained until she was given the ability to also bartend on the weekends. And although her attitude was terrible, DeeDee secretly welcomed the help since her normal crowd doubled with the combination of regulars and new patrons who noticed the buzz.

"Hey T!" Monique waved as she walked through the crowd toward the back of the bar.

Paul stepped through the *staff only* door, smiling big when he spotted Monique dressed in the new red, floor-length fur coat he'd bought her. Underneath she wore a black turtleneck, a pair of black leather shorts and matching thigh-high boots.

"Damn, you look good." Paul pulled her close, pressing his pelvis firmly against his.

"Thank you, baby." She kissed him then wiped her lipstick from his lips with her thumb.

"Where's your son?" He looked around.

"Outside smoking with his friends."

Paul nodded, "Alright, well when he comes in that'll be y'all's booth. I also had Theresa reserve a seat for you at the bar, since I know you like to people-watch."

"Did you get my wine?"

"She has it behind the bar. Chilled and ready."

Monique stared up into his eyes, in awe of how quickly they'd picked up where things left off. It was like no time had passed. Slowly but surely, he was melting her heart.

Paul helped her out of her coat, "I'mma put your coat in my office, you go ahead to the bar. I've got to go make a few calls and grab some chicken from the deep freezer in the basement."

"Okay."

Monique walked over to the bar toward a bar stool labeled *Reserved* and one of the young guys standing beside it turned and noticed her. He smiled charmingly; his eyes hidden behind a pair of square, frameless designer glasses.

"Let me get that for you." He reached out his hand to help her onto the stool.

"Don't fuckin' touch my mother." Tyree spoke coldly, walking up behind the man.

The guy turned around, standing eye level with Tyree's beard. He looked up and the expression on Tyree's face defied the expression *If looks could kill.*

"My bad man, just trying to be a gentleman." He threw his hands up in surrender.

Tyree didn't respond, he just stared at the man waiting for him to catch the hint. In an instant the man grabbed his drink and walked away.

Monique shook her head, "He was harmless."

Tyree ignored her statement and turned his attention toward Theresa and DeeDee, who were both serving patrons in the middle of the bar. He raised his hand, catching Theresa's attention and once she was done with her patron, she made her way down to their end of the bar.

"Hey, Mo! I got your wine right here. You want a big glass or small?"

"Big."

Theresa reached into the mini wine fridge beneath the bar top and pulled out a bottle. She grabbed a large glass from the hanging rack and poured until the glass was half full then slid it to Monique with a napkin.

100

"And what can I get you, handsome?" Theresa grinned, revealing her gold tooth.

"T, this is my son T.Y., the one I told you about. He just came home today, so we're celebrating." Monique interjected.

"Oh, nice! So, what can I get you?"

He pointed toward DeeDee, "You can get *her* for me."

Theresa looked over her shoulder and rolled her eyes, "I work this end of the bar."

"Then you can't help me." Tyree stated bluntly.

Monique placed her hand on his arm, "Paul reserved the booth over there for us. So, you and your friends don't have to stand all night."

"Alright." He nodded and walked away toward DeeDee's end of the bar.

Monique shook her head, "Sorry about that, I'd blame it on jail but he's his father's son."

"It's cool, girl. Let me go help them." Theresa walked over to a group of girls waiting to order.

Monique sipped her wine and people watched as *"Get it Sexyy"* by *Sexyy Red* came on and the women in the bar went crazy, twerking in the middle of the floor and on the booth seats.

Amidst the chaos, Khalil and Korena walked into the bar trying to avoid hair flips and the plethora asses being shook. Monique waved to them and once they spotted her, they headed over.

"Hey, Ma." Korena hugged her.

"Hey, Pooh!" Monique ran her hands over Korena's belly, "You're starting to get big girl."

"Ma, please. Not too much."

Monique chuckled, sipping her wine, "Hey, Khalil."

He nodded, "Hey."

Khalil was one hundred percent against his pregnant woman going to a bar at 11 o'clock at night, but she'd insisted that she needed to see her brother and couldn't wait until the next day. So, he decided to chaperone and just as he expected, the place was crowded and filled with smoke. And to make matters worse there were street niggas throughout the bar and he knew they were carrying, because security didn't even check him, and he was. Khalil shook his head in frustration and started the mental time clock for their departure, because they definitely wouldn't be there long.

"You walked past your brother." Monique pointed to Tyree who was now talking to DeeDee, or more like flirting.

Korena gasped, "Oh my God. I didn't even see him."

"T! Come here really quick." Monique shouted over the music.

Theresa wrapped up her transaction and walked over, "What you need, Mo?"

"Can you go tell T.Y. to come here? His sister's here."

Theresa reluctantly shook her head in agreement and walked over to DeeDee and Tyree. After a brief exchange, Tyree came walking over to them.

"T.Y.!" Korena exclaimed, throwing her arms around her brother's neck.

"Hey big head." He hugged her back and cracked a slight smile. Something only his siblings could get out of him.

Tyree released her but Korena held on, unwilling to release him.

"Come on man, let me go so I can get a good look at you."

Korena slowly released her grasp and stepped back with tears in her eyes. Tyree sighed at the sight of tears in her eyes, but his attention was quickly shifted to her belly.

"You're pregnant?"

She rubbed her belly with one hand, grabbing Khalil's hand with the other. Noticing the gesture, Tyree locked eyes with Khalil and the two stared each other down, not saying a word.

"Alright folks, we're gonna slow things down a bit, give y'all a chance to cool off." The DJ announced, playing *"ICU"* by *Coco Jones*.

"T.Y. this is Khalil." Korena broke the silent tension.

"Where I know you from?" Tyree quizzed.

Khalil looked him up and down but didn't respond. He knew exactly who T.Y. was and that was part of his apprehension for the family reunion he was forced into.

Tyree smirked then let out a subtle chuckle before walking away. He waved his friends over and pointed them toward the reserved booth, then returned to the side of the bar where DeeDee was.

∞∞∞∞

EARLIER THAT DAY

DeeDee stood at the far right of the bar, closest to the entrance, cleaning glasses in the bar sink.

"Hey boo."

She looked up and huffed, rolling her eyes, "What are you doing here Zhaniece?"

"Damn, we're using government names now, De'Shaye? I just came to check on my favorite cousin; see how things were going. This place looks way better than when I first scoped it out. Looks like you lucked up and hit the jackpot." She smiled.

DeeDee sighed, "What do you want?"

"Damn, why do I have to want something?"

"Because you always want something. I knew when you recommended this spot, it came with strings. I was just waiting for you to pull them." DeeDee huffed.

Zhaniece grinned, "That's not true...however, I do need a favor."

"Exactly." DeeDee shook her head, placing the last of the clean glasses on the hanging rack.

"It's nothing crazy, I promise."

"I know it ain't, because I told you when I moved up here that I was starting over. No more scamming and shit." DeeDee stated matter-of-factly.

"And that's why what I'm asking for is low lift shit."

DeeDee threw her hand on her hip, "What do you want?"

"Just a little intel."

"Intel? On who?"

Zhaniece leaned over the counter, "The nigga in charge."

DeeDee shook her head, "I knew there was a reason you sent me here. Nothing's every just a kind gesture with you."

"Yea, yea, I have ulterior motives. We've established that. Now, can I count on you or what?"

DeeDee pointed in her face, "I'm not sleeping with anyone to help you, so let's establish that before you proceed."

"I'm not asking you to. I just need you to keep tabs on that nigga and let me know his movements. Where he goes, who he's usually with and if anyone suspicious comes by the bar. Shit like that."

DeeDee huffed, "Fine. Which nigga are you referring to? Because theirs technically two owners."

Zhaniece sucked her teeth, "I ain't talking about that lame ass nigga, Lou."

"And how would I know? It's not like I know what you're up to. And I honestly don't want to know."

"I respect that. That's why I'm only asking you for information."

DeeDee leaned forward over the bar, "Is this information somehow going to lead to *Lou's* only having one owner?"

"You just said you didn't want to know what I was up to."

"I don't, I just…I like him. He's a good dude who's really looked out for me and I don't wanna see anything happen to him." DeeDee professed.

"Relax, he's not my target. I actually need his help, but I need more information on him for leverage, to assure his compliance." Zhaniece explained.

"Okay…you promise?"

"I promise." Zhaniece grinned, "Alright, let me get out of here."

She pulled the brim of her snapback hat down and threw on her hood. DeeDee watched has she walked out of the bar, feeling a knot in the pit of her stomach. As much as she loved her cousin, she knew Zhaniece was a walking catalyst for chaos and with that understanding she'd begun to mentally plan her escape route.

∞∞∞∞

One of the patrons beside Monique got up from their stool, headed for the exit.

"Grab that seat for Korena." She instructed Khalil, who stood with his back to the bar watching for Korena to return from the bathroom.

"Huh?"

"The stool." She pointed, "Grab it for your child's mother.

He nodded and grabbed the stool, sliding it next to Monique then resumed his surveillance. Tyree was now at the booth with his three homies, taking shots with several women.

"What the fuck are you doin' here, nigga?"

Khalil turned to find Mook, and his stoic facial expression lightened. He walked over to Mook and dapped him up, "Nigga, what are *you* doin' here?"

"One of my niggas just came home. Just stepped out to show him love." Mook nodded in Tyree's direction.

"How do y'all know each other?" Khalil inquired.

"I did a few jobs for him back when I was freelancing." Mook shared.

"Hmm...okay."

Just then, Tyree came walking over holding a bottle of Hennessey, "I finally remember where I know you from."

Khalil just stared at him.

Mook looked between the two of them confused, "So, y'all know each other, too?"

"Not exactly. But I definitely know who this nigga is...a certified crash dummy." Tyree smirked devilishly.

"Crash dummy?" Mook quizzed.

"Yea. The expendable nigga you send on all the suicide missions. Usually, a fatherless nigga looking for acceptance." Tyree glared at Khalil with a slight grin, watching to see if his words were landing how he intended.

Khalil, however, remained composed, never breaking eye contact as he clenched his jaw.

"Nah, that don't even sound right." Mook shook his head.

Tyree shrugged, "You're right. Maybe I'm mistaken. I've been locked down so long I can't tell one memory from the other some days."

He took a long swig from the bottle of Hennessey, eyes still locked with Khalil, then walked away as if the exchange never happened.

Mook looked over at Khalil and sensed his energy, "That nigga love's fuckin' with people. Been that way since I met him. Don't let him get in your head."

"He ain't in my head." Khalil finally spoke.

"Alright. Well, I'll holla." Mook nodded then walked over to Tyree's booth just as Korena returned to the bar.

"The bathroom was surprisingly really clean." She shared.

"You ready?" Khalil asked, ignoring her statement.

"No, why? Are you?" She inquired, taking a seat on the stool beside her mother.

"Yup. Especially after that lil tense moment he just had with your brother." Monique chimed in.

"What moment? What happened?" Korena looked from Monique to Khalil.

Neither of them said anything.

"It's almost eleven-thirty. I'll give you 'til eleven forty-five."

"Tyson and Eesha aren't even here yet." Korena retorted.

Khalil shrugged, "They better get here before eleven forty-five." She sucked her teeth and rolled her eyes.

"Or we can leave now." Khalil threatened.

Korena huffed, "Fine."

"That's what I thought."

Monique chuckled to herself; seeing her daughter so submissive was new for her. And although she had no intentions to admit it, she was actually starting to like Khalil. It'd become clear what Korena saw in him; he reminded her of Big TY.

"Oh, there goes Tyson!" Korena exclaimed, waving to get his attention.

He spotted her and started making his way through the crowd, toward them. After hugging his mother, he hugged Korena and playfully poked her in the stomach.

"What's up." He extended his hand toward Khalil, who reluctantly shook it.

Tyson dismissed the weird vibe he was getting from Khalil and turned his attention back to his mother and sister, "Where's he at?"

Monique pointed, "Over there."

"Damn, that nigga got husky as hell." Tyson blurted.

"He had plenty of time to do push-ups." Korena laughed.

"Real shit." Tyson shook his head, "Nigga almost doesn't look the same."

"Go head over. I'm sure he'll be just as shocked to see you after all these years. You're not the same lil' boy he last saw." Monique interjected.

Tyson nodded and took a second to mentally prepare himself before walking through the crowd. When he walked up to the booth, a girl was shaking her ass on Tyree's lap as if they were in a strip club and one of Tyree's homies put his hand on his chest, stopping him like he was security.

"Aye, nigga! Don't touch him." Tyree stopped the girl from dancing and stood up, putting down the bottle of Hennessey in his hand.

"Sonny." Tyree extended his hand and pulled Tyson into a quick embrace, "Look at you lil nigga, you starting to look like a grown man."

"Oh shit, lil Sonny. I ain't even recognize him." Tyree's homie Brix smiled.

Tyson shook his head, "You know I hate that name."

"What, am I supposed to call you Ty?"

Tyson shrugged, "I mean, yea. That's my name."

"That's too close to T.Y. and you ain't earn the respect that comes with this name, yet."

Tyson sported a look of confusion and annoyance. Although he missed his brother, primarily because he kept their mother in check, he didn't miss the way he asserted himself as *King of the Castle*. T.Y.'s word was law and anyone who crossed him felt his wrath. They were just members of his royal court; supporting characters in *his* movie and they'd need not forget it if they desired peace.

"Ayo Mike, go grab another bottle from the bar for my lil brother." Tyree commanded his other friend.

"Nah, you ain't gotta do that. I can't stay long, I just wanted to come see you and maybe take a shot." Tyson asserted.

"What you mean you can't stay?" Tyree pressed.

"I've got to work in the morning, plus I promised my girl I wouldn't be out too late." Tyson explained.

Tyree stared at his brother, unmoved by his words, "Mike. Go get the bottle."

Tyson sighed, rubbing his temples in frustration. He pulled out his phone and texted Brielle that he was going to be later than expected and that he was sorry.

Mike made his way through the crowd just as Myeesha came walking into the bar. She looked around and immediately spotted Monique and Korena.

"Hey, fat girl!" Myeesha rubbed her hands over Korena's belly gleefully.

"Uhn, uhn, don't piss me off. Mommy already called me *big*." Korena whined.

Myeesha laughed, "You're pregnant, girl! Did you think you'd stay the same size?"

"Whatever." Korena rolled her eyes.

"Hey, brother-in-law." Myeesha playfully slapped Khalil on the arm.

He turned his attention from the crowd to Myeesha and gave a faint smile, "What's up?"

"What's up." She mocked him, "Damn, that's all I get?"

Khalil sighed and leaned in to hug her, "Hey, Sis."

"That's better." She playfully scolded.

Turning her attention to Monique, who was sipping her drink watching with a visible attitude.

"Hey, Ma." Myeesha gave a forced smile.

"Myeesha."

Myeesha laughed to herself then turned her attention back to Korena, "Where's Tyree?"

"Over there with Tyson." Korena nodded in their direction.

"Oh, I see him. Let me go hug my brother." Myeesha smiled big, taking off her bubble coat revealing the long-sleeved body-con dress she had on, "Put my coat on the back of your chair and hold my purse."

"We're actually about to leave." Khalil informed.

Myeesha gasped, "What? No, don't leave yet. I just got here, and I haven't hung with my siblings all together in years."

Korena looked up at Khalil with pleading eyes, waiting for his response.

He sighed, "Fine. You've got til twelve, then we're leaving."

Korena smiled brightly, taking her sister's coat and purse. She watched as Myeesha moved through the crowd, her hips and ass catching the attention of men and women alike.

"T.Y.!" Myeesha shouted loudly.

Tyree looked up with an annoyed expression that quickly melted away when he saw his partner in crime.

"Eesh! My mothafuckin' right hand." Tyree pushed the woman on his lap aside and stood up, pulling his sister into a hug.

When they released from the embrace, Myeesha was dabbing tears from her eyes. She stepped back, taking a good look at him and then punched him in the chest.

"Still hit like a nigga I see." Tyree smirked.

"And you better remember it. Cause you leave me alone with Monique again and I'mma knock your ass out." She threatened.

Tyree nodded, "Trust me, the next time I leave it's gonna be in a box."

"Don't say that." Myeesha scolded, fully aware of how serious her brother was.

"What you drinkin', Eesh?" He disregarded her words.

"Doesn't matter, as long as it's not dark. I've got early appointments tomorrow."

"Sonny over here babysitting the tequila, you can take his bottle." Tyree nodded to Tyson, who was sitting in the booth, looking like he'd rather be anywhere else.

"Hey, Ty." Myeesha smiled.

He stood up and hugged her then offered her his seat.

"I'm about to go." Tyson whispered to her.

"Wait, no. I need to get a picture of us all together." Myeesha pleaded.

Tyson huffed, "Alright."

DeeDee twerked to the sounds of "*Wanna Be*" by *Glorilla*, as she poured tequila into the blender, making one of her signature frozen drinks.

"Go Dee! Go Dee!" The women at the bar cheered her on.

She pressed the button on the blender and proceeded to bend over shaking her as harder. When the song finally ended, she stood up giggling and turned around, high-fiving one of the girls.

"Shaye!"

DeeDee's eyes became big as saucers, "Mom?"

"Surprise!" Her mother exclaimed, leaning over the shoulder of the women sitting at the bar.

The two women scooted over, making room for her to step up to the bar and she extended a card in a green envelope.

"Happy Birthday, puddin'!"

One of the women at the bar gasped, "It's your birthday? Oh, bitch pour us another shot."

"No, no. My birthday isn't until Tuesday." DeeDee informed, taking the card from her mother and tucking it into her purse beneath the bar.

"Close enough!" One woman laughed.

DeeDee smiled and grabbed the bottle of tequila they'd been drinking and poured a shot for all three of them.

"You want one, mama?" One of them offered.

Her mother shook her head, "No, I'm good. Thank you."

DeeDee spotted her patron waving and remembered the drink she had in the blender. She poured the frozen drink into a tall glass and decorated it with candy before handing it to the woman.

She then waved her mother over to the side of the bar and lifted the bar flap, "Who are you here with?"

"Your father. He let me out at the door while he searched for a spot."

"Y'all really shouldn't be out here, in this part of the city this time of night." DeeDee warned.

"De'Shaye Antoinette, how many times do I have to tell you I grew up running these streets. Your father is the one who grew up like a Huxtable, not me." Her mother stated boldly.

DeeDee sighed, "I hear you, but this ain't the same city you remember."

"Girl, just hug your mother and tell her you miss her."

DeeDee obliged, "I missed you. But can you please go, I won't be able to focus worrying about y'all."

Her mother huffed, shaking her head, "Fine. I'll wait for your father to come in, so he can see you. Then we'll head to the hotel."

"Hotel? Why aren't y'all staying at the house?" DeeDee quizzed.

"Um, excuse me but you have patrons trying to get your attention." Theresa walked up behind DeeDee.

DeeDee rolled her eyes and exhaled heavily.

"She'll be over in a minute." Her mother interjected, sensing the unpleasant vibe between her daughter and the woman.

"You can't be back here." Theresa retorted, staring her up and down.

"I'm talking to my daughter."

"And you can do that on the other side of the bar." Theresa spat.

DeeDee turned around, "Don't talk to my mother like that."

Her mother pushed her aside and stepped in front of her, "I suggest you head back to your end of the bar before I knock that gold tooth down your throat!"

"Bitch I ain't scared of you or that lil hoodrat daughter of yours!" Theresa barked.

"Bravery ain't never kept a bitch from getting her ass whooped!" Her mother stepped forward.

"Kat!"

All three women turned to see DeeDee's father standing at the side of the bar, wearing a pissed off expression.

"Come on, mom. She ain't worth it." DeeDee tugged at her arm.

Kathy huffed and reluctantly stepped away and Theresa did the same. She walked over to her husband, and he slid his arm around her waist.

"What the hell is going on?" He questioned.

"Nothing, D. Don't worry about it."

DeeDee walked over, "Hey, daddy."

"Hey baby girl." He pulled her into a hug.

"How long are y'all here?" She inquired.

"Til Wednesday." Kathy chimed in.

"And why aren't y'all staying at the house? There's plenty of room."

Her father Darryl sighed, "Because your mother and grandmother can't manage a full day without bickering and I don't have the patience for it. But we'll be by the house though."

DeeDee shook her head, "Okay, well I don't have to be here until seven-thirty tomorrow. Y'all wanna do lunch or early dinner?"

"You're really putting us out?" Kathy gasped in faux offense.

Darryl took Kathy by the hand, "It's fine, I'm tired anyway. We'll see you tomorrow baby girl. Be safe and text us when you get in."

"Okay. Love you." DeeDee leaned in and hugged her parents.

"Love you too." They responded in unison.

Darryl moved Kathy in front of him and ushered her toward the exit. Once they stepped outside, it started to rain.

"Where'd you park?" Kathy asked, watching the downpour pick up in speed.

"At the other end of the block."

"Uhn, uhn. I'm not getting my hair wet. You go get the car and I'll wait here under the awning.

"Alright." Darryl quickly hustled down the block.

Kathy stepped back a little further under the awning as the wind blew and a few raindrops hit her face.

"Excuse me."

She turned to see a man trying to open the door. Kathy stepped to the right for him to open the door all the way and he gently nudged the woman with him out the door.

"Excuse us." The young woman smiled.

Kathy looked down and noticed the woman's pregnant belly, peaking through her open coat.

"You might wanna zip up. Don't wanna get sick." Kathy suggested.

The woman smiled and tightened her coat, "Right."

"Wait here and I'mma pull the car up." The man instructed.

"Okay."

He jogged to the left, trying to avoid the rain and Kathy watched the young woman watch him until he was out of sight.

"How far along are you?" Kathy asked.

"Huh? Oh, um, almost 4 months." She rubbed her belly.

Kathy sighed, "I remember that feeling. Nothing will ever compare."

"Really?"

Kathy nodded, "Yup. It's the closest I've ever felt to God. Partnering with Him to create this beautiful little life. It's a miracle that's become so common we don't always cherish it."

"I never thought of it like that." She stared down at her belly as she continued to gently rub.

"There's my husband." Kathy spotted the blue SUV they'd rented, "It was nice talking to you."

"Same."

"What's your name?"

"Korena."

Kathy extended her hand and Korena shook it, "I'll be keeping you and your baby in my prayers, Korena."

"Why?" Korena asked sincerely.

"What do you mean, *why?*"

Korena shrugged, "I mean, you don't know me."

"But I do...you're a woman about to bring life into the world, for the first time. And as much joy as that can bring, I know firsthand the fear and uncertainty that accompanies it. So...I'll be praying for you." Kathy smiled.

Korena nodded as a tear fell from her right eye, "Thank you."

Kathy walked over and took her by the hand, "You're gonna be okay. You and your baby."

"You ready?" Darryl stepped onto the curb holding an umbrella.

"Yea, I'm ready. Nice meeting you, Korena."

"Nice meeting you too."

Just as Darryl took Kathy by the hand, Khalil walked up.

"What's wrong?" He asked, noticing the tears in her eyes.

She shook her head, "Nothing, I'm good."

"You sure? Did somebody say something to you?" He asked, turning his attention toward Kathy and Darryl.

"She's just experiencing the emotions of motherhood." Kathy smiled assuredly.

"Yea, I'm okay. Really." Korena rubbed his arm, but he never broke eye contact with Kathy.

"You good, man?" Darryl interjected.

"Khalil." Korena gently tugged at his arm.

Kathy stepped forward, "Khalil?"

Darryl stared in confusion, "You know him?"

"I, uh…" Kathy placed her hand on her heart, unable to speak.

Korena stepped in front of Khalil and gently turned his face toward hers, "Baby, what's going on? Are you okay?"

"I think I know her." He whispered; eyes still locked on Kathy.

"From where?" Korena asked, looking over at Kathy, whose face was wet with tears.

His eyes began to water, "I…I think she's…"

Khalil shook his head and roughly wiped his hand over his face, recomposing himself.

"She's who?" Korena pressed.

"Nobody. Come on." He grabbed her by the hand and led her to his truck, which was parked to the left of the entrance.

He helped Korena into the truck and closed her door and shook his head as if trying to shake the thoughts flooding his mind.

"Wait!"

Khalil stopped in his tracks feeling someone grab him. He turned to see Kathy and shook his arm out of her grip.

"Don't touch me."

Kathy cried, "I'm so sorry."

"For what? I don't know you." Khalil sneered, turning back around and heading for the driver side.

"Khalil, please! I know I hurt you, but you have to believe me when I say, it was never my intention."

He stopped and turned to face her, "Look lady, I don't know who you think I am. But you've got the wrong person."

Darryl walked over and gently pulled her away, "Come on, Kat."

"I love you!" She exclaimed.

Khalil climbed into the driver seat, violently wiping tears from his eyes as he started the engine.

Korena placed her hand atop his, "Baby…is that your mother?"

He snatched his hand away, putting the car in drive and pulled out into traffic.

Chapter Eight

Paul waited by the back door of *Lou's*, that led out to a small side street, as a blacked-out truck pulled over. After a moment the back door opened and out stepped Captain Dave Howard dressed in formal black-tie attire, wearing a pissed off expression.

"This shit couldn't wait until tomorrow?" Capt. Howard fussed.

Paul didn't respond, he just held the door open waiting for him to step inside. Once the two of them were inside, they walked down to the basement.

WHAM!

Paul threw a right hook, catching Capt. Howard off guard and almost knocking him off his feet but he was able to catch his balance.

"What the fuck was that for?"

"It's been four months since my son was murdered and you have yet to give me anything useful, Dave! I'm starting to think you're playing me." Paul spat, squared up for another punch.

Capt. Howard touched his mouth where blood seeped and looked at him in bewilderment, "I'm not playing you; P. I swear. I put my best detectives on it but the only lead we had was the delivery guy and he's adamant that he doesn't remember anything."

"That's bullshit! The nigga is lying, he's clearly been paid off or scared into staying quiet." Paul shouted.

"Look man, I'm with you. I've tried everything I can to get him to talk, but I have limits to what I can do, especially with Internal Affairs down my back since the shit with Shaw!" He explained, rubbing his jaw.

"You always been pussy. Pussy and a sucka for pussy. How you made Captain is beyond me. All that power and you scared to fuckin' leverage it."

"Paul, it's not that simple. The systems are more advanced now. Everybody got cameras and recording devices hidden everywhere. Shit, and then there's all the doorbell cameras. This ain't the 90's man. We're in a fuckin' surveillance state. I'm putting myself at risk just showing up here." Capt. Howard reasoned.

Paul just stared at him, unmoved by his speech and plea for sympathy, "Give me his name and address."

"I can't do that."

"Nigga, I'm not asking."

"I can't do it, man!"

"And why the fuck not?!"

Capt. Howard sighed, "Because…his lawyer filed to have his identity sealed off and the only people with access are me and the two detectives on the case. If something happens to him and I.A. checks the logs, it's a wrap for me."

"Then used somebody else's log-in. I don't care how you get it done, but you better get me that name and address by Monday or it's going to be a police procession escorting your family to your grave." Paul gritted in his face.

"I…I'll see what I can do."

"Get it done, Dave. Don't make me have to stop by west 11th street." Paul threatened.

"Alright, man. I got you. I'll figure something out."

"You better."

∞∞∞∞

Brandon waited a moment before getting up from the pew and making his way out the front doors of St. Anthony's. Discretely surveilling his surroundings, he spotted Niecy in a blacked-out Mustang with her window rolled down. She nodded for him to come over and he quickly walked over to the car and got in.

"You better not try no shit." Brandon threatened, flashing the gun in his waistband.

Niecy giggled, "Nigga relax. If I wanted you dead, I would've shot you when you went into the confessional."

She raised her left hand and revealed a Glock 42 that was outfitted with a silencer. Brandon just stared at her, eyebrow raised, trying to size her up. *Did she really say she would've shot him inside the church?* The woman before him was indeed a different breed and the revelation of her nonexistent morality both frightened him and turned him on.

"Where're we going?" He questioned.

"Nowhere. We're just gonna ride around. I find that discussing serious business on the go, limits the possibility of interference or information being intercepted." Niecy explained as she pulled out into traffic.

"So, you gonna start sharing or what?" Brandon pressed, growing impatient after riding in silence for almost 20 minutes.

Niecy chuckled, "Cálmaté, Papi. Geez, you're impatient."

"Nah, I just don't like my fuckin' time being wasted."

"Trust me, nothing I do is ever a waste of time. I was just testing you to see how long you'd let me ride around before saying something."

Brandon sucked his teeth, "Enough with the bullshit. Tell me who shot my mother, so I can put the nigga in a plot next to her."

"Like I told you before, I'll tell you details on a need-to-know basis."

"Look, I'm not trynna be on no extended dummy mission, playing some long-game bullshit. So, your little plan better not take longer than a week or so. Otherwise, I'm going back to handling shit my way."

Niecy giggled, "You're too cute."

"Yea, I'm fuckin' gorgeous." He spat sarcastically.

"Trust me, you'll be pressing that peashooter against the skull of your mother's killer in no time. But for clarification, the person responsible ain't a nigga, it's a bitch."

Brandon shrugged, "My gun goes both ways."

"So do I." Niecy winked.

Caught off-guard by her candor, Brandon cleared his throat, "So, what else are you willing to share about this mystery chick?"

"She's related to a major player in the streets who just got released. And a nigga like him ain't coming home to play civilian. He's going to be looking for a chance to reclaim what he left behind, and that's where we come in." She explained.

"What's his name?"

"I'll tell you when it's time."

Brandon huffed, "Okay, so what am I supposed to be doing in this elaborate plan of yours?"

"You're going to offer him ten bricks in exchange for a spot on his team."

"Ten bricks!" Brandon blurted, "Where the fuck am I getting that kind of weight from?"

"I heard about how you used to move weight, before you got knocked. You're telling me you ain't got no money stashed or connects you can borrow from on consignment?" Niecy quizzed.

"I just came home! Ain't you the one who rolled up talkin' about how my connections in the streets were either dead or locked down?" Brandon retorted.

Niecy burst out laughing and Brandon just stared at her, confused by her amusement.

"You know what, let me out up here."

"No, no…I'm sorry." She composed herself, "It's just your face. You really think I'd expect *you* to have that kind of weight or money. Nigga, no offense but look at you."

"Fuck you! Niggas with real money don't wear it." He spat.

"And niggas with no money say shit like that."

Brandon tugged at his door as they pulled up to a red light, "Yo, for real, unlock the fuckin' door."

"Ugh! Y'all niggas are so sensitive." Niecy huffed.

"Unlock my door."

"For what? So, you can run home cause your feelings got hurt? Man the fuck up and chill." Niecy barked, speeding up once the light turned green.

Brandon stared at her like she had three heads. After a moment, he looked away, releasing a deep sigh and recomposed himself.

"So, where are we getting the weight?" He asked.

"Don't worry about it. When you need it, you'll have it. You just make sure you don't let that sensitive ass ego of yours cause you to fuck this up. You only got one shot with this nigga."

Brandon nodded, "Alright…when's the meet up?"

"I'll let you know."

"You know, keeping shit that close to the vest can lead to mistakes. You need to trust someone enough to run shit by them, so they can catch any errors."

Niecy chuckled, "And is that someone supposed to be you?"

"That would make sense, since I'm the other half of this operation."

"The only nigga I trusted to divulge my plans to was executed by the same bitch who killed your mother, so I'll pass."

"Man, whatever."

Suddenly Niecy pulled over next to stairs leading to the train and unlocked the car doors.

"Get out."

"What? *You're* mad now?"

"Nigga please. We're done talkin', so you can get your ass out. Meet me at the matinee show for *Lion King* Tuesday, you'll have a ticket at the box office."

"The *Lion King*?" Brandon repeated in confusion as he opened the car door.

"Yea. Now get out and don't slam my door."

Brandon shook his head and sighed, stepping out of the car. No sooner than he closed the door behind himself, Niecy sped off into traffic, almost side-swiping a yellow cab.

∞∞∞∞

Maleah put her truck in park then shut off the engine and just sat silently with her eyes closed. It'd been a long, busy day and the fact that she and Xavier had hardly spoken since the day Eric showed up, made it feel ten times longer.

After their little confrontation, Xavier decided to stay at his place. Stating that his day was stressful, he had a migraine and just wanted to sleep…alone. But Maleah knew that was code for *Don't bring yo ass over here!* And she happily obliged, still a bit overstimulated by Eric's unexpected visit and news of him joining the team. So, she gladly took that opportunity to decompress and stretch out in her king bed for the first time in months.

120

VRRRRBBBBB!

Her cellphone vibrated and when she grabbed it, she saw that it was an alert from the apartments kiosk system, informing her that a guest on her approved list had signed in.

"Who the hell?" She quickly opened the app and saw Xavier's name in bold.

Maleah huffed, "I really am not in the mood for this."

She dropped the phone back into her purse and closed her eyes again while pressing the recline button on the side of her seat. Once she was in a comfortable position, she kicked off her shoes and flexed her toes. Before she knew it, she'd drifted off the sleep.

TAP! TAP! TAP!

Maleah jumped up, startled out of her sleep to Xavier staring into her window with a look of confusion. She adjusted her seat back to the upright position and stuffed her feet into her heels before grabbing her purse off the passenger seat.

"Why are you sleeping in your truck?" He questioned, opening the door and helping her out.

"I just needed a minute before going inside."

"Because you saw I was here?"

Maleah sighed, "Yes..."

Xavier held the door open for her as they stepped into the building and walked over to the elevator. He pressed the elevator button then turned toward her.

"Why?"

"Because I'm exhausted and I didn't anticipate round two tonight."

DING!

The elevator doors opened, and they stepped inside.

Xavier pressed the button for her floor, "Round two? I'm not trynna fight, I just wanted you to see how your actions hurt me."

Maleah looked over at him, making eye contact for the first time since he'd helped her out of her truck. The sincerity she saw tugged at her heart.

"Look, I'm sorry. It wasn't my intention; I was just caught off guard." She explained.

The elevator doors opened to her floor and they both stepped off, headed for her apartment.

"What was the nature of y'all relationship?" He inquired as they entered her apartment.

Maleah released a sigh and kicked off her shoes then picked them up. She'd been dreading this conversation in particular, mainly because she didn't know how he'd react to her lying by omission.

"Let me shower and get comfortable, then I'll tell you anything you want to know."

"Alright." Xavier reluctantly agreed.

He took off his coat, hung it in the closet then stepped out of his shoes, before sitting on the couch and turning on the tv.

After about thirty minutes he muted the tv and heard the sound of the shower, "She's still in there?"

Xavier got up and went into her bedroom. The smell of vanilla filled the room as steam from her ensuite bathroom crept out the doorway. He could hear the sound of Maleah humming along to the sounds of *Alex Isley's* song *"Still wonder"*. He leaned against the door frame and watched her through the foggy shower door, swaying with her eyes closed as she gently scrubbed her body.

Mesmerized by the sight of her and the mellow sounds of the soulful crooner, he rested in the moment and took in the lyrics of the song.

"It's a hard pill too, cause I still wonder about you."

The words hit him in the chest like a wrecking ball and reinforced his concerns, that Maleah indeed had feelings for the *London Loverboy*.

When the song ended, she'd rinsed the last of the soap off her body and reached over to turn off the shower. Noticing a figure in her peripheral vision, she turned with a startled expression.

"Didn't mean to scare you. Just came to check on you."

Maleah stepped out of the shower, wrapping her towel around herself, "Sorry, I wasn't intentionally taking long. The shower just felt too good."

Xavier nodded, "I understand."

Maleah walked over to the sink and brushed her teeth, then proceeded with her nighttime skincare routine. Xavier just watched silently, tussling between the doubts flooding his mind and his unshakeable love for her. As much as he desired to believe it was all in his head, memories of Rochelle's betrayal nagged at him, encouraging him to leave no stone unturned.

"Excuse me." She stood in front of him, waiting for him to step aside.

Xavier let her pass and watched as she sat on the side of her bed, moisturizing her body. Once her skin was fully coated in shea butter and glistening, she slipped into a sage green, silk nightgown.

"Okay." She exhaled, "Let's talk."

He rubbed his chin and walked over to the velvet chaise sofa at the foot of her bed. He took a seat, and she sat with her legs folded on the bed.

"You love him?" Xavier cut straight to the point.

"No...but I thought I did at one point."

"You thought you did?"

"Yea. Dating Eric was like a *fever-dream*. A whirlwind international romance that felt like a Harlequin romance novel. But just like a novel, it wasn't real." She shared candidly.

"What happened?"

"He reeled me in with his charm, wined and dined me, but when we decided to make things official, I got word that I was being considered to head the New York office."

Xavier silently processed her words before responding, "So, you two broke up because you were moving back to the city and what, he hated it too much to visit?"

"Not exactly. It was a bit more complex than that."

"Okay. Break it down for me."

Maleah closed her eyes and took a deep breath, releasing it audibly, "My plan was to turn down the job offer and remain in London. I even started the paperwork to change my temporary work visa to a global talent visa."

"What made you change your mind?"

"I...I, umm..." Maleah twisted and pulled at her fingers, trying to force the words out.

Xavier's chest got tight with concern, "You what?"

"I...found out I was pregnant."

In an instant it felt like the room was spinning and Xavier looked away trying to digest her unexpected admission.

"I was so overwhelmed but excited at the same time. It felt like a clear sign that Eric and I were meant to be." She continued somberly.

Xavier stood up and began pacing the floor, "What happened to the baby?"

She cleared her throat, caught off guard by his directness, "I surprised him with the news during an elaborate dinner I planned and to *my* surprise, he was not happy."

Xavier stopped in place and turned to face her, met with her teary gaze, "He forced you to get rid of the baby?"

"No." Maleah wiped her eyes, "Eric's much too clever for that. He instead showed little interest and became distant. And when I confronted him about it, he said that he wasn't about to alter his life to accommodate a decision *I* made."

"What the fuck?"

She shrugged, "Yup. So, I read between the lines and decided to terminate the pregnancy, unwilling to be a single mother in a foreign land…I'd accepted the job offer, scheduled the procedure and started moving out of my flat all before the end of the week."

"Damn…" Xavier exhaled, leaning back against her dresser.

"He then had the nerve to flip shit on me, accusing me of doing it for my career and saying how he understood. Then offered me his forgiveness and proposed we start over. Little did he know, I was already back in New York."

"Hmm…" Xavier didn't know what to say, he just replayed her words in his mind. He definitely hadn't expected the conversation to go in the direction it went.

"Yea, so whatever tension you felt between Eric and I, was just me trying to maintain my composure as he used his charm to further gaslight me. As far as he's concerned, it basically never happened and clearly, he still thinks things are salvageable."

"Why didn't you tell him we were together?" He pressed.

"I'm sorry for that. I was honestly just blindsided and doing my best to not let him get a rise out of me. But I did tell him…when I walked him to the elevators, I made it clear that you and I are together and that I'm *very* happy."

"You did?" Xavier stared into her eyes in search of any sign of dishonesty.

"Yes. I even warned him to stop the flirty shit because I couldn't protect him from the consequences." Maleah assured.

Xavier exhaled, satisfied with her words and reassured of his position in her life. But he made a mental note to pay Mr. Yeboah a visit to make it even more clear that pursuing *Mal* would be a huge mistake.

"Come here." Maleah stretch open her arms.

Xavier slowly walked over and was enveloped in her embrace as she pressed her face against his abdomen. He looked down at her and she leaned back, meeting his gaze.

He sighed, "I love you."

"I love you too."

Xavier leaned down and kissed her passionately as she caressed his back. He broke free from the kiss and pulled his sweatshirt over his head, revealing his perfectly sculpted physique. Maleah leaned forward and planted soft kisses around his belly button as she slid her hands into his sweatpants.

"Mmm..." He moaned, feeling her soft hands wrap around his member.

Maleah stared up at him as she stroked him with both hands, "I'm sorry if I made you feel like my heart was anywhere else."

Xavier bit down on his bottom lip as her grip and pace became more intense, "Fuuuuck..."

"I love you, more than I could ever articulate." She cooed.

"I love you too, ugh..."

Maleah slowly slid him into her mouth, causing his eyes to roll to the back of his head. He gently slid his right hand behind her neck and squared his stance to maintain his balance.

"Oh, fuuu...."

His toes curled, gripping her plush rug as she pulled him close, swallowing all of him.

"Whew, shit...you been holding out on me." He moaned, caressing her neck.

Maleah picked up her pace, sucking like a hoover vacuum and within minutes Xavier was up on his toes, hand full of her hair, experiencing a mind-numbing orgasm.

"You good?" She smirked, wiping her mouth and chin with the back of her hand.

Xavier exhaled, shaking his head with his eyes closed. After a moment he opened his eyes and looked down at her, "You ain't never done that before."

She giggled, "I save it for special occasions."

"I see why."

"I'll go get the washcloth." Maleah stood up from the bed and headed into the bathroom.

Xavier stepped out of his sweatpants and followed behind her, fully naked.

"Uhn, uhn, here." She extended the warm, wet cloth to him.

He grinned, "You're not gonna do it for me?"

Maleah looked down and watched in real-time as he became erect, "It hasn't even been ten minutes and you're already hard again."

"You should know by now; the first one is just the appetizer and I'm a five-course kind of nigga." He winked.

"Xavier..." She whined, "I meant it when I said I'm exhausted. I just gave you all the energy I had."

He grinned, "Now it's my turn. Plus, think of how good you'll sleep afterward."

Before she could respond, he cupped her ass and lifted her onto the sink. He kissed her passionately while running his fingers over her labia, then pressed two fingers inside.

"Ugh...baby." She moaned.

"Mhmm...ain't tired no more, are you?" He watched as her eyes rolled to the back of her head.

She dropped the cloth on the sink and grabbed his wrist, thrusting her hips forward, "Mm...that's my spot."

Xavier gently pushed her back, leaning her against the mirror and placed his free hand on her pelvic area. As he pressed down firmly, he moved the fingers inside her in an upward motion. He gradually increased his speed and the rapid pressure he was applying to her G-spot caused her legs to begin shaking.

"Oh fuck, oh fuck...baby!" Maleah exclaimed.

Xavier was locked in, never breaking his rhythm despite her convulsions and before he knew it her back was arched, and she was squirting.

Maleah's legs shook uncontrollably as she tried to catch her breath and Xavier planted sweet kisses from her stomach up to her breast.

"You good?" He teased, massaging her thighs.

"Very funny." She rolled her eyes, "Help me up."

Xavier took her by the hands and helped her lean up from the uncomfortable slouched position she'd fallen into. Maleah pulled her nightgown over her head and tossed it atop the laundry basket in her bathroom.

"Now I've got to take another shower." She pushed him backward and climbed off the sink.

"We can take one together...afterward." He picked her up and carried her into the bedroom.

"Okay, but no sex in the bed. Unless you plan on sleeping in the wet spot."

"Alright." Xavier grinned, "I always wanted to bend you over that island countertop.

∞∞∞∞

"Ayo, boss, Mook's out here asking to speak with you. You want me to send him in?" One of Chris's bodyguards spoke through the cracked office door.

"Mook? What the fuck does he want?"

"I don't know."

Chris huffed, "Alright, send him in."

Mook stepped inside the office grinning like the menace he was.

"Wipe that smile off your face and tell me what you need, Mook?" Chris instructed.

"I've got an opportunity for you." Mook proceeded to smile.

"Spit the shit out, nigga. You've got 60 seconds before I put you out."

"Alright, my bad. So, a partner of mine just got out a few days ago."

"Nope." Chris cut him off.

"You ain't even let me finish."

"For what, Mook? So, you can ask me to give some nigga I don't know a spot he ain't earn? No. If you want to help the nigga, do it on your own time with your own resources."

Mook huffed, "It's not even like that. You know the nigga."

"Who is it?" Chris quizzed growing frustrated.

"T.Y."

"The nigga that used to run with Chuck? The answer just went from *No* to fuck no!" Chris spat.

"They used to do business but he ain't fuck with the nigga like that. Just give him a shot. The nigga ain't been back more than 72 hours and he's already commanding respect. Niggas is itching for his leadership, and I think he'd be a great replacement for Lucky." Mook bargained.

"Lucky already has a replacement."

"Gary? The same nigga that let a couple of young niggas rob him? The nigga I had to help recover his bricks and money, so you ain't lose profit? He's pussy!" Mook spat.

"Maybe I should put *you* in Lucky's spot."

"Nah, nah...I prefer moving in the shadows. But I think you should really consider T.Y."

Chris exhaled heavily, "I'll think about it.

"That's all I'm asking."

TAP! TAP!

"Boss man. It's a nigga out front saying he's supposed to be meeting with you. Says his name is T.Y."

Chris looked over at Mook, "Nigga you brought him here?"

"I told the nigga to stay in the car."

All of a sudden, they heard a commotion on the other side of the door.

"What the fuck?" Chris pulled his gun from behind him.

He stood up and listened for a moment, then walked around his desk to the door. Mook followed behind, holding a Glock 45 at his side. When he opened the door, there stood Tyree, staring down at Chris's driver, who was on the floor with a bloody lip. His bodyguard was in a defensive stance with his gun pointed at Tyree's head.

Tyree turned, causing the red dot to move from his temple to the center of his forehead, "Tell this pussy nigga to put the gun down."

"Say the word, boss man. I'll put this nigga down."

Chris flexed his jaw and sighed, "It's cool Lenny."

"Lenny?" Tyree smirked, "Pussy ass name."

"It can be the last name you speak, try me!" Lenny barked.

Chris placed his hand on Lenny's arm, "I said we're cool…for now."

Lenny reluctantly lowered his gun and rested it at his side.

"Nigga, I thought I told you to stay in the truck?" Mook interjected.

"What I look like, yo bitch?" Tyree sneered.

"T.Y. you know it's not acceptable to just show up like this. This really could've gone left for you." Chris warned.

Tyree smirked, "Yea okay. Anyway, I hear you've got a position that needs to be filled."

"You're what, three days out? Don't you want to spend some time with your family. Get reacclimated with the outside world." Chris questioned.

"You can either put me in position or I'll create an opening by taking that pussy nigga Gary off the map. Your choice."

Chris gripped the gun in his hand, "You're threatening me?"

"Just making sure we're on the same page."

"So, if I don't give you Gary's spot, you're gonna murk him? Nigga, you could kill him tonight and it won't bring you any closer to taking his spot." Chris shrugged.

"You're a smart businessman, so I know you don't want to risk a dip in revenue because of pride. You need someone that can not only hold shit together but take it to new heights. That nigga Gary only got vision enough to break even at re-up."

Chris took a deep breath and scratched his head with the tip of his gun, "You want Gary's territory, then you're gonna have to take it. But I'm not giving any orders. If you can manage a transition of power without a ton of bloodshed and making shit hot, I'll give you my seal of approval and grant you protection."

"I don't need either. I just need product." Tyree retorted boldly.

Chris chuckled, "That's what you think. But when shit gets messy, I'm the only thing standing between you and another stent upstate."

"The only way I'm going away again, is in a body bag."

"Well, you show up here again without being summoned and Lenny will shoot you on sight, expediting that." Chris stated matter-of-factly.

"Be expecting a call about your boy Gary in a few days." Tyree disregarded his threat.

"All the rest of our dealing, if you manage to pull this off, will go through Mook. He knows how to reach me."

The two men stared each other down for a moment then Mook walked over to Tyree.

"Come on, T.Y."

Tyree waited a moment longer then turned to follow Mook out the front door.

Chapter Nine

Officer Sean Ramirez walked briskly toward the detective's division, excited about the information he'd just received.

"What's that smile for, Ramirez? You got something for me?" Lydia looked up from her third cup of coffee.

"Not *something;* I may have found the thing to solve this whole thing." Sean beamed with pride.

"Okay, so spit it out." Det. Abrams interjected.

Sean exhaled dramatically, "Okay, so you know how we've been trying to figure out the link between my mother and Charles Campbell; whether or not it was just unfortunate coincidence or if he'd been seeking spiritual guidance from her?"

Lydia nodded with an impatient but engaged expression on her face.

"Well…it turns out it was the former. Him being there was random. I believe that he ran inside attempting to seek safety from the person pursuing him." Sean continued.

Det. Abrams huffed, "We've already come to that conclusion. I thought you had something groundbreaking to share."

"You know he was being pursued, but I think I know by *who*." Sean rebutted confidently.

"Alright, so who is it?" Lydia pressed.

Sean opened the folder in his hand and pulled out a picture, facing it toward them, "Him."

Det. Abrams shrugged, "Who the fuck is he?"

"This is Anthony Waters. The name that was written on the back of the book found at Det. Hanson's home."

Lydia grabbed the picture and examined it, "Damn, he's fine…what makes you think it was him?"

"His son was murdered last year, and Det. Hanson was assigned the case." Sean shared, handing the folder to Det. Abrams to look through.

Det. Abrams looked through the files and then passed the folder to Lydia so that she could also take a look, "Okay, so her log history shows she looked into him after the murder of his son. What are the rest of the dots? Because I'm not seeing the connection."

"Hanson's primary person of interest was this guy." Sean pointed to an intake photo of Peewee aka Percy, "And there's record of Hanson implicating him as an informant of Det. Johnson."

"Hold up. Interrogation logs and search history aren't available without a shitload of paperwork and approval, so how's a Beat cop like you getting this info?" Det. Abrams questioned.

"Aaron, let him finish." Lydia interceded.

"If you must know, I do have a friend who works in Internal Affairs. But everything is above board. I had them notate that it was for this case and put my name down as the requesting officer. So, if any blowback comes, it'll only hit my house."

"If I must know?" Det. Abrams scoffed.

"Aaron, please." Lydia sighed.

Det. Abrams threw his hands up and leaned back in his chair.

"Ok, so like I was saying Perciville Brundis, street name Peewee was apparently an associate of Det. Johnson."

"Okay, so Percy aka *Peewee*, allegedly murders Mr. Waters' son. How does Mr. Campbell fit into all of this?" Lydia leaned forward intrigued and partly envious of how well he was putting the pieces together. Her jealousy was only tamed by the fact that she could just take the credit when the case was closed.

"Well, some of the evidence we retrieved from Det. Hanson's home was documents profiling our second victim, Charles Campbell. And when I looked into Campbell's file, Officer Brian Shaw was listed as the arresting officer. The same officer whose corruption case ended up setting Mr. Campbell free. So, I believe Campbell's connection to the former partner of Johnson, who's also dead *allegedly* at the hands of Det. Hanson, isn't coincidence." Sean took a deep breath before continuing, "My theory: Charles, Percy, Johnson, Hanson, Shaw and Mr. Waters are somehow connected. And my gut is telling me that Mr. Waters may be responsible for more than one of these deaths…my mother was just collateral damage. I mean how coincidental is it that he's the only one, that we know for sure is still alive?"

Lydia sat in thought, staring at the files in the folder, flipping occasionally between pages, "Hmm…this is a solid theory. However, without some concrete link tying Waters to Campbell, it won't stick. The most I can give you is that he may be the reason why there's still a BOLO out for *Mr. Peewee*."

"Right. I figured that, so I was thinking we should go and talk to Det. Hanson, get her to share whatever she knows about Mr. Waters and see if we can find a link that way. I mean, she had to be looking into him if she wrote his name down."

"Or she could've just been making a list of the victims' next of kin. Especially since there's nothing in her reports about him being anything more than the father of the victim." Det. Abrams quipped.

"Father to a victim that was shot execution style and found possessing an illegal firearm. Not to mention the other victims on scene had drugs on them." Sean rebutted.

"So, his son was in the streets and now that makes him a murderer? You of all people should know how damaging it is to assume guilt of a person by association." Det. Abrams sneered.

Sean stepped forward, "What's that supposed to mean?"

"You know exactly what it means, Beat cop!" Det. Abrams stood up from his desk.

Lydia slammed the folder down, "Enough! Sit down, Dammit. You two and your dick swinging contests are going to make me castrate you both!"

A couple of detectives around the room looked up for a moment and then went back to what they were doing. Det. Abrams sat back in his seat, adjusting the collar of his shirt in frustration and Sean stepped back, taking a seat in the chair beside her desk.

Lydia sighed, "Now…Ramirez, there's way too much red tape around Hanson at the moment. Cap has instructed us to steer clear of everything regarding her case and I'm not risking my badge."

"Okay…well, what if I do it?"

She just stared at him with a perplexed expression, "You? The man responsible for her fiancé's current condition?"

"Yes…if I offer to sign a written statement saying that excessive force *was* used and that the arresting officer intentionally didn't call for medical support, maybe she'll help us." Sean admitted nervously.

"Nigga, what?" Lydia belted, "You've got to be fuckin' kidding. Did I not *just* emphasize the thin ice we are on as a department?"

Sean nodded, "Yes. You did. And please don't call me that."

"My apologies." Lydia chuckled sarcastically, throwing up her hands, "But the answer's no. You'll need to find another way."

"What other way is there? There's only two witness statements and they were both dead ends." Sean huffed.

"You read the witness statements? I didn't see them in this folder." Lydia pried.

"I read the one from the delivery guy who was out front at the predicted time of death. But the other one was sealed off…" Sean shared, and the look on Lydia's face sent the wheels in Sean's head spinning a hundred miles per hour, "Wait…I know people can request to have their identity sealed for safety reasons, but why would they need to do that if they didn't see anything?"

"Lower your voice." Lydia spoke through clenched teeth.

Sean shot up from his seat, "So, the other witness does know something? What the hell? We could've gotten justice for my mother, and you all are sitting on pertinent information?"

"Ramirez." Lydia looked around to see if anyone was listening, "Sit down."

"No! Not til you tell me what the hell is going on. I've been doing all of this work to find a viable lead and you have an ace in your possession." Sean huffed, grabbing the attention of a few detectives across the room.

"Ay! Sit down, before I sit you down." Det. Abrams threatened.

Sean stared at them in bewilderment, overwhelmed by his own insinuation.

"Sean, sit down. Please." Lydia spoke calmly, "It's not what you think."

He reluctantly sat back down, "Then what is it?"

Lydia sighed, "The second witness gave a similar statement to the one you read, but...they were accompanied by attorney Stephanie Desoto."

"Am I supposed to know who that is?" Sean sneered.

Lydia huffed, annoyed by his newfound backbone, "She's a high-powered criminal defense and corporate law attorney."

"She sounds way above those guys' paygrade. They were unloading fruit from a community garden organization." Sean asserted.

"Exactly. Our guess is, she was sent by someone powerful that doesn't want us digging further." Lydia shared.

"So...what, you're just going to let my mother's murder become a cold case? Is that why it's taking so long?" Sean quizzed.

"No, no...we're still pursuing this. There's just...some parameters we have to work around. It's part of the game; people with power creating invisible roadblocks." Lydia explained.

"So, corruption?" Sean blurted.

Lydia looked around then leaned in, "Do you like your job?"

Sean sucked his teeth, "What, now *you're* threatening me?"

"No smart ass, she's trying to save you." Det. Abrams barked.

"You need to tread lightly, before you end up on Cap's shitlist. Cause like I told you before, I'm not putting my badge on the line. I'll gladly throw your ass to the wolves. You hear me?" Lydia threatened.

"Yea, I hear you." Sean sighed then sat silent in thought for a minute, "So, who *does* know the identity of this witness? Because someone had to interview them...it was *you*, wasn't it?"

Lydia leaned back in her chair and sighed, then covertly nodded *Yes*, "But my hands are tied. If we pursue, Desoto has threatened extreme legal action and with the current shitstorm at our doorstep, it'd be the end of our careers indefinitely. Unless you're open to policing some small town in *East-Bubbafuck, Nowhere*."

"What if...I got the name on my own and pursued this off-duty, under the guise of being a grieving son?"

Lydia stared at him with a blank expression, "Comprehension wasn't your strong suit in school, was it?"

"Look, I get it. There's a possibility that they tell Desoto but there's also a chance they'll feel sympathy. If things go sideways, I'll take all the heat; this conversation never happened." Sean professed desperately.

"You're damn right this conversation didn't happen and you're not going to go searching for him." Det. Abrams spat.

"Him? So, our witness *is* male. Hmm…I figured there had to be more than one delivery guy on site." Sean spoke aloud to himself.

"Ramirez!" Lydia slammed her palm against her desk, "Enough. You need to listen to us. If you go digging, you'll not only get yourself caught up in some shit you can't get out of but your little friend in I.A. will be pulled in for violating legal agreements to keep the witness' documents sealed."

Sean mulled over her words and exhaled heavily, "Fuck. So, what the hell do we do?"

Lydia leaned her head back and rubbed her temples, "I might have a play. But it's not guaranteed to be fruitful."

"What you thinkin', Lyd?" Det. Abrams leaned in.

She sighed, "Ava's father."

Det. Abrams grimaced, "Damn. Okay…you're sure?"

"No other choice. He's the only way I can get communication to Brenda without raising eyebrows. We meet for our court appointed drop-off Friday; it's his week with Ava."

"I'm assuming Ava is your daughter, but who's her dad and how's he connected to Hanson?" Sean interjected.

"Don't worry about all that, just let me try this. I'm not even sure he'll agree to help, but it's better than you getting us hit with another lawsuit." Lydia sighed heavily.

Sean stared at them in pure confusion, "Why are you two being so secretive? What, is he a guard at the prison or something?"

"No one's being secretive, there's just nothing to discuss." Lydia bucked, "You know what you need to know, nothing more."

Sean huffed and threw his hands up, "Fine, so you'll get him to ask Hanson about Anthony Waters and if he had involvement with any of the recently deceased or missing?"

"Like I said, I'll try."

"So, what if it ends up being another dead end? What if he says no or Hanson has less information than we have? I still think you should consider a work around with the second witness."

Lydia huffed, "Jesus Christ, Ramirez! Can we focus on one potential shitstorm at a time?"

"Fine..." Sean stood up and grabbed the folder off her desk.

"Don't go doin anything stupid, Beat cop!" Det. Abrams shouted toward Sean's back as he headed down the hall.

DING DONG!

The doorbell rang just as DeeDee was about to head upstairs. She huffed and reluctantly walked over to the door. When she opened the front door, she was met by the menacing grin of her cousin, Niecy.

"You know, most people call before they come by." DeeDee huffed.

Niecy grinned, "I'm not most people."

"That's for sure." DeeDee quipped as she closed the door.

Niecy took off her coat and tossed it on the banister, then made herself comfortable on the sofa, "So, what you got for me? Your text was so cryptic I got excited."

DeeDee huffed and plopped down on the other end of the sofa, "You're not gonna believe who I saw."

"You're right, so let's just skip the theatrics and tell me."

DeeDee rolled her eyes and pulled out her phone, "Don't get smart cause I can keep the information to myself."

"Alright, alright. You're so testy."

"This is who I saw." DeeDee slid her phone across the sofa.

"Oh shit...did you hear what they were talking about?"

"Nope. When I went to use the employee bathroom in the back, I heard someone shouting and it sounded like it was coming from beneath me. Then as I was leaving out the bathroom, I saw the basement door open, so I stepped back inside and peeked out. That's when I saw him."

Niecy smiled big as she stared at the photo, "I knew I could count on you. Always could."

"Yea well this is where I get off the crazy train, because anything involving a police captain is bound to lead to jail time or worse. Especially with all the stuff I've seen on the news about the corruption and officers killing each other."

"Relax, ain't nothing gonna happen to you. But that's fine. This is more than enough to get what I need done, done. Thanks, cuz!"

VRRRRRBBBB!

Just as Niecy was about to pass the phone back to DeeDee, the phone vibrated as a call came across the screen. There was no contact photo, but the name read *"SMILEY"* with a smiley face emoji.

"Smiley?" Niecy read aloud.

DeeDee reached over snatching her phone, "Alright, if you need nothing else, I'm about to go take me a nap before I have to go in."

"Damn, the dick must be good if you're keeping it that close to chest." Niecy teased.

"Bye, Zhaniece." DeeDee rolled her eyes, pressing decline on the call for the second time.

"Alright, I'm out." Niecy laughed as she stood up from the sofa and put her coat back on.

DeeDee stood up and walked her to the door. Once Niecy was at the bottom step, she closed the door, and the phone began to ring again but it was a Facetime call.

She plopped back down onto the sofa and pressed *answer*.

"Why yo ass sending me to voicemail?" The man barked.

DeeDee sighed, "I was with family."

"So."

"How can I help you, sir?"

"Turn the camera so I can see the room." He demanded.

DeeDee sucked her teeth, "Why? What, you think I got another nigga here with me?"

"Turn the camera."

"You turn your camera. All I'm looking at is the sunroof." DeeDee quipped.

"I'm driving."

"And I'm relaxing before I have to go to work." DeeDee shrugged, stifling a giggle knowing full well that she was pissing him off.

He released a subtle chuckle, "You gonna make me fuck you up."

"Whatever, Smiley." She giggled.

"Ay, didn't I tell you to stop calling me that?" He scolded playfully.

"Too late, it's your name in my phone. It's official."

He sighed, "What time you work tonight?"

"Why? You coming to see me?"

"Not tonight, but right now, yes."

DeeDee laughed, "No you're not."

"I'm already pulling down your block."

"I told you I take care of my grandmother."

"I remember. That's why you're gonna bring your ass outside and take a ride with me." He rebutted.

"So, no rest for me?"

"You're off tomorrow."

DeeDee sighed, "Fine. Let me go pack my bag."

"Your *hoe-bag*?"

"Watch it! Before I change my mind."

"Whatever man, I'm parked across the street. Just hurry up."

"I'll be ready when I'm ready. Don't rush me."

He chuckled, "You talkin' big shit. Wait til I get my hands on yo ass."

The call ended and DeeDee giggled as she made her way upstairs to grab her things.

∞◇∞◇∞

Maleah looked up from her computer, hearing the sound of someone knocking at her office door.

"Whatever it is, it'll have to wait until Monday."

The door slowly opened revealing a grinning Eric Yeboah, surprisingly dressed in a grey sweatsuit and a pair of silver and white New Balance sneakers. He stepped inside and closed the door behind himself.

Maleah rolled her eyes, "Who let you in here?"

"Damn. Where's the love Mal?" He grinned.

"Back in London, Bruv. You should go join it." Maleah rebutted sarcastically.

"You're still bitter about how things ended? I thought you'd be past it, especially with how well things are going for you here." Eric made

139

himself comfortable, taking a seat on the new burgundy velvet sofa she added to her office decor.

Maleah chuckled, "Nice try. But your manipulation tactics have no sway over me anymore. As I told you before, I am very happy. I'm in a loving and healthy relationship with a man who's shown me that emotional intelligence, accountability and vulnerability aren't unicorn traits. I wasn't asking too much, just asking the wrong man."

The look on Eric's face let her know that her words had pierced and landed how she'd intended. Satisfied with her rebuttal, Maleah began logging out of her computer and packed up her things in her work bag.

"If that's all, you can leave now. And please, don't make this a habit. I have an assistant for a reason. Send all of your work-related inquiries through her." She instructed as she stood from her desk and walked over to her closet, pulling out her coat.

"Our kid would've been three, this year." Eric's words stopped Maleah in her tracks.

She stared down at the floor, counting in her head as she tried to regulate her breathing, "Get out."

"I'm not trying to upset you…it's just, turning 35 has had me introspective and thinking about how much time I wasted. You and I could've been married with a kid, but I fucked that all up." Eric professed sincerely.

"Get. Out, Eric!" Maleah shouted, staring him in the eyes.

"Come on, Mal. You can't tell me you haven't thought about it. What we could've been. How things would've turned out had I responded differently. We were perfect."

"No! No, we weren't. You were self-centered then and clearly have not changed."

Eric stood up from the couch and walked over to Maleah, "That's not true. I've changed a lot since then. If you give me a chance, I can show you."

"Eric, please just go."

"You're only fighting me this hard because you know you still love me. And it's okay, because I still love you too." Eric brushed loose hairs from her face.

"Stop!" She slapped his hand away.

Eric stepped back with his hands up, "I'm not trying to upset you. But we both know it's the truth."

"I don't, nor have I ever loved you. And you never loved me either. You just loved the idea of me."

"That's not true. Was I selfish yes, but I did love you. I *do* love you." Eric professed.

"So, you waited all this time to tell me? Why now?" She rebutted.

Eric shrugged, "Because I'm a fool."

"You're right." She nodded, "A damn fool to think I'd fall for your bullshit after everything you put me through."

"Everything *I* put *you* through? *We* hurt each other, but I'm willing to let the past go for the sake of our future."

"There is no future, Eric! What the fuck don't you understand? You forfeit your shot when you left me to make the most difficult decision I ever had to make, alone!"

Eric shook his head and paced in front of her desk, "How can you say that? I never told you to abort our baby. I just…I needed time to wrap my mind around the whole thing. I wasn't ready."

"Neither was I! But that wasn't an excuse to shut me out. I was willing to stay in London and start a whole new life with you, leaving everything I knew and everyone I loved back here. And you basically ghost me for weeks?"

"Mal, I'm sorry. I was just scared. But I did eventually come back, ready to figure things out and even when you told me you had the procedure, I *still* wanted to work on us. Because I love you."

Maleah rubbed her forehead, staring out the floor to ceiling windows of her office as tears fell from her eyes, "It was too late then and it's definitely too late now. There will never again be an *us*."

"Don't say that."

Maleah sighed heavily, her back still facing him, "Just go, Eric."

"Not until you agree to giving me another chance."

"Eric, what part don't you understand? The fact that I'm in a relationship or that I will *never* be with you again?"

"I don't care who you're with. You will always be mine."

Maleah didn't respond, she just silently watched the hustle and bustle of the city below.

"You hear me, Mal?"

"You should go." Maleah instructed calmly.

"What's going on here?"

Maleah turned to see Xavier standing in the doorway.

He looked over at Eric and then back to her; noticing the redness of her eyes, he immediately walked over to her.

"I'm fine." She assured, placing her hands on his chest.

The look in his eyes let her know that he was one second away from putting Eric on his head.

"You don't look fine. You look upset." He spoke through clenched teeth.

"X, baby, I'm good. I promise."

"Yea, she's good bruv. Just a little emotional, reminiscing on the past." Eric chimed in.

Maleah closed her eyes and inhaled deep, "Baby, please don't even respond."

"It's cool. We'll finish this conversation another time, Mal." Eric stood up from the couch and headed for the door.

Xavier removed Maleah's hands from his chest and followed him, "Let me holla at you really quick."

Maleah slapped her palm against her forehead and sighed heavily, watching the two men exit the office.

Eric turned to find Xavier closing the office door behind him. He released a brief chuckle then turned back around and headed for the elevators.

Once they were in front of the elevators, Eric turned to face Xavier, "What, are you about to do the whole threatening boyfriend act? Because I promise you, it won't mean shit to me."

"What's your plan, huh? Convince *Mal* to leave me and take you back?" Xavier quizzed.

Eric chuckled, "I ain't got to do no convincing. You saw her face when you walked in there. She still loves me. You're just some poorly dressed placeholder."

Xavier rubbed his chin and shook his head, "Look, I'm going to do you the courtesy of making this plain for you, because I don't want anything to get lost in translation. You press up on my woman again and there won't be any conversation. Ya' get me, bruv?"

"Oh really?" Eric walked closer to Xavier, "What *will* happen, then? If you don't mind me inquiring, *homie*."

"What's understood ain't got to be explained." Xavier responded calmly.

"Hmm…well let me make something clear, so *you* understand. Mans like you could never put fear in me. I'm from South London, Peckham to be exact; if you're not familiar, look it up but either way I'd be careful tossing threats."

DING!

The elevator arrived and doors opened as the two men stood in an intense stare down. Eric stepped onto the elevator with a menacing grin and Xavier walked back through the office doors, shaking his head.

"This nigga gonna make me kill him." He muttered to himself.

"What?"

He looked up to see Maleah, "Nothing. You ready?"

"Uh, yea. What happened out there?"

"Nothing. Don't worry about it."

"But I am."

"We just had a talk; man to man."

Maleah stared at him like she wanted to pry further but decided against it, "Alright."

Xavier took her by the hand and led her to the elevators.

Brynn sat in the driver's seat of his blacked-out Cadillac Escalade, watching back the footage of his post-trial conversation with the press. Reporters swarmed around him as he descended the stairs of the courthouse, accompanied by a private security escort that hurriedly rushed him toward a black SUV. Before entering the truck, Brynn stopped and turned to face the crowd of media correspondents.

"Attorney James! Attorney James! After today's hearing, what do you think the odds are of Det. Hanson being released without any charges?" One of the reporters shouted.

"Well, I'm not a man of odds, I deal in absolutes and what's absolute is that the evidence presented to the court today proves beyond a doubt that Det. Johnson, may he rest in peace, was clearly living a double life. Cop by day and drug dealer by night, using the thin blue line to literally get away with murder and even went so far as to try and pin the murder of his ex-partner, on my client. As I've stated before, the only thing my client is guilty of, is sniffing too close to a fox hole and unfortunately getting bit by a rabies-stricken system." Brynn boasted like an Alabama preacher.

"If she's innocent and the evidence proves it, then why haven't they released her?" Another reporter asked.

Brynn chuckled, "Because…this isn't about justice, this is politics. And politics is nothing more than theatre. They want to drag this case along for the sake of spectacle and media ratings, and the slim possibility that they can sway public opinion to get people onboard with their plan to execute a public lynching in modern day America. But like the great prophet Iyanla Vanzant said *NOT on My watch!*"

Brynn suavely turned and his security opened the back passenger door for him.

"Attorney James! One more question!" A young woman reporter shouted.

"No more questions. Back up." Brynn's Security barked.

Brynn rolled down his window, "Go head sweetheart, but make it quick before my driver pulls off."

"Do you feel any conflict of interest representing this case? I mean, with your child's mother being a detective on the same force as your client. Doesn't this case hit a little close to home for you?" The young reporter asked nervously.

Brynn just smiled and rolled up the window as his driver pulled out into traffic.

"These new reporters are damn near detectives. Shit." He muttered to himself as he swiped the screen revealing another video from a different angle.

BEEP!

A blue midsize SUV pulled up behind Brynn's truck and he sighed heavily at the sight of his ex-girlfriend exiting the vehicle. He watched through his side mirror as she helped their five-year-old daughter out of the backseat. Brynn exited his truck as they walked over and immediately directed his attention to his daughter.

"Hello, Brynn."

He looked over at her with confused expression, "Lydia."

"Can I talk to you for a second?"

"I missed my Avy-wavy." Brynn kissed his daughter on the forehead as he picked her up and she giggled.

"I missed you too, daddy." Ava cooed.

"Did you hear me?" Lydia interjected.

Brynn proceeded to ignore her, swinging Ava's bookbag over his shoulder as he carried her to the truck. Once he placed her inside, he walked around to the trunk and pulled out a booster seat.

"Really, Brynn? You're just going to ignore me?" Lydia walked over to him.

"I thought we agreed to keep communication to a minimum? Keep shit running smooth with no issues." Brynn replied dryly.

"I know, but we're adults who share a child. We should be able to amicably interact without it always being a fight."

Brynn furrowed his brow, staring at her in confusion, "Who the hell are you and what have you done with Ava's mother?"

"What are you talking about?"

"Lydia Diane Vance. You can cut the shit." Brynn chuckled, "The whole *minimal communication* thing was your idea, so why're you trying to amend it all of a sudden? You need a favor, don't you? What, you want me to keep Ava an extra couple of days so you can playhouse with that partner of yours?"

Lydia scoffed, "Aaron and I are just friends."

"Whatever. I honestly don't care." He shrugged, "Then what is it? Because this kid swap is now broken the record for how long it typically takes."

Lydia stepped closer and whispered, "It's regarding one of your clients."

"Nope." Brynn responded immediately, opening the back door of the truck and securing the booster seat.

"You didn't even hear the ask."

"I don't need to. Whatever it is, the answer is no. You and I talking about anything besides Ava is a conflict of interest." Brynn rebutted as he strapped his daughter into her booster seat and closed the door.

"Brynn please. I promise what I need won't interfere or taint your case." Lydia pleaded.

"You can't guarantee that. Us even being seen together could cause problems. All it takes is one well-crafted rumor and photo to accompany it and my credibility is shot. You and I both know that the court of public opinion wins more cases than real litigation, these days." Brynn rebutted.

"What if I agree to let you take Ava for the whole summer?"

"What?" Brynn turned to face her, "You'd really barter your child for my help? This really must be important."

"It's not a barter. I was considering letting you have her anyway. She's been asking to spend more time with you…but, yes. I really do need your help. This case is going on four months unsolved, and I've got a cop who is threatening to upend everything I worked for because he has personal ties to one of the victims."

"You're talking about the murder of Charles Campbell and the Parishioner."

"Yes…I believe your client may have some connections to one of our suspects. I just need to know what she knows about our suspect and if she can concretely tie him to Campbell." Lydia expounded.

Brynn sighed, "June to September?"

"Yes. The whole summer. But I will be visiting throughout. I'm not gonna just ghost my child for three months."

"Fine. Send the details to my assistant and I'll see what I can do." Brynn instructed.

"I can't do that. This needs to be as lowkey as possible. Just you and me, for now."

"Lydia, I'm lead council in a case against the NYPD involving corruption and two murder charges. I barely have the bandwidth the remember my schedule from day to day. If you don't send it to Tori, I may end up forgetting."

"Brynn, please. I need this handled discretely."

He huffed, "Fine. But you owe me more than a full summer. I'm sending you a bill."

Lydia threw her hands up and shrugs, "Whatever you say."

Brynn shook his head and climbed into the driver's seat, closing the door behind him. Lydia stood and watched as he pulled down the street and disappeared around the corner.

Lydia chuckled to herself, "Tuh. Yea, right! I am not giving that fool my kid for the whole summer."

Chapter Ten

DING DONG!

Marla Howard rushed to the front door wearing a flour covered apron, as the sweet sounds of *Anita Baker's "Sweet Love"* echoed through the speakers of her vintage record player.

"Coming!" She shouted as the bell rung again.

"Good evening. Is Dave home?"

"Uh, no but he should be shortly. Who should I say stopped by?"

"Tell him Larry, his old golfing buddy, I was just in the neighborhood and figured I'd stop by to grab something he picked up for me."

"Oh, wait. There he is, he just pulled up." Marla pointed toward a grey '68 Camaro pulling into the reserved parking space in front of their brownstone.

"What's going on?" Capt. Howard asked trying not to sound nervous.

"Larry said you had something for him." Marla informed.

"Yea, I came by to get that thing from you. Remember?" Paul smiled.

"Oh, yea...uh about that. I don't have it yet, I'm gonna need a few more days."

Paul just stared at him with a wicked smile, causing Marla to grow uncomfortable.

"How about y'all come in off the stoop and discuss whatever business you have in the den." She suggested.

Paul nodded, "Good idea."

"No, uh actually I wanted to show…Larry the new upgrades on the car." Capt. Howard nervously interjected.

Marla rolled her eyes, "You and that damn car."

"Come on, Pau-Larry. Let me show you."

Paul waited for a moment then obliged, meeting him at the bottom of the stoop.

"I'll be in, in a minute." Capt. Howard nodded with a faux smile.

Marla nodded, sensing something off about his demeanor but after a moment of surveying Paul, she went back inside and closed the door.

The two men walked over to the '68 Camaro and once they were beside the drivers' side door Capt. Howard threw his hands up in surrender.

"Look, I know you said Monday but…" Capt. Howard's words were cut short by the feeling of something cold and metal pressed into his side.

Paul leaned against the car, concealing the gun in his right hand, "But what nigga? You thought I was fuckin' joking?"

"No, no. I swear, it's just been a lot of eyes on me, and I've been swamped with meetings and press conferences."

"Do I look like I give a fuck?" Paul gritted.

"I know, I know…I get it. Believe me, if it was my kid, I'd be ready to move heaven and earth too. I'm just caught between a lot of obstacles." Capt. Howard explained.

"You don't know shit! You and that baren old bitch have no clue what I'm feeling." Paul pressed the gun harder into his side.

"You're right! You're right."

"But you will know the pain of burying a loved one, real soon, if you don't get me that fuckin' name and address." Paul gritted.

Capt. Howard just looked at him with a helpless expression and his silence and hesitation instantly enraged Paul.

"I see…" Paul nodded, chuckling to himself.

He took the gun and slammed it against the drivers' side window, smashing it.

"What the fuck!" Capt. Howard shouted.

Paul didn't respond, he just proceeded to unleash his wrath on the mint condition, custom painted '68 Camaro. He broke the side view mirror off, kicked a dent in the drivers' side door then pulled a knife from his jacket and cut holes in the cloth top.

"Come on man, stop! Please!" He grabbed Paul by the arm.

Paul snatched away and threw a left hook, knocking him onto the pavement, "Give me the fucking name! Now!"

"I…I can't. At least not until the case is over."

"Dave! Dave, what's going on? Are you okay?" Marla shouted from the top stoop.

"I'm fine, babe. Just go back inside. We're just having a little brotherly dispute." Capt. Howard assured as he got up from the pavement.

Marla sucked her teeth, "Are you back gambling? Or is this about a whore you didn't pay? I swear to God Dave, I'm sick of this shit. I thought you were done with that shit! How much does he owe you, sir?"

"Just go back inside, Marla!" Capt. Howard walked over to his wife as she came down the stairs.

She looked past him at Paul, "Larry, if that's even your name, how much to make all this go away?"

"He knows exactly what I want." Paul responded coldly.

"Well, whatever it is, we'll pay it." Marla professed.

"Marla, please. Just let me handle it."

"Shut up, Dave!" She pushed him aside, "How much?"

"I'm not here for money." Paul informed.

"Then what?"

"Like I said, he knows."

Marla turned toward her husband, "Whatever it is, give it to him. Now!"

Capt. Howard huffed, "Marla, it's not that simple."

"Now, Dave! Or I'm leaving you for real this time and when I do, I'm airing everything out. You won't have a nickel left to your name or a reputation to stand on." She threatened.

"What? You don't even know what he's asking me for?"

"I don't care! Do it!" She shouted, "I'm too old for this shit."

Marla huffed as she stomped up the stoop into the house, slamming the door behind her.

"Hmm... maybe I won't kill her. Maybe I'll give her the relief she clearly deserves." Paul chuckled.

Capt. Howard just stood staring at the front door of his home, his back facing Paul.

"Fine. I'll do it. But once I do this, you and I are done."

"Nigga, we're done when I say we are. Now give me the name."

Capt. Howard huffed, "Vincent Ruiz. I'll have to wait til I go in on Monday to get the address."

"Bullshit. I know you have a computer with access here. Go get me the address, nigga." Paul demanded.

Capt. Howard reluctantly trudged toward the stoop, into the house. After about ten minutes he came back, pulling a folded piece of paper from his pocket.

"This is a list of his last known addresses."

Paul shook his head, "Now was that so hard?"

"Man, if they see I pulled his file I'm fucked." He huffed.

"Then you better cover your fuckin' tracks. Either way, it's not my fuckin' problem."

Capt. Howard sucked his teeth, "Yea, alright man."

Paul reached out his hand and he reluctantly shook it then he pulled Capt. Howard into a close embrace.

"Ah fuck!" Capt. Howard belted.

Paul had taken his knife and jammed it into his thigh quickly then pushed him back from the embrace.

"That's for making me have to come find you, nigga." He barked.

"Fuck! That was unnecessary!"

"So was this fuckin' trip across town! Now give me your phone." Paul rebutted.

"For what?"

"Nigga, are you serious?"

Capt. Howard pulled the phone from his pocket and tossed it to Paul.

"Password."

"Dave."

"What?"

"Just press the corresponding numbers for the letters in my name."

Once Paul got the phone unlocked, he scrolled to the doorbell camera app. He went in and deleted the footage from their interaction and his arrival at the home.

"If this information turns out to be bullshit, my next visit won't be as pleasant." Paul tossed the phone back and it hit him in the chest before hitting the ground.

∞∞∞∞

Brandon laid across the couch, knocked out, as the tv played re-runs of sports highlights from the game earlier that day.

VRRRRRRRB!

His burner phone vibrated on the coffee table, startling him out of his sleep.

"Yo?" He answered groggily, trying to sound alert.

When he got no answer on the other end of the phone, he opened his eyes and looked down to see it was a text message from an unknown number that read, *"Light a candle. Now."*

Brandon quickly hopped up from the couch, grabbed his jacket and stuffed his feet into a pair of black Timbs. He quickly jetted out the front door almost knocking his brother and niece over.

"Where are you running to? What's wrong?" Sean quizzed.

Brandon huffed, "Do I question what you got going on?"

"No, but I'm not the one living at *your* house."

"Look, I ain't got time for this. I've got business to handle."

"Yea, whatever. Just make sure you stay wherever that business is until the morning, cause my doors lock at 10pm." Sean instructed.

Brandon just flagged his brother off as he hurried down the street, searching for a rideshare on his phone.

Once he arrived it front of the church, Brandon quickly hopped out the tiny prius and looked around in search of Niecy's mustang.

BEEEEEP!

He turned to find a green minivan across the street. The window rolled down halfway, and Niecy waved him over.

"What happened to the mustang?" He asked as he climbed in the front seat.

"Who's he?" A little voice came from behind him.

Brandon quickly turned around, startled by the unexpected voice, "Who the fuck?"

He was shocked to see three little girls in the backseat, looking to range between ages of seven and ten.

"Ay! Watch your mouth." Niecy scolded.

"Are these your kids?" He whispered.

"Nigga, please. You think I'd have you around *my* kids?" She laughed, "These are my homegirls' daughters. I promised them a trip to *Dave & Buster's*." Niecy stated nonchalantly as she pulled out into traffic.

"At...nine o'clock at night?" Brandon quizzed.

Niecy shrugged, "It's more fun at night."

Brandon stared at her with a confused expression, "So, what the hell am I doing here? Helping you chaperone? I thought this was *the* call."

"Nigga, relax and put your seatbelt on. You should realize by now that nothing I do is just for the hell of it?"

Brandon did as he was told and reclined in his seat as they rode to the sounds of *SZA's song "30 for 30"*.

Once they arrived, the girls hopped out and held hands as Niecy led them across the parking lot into the building.

"Alright, y'all meet me back here in an hour and we'll get something to eat." She instructed, handing the oldest one the playing cards.

The girls quickly ran off in the direction of racing games and Niecy proceeded toward the ticket redemption counter.

"Alright, so what are we really doing here?" Brandon whispered.

Niecy rolled her eyes, "If I tell you to relax one more time, I'm gonna make your ass wait in the car."

Brandon sucked his teeth and just quietly followed her. After waiting a few minutes, the guy working the counter came over to them all smiles. He was a tall, skinny guy with acne, braces and large square glasses that had lenses so thick it made his eyes look pea sized.

"Hey, beautiful."

"What's up, Greg."

He stared at her lustfully, "What do I owe this unexpected pop-up?"

"I'm here to redeem my prize." She cooed.

"Hmm…that's all?"

Niecy giggled, "Yea…today."

"You got your card?"

Niecy pulled a game card out of her bra and slid it across the glass countertop. Greg placed his hand atop hers then picked up the card, sniffing it not-so-discreetly. Brandon rolled his eyes and walked away to sit inside a shooting game, disgusted by his blatant lust for Niecy.

Greg scanned her card to see the number of tickets on it and then printed a slip, handing it to her.

"Which one you want?"

"Umm…" Niecy pretended to look around, "I'll take the giant green bear."

"That one's for display only, but I might have one in the back. Give me a sec." Greg winked.

After a few minutes Greg returned with a giant pink monkey, "This is all we had in the back."

"I love it. Pink's my favorite color."

"Mine too. Favorite flavor too." Greg bit his bottom lip.

Niecy giggled, "Behave."

Greg threw his hands up, "My bad. You're right."

"B! Come get this for me." Niecy shouted toward Brandon.

He reluctantly got up and walked over, "I'm not your damn baggage handler."

"Ay, my man, watch how you talk to the lady." Greg defended.

"Shut the fuck up, Urkel. Before I put your face through the fuckin' display." Brandon barked.

Niecy placed her hand on his shoulder, "Chill out, before you make shit hot."

The look in her eyes told him there was more to the exchange than it appeared. He reached over and took the stuff animal from Greg and the weight of it instantly let him know it was a decoy.

Leaned in, "Is this…"

"Here, go put it in the car, so we don't have to carry it around all night." Niecy handed him the keys, "And don't get no stupid ideas

154

because I know where you lay your head. Or should I say on who's couch."

Brandon paused, reading the threat within her tone and in her eyes. He snatched the keys from her and made his way toward the exit. When he returned, he found Niecy sitting at a high-top table sipping a frozen drink.

"It's the middle of the winter and you're drinking a margarita?" Brandon took a seat across from her.

"Yup. Would you like one?"

"No. What I want, is to know why the fuck we're sitting here with several bricks of coke in your van." Brandon whispered.

"Correction, it's not my van. It's my homegirls' van. And again, relax. The only people who know it's in there is you, me and Gregory. And his nose is so far up my pussy, I could get my period, and the nigga would drink it like Kool-Aid." Niecy giggled.

"That's fuckin' disgusting. How do you even fuck with a nigga like that? He *looks* like he smells." Brandon scoffed.

"First of all, I don't fuck him. But...I do let him watch me masturbate when I'm feeling generous. Fair trade for his storage services." She shrugged.

"So, this is where you stash all your shit?"

"Aht, aht. Don't go trying to figure out how I operate. This is just where I hid the keys."

Brandon shook his head, "Chiflada."

Niecy laughed, "And don't you forget it."

"So, what's the next move? I'm assuming you set up the meeting with the nigga I'm supposed to pitch the partnership to." He leaned in and whispered.

"You'll know what you need to know, when you need to know. For now, just order you a drink or go play some games." Niecy slid her game card across the table.

"The only person interested in playing games is you." Brandon huffed.

"Fine. Suit yourself." She shrugged, taking a large gulp of her drink and then stepping down from her stool, "I'm gonna go play air hockey. Order me the appetizer trio when the waitress comes back."

Brandon rubbed his forehead in frustration as he watched Niecy bounce through the game floor gleefully.

∞◊∞◊∞

"Bae, can you come zip me up?" Korena shouted toward the ensuite bathroom.

Khalil came walking out with a toothbrush hanging from his mouth, "I thought you was putting on the other dress?"

"No. I looked like somebody's grandma in that thing."

"So, you made me sit in that store while you tried on all of them dresses, just to wear something that was already in yo closet?" He fussed as he tugged at the zipper.

Korena sucked her teeth, "Whatever, just zip me."

"I'm trying! The damn dress doesn't fit."

She gasped, "I have not gained that much weight, you've probably got it snagged on the lining."

"Man, it ain't snagged on shit. The dress was tight as fuck before you got pregnant. It's only going to stretch but so much."

"Just stop, let me see something." Korena lifted the dress over her belly, "Now try it."

Khalil tugged at the zipper, and it finally went all the way up. Then Korena pulled the tight bodycon fabric down over her belly.

"See, I told you."

Khalil shook his head, "That's ridiculous. You're willing to smush my kid to wear this little ass dress?"

"Relax. The baby ain't smushed. At four months, it's about the size of an avocado." Korena quipped, rubbing her favorite vanilla musk oil behind her ears.

Khalil shook his head and went back into the bathroom, returning a few minutes later to finish getting dressed. He dapperly donned a black, cross-body lapel suit with silk trim, a black button-down shirt and a thin gold chain around his neck.

"Well, don't you look handsome." Korena smiled, watching him unwrap his du-rag and then brush his waves.

He smirked, "I always look good."

"Hmm…sometimes." Korena teased.

She walked over to his side and slid her arms around his waist and stared up at him while he brushed his beard in front of her standing mirror.

"Why're you looking at me like that?"

Korena sighed, "I know you said that you didn't want to talk about it, but I really think you should at least talk to X about...your mother."

He gently pushed back from her embrace, "No."

"But why not? That's your brother and you two are good now. I saw how seeing her shook you and keeping that bottled up isn't healthy."

"I wasn't *shook*, just caught off guard." He rebutted defensively, "And you're one to talk; aren't you the same one who kept a secret from her best friend for almost 15 years?"

Korena just stared at him in silence. She'd known Khalil to be hot tempered at times but never intentionally hurtful, especially not with her.

"I get it. That's a trigger point for you. But I'm not your enemy, so you can save that fight for the mothafuckas outside our home. I love you and I just want you to get the closure you need to really heal...if not for yourself or me, do it for our child."

Khalil sighed, grinding his teeth in frustration while he rubbed his forehead, "Fine. I'll talk to X. When I'm ready."

"Before this baby comes."

He huffed, "Korena."

"Khalil.", She mocked his stoic voice.

"This shit ain't a joke. This is my life." He fussed.

"Our life." She rubbed her belly, "And I ain't jokin' either. I want what's best for you Khalil and if that means I've got to fight with you to achieve that, I will."

Korena walked up to him and placed her hands on his face, caressing his cheek with her thumb. He looked her in the eyes then leaned forward and kissed her sweetly.

"You ready?" He asked.

"Yea."

Korena grabbed her purse off the ottoman and pulled her favorite black heels from the box that was beside it.

"Where do you think you're going in those?" Khalil quizzed.

"What's wrong with these?"

"You're not walking around in them skinny ass skyscrapers, so your pregnant ass can lose your balance and fall."

She sucked her teeth, "Khalil, I've been wearing six-inch heels since I was fifteen. Ain't nobody gonna lose their balance."

"Yea, but you ain't walked in heels that high with a baby in your belly, fucking with your equilibrium."

Korena huffed, "Khalil."

"Korena."

After a thirty second stare off, she sucked her teeth and tossed the heels into her closet then grabbed her black, three-inch, chunky heel Mary janes.

"Better?" She sneered.

"I guess."

"Nigga, it better be. Because I for damn sure ain't putting on flats." Korena retorted.

"Just bring yo ass on."

Khalil grabbed her shoes from her and took Korena by the hand, leading her downstairs to the front door of her townhome. Korena kicked off her slippers and stepped into her shoes with Khalil's help then he grabbed her Black and white Houndstooth coat from the closet and helped her into it. Once she was good, he slipped on his aqua marine colored ostrich skin loafers and then put on his wool trench coat.

"Watch your coat." He instructed as he tried to close Korena's car door.

Just as she pulled her coat inside, Khalil noticed a car with heavy tint on the windows creeping slowly down the street.

"What's wrong?" Korena asked as she tried to see what he was looking at.

"Hand me the gun from the armrest." He instructed, never breaking eye contact with the vehicle as it crept closer.

Without hesitation, Korena grabbed the gun and slid it to him. Khalil put the gun behind his back and took the safety off.

"Be careful." She grabbed his arm.

"Close the door."

Khalil cocked the gun, putting a bullet in the chamber then slid it into his pocket and slowly walked down the driveway, just as the car

158

stopped. He stood with his finger on the trigger, ready to shoot when the passenger side window rolled down.

"Boo." Tyree grinned.

"What the fuck you want?" Khalil asked coldly.

Tyree looked him up and down, "Nigga, this my lil sister spot, I'll pull up whenever I want."

"Yea, well that's *my* woman. And I pay the mortgage here." Khalil rebutted.

"So? Just because you're fuckin' and spending money on her doesn't mean you run shit. It just makes you a trick."

Khalil rubbed his free hand over his face, trying to maintain his composure despite the overwhelming desire to release the emotional tension he'd been carrying.

"What the fuck is your beef with me?"

"For one, my sister can do way better than the 2nd hand crash dummy of an OG." Tyree shrugged, "And...I honestly just don't like you."

"Well, you're just gonna have to get over it, cause I ain't goin' no-fuckin-where." Khalil spat.

Tyree grinned, "You sure about that?"

Khalil's cold stare was all the response he chose to give.

"Me and my woman are headed out, so if we're done here, you can get the fuck on." Khalil instructed calmly.

"Oh really?"

"Really."

Tyree shook his head, "I don't like your tone."

"I don't give a fuck." Khalil shrugged.

"You know...I was thinking, Mike here would make the perfect stepdad to our newest edition to the Moore clan." Tyree taunted with a devilish smile.

"I don't know about that. But he'd definitely make the perfect pallbearer at your funeral. What you think Mike?" Khalil quipped.

"Fuck you!" Mike spat.

"While we're on the topic of stepdads, does yours know you set his son up?" Khalil quipped.

Tyree's entire demeanor shifted, "Be careful talkin' about shit you know nothing about."

159

"Are *you* sure about that?" Khalil grinned.

Tyree leaned up in his seat, "You're threatening me?"

"Not at all Big TY. Oh, my bad, that was your pops, right? Funniest thing happened the other day…your mom and sisters said I remind them of Big TY. Crazy, right? Especially since that's who you're trying so hard to emulate."

Tyree clenched his jaw then released it with a smile, "Nice try. They ain't say that shit."

"Okay.", Khalil shrugged.

Tyree shook his head, "Niggas always think they're funny until their choking on their last breath."

"If only I was joking."

"Yo, who is this nigga talkin' to?" Mike opened the drivers' side door, ready to hop out.

"Chill out, Mike. We ain't here for that. Plus, I know you see my pregnant sister in the car over there." Tyree scolded.

"My bad, T.Y." He huffed, slamming his door shut.

Tyree turned his attention back to Khalil, "You can take your finger off the trigger, nigga. Like I said, I ain't come here for that *today*, I just came by to put my eyes on where my sister stays, in case I have to make a late-night house call."

"Make sure you call ahead, next time. I'd hate for you to get shot, mistaken for an intruder." Khalil quipped callously.

Tyree laughed, "Picture that. A crash dummy taking out a tank."

"You know, you keep throwing that word around but maybe you should be asking yourself why this so-called crash dummy is still very much intact?"

Tyree smirked, "Cause it ain't ran into the right wall."

"Feel free to test that theory anytime. We'll see who the dummy is."

"Ayo, you hear this nigga? *We'll see who the dummy is.*" Tyree taunted as him and Mike laughed, "Come on, let's get out of here before tough guy bursts a blood vessel trying to look scary."

Mike pulled off immediately as the sound of their laughter and *Jay-z's* "*Money, Cash, Hoes*" played at a disrespectful volume.

Khalil walked back up the driveway to the car and took a moment before getting in. He cleared the chamber on the gun, put the safety back on and placed it back inside the armrest as Korena stared at him with a concerned expression.

"Relax, everything's fine." He started the car and put it in reverse.

"Relax? You just had me pass you a gun like you're still in the streets and got OPPs lurking. Who the fuck was that?"

"I ain't in the streets."

"Ok, so then who the fuck was that?" Korena stared at the side of his face waiting for a response.

Khalil huffed, "Your brother."

"T.Y.?"

"Yes."

"What the hell did he want and why didn't he get out the car and say something?" Korena quizzed.

"He ain't want nothing."

"That doesn't make any sense, what were y'all talking about? What did he say?" Korena pressed.

"Korena, what did I just say?"

"Nothing! That's why I'm trying to get more details. You say my brother pulled up, doesn't get out to speak to me and that he didn't want anything meanwhile your ass is all tensed up around the shoulders. He clearly said something to piss you off." Korena ranted.

"Let it go."

Korena considered pressing the matter further but the look on his face told her to just leave it be, so she did. But she indeed intended to call her brother tomorrow to see what his impromptu visit was all about. Her gut was telling her there was some animosity between her brother and Khalil, but she couldn't figure out why. Khalil told her that he only saw her brother in passing but didn't really know him well, so what was the beef?

Chapter Eleven

After almost an hour of watching Maleah try on one dress after another, she and Xavier were now in his car on their way to dinner for Valentine's Day. She'd finally settled on the very first dress she tried on, which was a plum red, off-the-shoulder cashmere sweater dress. The dress was so long, her gold metallic heels barely peeked from beneath when she walked. Her hair was pinned up with soft ringlet curls, and a few free-hanging pieces. The golden shimmer of her exposed chest, shoulders and back was complimented perfectly by the warm Arabian fragrance she wore. Maleah looked so good, that Xavier almost considered canceling their dinner plans and making her the *meal*.

"I hope wherever you're taking me, has some good fried calamari. I've been craving it all week. Are we going somewhere Chef Pierre is spotlighting? Because I'd love you ten times more than I already do." Maleah rambled, fantasizing about the flavors.

"Will you relax and just let me surprise you." Xavier laughed.

She giggled, "Okay, okay. My bad, I'm just excited and lowkey really hungry."

"We'll be there soon." He assured, "I just need to stop by my place really quick."

"Why? What'd you forget this time."

"Ay, don't say that like I'm always forgetting things."

Maleah laughed, "Not always, but out of the two of us, you're the one who typically has to double back for a phone or keys."

"That happened like twice and, in my defense, one of those times we'd just finished rearranging your desk, so I was a little disoriented." He smirked.

"Yea, well what's your excuse this time? Because we haven't had sex in 24 hours." She teased.

"That's the reason, right there. Doc said I'm supposed to take two a day, three if symptoms worsen and you be depriving me of my medicine." He joked.

Maleah laughed, "You're so corny."

"And you love it." Xavier quipped as he parked in front of his Loft's building.

He leaned toward her, his face inches from her and exhaled as he took in her beauty and aroma.

"Hurry and go get whatever you left." She whispered as his breath tickled her lips.

Xavier leaned closer, brushing his lips against hers, "What if we don't go?"

"What if you don't get your medicine for a couple more days?" She caressed his beard.

Xavier smiled hard trying to stifle a laugh, "Alright, come on."

"Come on? Why do I have to get out?" She questioned in a slightly bratty fashion.

"You know damn well I'm not leaving you out here in this car."

Xavier shut off the car and stepped out then walked around to her side and helped her out. He chivalrously ushered her through the main entrance to the private elevator that led to his loft, on the top floor of the four-story brick building.

"What did you forget?" She asked again, as the elevator arrived at its destination and the doors slowly opened.

The smile on his face confused and excited her, then the sound of "*ICU (Vmix)*" by *VEDO* grabbed her attention.

"Come on." Xavier took her by the hand and led her out of the elevator.

Maleah gasped, covering her mouth, "Oh my God! X?"

He smiled at the shock and overwhelmed expression on her face. The two walked hand in hand through rose petals that covered the floor. Maleah looked to their right and in the kitchen, she saw there were several of her favorite dishes plated fancily, including the fried calamari.

"Oh my God!" She gasped, "Chef Pierre?"

"Yup." He smiled, "I had him make all of your favorites, even the…"

"Congolese cocoa brownies and coconut vanilla-bean sorbet?"

Xavier nodded with a smile as he let her toward the front of his loft, where the floor to ceiling windows were covered by long, red velvet curtains that extended onto the floor, creating a runway. Maleah, in awe, looked around at the dozens of polaroid photos hanging from the ceiling, each with loving notes written on the back. Then she looked to her left and noticed two violinists who were playing along to the music.

She grabbed his arm tightly, "This is too much…you did all this for Valentine's Day?"

"I did all of *this*, for *you*." He whispered.

Once they'd stepped onto the velvet curtain, Maleah stood frozen as she looked at the various photos attached to the curtain with a sign that read "*The moment's you're most beautiful to me.*"

Each photo was a candid from Xavier's POV. There was a screenshot of her laughing hard on a facetime call, a picture of her looking silly in a pink bunny rabbit onesie, one of her cooking in his kitchen, while wearing an oversized t-shirt with her hair looking crazy and there were also various photos of her sleeping in random places: Passenger side of his car, on his private plane, at a NBA game and in a movie theater.

Maleah giggled to herself then felt herself growing emotional as she stopped at a photo of herself asleep on Xavier's chest. The visible peace on her face and the abrupt revelation of safety resonated in her soul. It was a beautiful assurance of how much life had changed and reaffirmed what her therapist helped her realize; she was *Loved*.

Just as the soulful crooner uttered the closing words of the song, "*Thank you for my wife…*" Maleah turned to find Xavier on one knee, holding open a blue velvet ring box, showcasing a 10 carat Canary Yellow Diamond ring with a band that was shaped like vines.

"Oh my God! Baby!" Maleah squealing as tears began to flow from her eyes, "What are you doing?"

"What do you mean, what am I doing?" He chuckled, tears forming in his, "Maleah Naomi Jones…I Love you."

She held her hand over her mouth, lost for words and overwhelmed with emotions. This was a moment that'd been theory for so long and at one point felt so much like a fantasy that she opted to not think about it at all and just be present, enjoying what she did have.

"Baby?" Xavier interrupted her train of thought.

"Huh?"

He gently grabbed her thigh, "I said, will you marry me?"

Maleah stared down into his eyes and felt like her knees were about to give out, "...Yes."

"Yes?" He exhaled a breath he didn't realize he'd been holding.

Maleah nodded her head as more tears fell, and Xavier removed the ring from the box and slid it onto her finger then stood and pulled her into a tight embrace.

The song *"Stairway to Heaven"* by *The O'Jays,* began to play and the violinist played along as they kissed passionately.

"Congratulations!"

Maleah broke away from the kiss, startled by the sight of all of their friends in the kitchen area. Lisa, Sky, Chris, Isaiah and his wife Keira, and Khalil. Before the question could fully form in her mind, she noticed Korena off to the side, seemingly hiding behind Khalil and Isaiah.

She looked up at Xavier as more tears began to fall and he pulled her into a tight embrace, kissing her sweetly.

"I love you." She sniffled.

"I love you too."

Lisa and Sky gleefully skipped over, Chris and Isaiah followed behind.

"Oh my God! Let me see!" Sky squealed, pulling her to the side.

Maleah extended her hand, and the women gasped and giggled with excitement.

"Congratulations, man!" Isaiah dabbed up Xavier and the two shared a brotherly embrace.

"This one better stick." Chris joked.

Xavier sucked his teeth, "Ay, chill out."

Chris burst out laughing and shrugged, "Just sayin'."

"Yea, whatever, nigga." Xavier chuckled.

Khalil walked over to the men, leaving Korena in the kitchen with Keira.

He and Xavier embraced briefly, "You ready to do this, for real this time?"

"Ay, what's wrong with y'all niggas? My woman is right there."

The fellas laughed heartily, and Xavier tried to fight his own laughter, shaking his head at them.

"Nah man, we're just fuckin' around. I know this one is different. Even I can admit, that's your wife." Chris professed.

"Wow, Omarion. Is the icebox where your heart used to be, melting?" Isaiah gasped in faux shock.

"Shut yo corny ass up. My heart ain't cold, nigga. It's actually very warm…for a plethora of women." Chris glanced across the room at Sky.

Xavier looked over to see who he was checking out and immediately shook his head, "Don't even think about it."

"I'll think whatever I want." Chris grinned, watching Sky's every movement, "You know I love tall women."

"Nigga, didn't I tell you she's engaged?" Khalil interjected.

Chris chuckled, "And didn't I say, I don't give a fuck?"

"That's messed up. Just because you don't respect monogamy doesn't mean you should disrespect another man's situation." Isaiah added.

Chris shrugged, "I don't give a fuck about none of that, so spare me the lecture. My mind is made up and the only way I'm backing down is if *she* tells me no."

"That's foul." Isaiah shook his head in disapproval.

"Just let it go, Zay. You know how he is."

"Yea, *let it go, Zay*." Chris smiled, "I'll be back."

Chris walked away from the men and walked over to where the women were standing.

"Congratulations." He nodded at Maleah.

She smiled bright, "Thank you."

"You're very welcome." He smiled then turned his attention toward Sky, "You look absolutely beautiful in that dress. Pink satin was made to be draped against your skin."

"It's actually silk." Sky corrected.

Chris threw his hands up, "My apologies. Of course, a woman as opulent as you would wear nothing less."

Sky blushed, "I appreciate the compliment."

"And I appreciate you gracing me with your essence." Chris's words oozed with vibrato.

"I'm sorry, what's your name again?"

"Chris." He extended his hand.

Sky placed her soft manicured hand into his firm grasp, and it gave him chills.

"Sky."

"It was nice meeting you, Sky. Hopefully this is just the second of many chances I get to delight in your presence." He gently kissed the back of her hand and then slowly released it, "If you ladies excuse me, I have to go make a phone call."

"No problem." Maleah smiled like a little kid who just witnessed something they shouldn't.

Chris walked away toward the bedrooms at the back of the loft and the women all turned their attention to Sky.

"What the hell was that?" Lisa quizzed.

Sky shrugged, "Girl, I don't know. I've only met him once and we definitely didn't talk much beyond a basic hello."

"Hmm...well, didn't seem like you were opposed to his flirtation." Lisa quipped with a sarcastic grin.

"What was I supposed to do, tell him to beat it? It was just harmless flirtation and...honestly the first bit of attention I've gotten in weeks." Sky shrugged.

"Where *is* Jared?" Maleah questioned.

Sky shook her head, "You don't even want to know."

Maleah grimaced, "With his mom?"

Sky reluctantly shook her head, *yes.*

"Damn and I thought I had it bad with Victor being out the country on business." Lisa frowned her face.

"So, he chose to spend his Valentine's Day with his mother, instead of you?" Maleah questioned in irritation.

Sky sighed, "He says she's been feeling particularly lonely around the holidays, with his dad being gone and she feels like she's losing him now that we're engaged."

"Wait, hasn't his dad been dead since he was sixteen?" Maleah quizzed.

Sky huffed, "I know…it sounds ridiculous because it is. But my therapist brain also knows that grief is cyclical and can come in waves."

"Nah, that's B.S., she's manipulating him like those moms who treat their sons like their husband." Lisa asserted.

"You're not wrong, but you know what, we're here to celebrate Leah's engagement, not talk about my man's mommy issues. We'll save that for our girls' night."

∞∞∞∞

Brandon pulled up behind a warehouse in a car Niecy loaned to him and put the car in park. He pulled out his burner phone and texted an unsaved number: *"Here."*

After a few minutes, a side door opened revealing a man dressed in black. The man nodded at him and then went back inside leaving the door ajar.

Brandon huffed and swiped his face with his hand, "Alright. Let's do this shit."

He stepped out the car, went around to the trunk and pulled out a huge duffel bag before heading inside the building. Once inside he was immediately stopped by two men who patted him down and a third guy grabbed the duffel bag from him.

"Ay, what you doin?"

"Shut the fuck up and come on." One of the men barked.

Brandon huffed and followed, knowing he was too outnumbered and definitely outgunned to protest further.

"I know you, nigga?"

Brandon searched the room to see who was speaking. The authority of the voice let him know whoever it was, was who he was there to meet.

"You deaf, nigga?"

His gaze immediately diverted to a man sitting at a table, in the corner of the room, playing a game of solitaire.

"T.Y.?" He muttered to himself, trying to mask his shock.

"Yo, Mike get this nigga out my sight." Tyree barked.

"Wait, wait. No, we don't know each other, but I'm here to change that."

"Nigga, state what you want before I lose my patience.", Tyree commanded coldly, never looking up from his card game as he intently flipped and moved cards around the table.

"I'm here to offer a partnership. Help you make money."

"Who the fuck said I need help?"

"I wasn't saying it like that. I mean, who couldn't use more money?"

"Yo, get this nigga out my face."

The two men who patter him down immediately drew guns and walked toward Brandon.

"Ay yo, what the fuck? I came here to do business." Brandon huffed and threw his hands up.

"I don't do business with mothafuckas I don't know."

"Wait, what? Then why'd you agree to the meeting?"

"Free product." Tyree shrugged.

Out of nowhere the sound of a woman laughing echoed and Niecy came walking from behind him.

"Relax, Papa. Just had to test and see if you'd bitch up under pressure." She grinned.

"Why does everything have to be a game with you?" Brandon huffed.

"This ain't a game." She rebutted seriously.

"Yo, I don't know T.Y. this nigga smells like pussy to me. Let's just keep his shit and dump his ass in the Hudson."

"Now, Mikey that's not nice. Didn't I tell you Brandon was my cousin? How am I gonna look my aunty in the face knowing I got him killed?" Niecy cooed.

Mike sucked his teeth, "He ain't *my* cousin."

Niecy walked over to Tyree and leaned over the table, exposing her cleavage, "You're really gonna let them kill my cousin?"

Tyree looked up, staring from her breast up to her alluring eyes and sighed, "The nigga gets a trial run, but if I don't like him, it's a wrap. And the only way out this mothafucka is in a box or a bag."

"That's fair. Right, B?" Niecy looked over her shoulder at Brandon.

Brandon reluctantly nodded, "Yea."

Niecy turned her attention back to Tyree and grinned seductively, "Am I seeing you later?"

"Maybe." Tyree responded nonchalantly, returning his attention back to his game of Solitaire.

Niecy quickly grabbed several cards and stacked them on another and Tyree's face frowned up then subsided to a slight grin once he realized she'd made a good move.

"See you later." She winked then walked over to Brandon, "Let's go before he changes his mind."

"I thought he was supposed to be paying for the bricks?" He whispered.

"Nigga, did you buy them?" Niecy retorted.

Brandon sighed and followed her out of the warehouse. He watched as she walked out the lot then got into his car and sped out the lot. Once he spotted her, he pulled up beside her mustang and beeped.

Niecy rolled down her window, "What?"

"Why you ain't tell me the nigga you were planning to set up was T.Y.?"

She looked around and frowned, "Shut the fuck up! We ain't talkin' about this here."

"Then where? Because I need some mothafuckin answers before I go back in there and blow up your whole plan." Brandon threatened.

"Nigga, what? After I just saved your bitch ass?"

"You're the reason I'm in this shit in the first fuckin' place!" Brandon barked.

Niecy looked around again and bit her lip in frustration, "Follow me."

"Where?"

"Just fuckin' follow me, dummy!"

Brandon reluctantly back his car up so she could pull out of her parking spot, and he followed her. After a twenty-minute ride of trying to keep up with her, they pulled up on a residential block in Harlem and Niecy hopped out her car. She walked up the stoop of a house and then waved at Brandon to follow her. He cautiously exited his car and followed her into the house.

"Bitch nigga!" Niecy spat as she cracked him in the jaw with the butt of her gun.

"Ah, what the fuck!" Brandon grabbed his jaw as he stumbled through the entry way into the living room of the home.

"Don't you ever threaten me again, nigga!" She shouted.

Brandon charged at her, knocking the gun from her hand and the two fell into the sofa.

"I'm sick of your fuckin' games!" He gritted while trying to restrain her arms.

Niecy struggled to get free, "Get the fuck off of me! Are you crazy?"

"No! Not until you tell me what the fuck your plan is. Cause I'm not about to blindly go up against one of the most dangerous niggas in the city."

After an unsuccessful struggle, Niecy finally stopped fighting and sighed. Brandon stared down at her, watching her breathing slow and carefully released her. He jumped up from the sofa expecting her to swing but she just laid in the same spot with her eyes closed. And for a split second, he found himself admiring her beauty.

"I didn't tell you, because I knew you might bitch up and back out." She spoke callously as she sat up.

Brandon rubbed his jaw, still in pain, "I ain't no bitch, but you're damn right I'm backing out. T.Y. ain't the kind of nigga you fuck around with on no scheming shit. And you're talking about taking out his sister? You're fuckin' insane."

"Fuck him and his bitch ass sister! I don't care who that nigga's supposed to be, he ain't shit to me but an obstacle for my revenge." Niecy spat.

"Wait, hold up. So, you're telling me his sister killed the nigga Chuck and my mother?" Brandon questioned.

"What you know about Chuck?"

"I know that's who you're doing all this for but more importantly, I know him and T.Y. are two crazy mothafuckas cut from the same lunatic cloth." Brandon shared.

"T.Y. ain't shit! Don't ever compare my nigga to him. You ain't seen crazy." Niecy boasted with a crazed look in her eyes.

Brandon shook his head, "Yea…I ain't doin this shit. I'm out."

"No, you ain't nigga! You heard T.Y., the only way out is in a box or a bag."

"I'll take my chances." He shrugged.

Niecy chuckled maniacally, "Have you learned nothing by now? Nigga, I'm a collector of people, places and things. Whatever I need to make my ends meet."

"What the fuck is that supposed to mean?"

Niecy pulled out her cellphone and opened a video then passed it to Brandon, "Press play."

Once he did, he saw a backstage view of his nieces' dance recital from the week before.

"How the fuck?" Brandon gritted, "Bitch, I'll kill you."

"And the person that took that picture, will kill little Addie." Niecy smiled.

"Since you know so much, I'm sure you know who her father is. How you know I ain't tell him all about you?"

She shrugged, "Probably because your square ass brother is so law abiding that he'd have us *both* arrested. And we both know, you're terrified of going back, no matter how tough you act. I heard from a source up at the prisons, that you turned Muslim for the protection. What, your Celly tried to break your pinata with his stick?"

"Fuck you, bitch! Ain't nobody touched me!"

Niecy laughed, "Relax, I know. I made sure of it. Can't have a nigga who can't protect his own assets working for me."

"I don't work for you!"

"Aw…but you do. I'd think you knew that by now. You're just a pawn on my chess board; a domino waiting to be slammed on the table wherever I deem fit. You will do what I say, when I say, or I'll tip your whole life over."

"You think I won't kill you." Brandon gritted, pulling the gun from his waistband.

"I know you won't." She replied unfazed, "You're really slow at the whole comprehension thing so let me spell it out: You killing me won't be the end of your problems, it'll just be the beginning. I have several contingencies in place to assure my loss is your loss. It's called leverage, Papi."

Brandon stood tense, grinding his teeth in frustration as he tapped his finger against the side of his gun.

"If I help you, once this shit is done you leave me and my people alone."

She chuckled, "Oh, honey. You have no leverage to make demands, so quit while you're ahead."

"I know where you live." Brandon pointed around at the house.

Niecy burst out laughing, "Nigga, you really are dumb. You actually think I'd bring you to *my* house? This is a place I rent to a queer white couple at an astronomical mark-up via a third-party system. But nice try."

Brandon looked around at the pictures on the fireplace mantal, displaying two white men lovingly embracing. He frustratedly exhaled and stuffed his gun back into his waistband.

"That's better. Now hand me my gun off the floor and let's go. I can't remember if they come back from vacation tonight or tomorrow."

∞◇◇∞

"Ma, what're y'all still doing here? I thought y'all went back to Atlanta? Y'all called when you got to your gate." DeeDee was surprised to see her mother and father walking into *Lou's*.

The *Lakers/Warriors* game was on earlier that night, so the bar was packed with hardly anywhere for them to sit, so they just stood at the side of the bar.

"Hey, baby. We were supposed to but…your mother has some things she needs to handle." Darryl informed, being particular with the details he shared given the environment.

"What? What things?" She asked while multitasking the pouring of several beers and a mix drink.

Kathy sighed, "I'll tell you later, but right now I need your help."

"Need my help with what?" DeeDee lifted the bar flap and stepped from behind the bar.

"There was a guy here, the night we surprised you and I wanted to know if you could help me find him. You know, could you like ask around and see if anyone knows him?" Kathy asked discreetly.

"Why're you looking for him? Did he disrespect you or something?" DeeDee pried.

"No. Nothing like that." Darryl interjected.

"Look, it's too much to discuss here, but I promise I'll tell you everything later, I just need your help."

DeeDee sighed, "Alright, as long as you're fine. Do you have a picture of him?"

Kathy sighed, "No. I was hoping maybe you could check the security camera's or something."

"Hmm…alright, I'll see what I can do. I can't make any promises though."

"We really appreciate your help, baby girl." Darryl placed his arm around her and pulled her into a hug.

"No problem. So, when are y'all planning to leave?"

Kathy looked over at Darryl and shrugged, "I honestly don't know."

"You don't know?" DeeDee frowned in confusion.

"Hey! You've got patrons trying to get your attention!" Theresa shouted from behind the bar.

The look on Kathy's face caused DeeDee to step in front of her mother, blocking her view of Theresa, "Ma, it's okay. I'm fine. I'll call y'all later."

"That bitch is gonna make me crack her head against that bar." Kathy grumbled through pursed lips.

"I know, I know… but she ain't worth it."

"Come on, Kat." Darryl took her by the hand.

Kathy grabbed DeeDee and kissed her on the cheek, "Be safe baby and text me when you get in. I don't care how late it is."

"Okay."

They shared one more, brief embrace then Darryl and Kathy left *Lou's* leaving DeeDee with many questions.

∞∞∞∞

Shortly after the proposal, the serving staff arrived and assembled a few high-top tables and chairs. Once everyone was seated at their respective tables, champagne was poured, and Isaiah made a sweet, slightly cheesy toast to Xavier and Maleah's Love.

"To Love." He boasted.

"To Love!" Everyone shouted in unison.

They all sipped from their glasses as *Ashanti's* song *"Baby"* started to play. The women all swayed and sang along, cooing about their love for the song as the men talked amongst themselves.

Xavier swayed with Maleah to the music, but she was distracted by the sight of Korena sitting by herself, at the island countertop, eating fruit.

"You know, Khalil told me she was really excited to be here. She didn't want to miss this moment, even though she knew you probably wouldn't speak to her." He whispered.

Xavier's words poked at her heart, "Really?"

He slid his hand around her waist and massaged her belly, as he rested his face in her neck, "Really."

Maleah inhaled deeply then exhaled, "I'll be right back."

Xavier released her and she walked slowly over to Korena, whose attention was fixed on her phone.

"Can I talk to you?"

Startled by Maleah's unexpected presence, she started choking on the grape she was chewing.

"Oh my God, I'm sorry. I didn't mean to scare you." Maleah gasped.

Korena coughed, releasing the fruit into her hand and placed it on the plate. She looked up and saw everyone including Khalil staring with a look of concern.

"It was just a grape." She waved him off.

He looked at both of them then over at Xavier who nodded in reassurance that everything was cool.

"Sorry about that. Are you okay?"

Maleah's question, as simple as it sounded, felt heavier than a ten-ton elephant. Would she survive the assault of a grape without residual trauma? Yes. But was she *okay?* No. In a twisted turn of events or what some would call fate, she'd ended up on the outside looking in on a moment she had vivid memories of fantasizing about with her best friend.

"I'm...honestly no." Korena quickly swiped tears from her eyes, "But I'm really happy for you."

Maleah gently took her by the hand, "Come with me."

"Okay." Korena nervously stepped down from her stool and followed her to the master bedroom.

Once they stepped inside the room, Maleah turned around and pulled Korena into a tight embrace. She was shocked at first then immediately wrapped her arms around her waist and wept into her shoulder.

"I...I'm so sorry." Korena cried.

Maleah stared up at the ceiling, tears rolling down her cheeks, "I know..."

They stood, hugging and rocking side to side as they cried.

"I missed you." Maleah whispered.

Korena hugged her tighter, "I missed you too."

After standing in each other's embrace a moment longer, they separated and let out a chuckle at the sight of their faces in the mirror beside them.

"I promise, I never meant to hurt you. When I found out what he did to your dad, I swear I made it my mission to get him away from you. I just...I was too afraid of you hating me, if you found out the truth. It was selfish, I know. And I am forever sorry for the pain it caused you." Korena professed sorrowfully.

Maleah stared silently at her for a moment then grabbed her by the hand, "I forgive you."

Those three little words toppled Korena, causing her knees to become weak as she wept. Maleah reached out and caught her as they slowly lowered onto the floor.

"Why?" Korena looked up at her.

"My therapist helped me to see that none of us are the sum total of our worst mistakes. We are a summation of both good and bad...and when I did the *math*, the answer was always the same. You are my sister. My best friend. And, if I can forgive a man whose ex tried to literally kill me, and accept his proposal less than six months later, I can forgive the woman who has *always* had my back."

Korena sat silently, staring at her as she let the sentiments of her words absorb into her heart.

TAP! TAP!

They both looked over at the bedroom door where Xavier and Khalil stood with unsure expressions.

"Everything alright in here?" Xavier questioned cautiously.

"Yes. We're fine, we don't need a chaperone." Maleah quipped.

Xavier placed his hand on his chest in faux offense, "Damn, that's how you talk to your Fiancé?"

"I love you." She smiled, "Now please go and close the door behind you."

"You good?" Khalil looked at Korena.

She nodded, "Yea...we're fine. I'm okay."

Instantly she started crying again and Khalil moved to step around Xavier, but he put his arm up to stop him.

"Aye man, watch out." He huffed.

"Relax man, they're just having a moment. Let them work it out."

"I'm fine Khalil, for real..." Korena assured, "These are happy tears."

He sighed and turned to head back out the room, "Women."

Xavier just laughed and followed him out the room, closing the door behind himself.

"Relax, man. They're alright. You know them woman love a good cry." Xavier nudged Khalil, noticing his energy was off.

He sighed, "Man, I wish that was all I had to worry about."

"What's up?"

Khalil rubbed his forehead in frustration, "I feel like I'm being tried on every side and I'm trying hard as fuck not to crash out but I'm about two seconds from catching a body."

"What y'all niggas over here whispering about? I hope y'all letting them women sort their own shit out." Chris walked over, smiling big.

"We're good man. They figured their shit out." Xavier assured.

Chris looked over at Khalil, "Then why this nigga look like he's ready to put somebody in the ground?"

"I'm good."

"Bullshit. You ain't said much all night and the only time you're this quiet is when you're locked in, ready to hurt something." Chris rebutted.

"Just tell us what's going on." Xavier pressed.

Khalil looked around and sighed, "Fine. Let's take a walk."

Chris and Xavier nodded in agreement then they headed for the elevator, grabbing their coats off the rack beside it.

"Everything alright?" Isaiah walked over.

Chris nodded, "Yea, we're good man. Hold shit down, we'll be right back."

The elevator doors finally opened, and they stepped on, riding down in silence. Once they stepped outside, they walked to the corner posted up on the side of the building.

Chapter Twelve

Pulling up to the second address on the list Capt. Howard gave him, Paul put the car in park and turned off the engine. He looked around through his rearview mirrors and once he felt the coast was clear, he pulled the brim of his hat down and threw on his hood, cautiously exiting the car. He huffed and gritted his teeth at the squeaky hinges of the gate as he attempted to close it quietly. And as soon as his foot touched the top step, the living room light came on and someone peeked out.

"Who is it?" The sound of an elderly woman's voice came through the door.

"I'm a friend of Vince. Is he home ma'am?"

"Vinnie doesn't live here anymore, please leave before I call the police." The woman warned.

"No need for that, just came to drop something off to him." Paul spoke calmly.

"What?" The woman shouted through the door.

"I said…I have something for him."

"No not you." She replied.

Paul listened closely and could hear someone whispering to the old woman as she attempted to whisper back but was failing terribly.

"It's fine ma'am. I'll just leave it on the steps for him." Paul informed as he walked down the steps.

He got in his car and pulled off, but made a hard U-turn at the end of the block, speeding back up the block catching Vincent standing in the open door. Vincent quickly closed the front door and Paul pulled over and hopped out his car. Running through the narrow pathway beside the house, he pushed through the gate and was met by a Pitbull chained to the fence.

"Shut the fuck up before I shoot you." He gritted at the dog.

Paul climbed the back steps and shot at the door, then used his shoulder to force it open. The elderly woman screamed at the sound of the door slamming against the wall, as Vincent tried to quickly push her upstairs.

"I just want to talk Vincent." Paul spoke calmly.

"Bullshit! You just want to talk but you broke down my grandmother's door holding a gun." Vincent shouted.

"Please, don't hurt him! Dios mio." His grandmother shouted.

"Abuelita, go in the room and call the police."

Paul pointed the gun at him, walking further into the living room, "I wouldn't do that, mama. Not if you want Vinnie here to survive the night."

"What do you want man? I already told the cops I didn't see shit. So, whoever sent you is safe." Vincent professed desperately.

"I ain't here to keep you quiet, I'm here to find out *who* you saw that day." Paul informed.

Vincent threw his hands up, "I didn't see anything, man."

"Bullshit. Why have your identity protected if you didn't witness anything?" Paul huffed.

"Because of shit like this."

"You're lying. I know you saw something. So, just tell me and I'll be on my way." Paul rebutted.

"Look man, you don't know what you're asking. Even *if* I did know something, telling you would put my life in danger in more ways than one."

"Mothafucka, do you not see this gun? Your life is currently in danger." Paul walked closer to Vincent, pressing the nose of his gun against his cheek.

"Okay, man. Alright, alright! I, uh…I did see a guy. Big, brolic darkskin dude." Vincent confessed fearfully.

"If I show you a picture, you think you'd know his face?" Paul questioned.

Vincent shook his head as tears formed in his eyes, "Yea."

Paul pulled out his phone with his freehand and scrolled through his phone while still pressing the gun into Vincent's cheek.

"Was it him?"

Vincent squinted at the photo and then reluctantly shook his head *Yes.*

"You're sure?"

"Yea, man. I'm sure. I remember seeing him sit in the pews, praying then he went to the back." Vincent shared.

Paul nodded, "Thanks for your cooperation."

"You know, if the people who paid me to stay silent find out I told you, we're both dead." Vincent shared as Paul walked back toward the back of the house.

He stopped in his tracks, "Who's gonna tell them?"

Vincent's silence let Paul know that mercy couldn't be shown, as much as he hoped. He immediately turned and pulled the trigger, shooting him in the chest three times. Vincent stumbled backward into the coffee table and his grandmother screamed as she tried to hurry down the stairs.

"Vincent!" She wailed.

Paul quickly made his way out the back door.

∞∞∞∞

"Biiitch, yes! Hella messy! I know!" Brielle cackled.

She was sprawled across the couch in the living room of her apartment, on a facetime call with her twin sister Brianna.

"So, this nigga about to have project twins?"

Brielle giggled, "Yup!"

"Damn...I'd love to be a fly on the wall when she finds out. Actually, I wanna be a fly on the wall when her mama finds out, with her wannabe bougee ass! Acting like you ain't good enough for her son, meanwhile her daughter about to be a stepmom." Brianna boasted.

"Girl, you know I can't wait to rub this shit in her and Korena's faces!"

"When is Porsha planning on telling them?" Brianna questioned.

"She says she wants to wait until she has DNA results to back-up what she says."

"That's smart but how's she gonna get the test results if the nigga refuses to even speak to her?"

Brielle shrugged, "I don't know. I told her we should just pull up on the nigga and threaten to tell the family if he doesn't."

"Wait, hold up, ain't Tyson there with you?"

"Yea, he's here. He's knocked out in the bedroom. I finally gave him some coochie and the nigga was out like a light." Brielle smiled.

"Ew, please. Not too much. I was just wondering, because your ass surely ain't whispering."

"Girl, please. He can't hear shit. Watch this..." She placed the phone on her lap, "Ty! Ty! The house is on fire! Ty!"

After a few minutes of silence, she picked the phone back up with a sarcastic expression.

"Damn. That nigga really is knocked out." Brianna laughed.

"Exactly. It's terrible in case of a real emergency but good for when I want to be messy. That's why I'm scared to leave my baby with him, sometimes."

"Nah, Elle that's his son. He wouldn't let anything happen to T.J." Brianna challenged.

Brielle rolled her eyes, "Yea, while he's awake."

Brianna laughed, "You're so dramatic."

"Whatever. You just heard me scream bloody murder and the nigga didn't even budge."

"Why yo ass out here screaming?"

Brielle jumped, startled to find Tyson walking into the living room in just a pair of boxers.

"I gotta go girl, I'll talk to you tomorrow."

Brianna just laughed and ended the phone call.

"Who was that, your sister?"

She nodded, "Yea. I was just staying on the phone with her until she got in from her date."

"Hmm...so, why was you yelling?" He asked sleepily.

"That was just me joking around with Bri. Go back to bed." She assured.

Tyson smirked, "You gonna help me?"

"If I do, can we go to the Gucci outlet this weekend?"

He smirked and shook his head, "Fine. But five hundred is your limit."

"Seven."

"Six."

"Six-fifty."

"Fine. Now bring yo ass in here so I can get my money's worth."

Tyree turned and headed back into the bedroom and Brielle leapt up giddily and pranced into the bedroom behind him.

∞∞∞∞

"Alright, so what's up?" Chris questioned.

Khalil audibly huffed, "Nigga, I don't even know where the fuck to start!"

"I don't care where you start, just do it before the temperature drops any lower." Chris stated bluntly.

"Yea, I ain't trying to rush you but it is cold out here." Xavier agreed.

"Alright, alright. So, I guess I'll just go from bad to most fucked up."

Chris shrugged, "Dealers choice."

"Well, first…Porsha's ass is pregnant, and she swears it's mine."

"Damn, nigga. That's the *bad?* I'd consider that fucked up. Shit, you about to have project twins." Chris blurted.

"Nigga, I ain't having no fuckin' project twins."

"You sure it ain't yours?" Xavier interjected.

"Man…I really don't think it is. I think she's just trying to fuck with me because I'm with Korena, now." Khalil huffed.

Chris laughed, "Go ahead and buy a double stroller, nigga."

Khalil sucked his teeth, "Man, fuck you."

"Don't get mad at me cause you ain't wrap your shit tight."

"So, I'm guessing you haven't told Korena." Xavier stated knowingly.

"Hell no. The last thing I need is for her ass to get all worked up and end up in the hospital, again."

Xavier threw his hands up, "I was just asking, no judgement here. I definitely don't know what the fuck I'd do in your situation."

"Thanks. That's really helpful." Khalil sighed.

"Nigga, it's simple. Just go get a DNA test, see if the baby is yours and if so, tell Korena after *y'all* baby comes. Her reaction gonna be the same regardless of when you tell her, but at least you won't have to worry about her losing the baby." Chris suggested matter-of-factly.

"Man, I guess…"

"Nigga, you guess? You better man the fuck up and take care of your responsibilities. Don't do that kid like your peoples did you; if it's yours, figure out how to make that shit work." Chris instructed.

"Alright man, I hear you."

"So, what else happened that could be more fucked up than project twins?" Xavier quizzed.

"Stop saying that shit." Khalil huffed, "But…to make matters worse, I've got Korena's brother making passive threats. And I really feel like this nigga gonna make me get in my bag and end up putting him in one."

Chris shook his head, "That can't happen."

"I don't want it to, because I know that shit will fuck Korena up, but it's looking like that's going to be the end result." Khalil rebutted.

"Nah, I mean that really *can't* happen. With out telling you more than necessary, just know he's handling some shit for me and is currently under my protection until otherwise." Chris informed.

Khalil scoffed, "What? You got that nigga T.Y. working for you?"

"Something like that."

"So, if I go at the nigga I gotta go through you?"

"Something like that."

"And what about the threats that nigga is making toward me? I'm your fuckin' brotha!" Khalil spat.

"Nigga, chill out. I ain't gonna let that nigga do shit. You're good."

Khalil sucked his teeth, "I don't need your protection, I just need you to keep your people out my way if it comes down to it."

"It ain't gonna come down to nothing, cause like I said neither him nor you are going to do shit." Chris directed sternly.

"You really think that nigga's gonna take orders from you?" Khalil quizzed.

"He will if he wants to remain *employed*."

184

"Yea, whatever. Well, I'm telling you now, if the nigga tries me, it's a wrap. So, start vetting his replacement."

Chris shrugged, "I made my stance clear; you can do with that information what you will. But any money I lose, *you* will be responsible for recouping."

"Say less."

"Alright, so now that we've covered the extra baby and potential murder charge, what else is there? You're snorting coke, poppin X, eating shrooms? Is it crack?" Xavier tried to make light of the tension filled situation.

"Fuck no! But…the shit definitely felt like a hallucination or what mothafuckas be calling *fever dreams*."

"What happened?" Xavier inquired.

Khalil exhaled hard, "Man…"

"Damn, it's worse than another baby and killing your girls' brother?" Chris questioned.

"Nigga, yes…"

"Well, what the fuck happened, spit that shit out nigga." Chris asked impatiently.

"I…I think I saw my mom's." Khalil reluctantly shared.

"You think? What you mean? You saw her somewhere and recognized her?" Xavier questioned.

"Nah…I saw her when I was out with Korena and her people. They were celebrating her bitch ass brother and when we left, I ran to get the car. When I came back, I see a lady and her husband talking to Korena and I noticed tears in my girl's eyes so instantly I'm asking what's up. Long story short, Korena says my name and the lady repeats it and hearing her say it instantly sent memories flooding my brain. I knew immediately it was her." Khalil explained, trying hard to suppress his emotions.

"What the fuck…so she's been in New York all this time? How did she look? Was she clean or on something?" Xavier rapidly questioned.

"Nigga, I don't know. I honestly didn't stand there long enough to ask or really look at her. Once she started apologizing and crying, I got the fuck out of there." Khalil shrugged.

185

"So, what you gonna do? You gonna go look for her and get closure?" Chris asked.

"Nah, I don't need no fuckin' closure. I'm not about to sit down and let her unload her guilt on me so she can feel better about abandoning me. Fuck her!"

"You don't mean that." Xavier asserted.

"Yes, I do!"

"No, you don't, you're just hurt, and we get it. What she did was fucked up. But we've all lived enough life to know firsthand that it be fucking everybody up. And hearing her story might help you let go of some of that anger, nigga." Chris added.

"He's right, Kha. And you're about to bring new life into this world..."

"*Two* new lives." Chris inserted.

Xavier shook his head, "You're not helping."

Chris threw his hands up, "My bad, just reciting the facts."

"Getting closure is a necessary part of being a parent, otherwise you unintentionally transfer your baggage to your child. And you know this not only because of your experience but you also witnessed me grow up calling my grandma *mom*. After my mom and pops split, and she got sent back to Antigua, she became so bitter and angry that she ceased communication. To this day, I only hear from my mother via postcards she sends twice a year from whatever Caribbean cruise she's working."

"I hear you."

The men stood in silence for a moment, just the sounds of the cold night winds whipping through the streets and the faint sound of music coming from Xavier's loft, filled the night air.

"Alright, well this was a productive pow-wow. So, Kha is going to get the DNA on that baby, leave T.Y. to me and hash shit out with his moms?" Chris debriefed.

"Yes, unlikely and maybe." Khalil shrugged.

"Whatever, nigga. You're grown, do shit the hard way if that's what you prefer." Chris chuckled, "Gimme the key, so I can go back inside."

Xavier tossed him the key fob and he walked away, leaving them standing outside in silence.

"You good, man?" Xavier asked sincerely.

186

Khalil shrugged as a single tear fell from his left eye, "Man, I don't know."

Xavier pulled him into and embrace, "You gonna be alright. I've got your back."

Khalil reluctantly obliged the embrace, patting Xavier on the back, "Thanks, man."

Then released from the embrace and Xavier patted him on the shoulder, "You're my brother. I ain't gonna leave you out here on your own. Shit, I'll babysit that second kid, help you bury T.Y.'s body and go with you to talk to your mom."

The two men shared a brief laugh and then Khalil regained his composure, "Alright, let's get the fuck out this cold."

Xavier led the way and as he scanned his phone to open the doors to the building a black sedan pulled slowly down the street.

"You strapped?" Khalil whispered.

"Nah, my shit is upstairs in the safe."

"Fuck. My shit is in the armrest."

The two of them kept their eyes locked on the vehicle and as it crept closer the window rolled down, revealing Tone's smiling face.

"Tone? What the hell is he doing back here?" Xavier questioned.

"I don't know but it's probably nothing good."

Xavier sent a text on his phone, "I wonder if Jay is with him."

"You texted Chris?"

"Yup."

Khalil nodded then walked over to the truck, "Nigga, what are you doing back in New York?"

Tone grinned, "Just came to keep you legit businessmen on your toes."

"Yea, whatever. Chris knows you're here?" Khalil questioned.

"You're asking like that nigga's my handler or something. I ain't gotta check in with him."

Khalil threw his hands up, "It ain't even like that, I was just asking."

"You done spoke that nigga up." Tone huffed when he spotted Chris walking out the building, "What y'all niggas having a party?"

"Something like that. X just proposed to his girl." Khalil shared.

"Oh shit, that's what's up. Did he tell Jay?"

Khalil shrugged, "I don't know."

"She's gonna be pissed if he didn't." Tone chuckled.

"I thought I told your old ass to take a vacation?" Chris huffed.

Tone laughed, "Nigga, my life is a fuckin' vacation. And since when do I take orders from you?

Chris smirked, rubbing his chin, "You know what, you're right. Do whatever the fuck you want. Y'all niggas clearly think I'm a fuckin joke and my word means shit. So, y'all are all on your own and please don't call me when shit hits the fan."

He walked away and went back inside the building, without another word.

"He big mad." Tone smirked.

Khalil sighed, "Yea. He's just used to running shit, but he'll be alright. Anyway, what you back in the city for?"

"See family, handle some business and tie up a couple loose ends."

"How long you here for?"

"Damn, nigga. What're you surveilling me?" Tone joked.

Khalil sucked his teeth, "Man whatever, I was just asking. Plus, I might need your help with something. Chris ain't gonna help me, clearly, and I ain't trynna involve X in this shit."

"But you want to involve me?"

Khalil shrugged, "If you're willing. Otherwise, I'll handle the shit myself."

"Let me get my shit situated and I'll come see you." Tone informed.

"Alright, say less."

"Tell that nigga, X to come here." Tone instructed.

Khalil walked back over to Xavier, and he came reluctantly walking toward the truck.

"What you need?" Xavier asked trying to hide his disinterest.

"Damn, that's how you greet your brother?"

"My bad, what's up Tone?"

"First of all, congratulations. I hear I'm about to get a new sister-in-law." Tone smiled.

Xavier nodded, "Thanks man, I appreciate it."

"Why you look like you ain't happy to see me?" Tone quizzed.

"Because…the last time you were here my sister was in my office crying while you were doing God knows what." Xavier huffed.

"Fair enough…but we're good, your sister is good. And speaking of Jay, did you tell her you were proposing?"

Xavier sighed, "No. I hadn't told anyone before a few days ago. It was sort of *spur of the moment*."

"Hmm…well, you better call her, soon. Because if she finds out through social media, she's going to cuss you out." Tone warned.

"I know…I'mma call her. She here with you?"

"No, her and the girls are on a Disney cruise, but they'll be here next week."

"Why you ain't with them?"

Tone smiled, "Tie up some loose ends."

"You think that's smart with your wife and daughters here?"

"Let me worry about my family."

"They're my family too."

"You're right…that's actually why I was stopping by." Tone grabbed an envelope from the armrest and handed it to Xavier.

"What's this?"

"Legal documents giving you parental rights if anything ever happens to me and Jay." Tone explained.

"What? Why would something happen? What the fuck you into?"

"Relax, everything is fine. We just decided, after our last visit, that we needed to put plans in place in case unforeseen circumstances arise. And since the girls don't have godparents, we decided you'd be the best person to take care of them."

Xavier sighed, "You sure everything is cool? If my sister is in any kind of danger, I need to know."

"Jay and the girls are safe. Honestly, these documents were mostly her idea. I ain't gonna let anything happen to my family and I already know if something happens to me, Jay has you."

"Alright…but if things go left with those *loose ends*, promise you'll let me know. I ain't trying to see anything happen to you either." Xavier professed.

"I appreciate that, I really do. But I'm straight. You ain't gotta worry about me."

"Alright. Well, I'll have my lawyer look over these then I'll sign and get them back to you."

Tone nodded, "Alright, no rush. But make sure you call your sister, before your girl starts posting. Cause I know she bought that WIFI package on the cruise and she stays lurking on ya' girl's page."

"I got you."

Xavier tucked the manila envelope under his arm and walked back to the building where Khalil was now standing inside the doorway.

"Everything good?" Khalil inquired.

Xavier exhaled, "Yea…but my gut's telling me, not for long."

∞∞∞∞

It was almost 2AM as DeeDee laid across the bed of her hotel suite wearing red lace lingerie and eating an assortment of chocolate covered fruit.

VRRRRBBBBB!

Her cellphone vibrated on the nightstand and the name *SMILEY* flashed across the screen and less than a second later, the room phone started to ring.

She decided to answer her cellphone, "Hey, you downstairs?"

"Yea and this goofy nigga, at the desk, says I can't go up after hours without a room key. That's him calling you now."

"Okay, hold on." She picked up the room phone, "Hi, yes. He's, my guest. I asked that a key be left for him when I checked in."

DeeDee listened to the man apologize and then they hung up.

"I'm on my way up."

Before she could respond the call ended and she leapt up to check herself out in the mirror. Satisfied with her appearance, she sprayed on more of her favorite perfume and pressed play on her a playlist she specifically made for that night.

Tank's song *"No Limit (ft. Alex Isley)"* started to play and she laid back on the bed with her legs spread, giving full view to her bare lower half.

She heard the sound of the door opening and footsteps slowly entering the room.

"Damn…" He looked at her with pure lust in his eyes.

"Took you long enough." She purred.

He walked over to the foot of the bed and grabbed her by the ankles and slid her to the edge of the bed, resting her legs on his chest. Leaning forward, he caused her feet to stretch above her head and she slid her hands over his beard, pulling him into a passionate kiss.

"I've got a surprise for you." He whispered.

"A surprise?"

"Mhmm… remember that *special* thing we talked about. That you said you'd be down for, with the right person?"

DeeDee stared at him with concern, "The threesome?"

"Mhmm."

"Tonight?"

He grinned, "Yea…I found the perfect person."

"Choosing the person was supposed to be an *us* thing. And I said I'd consider it, not that I was ready." DeeDee rebutted.

"What you scared of?"

"It's not about being scared. It's about you checking in with me, before deciding to *surprise* me."

"Then it wouldn't be a surprise."

DeeDee sighed, "You know what I mean. Either way, the answer is no, so call your little friend and tell her not to come."

"She's already here."

"What? Where?" DeeDee pushed him back, trying to remove her legs from his shoulders but he had all of his weight on her.

"You're really going to make me send her home?"

She tried to sit up again, "Nope, cause I'm about to, once you get off me."

He took his time but finally leaned up, releasing her to sit all the way up. DeeDee grabbed her robe off the ottoman and stuff her feet in a pair of slippers as he watched her in amusement.

"Chill out. You don't have to do all that, I'll tell her to leave."

"No. I said I've got it.", DeeDee snatched the room door open, and her mouth dropped, "What the fuck?"

"DeeDee?"

He stared at the two women confused, "Wait, y'all know each other?"

"Clearly, T.Y.!" DeeDee shouted.

"Lower your fuckin' voice." He commanded.

DeeDee turned to Tyree, "Now do you see why picking the person needs to be an *us* thing?"

"Wait...*this* is Smiley?"

"Don't fuckin' call me that." Tyree glared.

"How the fuck do y'all know each other?" DeeDee quizzed.

"How do *y'all* know each other?" Tyree rebutted.

"She's my fuckin' cousin. Now, your turn." DeeDee quipped.

Tyree shook his head, "That's not important."

"He's right. It's not important. I'mma go ahead and get out of here."

"Uh, uh Zhaniece, not so quick. How long y'all been fuckin' around?" DeeDee pressed.

"*Zhaniece?* Who the fuck is Zhaniece? I thought your name was Tammy." Tyree interjected.

"It's my middle name." Niecy quickly rebutted.

Sensing some sort of scheme at play, DeeDee grabbed her by the arm and pulled her down the hallway toward the elevators.

"What fuckin' game are you running, Niecy? Were you planning on setting him up to rob him?" DeeDee interrogated.

"Lower your damn voice." Niecy gritted.

DeeDee gasped, "Oh my God, you were...what is wrong with you? Don't you get tired of this shit?"

"That's not what I'm doing. Contrary to what you think, I actually did come here to just get some dick with a side of pussy."

"Ew, please. Spare me." DeeDee frowned her face.

Niecy shrugged, "Weren't you just about to do the same thing before you saw it was me?"

"No. I had no idea about this shit. T.Y. called himself surprising me, all because we talked about threesomes, and I said I'd never done it but would consider it one day. But today was not that day. Anyway, if you're not up to anything, why the hell does he think your name is Tammy?" DeeDee ranted rapidly in a hushed tone.

Niecy peeked behind DeeDee and noticed Tyree was nowhere to be seen and she leaned in, "Look, you remember how you said you didn't want to know anything about what I was doing?"

"Yes."

"Well…file this under that and don't ask me anything you're not prepare to hear the answers to." Niecy warned.

DeeDee huffed hard, "What the fuck? Of all the niggas in New York, you had to pick the one I like to involve in your fuckin' schemes? I can't have shit good, fuckin with you!"

"New York is full of fine niggas. Just pick another one."

DeeDee gasped, "You're not planning on hurting him, are you?"

"I've got to go. Enjoy your Valentine's night. Even though it's technically the fifteenth. Oh, and stop using my fuckin' government name."

Niecy pressed the elevator button, and it opened immediately. She stepped on leaving DeeDee standing in the hallway with a perplexed expression.

When she got back to the room, Tyree was sitting at the table by the balcony doors. Too overwhelmed by what she'd just learned, she walked into the bathroom, flushed the toilet after a few minutes then turned on the faucet, to buy herself some time.

TAP! TAP!

"One second."

"Open the door, De'Shaye." Tyree spoke sternly.

She slowly opened the door and the look in his eyes let her know that she was about to be interrogated to the third degree.

"What's up?"

"What's your cousin's name?" He asked calmly.

"You invited her, why don't you know her name."

Tyree shook his head, "This ain't a game."

DeeDee looked up at him with distress written all over her face.

"Is it Tammy or Zhaniece?" He asked, walking up on her.

The way he towered over her, gave DeeDee chills, "I…I can't…"

"You can't what?" Tyree stared intensely into her eyes.

DeeDee looked away and sighed, "She's my cousin…my family."

"And I'm your man."

"Yea, but…you and I haven't known each other that long. I can't betray my family for you." She admitted.

Tyree chuckled, "Oh…okay. I see."

"Please, don't be mad. I'm not trying to choose between you to."

"But you already have." He backed out of the bathroom.

Niecy panicked, "No, I'm just trying to stay out of whatever this shit is. Fuck! If you hadn't tried to surprise me, we wouldn't be in this situation."

Tyree grinned as he opened the room door, "Relax. Don't worry about it."

"Where are you going?"

"We haven't known each other long enough for you to be asking where I'm going?" He responded callously as he stepped out into the hallway and closed the door behind himself.

"What the fuck, Zhaniece!" DeeDee huffed, slamming her fist against the wall.

Chapter Thirteen

"You've got to be fuckin' kidding me!" Lydia belted.

She was standing outside the jail, about to go in for her scheduled visit with Brenda Hanson when Det. Abrams called. The news of the confidential witness being murdered was not on her bingo card for the day and at 7AM without her necessary three cups of coffee, she was ready to rip a hole in someone's throat.

"Alright. Look, I'm about to walk in the prison, I'll call you when I get back to the city. Matter of fact, meet me at the pub, because I'm gonna need something stronger than coffee."

She hung the phone and shoved it into her pocket, taking a deep breath to compose herself then she made her way to the entrance.

"This way." One of the guards directed her.

After what felt like forever, Lydia was finally through processing and was met by one of Brynn's paralegals.

"Hi, Ms. Vance. I'm Sheila." The young white woman extended her hand.

Lydia looked at the woman's hand and nodded, "Nice to meet you. So, how's this gonna work?"

"Well, to keep you from having to log your name as a visitor, Mr. James had me put you down as co-counsel with the defense. So, I'll have to be present in the room with you, but everything shared will be legally confidential."

"Hmm…okay, well I'm going to need you to act like you've got an important call to step out for. Because we both know confidential is just a word in our line of work."

195

Sheila looked at her with offense, "You simply being here, given the nature of your relationship is enough to create a problem for you."

"You're threatening me?" Lydia stepped close to her.

Sheila shrugged and shook her head, "Not at all. Just pointing out the obvious."

Lydia sighed and rolled her eyes, "Whatever. Let's do this."

Without another word Sheila led her down a hallway and they stopped at a door where Lydia could see an exhausted looking Brenda, through the narrow window.

"Good morning, Ms. Hanson. Sorry for the early visit." Sheila smiled.

Brenda just nodded, then looked past her at Lydia with a confused expression.

"Vance?"

"Hey, Hanson. How're you holdin' up?" Lydia smiled awkwardly.

"Don't ask things you don't actually give a shit about." Brenda responded dryly.

Lydia and Sheila took a seat on the opposite side of the table.

"I do give a shit." Lydia rebutted.

Brenda gave a faint laugh, "No you don't. Because if you did, you would've come long before now and not with my legal team, which clearly means you need something."

"Come on, Brenda. You know I couldn't come here with all the heat your lawyer is bringing against the department. It would've been a death sentence." Lydia explained.

"And yet you're here now. Must be pretty important for you to risk your badge. Much more important than little ole me." Brenda sneered sarcastically.

"Look, Brenda I'm really sorry. And trust me, I planned on seeing you after things cooled down. But I have a kid and aging mother to think about. I can't afford to lose my job."

"Whatever. Spare me the sob story and cut to the chase. How can I assist you *Detective Vance?*"

The coldness Lydia saw in her eyes made her feel ten times worse than she already did. The once joyous, kind, justice seeking detective she knew was now faded into a jaded cynic with a callous spirit. The system has successfully broken Brenda Hanson.

Sheila cleared her throat, breaking the silence, "We're here to see if you can assist with one of detective Vance's open cases."

Brenda chuckled cynically, "Can I? Probably. Will I? Unlikely."

"What if I agree to in-camera, closed testimony of Johnson's misconduct?" Lydia blurted.

"Bullshit... I know your game, Lydia. You're good for making deals to get what you want then conveniently switching up. You're not about to take my help then turn around and give me some bullshit about being *scared* and changing your mind."

"I promise, that's not what this is. I'll sign written statements and all. I really need your help. I've got a parishioner who's dead after being caught up in the execution of a well-known dealer and the only viable witness lied about seeing anything, which I can't blame him because now he's also dead, despite his identity being sealed at the request of Stephanie Desoto. Oh, and did I mention the son of the dead parishioner is an eager beat cop, who's now been granted access as consultant on the case?" Lydia ranted frustratedly.

"Wait, Desoto? She's big time. Your witness must've been high profile." Sheila interjected.

"Actually, he wasn't. Which makes this shit even more complicated." Lydia shared.

"So, someone very powerful didn't want your witness telling what or *who* they saw, so they sent legal. But your witness ended up dead anyway?" Brenda questioned amused by her visible desperation.

Lydia sighed, "Yes...so, now my only lead is a name the eager beaver beat cop found, while doing some doodle sketch TV-detective shit on a book he found at your home."

"My home?" Brenda questioned.

Lydia paused, realizing in her rant she may have shared too much.

"It was a book found with the evidence that was taken from your home." Lydia amended her statement.

"That's not what you said."

"Yes, it is."

Brenda shook her head, "No, you said it was a book *he* found at my home. Who is he?"

"Nobody. Just an eager beat cop, like I told you." Lydia assured.

"Bullshit. And if you don't tell me the truth, I'm going back to my cell." Brenda scooted her chair back.

"Alright, okay! Okay…" Lydia sighed, "It's the cop…who was part of yours and Mia's arrest."

Brenda shook her head, "Oh yea, you've definitely lost your fuckin' mind. Let me get out of here before I leap across this table and get myself a new charge."

"No, wait! Just hear me out. Look…I know he's a complete idiot and a fuckin' wet noodle. Believe me, I get it. But I'm not doing this for him. I'm doing this to bring his mother's killers to justice. From what I've learned, she was a pillar in the community and a sweet woman. Hell, it's probably why he turned out so damn soft. But I say that to say, I'm asking you to help me help her, not *him*." Lydia professed.

"Why should I care about his mother? He didn't give a fuck about my fiancé, who's still in a fuckin' coma. All he had to do was call the ambulance like I asked, and she wouldn't be fighting for her life right now." Brenda rebutted angrily.

"I know…and he has to live with that on his conscience. But you don't have to live with knowing you could've helped this sweet woman but didn't because of her son's cowardice." Lydia reasoned as she pulled a photo of Adelaida Ramirez out of a folder and placed it on the table.

Brenda pushed the picture away, "Don't do that. Don't try and guilt me into helping you."

"I'm not. I just figured it might help, to see her face."

The room fell silent as Brenda looked over at the photo then away, staring down at her hands.

"What the fuck do you need from me?" She sighed, shaking her head in frustration.

Lydia pulled another folder out of her bag and opened it, "What can you tell me about him?"

Brenda grabbed the folder and looked over the photos for a moment before flipping through the other documents.

"What do you already know?" She questioned.

"That his name is Anthony Waters and he's the father of the sixteen-year-old who's murder you were investigating. The same investigation that leads you to cross paths with Johnson."

"Hmm...looks like you did your homework."

"Something like that. So, what can you tell me that I don't already know? Because he had to be important for you to write his name down." Lydia pressed.

"Or he could've just been on my list of family to question about the victim." Brenda shrugged.

"Was he? Or was he more?"

Brenda rolled her eyes, "If I tell you what I know, you have to sign written statements, right now, confirming Johnson's dirt."

"Not a problem." Lydia pulled out a legal pad and a pen and began to write down a statement.

After about ten minutes and three and a half pages, she slid the pad to Sheila, who read each page intently.

"Okay!" She nodded gleefully, "She's actually provided some decent information. There's misconduct, dates, times, cases by name and correlation to other information we received about stash spots. I'm going to step out and call attorney James. I just need your signature."

Lydia grabbed the pen and quickly scribbled her signature in cursive before sliding the pad back to Sheila, "You can keep the pad."

"Alrighty. I'll be back in a few."

Sheila exited the room and Lydia stared at Brenda who looked reluctant to speak.

"Okay, so I did my part. Now, what can you tell me?" She broke the silence.

Brenda sighed, "I didn't find much in the system, besides a domestic violence dispute. Which I dismissed at first since it was so long ago, and the woman involved had several arrests of her own. Looked like the typical domestic situation. But something told me to look again and when I read through one of the woman's statements, she mentioned something about being afraid of him because of who he worked for."

Lydia leaned forward, "Who did he work for?"

"She never said." Brenda shrugged, "But after meeting him the first time, I got a sense about him that he was more than just a grieving dad. And her statement was like confirmation."

"Did you ever find anything to corroborate your feeling or her statement?"

"Nope. But I made a mental note that if bodies started dropping in relation to my victim, he'd be the first person I'd look at." Brenda shared.

Lydia sighed, "That's all?"

"Yup."

"Well, that doesn't help me at all." Lydia huffed, "I need a way to directly connect him to Charles Campbell, in order to prove motive."

"What connections have you made so far?"

"So far, I've got Campbell connected to officer Brian Shaw, who was Johnson's partner at the time he arrested Campbell." Lydia informed.

"That's solid. Mia and I were planning on reaching out to him for information on Johnson. Have you found his girlfriend?"

"Girlfriend? No. What's her name?"

"Zhaniece Gregory. She used to work at the prison and supplied his ride home on release day."

Lydia slid a pen and the flipped over picture of Ms. Ramirez toward her, "Write her name down for me and I'll look into her."

Brenda obliged then slid it back, "I don't know if she'll be any help, but she may be able to tell you if Campbell and Waters had any dealings or beef."

"Thanks, I appreciate your help." Lydia collected the documents into the folder and stood up just as Sheila was coming back into the room.

"We all good here, ladies?" She smiled.

Lydia nodded, "Yup. We're done."

"Alrighty. Brenda, Attorney James and I will see you in a few days. Detective Vance, it was a pleasure working with you, despite our employers' current litigations." Sheila extended her hand and Lydia shook it.

"Keep your head up, Hanson. You've got this." Lydia knocked on the table.

Sheila and Lydia exited the room as two guards made their way into the room, to escort Brenda back to her cell. As they walked, Brenda fought the urge to cry, overwhelmed by the glimmer of hope she'd begun to feel. Lydia giving witness statement that could potentially help her case and getting to do what she loved for even a brief few minutes felt like possibility. After months of despair, she'd given up on the idea of freedom or resuming the life she once knew, but out of nowhere the light of hope shined, melting part of her cold, hardened heart.

∞◇◇∞

Maleah nervously walked up the stoop of her grandmother's brownstone, followed by Xavier. Just as she reached to ring the bell, the door opened, and Mama Fernandez stood with her hand on her hip and a knowing smile.

"Well, ain't this a surprise."

Maleah sighed, "I know…I've been meaning to come see you for a minute. Work has just been crazy."

"You know the phone still works. They even got the little video call thing, now." Mama Fernandez quipped.

"I know, I know. Go ahead, you can pop me." Maleah poked out her bottom lip and extended her hand.

Mama Fernandez grabbed her hand and pulled her into a hug, "Bring your crazy tail in here."

When they released from the embrace she looked past Maleah at Xavier with an inquisitive expression.

"Ma, this is Xavier…my Fiancé." Maleah shared nervously.

"Fiancé?"

"How're you doing, ma'am?" Xavier smiled.

"I don't know yet, but you can come on in so I can give you the third degree."

Xavier walked up the steps and followed them into the house. Once inside, Maleah led him over to the sofa where they sat across from Mama Fernandez.

"So, what's your name young man?"

"Xavier." Maleah answered.

"I asked *him.*"

"Xavier Smith, ma'am."

Mama Fernandez nodded, "And where are you from?"

"Well, I was born and raised in Harlem, but my mother's side is from Antigua and my father's people are from Georgia and the Carolinas."

201

"Hmm...okay. So, how'd you and my granddaughter meet?"

"Actually, we met over there by the park. I was coming from playing ball and she must have been coming to see you." Xavier shared.

"And what are your plans for my Granddaughter? How does her success tie into your life's plans and goals? Because her father and I didn't raise her to just be some man's arm piece or housewife." Mama Fernandez stated boldly.

Xavier cleared his throat, caught off-guard by her directness, "Well, I can assure you that I have no intentions of stopping your granddaughter from reaching every height imaginable in her career. To the contrary, my intention is to actually help her reach them."

"Yea, he's been nothing less than supportive to me. Xavier's not that kind of guy." Maleah chimed in.

"Not like the last one, who almost had you dropping out of school and in jail?"

Maleah gasped, "Ma."

"I'm just keeping it real or whatever it is you children say." She shrugged.

"I can guarantee you, I'm nothing like the last guy." Xavier assured.

"Hmm...okay. And how long have you two been seeing each other?"

Xavier did the math in his head, "About...four months, almost five."

"So, you think you want to marry my Leah after just four or five months of knowing each other?" Mama Fernandez questioned in disbelief.

"I *know* I want to marry her." He rebutted confidently.

"Oh, you *know*. Well, excuse me."

"When a man knows, he knows. I could've waited longer, but why wait when I'm certain that the woman beside me is the one I want to spend my life with?" Xavier expressed boldly.

Mama Fernandez nodded, "Okay...so, do you believe in God? Or better question, do you have a relationship with Him? Because a man who is not led by God will lead a woman and anyone else who follows, to their destruction."

Maleah gasped, "Ma."

Xavier patted her thigh, "Relax, we're good."

"Yea, if the question offends him then I know everything I need to. And *you* should take heed."

"To answer your question; Yes, I do believe in God but I'm not ashamed to say the relationship could use some work. I've grown up in the church with my grandmother being the minister of music and my grandfather being a deacon, but I strayed a bit when I left for college." Xavier shared candidly.

"Hmm…so, you've been baptized?"

"Yes, ma'am. November 3, 2001, at one of the oldest Baptist churches in the city off West 138ᵗʰ."

Mama Fernandez nodded, "I know which church you're referring to. I have a few friends who goe there."

"Oh really, would you happen to know a Xavier Edward Smith, he goes by Eddie? Or Thelma Smith?"

"Wait, you're Thelma's boy? We used to play bingo together." Mama Fernandez squinted.

Xavier smiled, "Yup. I'm Thelma and Ed's grandson."

Mama Fernandez gasped, "My Lord! It's a small world. How is she? I haven't seen her in years."

"She's doing alright. Covid tried to take her out but she's a fighter and a prayer warrior."

"Don't I know it! She prayed me through the loss of her father." Mama Fernandez pointed to Maleah, "She was one of the few people who consistently checked in on me that first year."

Maleah hugged Xavier's arm tightly as the emotions on her grandmother's face caused her to get a bit choked up, thinking about her father.

"I'll make sure to tell her that her old bingo partner asked about her." Xavier smiled.

"Yes, please do. Tell her Marie Fernandez said hello and that she's always in my prayers."

"Well, isn't this just perfect." Maleah sighed happily, "I was worried you wouldn't like him."

"Who says I do?" She quipped.

"Ma!" Maleah laughed.

Mama Fernandez chuckled, "I'm just kidding. But you two ain't off the hook. If y'all getting married, you need to do it the right way and I know Thelma would agree. So, make some time in them busy schedules of yours for the Lord and to set up marriage counseling at whatever church y'all plan on doing the wedding at. Y'all are doing it at a church, right?"

Maleah looked over at Xavier, "Uh, we haven't discussed all of that yet."

"Well, get to discussing." She rebutted, standing up from her chair and heading into the kitchen, "Y'all hungry?"

"Uh, nah. I'm good." Xavier replied.

"What you make?" Maleah stood up from the couch, following her grandmother into the kitchen.

The smell of fried catfish and red beans and rice brought back nostalgic memories for Maleah. One thing her grandmother loved besides God, was cooking. Ms. Marie Fernandez was known for her skills in the kitchen, something she learned in her youth growing up in Louisiana. At the age of 19 she fled to New York with her son; with desires to be a world class chef and to escape an abusive marriage, she brought the flavors of home with her. From Gumbo to Red beans and rice, catfish, crawfish etouffee and her beloved boudin, Mama Fernandez's cooking became the ministry in which she served her community. Whether feeding the congregation of her church, a neighbor in need or the homeless shelters, Mama Fernandez spelled Love: *F.O.O.D.*

"So, when y'all coming to church?" She inquired as she stirred the pot of red beans.

Maleah shrugged, "Uh, I don't know."

"How about tomorrow? You got work?"

"Hmm…no, actually I don't"

"Then it's settled, y'all coming to church with me tomorrow. Pick me up around seven forty-five, so we can get there and get a good parking spot by eight-thirty." Mama Fernandez instructed.

"Ma, I've got to check and make sure Xavier is available."

Mama Fernandez turned toward the living room, "Xavier!"

"Yes, ma'am?" He stood up from the sofa and walked toward the kitchen.

"We're going to church tomorrow, I need y'all here quarter to eight so we can get a good spot in the church lot." She informed.

Xavier looked over at Maleah confused, "Uh, okay…"

"Good. I'll see y'all bright and early. You want me to make you a plate for later?" Mama Fernandez grabbed a Tupperware container from the dishrack.

He looked around at everything, inhaling the pleasant aroma, "Uh, yea. Sure."

Without hesitation she began loading rice and beans into the container and then she grabbed another container and put a few pieces of fish inside.

"There's enough in here for both of you, unless little greedy grabber here gets to the fish before you." Mama Fernandez teased.

Maleah sucked her teeth as she nibbled on a piece of fish, "I am not greedy."

"Whatever. She used to stand by the stove while I fried fish, eating them as soon as they touch the plate. Just burning the roof of her mouth." She laughed.

"It's not my fault you make the best catfish." Maleah shrugged, "I wish you'd just give me the recipe for your batter."

"Then you'd never have a reason to come see me."

Maleah threw her arms around her grandmother, "Aw, don't say that. You know I love you. I'm going to do better at coming to see you."

"So, that means you'll be coming to church with me every Sunday?"

Maleah sighed, "Fine. I will do my absolute best to try and come to church with you more often. Sunday's will be our day unless I have to work or travel."

"Don't say it like you're doing it for me. It's *your* relationship with God and last I checked; he's been mighty good to you. You owe him some praise."

Maleah nodded, "You're right…"

"I know, now unhand me and pass me a plastic bag from under the sink, so I can bag this up for y'all."

Maleah grabbed a bag and opened it for her grandmother to place the two containers inside. Once she tied the bag, she handed it to Xavier and Maleah leaned around her to grab another piece of fish.

"I told ya'. Just greedy."

Xavier and Mama Fernandez burst out laughing.

Maleah sucked her teeth, "Whatever. Here, try it and tell me you wouldn't be willing to burn the roof of your mouth for this?"

Xavier took a bite of the fish in her hand and as soon as the flavors hit his tongue his eyes closed, Oh my God. The fish is so tender and fresh, while the batter is crispy. And what is that seasoning?"

Mama Fernandez smiled, "Chef secret."

He nodded, "I get it now."

"See, I told you." Maleah giggled.

"Alright, grab y'all a cold drink from the fridge and then y'all gots to go. I need to clean my kitchen and rest my bones so I'm well-rested for church in the morning."

"A cold drink?" Xavier repeated.

"It's one of the many Louisiana things she didn't leave behind; her cooking and what she calls sodas." Maleah explained as she walked over to the refrigerator and grabbed two cans of soda.

"Oh my God! I haven't had this in so long!" Maleah exclaimed, holding up a root beer.

Mama Fernandez smiled, "I know. I ordered on that grocery app you set up for me when you said you were stopping by."

"Aw, GiGi!" Maleah hugged her grandmother.

"You haven't called me that in years."

"I know…I'mma start doing that again, too."

"No, that's alright. We can save that for my great grandbabies. If you have some while I'm still here."

Maleah gasped, "Ma. That's not funny."

"I ain't joking."

"We won't make you wait too long." Xavier smiled.

"Excuse me but that's not up to you." Maleah poked him in the chest.

"Alright, alright. Y'all take that back to y'all's house. I need to clean and get ready for bed."

Xavier leaned toward Maleah and whispered, "It's only three-thirty."

She placed her hand on his chest, "I know…she likes to be in bed by six."

"What y'all over there whispering about?" Mama Fernandez quizzed.

Maleah smiled, "Nothing. We're gonna go ahead and get out of here. Thanks again, Ma."

She handed the bag of food to Xavier then hugged her grandmother. Then he stepped up and hugged Mama Fernandez as well.

∞∞∞∞

It was 12pm on the dot, three hours before *Lou's* opened, when Paul pulled up. He quickly checked his surroundings then got out his car and entered through the side door. Once inside, he locked the door behind himself, and he noticed a faint light coming from the back.

"What the fuck?"

Paul pulled his gun from his waistband and quietly made his way through the staff only doors. He noticed that the light was coming from Lou's office and released an annoyed sigh.

"I know Lou's ass ain't here." He muttered to himself.

As Paul crept toward his office door, he noticed the silhouette of a women through the crack in the door. He watched intently for a moment and the woman must have felt his presence because she walked over and peeked through the slit.

"Paul?"

He cautiously pushed the door open, still holding his finger on the trigger of his gun.

"Who the fuck are you and how'd you get in here?"

"Let's just say, I would've been your daughter in law had they not murdered your son." Niecy folded her arms, sitting on the edge of the desk.

"Look, I don't know nothing about that, but you need to raise up out of here before we have a problem." He threatened.

"Damn, that's how you treat family?"

"You ain't my damn family."

Niecy sighed, "Of course Charles didn't tell you about me. That's okay…we'll have plenty of time to get to know each other."

Paul shook his head, "You must be deaf."

"Don't you even want to know why I'm here?"

"You've got 30 seconds to remove yourself from the premises." Paul cocked his gun.

"Whoa, whoa. Chill out, dad. I come in peace."

"I'm not your fuckin' dad and you now have 25 seconds."

Niecy gasped, "You'd really kill the mother of your grandson?"

"Bullshit! My son ain't never say anything about a kid!" Paul spat pointing the gun at her.

"It's not bullshit. I have the C-section scar to prove it."

Paul shrugged, "Doesn't mean it's his kid."

Niecy laughed, "I knew you wouldn't believe me."

"You're damn right. And you're out of time." Paul sneered.

"If you value your freedom, you'll stop aiming that gun at me and relax." Niecy spoke calmly.

"What?"

"You heard me…I'm sure you wouldn't appreciate your relationship with Captain Howard being leaked. Especially after the recent murder of a witness whose identity was only known by a handful of people, Dave Howard being one of them. And since the murder that man witnessed was *your* sons', I'd say that'd make you suspect number one."

Paul glared at her, gun still raised, and she reached out lowering his hand, "Who the fuck are you?"

"Like I said, I'm family. And I'm here to simply make you a proposition that benefits us both."

He huffed, "Oh yea, and what would that be?"

"Can we sit?"

"No, I'd rather stand."

"Suit yourself." Niecy shrugged and made her way around the desk, taking a seat behind it.

"What do you want?"

"The same thing you want…to kill the person responsible for Charles' death. Oh, and my cut of the money you took from Charles' stash."

"What money."

"Judging by how quickly you answered, you know exactly what money I'm referring to."

Paul shrugged, "No clue what you're talking about."

"Please don't play games with me, I know he was communicating with you when he got out. I'm guessing he must've told you about the stash in case something happened to him, but what he didn't tell you is that part of that money was mine." Niecy spoke sternly.

"Says who?"

"Says the fact that I helped him get it and again, I'm the mother of his fuckin' child. *Your* only remaining heir."

Paul chuckled, "My only remaining heir? What the fuck is this, Game of Thrones? Look, whatever my son left *me*, is mine. So, if that's all you came for, you wasted your time."

"So, you don't care about your grandson?"

"I don't know shit about no kid. For all I know you're just some chick my son used to fuck, whose lookin' for a quick come up. Hoes been running that *it's yo baby* scam for decades." Paul scoffed.

Niecy shook her head, "You niggas love making shit difficult. Here I am, not only offering you legacy but to rid you of the people responsible for your son's death. Preventing you from having to look your woman in the eyes with a guilty conscience and your stingy ass won't release what's rightfully mine?"

"What the fuck my woman got to do with any of this?"

Niecy chuckled, "Don't tell me you killed the witness and didn't even get him to tell you who did it?"

"Who said I killed someone?"

She huffed, "Fine. If you hypothetically found the man who could identify your son's killer, I'd hope you got the information before hypothetically killing him."

"Who do you think killed my son?" Paul quizzed.

Niecy grinned, "I don't think, I *know*. And it'd be in your best interest to let me handle it for you, so your hands stay clean."

"And in exchange, I give you what?"

"Two hundred and fifty thousand dollars."

Paul arched his eyebrow, "And where the fuck would I get that, *hypothetically*?"

"From the 1.2 million dollars you hijacked. I know you haven't blown through it already; you couldn't have spent more than fifty grand in here." Niecy stated matter-of-factly.

"I have no idea what you're talking about. But, if I hypothetically had that kind of money, I would've put it into multiple business ventures to clean it. So, it wouldn't be liquid. *Hypothetically.*"

"Well, *hypothetically,* you better wire my money to me by Friday, or I won't just be leaking your relationship with the police captain, but I'll make sure your new lady learns of your ulterior motives."

Paul chuckled, "You're real bold with these threats, like I couldn't very *literally* shoot you right here, right now. And why the fuck do you keep bringing up my woman?"

"First of all, if you shoot me the information will definitely be leaked. I'd be a fool to come here without a contingency plan to have someone send it for me. And second, you really didn't get any info out of Mr. Ruiz before you shot him? That's amateur...you really need to accept my help."

"Who the fuck do you think shot my son?" Paul asked again, still a bit confused by her previous statement.

Niecy tilted her head, confused by the state of confusion on his face, "Who do *you* think did it?"

"I actually know who did, but I'm starting to see that *you* don't"

"Bullshit. I know who did it and either you help me to help you and stay out of my way or you'll be lying beside them on an autopsy table." Niecy threatened coldly.

"Who is *them*?"

Niecy grabbed a notepad and pen from his desk and scribbled down a long number before tearing out the page and sliding it across the desk.

"Send my money by Friday and stay the fuck out of my way." She stood up from the desk and headed for the door.

"What about my grandson?" Paul asked, amused.

"Fuck you! I flushed that lil nigga the moment I found out Chuck was dead." Niecy spat as she walked out into the hall.

Paul shook his head, "Crazy mothafucka. I knew she was lying."

He walked out the office and followed her to the door, watching as she climbed into her mustang and sped off. Paul took a mental snapshot of her license plate and quickly typed it into a text with the message: *I need all the information you have on the owner of this car.*

Chapter Fourteen

"Welcome to Henderson International Luxury Automotives, where your dream is made reality." Cyntoia the receptionist recited, never looking up from her phone.

"Is Chris in?"

The familiar baritone voice sent shivers down through her body and she looked up, locking eyes with a man who'd been a part of many of her fantasies since the day she'd first laid eyes on him.

"Uh, yea...he's in his office. What's your name, again?" She blushed.

"Oh, you remember me?" He grinned.

She looked away bashfully, "How could I forget."

He chuckled, "Tell him Tone is here to see him."

Cyntoia nervously pressed the button on the desk phone for Chris's office, "Hi, Mr. Henderson. I have Tone here to see you...oh, okay..."

"What did he say?"

Cyntoia looked up with an awkward smile, "Let's just say he used some less than professional words, to basically say he doesn't want to see you."

Tone chuckled, "It's okay, don't worry about it."

He walked past the desk, toward Chris's office and Cyntoia leapt up and watched nervously from afar as he knocked then pushed open the office door.

"Nigga, what the fuck? What part of *don't ask me for shit* wasn't clear to you?" Chris huffed, slamming a folder down on his desk.

"Relax. I ain't come here for help, I just need some information."

"Nigga, that's literally asking me to help."

Tone shrugged, "Alright, well I just need a little bit of help then I'll be out of your way."

Chris swiped his palm over his face in frustration, "What do you need?"

"I need to know where I can find the nigga Paul and where I can find those other two loose ends." He informed.

"I would ask what you plan on doing with this information, but I honestly don't have the energy for a part two of the shit you pulled last time you were home. All I'm going to tell you, like I told Khalil, if anything you do fucks with my business, you will be held responsible." Chris stated sternly.

"Held responsible in what way?" Tone inquired.

"In whatever way I deem necessary."

Tone chuckled, "Yea, whatever…you gonna give me the information or what?"

Chris laughed to himself, "You niggas really think I'm joking. Family or not, this shit will turn ugly if y'all fuck with my business."

"Yea, yea, I hear you, nigga. Ain't nobody about to fuck with your business. Unless you're telling me these mothafuckas work for you or something."

"No. I don't have no business with these niggas, but your shit has had a funny way of blowing back my way."

Tone sucked his teeth, "Nigga, that was one time."

"What do you call this, right now? You've literally brought your problem back to my door as I'm still cleaning up the previous one you created." Chris snapped.

"Nigga, I'm trying to solve this problem for good, so you don't have to worry about it anymore."

"I wish it were that simple, but worrying is inherent when it comes to dealing with you. You're like a bull in a fuckin' China shop! You just can't help yourself."

"Man, just give me the information and I'll be out of your way."

Chris exhaled hard, "Check Lou's. P is the new partial owner. The other two, I'll have to get back to you."

Tone nodded, "Alright, I'll check back in a few days."

"No. I'll call you when I have it."

"Whatever, nigga. Is this the place?" Tone held his phone up for Chris to see the place he'd searched online.

"Yea, that's it."

"Alright. Thanks for your cooperation. Oh, and tell Mook I might need his assistance."

"Anything else?"

"Yea. Give the girl at the front desk a raise."

Chris chuckled, "Nigga, if you feel like tricking then be my guest. I won't tell Jay."

"I ain't even mean it like that, she's just a sweetheart and I know your stingy ass ain't paying her enough." Tone rebutted.

"To answer the phone and greet guests? Yes, the fuck I do. I pay her more than enough. Just because you've got a lil crush doesn't mean I need to increase her pay." Chris quipped.

"Man, whatever. I'm out. I'll be in touch about them other two and don't forget to tell Mook what I said."

"Mhmm…" Chris nodded, returning to the paperwork on his desk.

∞∞∞∞

"Mr. Anderson, I have a Kathy Lewis trying to schedule an appointment with you." The receptionist came through the speaker of Khalil's desk phone.

"Okay, well did you find out who she is or what she wants? Is she an A&R or just some random woman off the street?" Khalil questioned.

"When I asked her what the purpose of the meeting was, she said it was a serious, private matter."

Khalil thought for a moment, "Kathy Lewis? I have no idea who that is."

"So, do you want me to tell her you're unavailable?"

"No, um patch her through. Let me see if I know her." He instructed.

The phone line beeped and then there was silence.

"Hello?"

"Yes, hello. This is Khalil Anderson; my receptionist said you were trying to schedule a meeting with me. Can you remind me of where I know you from?" Khalil spoke in a professional tone.

"Khalil, it's me. Your mother."

He immediately ended the call and leaned back in his chair, trying to calm his breathing as the room began to feel like it was closing in on him.

BOOP!

The desk phone beeped.

"Mr. Anderson, the same woman is calling back. She says the call dropped."

Khalil sat in silence staring at the wall.

"Mr. Anderson?"

"Get her number and tell her I'll call her back." Khalil responded then ended the call and got up from his desk.

He grabbed his cellphone and headed out of his office and down the hall to Xavier's. He knocked on the door then slowly opened it to find him sitting at his desk while Maleah sat on the edge of the desk, with her back to the door.

"My bad, I ain't know you had company."

Maleah looked over her shoulder and smiled, "Hey."

"Nah, you're good, bro. What's up?" Xavier nodded.

"It's kind of private. I'll just come by later."

"It's cool, I need to get going anyway. I should've been headed upstairs for my meeting ten minutes ago." Maleah interjected.

She kissed Xavier on the lips then stood up, adjusting her skirt and made her way out the office.

"What's going on? Is it problem A, B or C?"

Khalil plopped down on the sofa, placing his head in his hands, "Problem C."

"Damn...what happened?"

"Man, she just called up here trying to schedule a meeting with me. I don't even know how the hell she found out where I work."

Xavier shrugged, "Probably google. I mean, it's not like your name has changed and your information is publicly accessible."

"Bruh, why can't she just leave me alone? She's been gone all this time and I've been fine. Shit, she started a whole new family. I don't want to rehash the fucked-up parts of my life that I've worked hard to forget. And I damn sure ain't trynna give no old lady a fuckin' heart attack, but if she says the wrong shit, I swear I'm gonna snap!" Khalil ranted.

"What if all she wants to do is apologize? I know you think it doesn't matter, but Kha that closure might help you release some of the anger you be carrying." Xavier spoke sincerely.

"I'm not holding onto no anger. I'm fine. When people fuck with me, yes, I get angry but I ain't just walking around angry." Khalil argued.

Xavier threw his hands up, "Okay...well, if you ain't angry. Why can't you sit and hear her out?"

"Because...I *am* angry with her." Khalil huffed.

"And the only way to free yourself from that, is to just talk to her. Release that shit."

"I can't!" Khalil gritted, fighting back tears, "Because if I release everything, I've felt toward her, since the day she left me...it'll probably fuckin' break her. And I don't want to do that, because...part of me still loves her."

Khalil leaned over, resting his face in his hands and Xavier got up and walked over to him. He sat down beside Khalil and placed his hand on his back.

"I know it's hard man and it's fucked up...you didn't deserve that shit. Don't do this shit for her, do it for you and for your future children. You know, I went to church Sunday with Leah and her grandmother and the Pastor said something really profound...he said we forgive others for our own peace of mind. It frees *us*. And he said that unforgiveness is like drinking poison, hoping that the other person dies."

Khalil wiped his face and sat up, "Yo ass went to church?"

"I said all that and that's all you heard, nigga?"

"Nah, man." Khalil let out a faint laugh, "I heard you...you're right. I'm gonna call her and set up a meeting. I need to just face this shit so I can put it behind me, because I've got bigger shit to worry about."

"Yes, you do." Xavier smirked.

Khalil looked over at him and they both burst out laughing.

"I'm glad my life is a joke to you." He shook his head.

"Nah, it's not a joke. But you have to admit, it is a little funny."

"Whatever, nigga. I'm going back to work. Thanks for the pep talk, I guess." Khalil stood up and the two men dapped each other up.

∞∞∞

Brynn James, Esq stood at the front of the courtroom, looking dapper in a Yeboah Bespoke custom suit as he argued his case.

"Mrs. Shaw, may I call you Erica?"

Erica Shaw, the wife of the deceased officer Brian Shaw nodded, *yes.*

"Okay, so Erica. Is it true, you told the detectives that your late husband called your daughter, the day he was murdered?"

"Yes."

"Hmm…and the timestamp of said call was shown to be before estimated time of death and long after Detective Hanson left the premises."

"That's what I'm told."

Judge St. Claire leaned over, "Simply answer yes or no, Mrs. Shaw."

She nodded, "Yes."

Brynn turned to face the jury, "And as we've all learned from the autopsy and expert toxicologist, the drugs found in Mr. Shaw's body would've likely taken affect almost immediately after being administered, given the dosage. So, how then did my client administer the drugs ten to fifteen minutes prior to Mr. Shaw's overdose and he still had cognitive ability to dial his daughter and leave a very coherent voicemail? I'll answer that for you; he couldn't! The truth that is being so carelessly overlooked is that, if officer Shaw didn't do it himself then someone else was clearly there. And instead of doing real police work to find out who, the detectives investigating the case have chosen to take the lazy route of pinning it on my client. So, I motion to dismiss the charge of murder in first degree of officer Brian Shaw."

The courtroom erupted in gasps and whispering amongst the press and spectators.

"Objection, your honor! Counsel has no grounds to request dismissal. We provided more than enough evidence!" Leonard Eisenschmitt, Legal counsel to the Police department, shouted.

"I'm requesting dismissal of the charges on the grounds of insufficient evidence and lack of due process! The evidence provided by the NYPD has done nothing but expose the inadequacies in their investigative standards and practices." Brynn boasted to the press, causing the chatter to grow even louder, as the tension in the room rose.

Judge St. Claire tapped her gavel, "Enough! Everyone, quiet down. Mrs. Shaw, thank you for your cooperation, you can step down now. The court will take a brief fifteen-minute recess. You two, in my chambers, now."

The Bailiff's emptied the courtroom as Brynn and Leonard headed into the judges' chambers. After the recess concluded, everyone returned and took their seats. Brynn stood behind the defense table, sporting a maniacal grin as Leonard glared angrily.

"Alright, settle down. The court has reviewed the motion filed by the defense to dismiss Count II of the indictment, the charge of murder in the first-degree by poisoning, in the death of officer Brian Shaw. Having considered the motion, response by prosecution, the evidence presented and relevant case law, the court finds the following: Lack of sufficient admissible evidence and forensic analysis that lacks definitive links between the defendant and method of death. So, the court hereby finds that it would be contrary to the interest of justice and due process, to continue proceedings on Count II. With that being said, the motion to dismiss Count II is hereby granted.

The courtroom erupted in chatter as camera shutters could be heard snapping photos and people whispered amongst themselves.

"However, Count I, murder in the first degree by firearm in the death of Detective Richard Johnson, remains pending. That charge will proceed to trial as scheduled. Court is adjourned." She banged her gavel then stood and exited the courtroom to her chambers.

"Oh my God." Brenda gasped.

"I told you; I've got you. Now, just one more battle to win and then we file our civil suit to collect reparations from these fucks." Brynn whispered eagerly.

Brenda nodded, "Okay."

She tried hard to regulate her breathing and not get too emotional, because she knew there was still an uphill battle. But she couldn't deny the excitement she felt. The hope in her heart was growing expeditiously.

"You may have gotten the charges dropped for Shaw, but there is no way you're winning in the murder of Johnson." Leonard sneered.

Brynn grinned and winked, "See you at trial, Counselor."

∞∞∞∞

"Ayyyyyye! Go, Lis! Go Lis!" Maleah shouted gleefully.

The ladies stood around Maleah's living room, cheering on Lisa who was winding her waist to the sounds of *"What a Bam Bam"* by *Amara La Negra*.

"Show us how y'all do it in the D.R.!" Sky chimed in, sipping her glass of red wine as she swayed to the rhythm of the song.

Korena just sat on the sofa, all smiles, wearing a pink silk pajama set. They all had on matching pajamas, courtesy of Maleah. She'd planned their girls' night sleepover down to the smallest detail of creating gift bags with each of their favorite fragrances, skincare and make-up.

"Whew! I need a break." Lisa huffed as the song came to an end.

"Me too!" Maleah laughed, walking into the kitchen and bringing out the bottle of sparkling wine and non-alcoholic Moscato.

She refilled everyone's glass then headed back into the kitchen and returned with a large charcuterie board. After placing it down on the coffee table, she grabbed bags of pink dyed popcorn and some mini plates. Maleah handed each of the women their own popcorn and a mini plate for the charcuterie then took a seat beside Lisa on the assortment of plush pillows she'd scattered across the living room floor. Grabbing the remote, she turned down the volume on the sound system then changed the music to her *Chill Vibes* playlist.

"Agape" by *Nicholas Brittel* began to play, creating a beautifully mellow atmosphere.

They all released a collective sigh and then laughed at the unison moment of release.

"I really missed y'all." Korena whispered, breaking the silence.

The tears in her eyes caused Sky to reach over and grab her hand, squeezing gently. Maleah dabbed the tears that started to fall from her own eyes and Lisa released a heavy sigh.

"We missed you too." Sky spoke sincerely.

Korena nodded, "I know Leah and I already had a heart to heart, but I wanted to apologize while we're all together. I'm sorry I broke our sisterhood because of selfishness and fear. It was never my intention to hurt anyone."

Maleah got up and walked over, taking a seat beside Korena on the sofa, "We're not broken. Maybe a little bent up and dented, but not broken."

"Yea…any long-term relationship will experience its ups and downs, but longevity is granted to those who persevere." Sky added.

Korena looked over at Lisa, whose face expressed a mix of emotions, "It's okay. I'm not expecting you to forgive me right away or at all, honestly. I know how much you love Leah, and my actions hurt everyone involved, damaging the trust. All I can do is try to prove myself worthy of trust and this sisterhood, as time passes."

Lisa sighed, "I…I forgive you."

Caught off guard by her words, Korena exhale and the flood gates burst open. And like a domino effect, they all released tears.

"But don't you ever pull no shit like that again!" Lisa threatened tearfully.

"Trust me, I won't. I'm an open book. No more secrets, I promise." Korena smiled through tearful sniffles.

Sky reached over and pulled Lisa up and they all embraced in a group hug, "Aww! I love a happy ending!"

The released from the hug and sat in silence for a moment as the atmosphere shifted to a light, peacefulness.

Maleah stood up, "Alright, so what's the verdict? *Best Man, Best Man Holiday, Two can play that game* or *The Brothas*?"

"Definitely not *Best Man Holiday,* I've had enough crying for one night." Lisa asserted.

"I vote for *Two can play that game.* That's my fave Vivica movie!" Korena added.

Sky shrugged, "I'm good with whatever."

"Well, I vote *Best Man*, which makes you the tie breaker Sky. So, you have to vote." Maleah insisted.

Sky giggled, "Why do I have to decide. Can't you just put the names in a hat and draw one?"

"Nope, you have to decide."

"Well, then I choose *The Wood.*" Sky grinned.

Maleah sucked her teeth, "That's not an option."

Sky shrugged, "That's my choice. Take it or leave it."

"Actually, I haven't seen that in a while. I wouldn't mind a lil Omar Epps on my screen." Korena grinned.

"Looks like we're watching *The Wood.*" Lisa smiled.

Maleah rolled her eyes playfully, "I don't appreciate y'all ganging up on me."

"I'm sorry, but I can't watch Morris Chestnut hang that man from a building again. Not for at least two years." Korena smiled mischievously.

"Yea…you've watched it enough for a lifetime, Leah. I don't even think the cast has the lines memorized as well as you do." Lisa chuckled.

Maleah snatched the tv remote off the end table, "Whatever! It's a good movie. Y'all are just haters."

"It's okay, boo. I get it. It's your fixation movie; most people with anxiety have something they watch repeatedly for comfort. There's no surprises and your nervous system is also at ease because of the nostalgia." Sky offered sweetly.

"Thanks, Sky. Now, I really feel like a nutjob."

"We all have our *quirks.*"

Maleah flipped through her streaming apps and found *The Wood.* Once the opening credits started to roll, she dimmed the living room lights and got comfortable next to Lisa on the floor.

"I think Khalil is cheating on me." Korena blurted, catching them all off-guard.

"What?" Sky gasped.

Maleah scrambled for the remote and quickly pressed pause, "What do you mean, you think he's cheating? What happened?"

"Nothing big happened, but it's been little things here and there…I caught him hiding out in the bathroom on a call and ever since then he's been acting secretive. And now there's this weird energy between him and T.Y., who rarely ever interferes in my love life unless he's protecting me. So, it's got me question what Khalil's been doing that I don't know about." Korena divulged exhaustedly.

"Have you said anything to him about it?" Sky inquired.

Korena sighed, "No…because I've been trying to maintain some semblance of peace, for the baby's sake and I'm scared of what I'll find out. Plus, he's been on edge since…"

"Since what?" Maleah pressed.

Korena shook her head and stared up at the ceiling, "Promise me, this doesn't leave this room."

"Of course." Lisa nodded.

Maleah and Sky agreed.

"Okay…so, the night of my brother's welcome home celebration, we ran into Khalil's mom."

Maleah gasped and both Sky and Lisa looked confused.

"Why is that a big deal?" Lisa questioned.

"Because, he hasn't seen her since he was a toddler." Maleah shared.

Korena nodded, "She abandoned him in a vacant house…the police found him, and he spent the rest of his life, until he met X, in the system."

"Damn…that explains a lot." Sky sympathized.

"Yea…and this is the first time he's seen her since the day she left him. And he's been doing his best to hide it, but I can tell it's fuckin' him up." Korena admitted.

"Well, do you think maybe that's the reason why he's been acting all cagey and secretive?" Lisa inquired.

Korena shook her head, "No. He's been acting that way before that night. And my intuition is screaming at me that there's another woman."

"I don't know…from the way X describes it, he's never seen Khalil like this with anyone. He says he's never seen him in love, before you." Maleah shared.

"Yea, but love doesn't keep a man from cheating. Trust me, I know…" Lisa interjected.

"True…wait, what do you mean, you know? Victor cheated on you?" Maleah gasped.

"Yea…" Lisa nodded, "It was in the first year of us dating. He claimed he realized how he felt about me and got so overwhelmed that he just started doing shit to sabotage things."

"What made you decide to stay?" Korena inquired.

"I didn't. I broke up with him the moment I found out, but he persistently begged me for a month to give him another chance. I told him I'd consider it if he went to therapy, and we did couples counseling. He agreed and six months later, he proposed."

"Khalil would never agree to therapy or counseling. He barely wants to talk to me about his problems. I have to damn near force it out of him." Korena huffed.

"Maybe with the support and encouragement of X, he might be willing." Maleah suggested, "He and I just signed up for premarital counseling at the church."

"I don't know…I'll think about it." Korena shrugged.

"You know, therapy would be good for you too. To work out your feelings surrounding becoming a new mom and what that will trigger up from your own experiences with your mother." Sky added.

Korena sighed, "Please, don't even get me started on that. We're supposed to be having dinner at Monique's for the first time as a whole family. And I don't know if I'm ready for part two of what happened last time."

"Sounds like y'all may need a family session." Sky smiled.

"Oh, no. That definitely ain't happening. Getting Monique to agree to being told about herself? Girl, she'd probably slap the doctor." Korena chuckled.

Maleah laughed, "I can definitely believe that. Ms. Mo be wilding."

"She'd better be careful, 'cause not all therapists be on that *Kumbaya* vibe. Some of us definitely slap back." Sky boasted.

"Some of *us?* I hear you, Sky. Let them know. You ain't no Cosby kid, you may have grown up in Manhattan but them hands is from Queens!" Lisa chimed in.

The ladies laughed heartily for a moment then settled.

"So, what's the plan for the baby shower?" Maleah asked, "Is Eesha planning it?"

"Actually. I decided I didn't want a baby shower. Khalil and I can afford everything the baby needs and honestly waddling around a party, all swollen like *Veruca Salt* from *Willy Wonka,* in a gown doesn't sound like fun to me." Korena frowned.

"You know, you don't have to wait until your eight months pregnant to have your baby shower. I've seen women doing them in combination with the gender reveals, at like five or six months." Lisa shared.

"Oh, yea…that's a good idea. Wait, do you know the gender yet?" Maleah quizzed.

Korena shook her head, "No. I find out in two weeks."

"That's perfect! We can get them to put your results in an envelope and take it to a bakery so they can make a cute little gender reveal cake. Eesha and I can plan the gender reveal slash baby shower and it'll be cute and intimate; with only the people you choose. And since you're just starting to show, you'll still be able to stunt on hoes!" Maleah rambled excitedly.

Korena giggled, "I feel like *no* isn't an option."

"It's not." Maleah shrugged and burst out laughing.

"I think that's a good idea. In all the chaos you haven't had a chance to really celebrate motherhood or be celebrated." Sky asserted.

"What if we just do a cute little gender reveal at the house and then a trip for my b-day? I've been thinking about Miami or Vegas. I feel like that's a win-win; we can celebrate the baby and me." Korena suggested.

"You really don't want a baby shower?" Lisa asked.

Korena frowned her face, "Not really."

Maleah huffed, "Alright, fine. No Baby shower, but question: what the hell are you going to do in Vegas or Miami at five months pregnant?"

"Eat, gamble, lounge by a pool or the beach, see a show, gamble some more and go to a spa. There's plenty for me to do besides party and drink." Korena rebutted.

"Okay." Maleah threw her hands up, "So, intimate reveal and a trip for your birthday. Is this a *girls' trip* or are the men invited? Also, when exactly, so I can align my schedule."

"Um, I don't mind if the guys come. Especially since I know Khalil's hovering ass won't let me go far without him. And I was thinking the weekend before or after." Korena replied.

"Wait, your birthday is April fourth, right?" Lisa asked.

"Yea."

Lisa sighed, "Damn, I'll be out the country on a work trip in South Africa."

"Oh, wow! Nice. That's one of the places on my bucket-list." Sky gasped.

"That's okay. I plan on doing another trip after I drop this baby. I wanna be on somebody's island with blue water for at least a week." Korena smiled.

"When are you due?" Lisa inquired.

"End of July."

"Oh, that'll be perfect. A nice end of year trip while it's cold here." Maleah interjected.

"Yup, I plan on spending Christmas somewhere warm. By that time, the baby will be five months and can stay with my mama or Eesha while I get some much-needed rest."

"Well, I'm down for both. I've just gotta confirm with Jared, to see if he'll be joining me." Sky stated.

"That's fine. Don't feel pressured to do any of this. Besides, if I find out Khalil's been fuckin' around on me I'll be spending the end of the year in county. Because, once I drop this baby, I'mma kill him." Korena stated matter-of-factly.

"Lord." Maleah shook her head, "Well, I pray it's just a misunderstanding, because I know you're actually serious."

"As a heart attack." Korena pursed her lips and shrugged.

All of a sudden, the sound of *LL Cool j's "Doin it"* came from the bowl containing their cellphones.

"Uhn, uhn. I whose phone is that? Phones are supposed to be on silent during Girls' night." Maleah chastised.

"Don't look at me, my phone is off. Mia is safe with her father and mi madré is asleep this time of night." Lisa stated proudly.

Korena shook her head, "It's not me. That ain't my ringtone."

Maleah looked over at Sky, who smiled coyly, "Oop, not Ms. DND."

"Sorry, I thought I did silence it."

Sky hopped up and went over to the kitchen, grabbing her phone from beneath the bowl on the island countertop.

"Tell Jared that you'll see him tomorrow, this is our time; he'll survive." Maleah teased.

Sky didn't respond, she just stared at her phone with a childlike grin then proceeded to text quickly before turning off her ringer and returning the phone beneath the bowl.

"What did he say that got you grinning like that?" Maleah pried.

"Nothing." Sky fought back a smile.

Maleah stared at her in disbelief, "Jared said nothing, yet you're looking all hot and bothered after reading a text from him?"

"Unless it wasn't from *him*." Lisa smirked.

"Oop." Korena's eyes widened.

Sky gasped, "Lisa!"

Maleah turned to Lisa, "What do you mean, *unless it wasn't him?*"

"All I'm saying is…I noticed Sky made herself a new friend at your engagement party and I don't think he intends to keep things platonic."

"There were only close friends there, so who could she have possibly met? One of Chef Pierre's servers?" Maleah stared at her in confusion.

"Not everyone who came was coupled up." Lisa grinned.

Sky sucked her teeth, "Really, Lis? You're just gonna sell me out?"

Lisa laughed, "We said no more secrets in the sisterhood, I'm just helping you keep your word."

"Mhmm…" Sky shook her head.

"Oh, hell no, do not tell me you and…Chris?" Maleah exclaimed.

"What?" Korena gasped.

Lisa smiled and nodded, "Yup."

"Skylar!" Maleah whined.

"Whaaaat? It's not like we're doing anything. It's just harmless little flirtatious texts." Sky shrugged.

"Harmless? It looked like you wanted to get naked and climb into the phone after reading that text." Lisa teased.

"Sky, you're better than that. Apart from the fact that you're engaged, Chris is not *your* type of guy. Him and monogamy are like oil and water." Maleah chastised.

"Like salt to a damn snail." Korena chimed in.

"First of all, in the sister circle *we listen, and we don't judge.* Second, I just said it's nothing more than a few harmless texts. And third, but most importantly, what if I'm bored with *my type*?"

Maleah gasped, "What are you saying? You're thinking about leaving Jared?"

"No, no…I mean, I don't know. I'm just bored. Bored with the way things have been. It's the same ole routine: Bowling or movie date night, occasional stuffy Fundraiser Gala or Fraternity event, the same meal prep in rotation every week, Pizza Fridays, farmers market with his mother every Saturday, and that soulless Catholic mass on Sunday when he knows I'm a Pentecostal girl. It's just been the same thing every day for the past two years and I'm dying of boredom. I *need* a little thrill with my romance, and Chris facilitates that." Sky sighed.

The ladies just stared at her with looks of surprise on their faces.

"Wow…why'd you never tell us you felt that way?" Lisa broke the silence.

"Because…I was busy trying to convince myself that what I had was enough for me. That I was simply mistaking stability for boring. But after making a real effort to lean into things, it made it clearer that I'm not satisfied. And, if a patient of mine expressed these same sentiments, I would suggest they reconsider the relationship. Especially before making a permanent decision like marriage." Sky shared candidly.

"Damn…I thought you and Jared were happy. Y'all seemed like the perfect couple, next to Lisa and Victor." Maleah admitted.

Lisa scoffed, "Honey, don't measure your relationship against mine. There's plenty behind closed doors y'all don't see and only through much prayer and counseling, have we made it this far."

"Why does everything have to be so damned complicated." Korena huffed, rubbing her belly.

Sky sighed, "It doesn't have to be, if we do the hard things that allow ease."

"So, does that mean you're breaking up with Jared." Maleah pried.

"I'm definitely going to have a conversation with him about what I've been feeling. I don't want to end it…but if that's where things lead, I will. No matter how much it hurts." Sky rubbed her forehead, fighting back tears.

Lisa grabbed Sky by the hand, "Well, we're here for you, whatever you decide."

"Yea, we've got your back, girl." Korena chimed in.

Sky smiled faintly, "Thanks y'all."

"Yea, we've got you…But! I am in no way supporting this whole Chris thing." Maleah added.

"I don't know…" Korena shrugged, "I mean, Khalil was a whole different person before he met me. Maybe Sky could be the one to change him."

Maleah pursed her lips, "Now, Korena. No shade, but didn't you just finish saying you might spend your Christmas on Riker's if you find out Khalil been cheating?"

"Oop! Not too much! We're only a few months past your scuffle with X's crazy ass ex." Korena quipped.

Maleah gasped in amusement, "Touché, heffa!"

"Now, now ladies…*we listen…*"

"And we don't judge!" They all responded in unison and then burst out laughing.

"But I'm serious, Jared or not, please leave Chris alone." Maleah giggled.

Sky pouted, "But he's so fine."

"I can't argue with that." Lisa shrugged.

Korena threw up her hands, "I'm minding my business. I can't afford to catch anymore strays."

The ladies burst into laughter once more and Maleah snatched the remote off the floor.

"I'm putting on *The Best Man.*"

Sky playfully tried to wrestle the remote from her as Lisa cackled and Korena watched in amusement as she stuffed her mouth with popcorn.

Chapter Fifteen

"Vance! In my office, now." Capt. Howard commanded.

Lydia looked up from her computer then over at Det. Abrams. She stood up from her desk and made her way into the captains' office.

"What's going on, Cap?" She asked skeptically.

"Close the door."

Lydia stepped inside and closed the door behind herself, "What's up?"

"Have a seat." He spoke sternly.

"Uh, okay…" Lydia followed his instruction.

"I've just come from getting chewed up and spat out by the Chief, Police commissioner and the D.A., all because you apparently gave a signed witness statement to Hanson's legal team, testifying to the misdeeds and misconduct of Det. Johnson. Have you lost what's left of your got'damn mind?" Capt. Howard barked.

Lydia sighed, "I promise, I was going to tell you."

"When? Once the headlines announced that more officers are coming forward to confirm the corruption of the NYPD?" He slammed his fist against his desk.

"No! I didn't know it'd be admitted this quickly." Lydia replied.

Capt. Howard shook his head, "You've really fucked up this time."

"My testimony could be the perfect way to cast all blame on Johnson, who was in fact as terrible as the reports state! Let the heat of these allegations be buried with Johnson and Shaw. Paint them as lone wolves and the department can distance itself from the corruption stigma." Lydia ranted passionately.

229

"So, now you're offering legal counsel? The crossing of boundaries never ends with you. Ever since you were a rookie, you couldn't stay in your fuckin' place!" He spat.

"What? Are you serious, Cap? I'm one of, if not *thee* best detectives on the force. And any dirt I kick up, is only in response to mothafuckas throwing stones my way, first!"

"I don't care how you spin it; you've gone too far this time. And you did this shit the day after a confidential witness is killed! A witness, might I add, that *you* knew the identity of. This shit looks worse than bad and unfortunately for you, I'm gonna have to put you on administrative leave until further notice."

Lydia gasped, "You've got to be fuckin' kidding me!"

"Hand over your gun and your badge, Detective Vance."

"What? No! I had nothing to do with the witness being killed. Even when that fuckin' beat cop suggested I let him talk to the guy, I shot him down! I didn't leak that shit!" Lydia defended angrily.

"That's for I.A. to investigate. In the meantime, you are to handover all materials pertaining to any case you're working. You will be banned from all NYPD buildings until the investigation is concluded, so make sure to take anything of importance when you leave and communication between you and any officers, Abrams included, should be avoided otherwise they will be placed under investigation as well." Capt. Howard recited stoically.

"Cap., come on." Lydia pleaded.

"Gun and badge, Detective Vance. Or I'll have officers remove them from your person and escort you out. And I'm sure you don't want the spectacle."

Lydia reluctantly unclipped her gun and laid it on his desk, then slowly removed her badge and placed it down beside it.

"This is some bullshit and you fuckin' know it." She gritted.

"Watch how you speak to your superior, Vance. Or this can become a firing on the grounds of insubordination." Capt. Howard threatened.

Lydia clenched her jaw, fighting back the cuss words she wanted to hurl in his direction. She turned and exited the office and made her way back over to her desk while trying to maintain her composure.

"What happened, Lyd? What'd Cap say?" Det. Abrams stood up from his desk.

"I'll tell you later." She avoided eye contact, as she gathered her work bag and stuffed some of her things inside.

"Where are you going?"

She huffed, "Home."

"What? Why?" He walked over.

"What are we going to do now that our key witness is dead?" Sean came storming over to Lydia's desk.

"Calm down, beat cop. This ain't the time!" Det. Abrams barked.

"Enough with the *beat cop* shit! It's tired and I'm tired of it. I need to know what we're doing to solve my mother's murder without a witness to identify the shooter. Were you able to get any leads from Hanson?" Sean ranted frustratedly.

Lydia just ignored him as she logged out of her computer then pushed her chair under her desk and tossed her bag over her shoulder.

"Where the hell are you going?" He stepped in front of her.

"Ramirez, if you don't get out of my fuckin' way." Lydia gritted.

Sean folded his arms, "Not until you answer me."

"I'm going to give you three seconds."

"Get out of her face, beat cop before I get you thrown off this case and back on your beat!" Abrams barked.

Sean huffed and stepped aside, "I knew neither of you actually gave a shit about getting justice for my mother. That's why I begged to join the investigation."

"You don't know what the fuck you're talking about." Lydia pointed in his face.

"I know that you've been delaying the process, omitting key details and at the moment inconvenience arises you just back off." Sean rebutted.

"Back off?" Lydia stepped up to him, "Nobody fuckin' backed off, Ramirez. I did the complete opposite and now I'm being benched for it. So, before you go protesting through the halls, with this newfound backbone of yours, saying I don't give a fuck, consider what I sacrificed."

Lydia's passion caught the attention of some of the other detectives, who began whispering amongst themselves. In attempt to avoid further embarrassment, she walked past him out into the hallway.

Detective Abrams ran to catch up with her, "Cap benched you? For how long."

"Until I.A. completes their investigation." She huffed, pushing through the side door and stepping out into the lot.

"Investigation? Into you? Why because of the dead witness?" He inquired, following her to her car.

"Yup and the fact that I gave witness statements to Hanson's attorney, testifying to Johnson's misconduct." Lydia shared as she tossed her bag into the backseat of her car.

"You what? Why would you do that? We agreed to stay out of that shit, for this very reason." He fussed.

"Because it was the only way to get Hanson to agree to helping me and honestly, I hated Johnson. He was a racist and shady fucker, who almost got us jammed up a few times and he was also a fuckin' pervert. Hanson doesn't deserve to rot in jail for him, so it felt like a win-win to me." She shrugged.

"Yea, well I hope whatever she gave you was worth risking your career." Det. Abrams huffed.

"I don't know that it was, but if it helps you close the case, so be it. I'll work this shit out with my union lawyer, this ain't the first time they tried to get rid of me."

"So, what'd Hanson tell you?"

"She told me that she looked into Waters and found statements from an ex-girlfriend that alluded to some deadly connections and said that she'd consider him suspect number one if bodies started dropping in relation to her case." Lydia shared.

"So, still nothing concrete. I can't believe you risked your badge for that."

"Relax, Aaron. She also gave me the name of a woman who was apparently the girlfriend or at least lover of Charles Campbell: Zhaniece Gregory. Put a BOLO out on her and see what she knows. If she can tie Waters to Campbell, confirming any possible beef, that could be a strong enough lead to bring him in." She expounded.

Det. Abrams nodded, "Alright. Text me the full spelling of her name and I'll get on it."

"Speaking of texts, we're gonna have to keep communication to a minimum. Cap has informed that anyone I talk to on the force can be pulled into the I.A. investigation." Lydia shared.

"I don't give a fuck. You're my partner. My family. Let them investigate me. If all else fails, we'll open our own private investigation firm." He shrugged with a smile.

Lydia chuckled, "Vance and Abrams investigative services. That has a ring to it."

"Of course you put your name first." He shook his head.

"Absolutely. I'm simply better than you, so my name has to be first." Lydia smiled as she climbed into the drivers' seat.

Det. Abrams leaned against the door frame, "Whatever! Anyway, what're you gonna do with all your newfound free time?"

"I haven't thought that far ahead. But right now, I'm going to go pick Ava up from school early and take her to the movies to see that new animated movie she's been begging me to see."

"Sounds like a plan." He shut her car door and stepped back.

Lydia started the engine and put the car in drive, "Try not to kill the Beat Cop. I know he's a pain in the ass, but it's his mom. You'd be ten times worse if it were Ms. Tina."

He sighed, "Fine. I'll try, for you."

"Thanks, A-A-Ron." Lydia smiled.

"I hate that name."

"I know." She laughed.

He tapped the hood of her car, "I'll let you know how things pan out with this new lead."

She nodded, then pulled out of her parking spot and out of the lot. Det. Abrams stood and watched until she was out of sight with a look that faded from peace to stress.

∞∞∞∞

Khalil sat in his car, staring across the street at the brownstone that matched the address he was given. He took a deep breath and exhaled hard, then turned off the engine.

"Don't let this shit rattle you, Kha." He coached himself.

VRRRRRRBBBB!

He looked down at his phone and saw an unknown number pop up on the screen.

"Who's this?"

"It's me. Look, I ain't got a lot of time, I just need to know what you can tell me about that bar *Lou's,* over on Franklin Ave.? What type of crowd me in there, street niggas or old winos?"

Khalil shrugged, "I've only been there once and the night I was there, it was a mix of young bitches shaking ass, street niggas and old drunks."

"What's security like?"

"Just there for show. The niggas at the door only check who they think they can press, so majority of them young niggas was carrying." Khalil shared.

"Hmm…okay. What was you doin' there? You ain't the after-hour type."

Khalil sighed, "I'm not. But my girl's brother came home and they decided to celebrate there since her mom's boyfriend owns the spot."

"What's his name?"

"Who? The brother or her mom's nigga?"

"Her mom's nigga."

"I think his name's Paul."

"Nigga, you're real bold going up in there."

Khalil frowned in confusion, "What you mean?"

"You're telling me, you don't remember that nigga?"

"I've never met the nigga. Whole time we were at the bar, I think he was somewhere in the back. Why, who is he?" Khalil questioned.

"Nigga, that's P! Chuck and Rich's pops."

Khalil's jaw dropped, "You're lying."

"I put that on my kids."

"I thought the nigga was dead. When the fuck did he come back to the city?" Khalil quizzed.

"I don't know. But I know he ain't back to offer forgiveness."

Khalil huffed, "Shit…I'm supposed to have dinner with my girls' family tomorrow night, and I think the nigga is supposed to be there. "

"Well, it's a good thing no one but you, me and Chris knows what happened."

"Does he know what *you* did?" Khalil asked.

"I think so. That's why I'm here, to get ahead of whatever plot he's got in motion."

"You need help?"

"Nah, I've got it handled. Plus, you're too close to this shit. I'm trying to create as little collateral damage as possible."

Khalil nodded, "Alright. Let me know if you change your mind."

"I won't. But you keep your head on a swivel, I'll holla at you later."

The call ended and Khalil felt the overwhelming desire to start the car and just pull off. Just as he reached to start the car, he saw a young woman walking up the stoop. She rung the bell and shortly after Kathy came to the door and hugged her lovingly. When they released, Kathy looked past the woman and spotted Khalil parked across the street. She gestured for her to go inside and she made her way down the stoop and across the street.

TAP! TAP! TAP!

Kathy used her acrylic nails to tap on the drivers' side window, "You're planning on coming in?"

Khalil shrugged, staring straight ahead unable to face her. Kathy walked around to the passenger side of the car and tapped on the window again. He released a frustrated sigh then unlocked the car door and Kathy got in the car.

"I know you'd rather be anywhere else in the world right now, but I'm glad you came." Kathy spoke sincerely.

Khalil didn't respond, he just nodded.

"You wanna come inside? I cooked and everything." Kathy asked.

"Not really."

"Okay…so, you want to do this here?"

Khalil gritted his teeth, fighting the emotions rising, "I don't want to do this shit at all!"

The pain on his face and anger in his voice brought tears to Kathy's eyes.

"You have every right to be angry."

"I don't need you to tell me what I have the right to feel!" He slammed his fist against the steering wheel, startling her.

"I'm sorry, that's not what I meant." She spoke tearfully.

"Were you here, this whole fuckin' time?" Khalil spat.

Kathy shook her head, "No...I haven't lived in New York, since..."

"Since you abandoned me?"

His words pierced through her heart like a jagged knife through leather.

"It wasn't my intention to...abandon you, Khalil." She cried.

"Your intention? What could possibly be the intention behind leaving a fuckin' three-year-old in an abandoned house?" Khalil barked.

"I came back, Khalil! I didn't just leave you. I just...I was fucked up."

"Oh, so you decided to just leave me in an abandoned house while you went to go get your fix? Is that what you're telling me. Because that's not much better." He rebutted.

"That's only part of the truth."

"What other part am I missing? The part where you've clearly gotten clean and started a new family, never even attempting to look for me? I can only assume that the girl you just let in, is your daughter." He ranted.

"Yes, I got clean and yes, I started a family, but I also looked for you. I was there when the police came and got you, I even went to the hospital to try and get you." Kathy explained.

"Then what happened? Why did I spend the last thirty-plus years of my life without a mother or a father?" Khalil tried his hardest to fight back his tears, but a few fell.

"To understand, you have to let me tell you the whole story." Kathy pleaded.

"Fine." He shrugged, wiping tears from his eyes.

"You wanna go inside first?"

He clenched his jaw, "No. I have no desire to see the happy home you created without me."

"This isn't our home; this is just a short-term rental. Like I told you, I haven't lived here in years."

"I'm not talking about the fuckin' house, Kathy. I'm talking about your husband and daughter!" Khalil exclaimed.

Overwhelmed by his reaction, Kathy leaned away, "Sorry. I misunderstood."

TAP! TAP!

Both startled, Khalil and Kathy looked up to see who was knocking at his window. It was her husband, Darryl. Khalil reluctantly rolled the window down.

Darryl leaned down, "I just came to check on you, make sure everything was okay."

"I'm okay, baby." Kathy nodded.

"Alright. And what do you want me to tell DeeDee?"

"Just tell her I'll be in, in a few and we'll talk to her together."

Khalil scoffed, "So, you haven't told her about the child you left behind?"

"We planned on telling her today, but I wanted to talk to you first." Kathy informed.

"Mhmm…" Khalil shook his head in disbelief.

"Alright, I'mma let you two get back to talkin'. I'll see you in a bit, baby." Darryl nodded then headed back across the street, inside the house.

Khalil sat with his head in his hands, massaging his forehead as he tried to calm himself.

"You want me to start now, or you need a minute?" Kathy asked cautiously.

"Go ahead."

Kathy took a deep breath and proceeded to start from the beginning, where she met Khalil's father Kyle Anderson in the nineth grade.

Kathy was in love with Kyle from the moment they were paired together in Honors Biology. Kyle was a highly sought after Pop Warner athlete who had schools across the district trying to get him on their football team. And part of his appeal was that he was equally smart as he was talented on the football field.

Not long after the two met, Kyle asked Kathy to be his girlfriend, which of course pissed off the *popular girls* who felt they were entitled to him, but Kyle only had eyes for his *Kit-Kat,* as he called her. And much like many of their peers, the late-night phone calls and in-between-class make-out sessions led to a desire for much more. So, the night of the Winter Formal, they left early with a few friends and took the party to a friend's house, whose mother worked overnight. And, that night, Kathy lost her virginity to her first love.

"Where is he now?" Khalil interrupted.

"I looked him up, years ago and found out he lives in San Diego. He has a wife and two daughters, and coaches high school football." Kathy shared.

"So, what happened between y'all?"

Kathy continued her trip down memory lane, explaining how once she found out she was pregnant, she told Kyle, and he basically started to distance himself. He wouldn't talk to her in the hallway, answer any of her calls and when she went by his house, his mother would lie and say he wasn't there. Then one day, Kathy finally had enough and told his mother she was pregnant. And that was the moment that set everything into a downward spiral. They called Kathy's parents, had a sit down and discussed next steps as if Kyle and Kathy weren't even present. The parents agreed that Kathy would get rid of the baby and the two of them were no longer allowed to see each other.

"They were gonna make you get rid of me?" Khalil asked.

"Kathy nodded, "Yea…but I refused. I told them it was my body and my baby, and I wasn't about to destroy a gift from God just because they saw it as a curse. All that talk in church about loving God's children, and they wanted me to get rid of mine."

"So, what happened after that?"

Kathy calmed herself and then continued the story, sharing how distraught she was to know that Kyle agreed with their parents. They'd convinced him that having a baby would derail his dreams of becoming a professional athlete. But Kathy was determined to stand on her choice; she refused to get rid of her baby. The decision to defy her parents wishes led to her being kicked out of the house; they told her if she wanted to make adult decisions, she might as well start living like one for real. So, there she was, fourteen, pregnant and couch hopping from one friends' house to the next while trying to maintain her studies and conceal her growing belly.

"Damn...they really put you out at fourteen?"

Kathy nodded, "Yea...it was a different time, and social services wasn't what it is today, unfortunately."

"That's fucked up."

"Very, but I was tough." Kathy smiled through the tears.

She took a deep breath then shared how she ended up completely homeless, living on the streets, once she started to show. None of her friend's parents were okay with a pregnant kid in their home and she feared that if they called the police, her baby would be taken away. So, she got clever and started going into hotels during the night shift, acting like she was a guest there and would sleep in the bathroom until the morning staff would come. But they eventually caught on and she had to stay at a real shelter. Kathy hardly slept though, afraid of the men who slept less than a few feet from her cot.

"Is that why you started using? Because you were on the streets?" Khalil interjected.

"No...I didn't start that until a year or so after you were born." Kathy shared.

She told Khalil how she was stopped one day, while heading to school, by a woman who looked to be in her twenties. The woman resembled the singer/actress *J. Lo* and was dressed from head to toe in designer. She offered to give Kathy a ride to school in her green 1990 Mercedes G-Wagon. Kathy was exhausted from her long commutes and enamored by the woman's beauty, so she took her up on the offer. The whole ride to school, they talked; Kathy shared about her situation and the woman named Ramona, showed empathy and offered to help her out.

"Ramona told me that I reminded her of herself and shared how her mother also kicked her out when she was younger, so she wanted to do for me what no one did for her. Little did I know, Ramona had been watching me for weeks, looking to recruit me as one of Hurricane's girls." Kathy sighed.

"Hurricane?"

"Yea...Hurricane was a major drug dealer and pimp, who had a reputation for supplying any and every desire his clients could think of. He offered his clients women and men of all ages; I think the youngest I met was this twelve-year-old girl named Denice. Hurricane had zero boundaries, he even pimped out a few trans women to white guys on wall street and a couple downlow gangstas."

"That's foul."

"Don't I know it. I just got lucky that I was pregnant and none of his clientele had a taste for pregnant teenager."

Kathy went on to share how she decided to leave, once she realized that Ramona wasn't actually offering her a safe place to live with other girls in similar situations. She'd been involuntarily signed up to live and work in a whore house. But when she tried to leave, Ramona took her to meet Hurricane and the fear she felt in his presence, left her stuck. He'd basically told her that she wasn't allowed to leave but that her living there wasn't free; she'd have to make up the cost for her existence in the house as soon as she dropped the baby, but in the meantime, she'd basically be the maid and an errand girl for the house. Too afraid to challenge him and risk being on his bad side, especially while several months pregnant, Kathy decided to just stay and slowly plot her escape.

"The nigga kept you against your will?" Khalil quizzed, growing angry.

Kathy nodded, "Basically."

"And you said his name is Hurricane. You know his real name?" Khalil questioned.

"Don't even waste your time thinking those thoughts. I looked him up, years later, with the same intentions and it turns out Hurricane died in prison, from AIDS."

"Good." Khalil gritted.

She continued her story, sharing how she balanced being the house assistant with school for months, while taking in as much information as possible to plan her escape. Hurricane had people from all walks of life coming in to do business, buy sex and much more. From city workers, to lawyers, dealers and some men who looked like local politicians. Kathy found herself growing paranoid, that even if she did manage to leave, someone who knew Hurricane would tell him where she was. As she entered her nineth month, she became more overwhelmed by what it'd mean once she gave birth and feared even more bringing a baby into that hell house. She'd witnessed the young men Hurricane forced to turn tricks. Kathy refused to let that happen, so she mapped out her plan and decided to execute it that night. But her plan was interrupted by the labor pains that kicked in on her train ride to school.

"I cried and prayed that I was just imagining things, but the pain increased, and I knew for sure, I was in labor. Which meant, the time clock had finally wound down on my labor-free stay at Hurricane's manor."

"So, what'd you do?" Khalil inquired, fully engaged.

"Nothing I could do, honestly. An older woman shouted for help at the next stop, they helped me off the train and the paramedics took me to the hospital. I was just lucky that Ramona had my fake I.D. made stating that I was nineteen-year-old Samantha Brooks, so I was able to be admitted without issue."

"My birth certificate has your name on it, though."

Kathy nodded, "I know…I used my real name and gave you your father's last name. I honestly wasn't sure I'd survive long after Hurricane found out I gave birth and didn't want you having any connections to them via that fake I.D."

Kathy wiped tears from her eyes as she reminisced on how dark of a place she was in mentally. That was a time in her life where she didn't know if life was worth living, but she held on for Khalil.

"So, what happened? Did he find you?"

"No…I didn't wait long enough for him to. You were a quick birth, unlike your sister. Ten minutes after I was moved to the delivery room, your head was coming out. And no sooner than the nurse left with the paperwork for your birth certificate, I packed my bag full of every baby item they provided and packed you up."

"You left, right after giving birth?"

"Yup. I couldn't risk anything happening to you. So, I changed my clothes, wrapped you up and hid your little body in my coat and slipped out the hospital."

"Where'd you go?"

Kathy told Khalil about how she'd gone to a library, just for a safe place to sit down and rest when one of the librarians asked if she'd needed help. The simple question sent an already hormonal Kathy into a hysterical cry, leading to her and the woman talking about her current circumstance of homelessness. The sweet old woman ran and grabbed some pamphlets and made some calls, and by the end of the night there was a van from a shelter for abused women and their children. At first Kathy was opposed, specifically because of how far it was from the city. But after considering what that'd mean for her safety, she obliged and they were on their way to White Plains, New York.

"That was the safest place I'd been in nine months." Kathy professed.

"So, how'd we end up back in Harlem?" Khalil quizzed.

"After a year and a half of living there, working in the kitchen and building community, the non-profit lost funding and had to close."

"And they just put y'all back on the streets?"

"No, no…they offered us transfer to another facility further upstate, but I didn't want that. Living in some po-dunk town with cows and corn fields wasn't for me. I was a city girl…before that lil rap group."

"Even if it meant risking your safety?"

Kathy shrugged, "I was sixteen. In my mind, enough time had passed that Hurricane should've moved on. And as long as I stayed away from his territory, I thought I'd be fine. So, I packed us up and moved to Manhattan."

"Manhattan?" Khalil frowned.

"Yea. One of the women who worked at the shelter, had an uncle who owned a diner in the city and was willing to pay under the table. So, she recommended me and when she told him about my situation, he offered me a room in his boarding house not far from the diner." She explained.

Kathy expounded further, sharing how she worked hard while saving her money and even enrolled in night classes, twice a week, to get her GED. Life seemed to be improving, and her fears of Hurricane slowly became distant memories. Kathy was finally getting her life on track and had even made a new friend, an Italian girl named Lacey who was four years older than her. Lacey and Kathy became fast

friends; she loaned Kathy the money to enroll Khalil in daycare and
didn't rush her to pay it back and she even watched him for her when
she just needed a couple hours to herself.

"For the first time in a while, I felt like I was really living and
not just surviving; holding my breath for the next catastrophe."

"How did I end up abandoned, in a crack house?" Khalil
interjected.

"It wasn't a crack house. It was a house that was under
renovation. I wasn't a crackhead, Khalil." Kathy calmly rebutted.

"Then what were you, because the report in my case file says I
was the child of a drug addict." Khalil huffed.

"I did do drugs, but it wasn't crack."

"Crack, meth, heroine? What's the difference. It still led you to
leave me."

"You're right. It's just a bit more to it than just me choosing
drugs over you." Kathy replied.

"Ok, well tell me what happened then."

Kathy cleared her throat then proceeded to tell him about the
first night she'd hung out at Lacey's apartment. She'd invited Kathy
over and it was rare that she got invited anywhere. The other girls at
the diner and the few school friends she had, rarely extended invites
because she was the girl with the baby and no guaranteed sitter. So,
Kathy happily went, especially when Lacey said it was okay to bring
Khalil. She made sure to keep him up from his nap; to assure he'd sleep
the whole time, so when they got to Lacey's, she laid him in the room,
and they proceeded to party. Lacey ordered tons of food and Kathy
smoked weed for the first time.

"Little did I know, Lacey liked to lace her blunts. And since I'd
never done a drug in my life, I had no idea what weed was supposed to
taste like. I knew it smelled funny, but Lacey told me she smoked a
special kind, so I just figured I didn't know about all the types of weed.
But I trusted her." Kathy shrugged.

"What did she lace it with?"

"Cocaine."

Khalil shook his head and rubbed his hand over his face.

Kathy proceeded to share the details of how she quickly became
addicted and that she and Khalil started spending more and more time

243

at Lacey's to *party*. After a while, Lacey grew tired of supplying Kathy and told her she'd have to purchase her own supply. Unsure of how it worked, she'd just give Lacey whatever amount of money she said was necessary and Lacey would bring her back several rolled joints. Over time, Kathy started opting to stay home and get high, closing Khalil in the bedroom while she *hotboxed* in the bathroom. She'd eventually gotten so bad, that she missed shifts at work and barely finished her GED course. Despite Lacey's attempts to cover for her, she finally ran out of second chances and the owner of the diner fired her. Then he gave her two weeks to move out of the boarding house, after tenants complained that the bathroom smelled like weed after she used it.

"I'd lost my job and our home all in a matter of eight months. My only saving grace was that your daycare was twenty-four hours, due to the hospital staff that had children there and I'd paid ahead for the month. So, while you were sleeping safely at night, I slept wherever I could."

"What about Lacey? She's the one that got you fucked up. She couldn't let you stay with her?"

"I found out the hard way that everyone who calls you friends, isn't actually that."

Khalil sighed, "That's fucked up. So, that's how we ended up in the abandoned house?"

Kathy nodded, "Yea. After your month in daycare was up, I found a job at a dry cleaners but was unable to find housing. On one of our walks through a neighborhood I wished I could raise you in, I noticed there were newly renovated brownstones for sale. The sign out front said *open house tours would begin in the fall*, and I remembered one of the women from Hurricane's manor telling me she squatted in brownstones owned by wealthy white people who lived in Florida during the winter. I scoped the place out for a week and noticed no one coming or going, so I decided to try my luck. And lucky for me, the realtor or contractors left the key-box unlocked."

Khalil listened intently as she explained to him how she made a copy of the key at a neighborhood hardware store, set up a makeshift bed in a back room and snuck him into work with her, hiding him under the dry-cleaning racks, for weeks until she could afford childcare again.

"You were still using?"

Kathy nodded sorrowfully, "Yea…I'd just learned how to manage it, or so I thought."

"When did you end up leaving me?"

"It was late one night; I'd just gotten you to sleep, and I decided to take a walk while I smoked. And that's when I saw him, your father, walking hand in hand with a girl we went to school with. Her name was Sadé; we'd been sworn enemies since the seventh grade, and he knew she hated me. The sight of them together sent me over the edge, I jolted across that street and snatched her by the hair, giving her the ass whooping I owed everyone who'd wronged me: *My parents, Kyle, his parents, Ramona, Hurricane, Lacey!* I swear I would've killed that girl if Kyle hadn't pulled me off her." Kathy shook with rage, reliving the moment in her mind.

She went on to tell Khalil how she ran, after Kyle threatened to call the Police. Overrun with emotions, Kathy stopped in a nearby park and smoked the last two joints she had until she was barely conscious. By the time she woke up, the sun was rising, and she was so disoriented she didn't know where she was. When she finally got herself together, she'd ran back to the house but when she arrived, a man in a Dickie set and work boots was passing a crying Khalil to a policeman.

"What the fuck, man…" Khalil leaned against the steering wheel as tears fell from his eyes.

The visions of that day, flashed in his mind; for the first time those fragments were connected to a larger picture for him.

"I'm so sorry…" Kathy cried, placing her hand atop his shoulder.

Khalil snatched away, "Why'd you let them take me? Why didn't you come get me?"

"I did try, Khalil. I found out what hospital they took you to and when I got there, I overheard officers saying *whenever the mother shows up, she's going to jail.* So, I just sat in the ER waiting room, hoping for a chance to grab you and run. I stayed until security said I had to leave because visiting hours were over. But even then, I waited outside, sleeping on a bench until security woke me up to leave."

"So, you traded my freedom for yours?"

"There was no trade off. If I claimed you, they would've arrested me, and we'd still be separated."

"Yea, but at least I would've known you tried!" He shouted with tears in his eyes.

"Khalil, I did... but I was scared."

"You were scared? *You?* I was a fuckin' child! Snatched from the only life I knew and dropped into a fuckin' system that hated me so much I eventually hated my fuckin' self!" Khalil barked.

"I'm sorry, Khalil."

He slammed his fist against the armrest, "Stop fuckin' saying you're sorry and tell me why! Why didn't you keep trying?"

"I did..." Kathy cried, "I stayed at the hospital for days until I was sick from withdrawal. I ended up admitted for treatment and the hospital sent the psych doctor to evaluate me. It just so happens that his intern was Darryl, who saw beyond the lies I fed the doctor. He came back later that same day and pried the truth out of me in the sweetest way, then offered to help me if I'd let him."

"So, you just went on with your merry lives, clean sober and living happily ever after!" Khalil interrupted.

"No, no! That's not what happened. I accepted his help and was admitted to a rehab upstate. When I got out six months later, he solicited the help of his older brother, who was a jr. partner at a law firm. And despite his advisement against pursuing custody, because I'd likely be arrested, I still had to at least try. But, when he showed me the family you'd been placed with, I had second thoughts. They had a big house, were well-dressed and looked like they could give you a better life than a seventeen-year-old drop out, with no plan or place to stay."

Khalil chuckled cynically, "Those mothafuckas were far from the Cosby's. I spent the next three years being beaten and verbally abused by my drunk ass foster dad and his wife was just a weak doormat who was happy he took a break from whooping her ass when he beat us!"

"Khalil, I...I didn't know..."

"How could you! You didn't even bother to check on me for real! Just looked at a few fuckin' pictures and assumed I was cool." He violently swiped tears from his eyes.

"If I would've known..."

"You what? Would've came and got me? Huh? Bullshit!"

"Khalil, I would've never left you there had I known what was happening."

"Yea, well it's too late for all that, now. Luckily for me and my foster siblings, Ms. Dulaney finally got fed up and shot his punk ass. It's just too bad she shot herself too, so we were scattered back into the system and it's a lot harder for a six-year-old to get chosen than a two-year-old."

"Oh my God." Kathy gasped, covering her mouth.

"Yea, you ain't the only one with a fucked-up origin story, Kathy. I spent my life from ages six to eleven being tossed between group homes. Fighting niggas twice my size, cause the lil high yellow nigga with freckles is expected to be a bitch. It wasn't until I met my brother X, and his family took me in unofficially, that I finally experienced some sort of safety. Finally knew what it felt like to be cared for." Khalil gritted as tears fell from his eyes.

"I'm sorry..." Kathy cried, unable to utter anything else.

"You ain't ever wonder about me?" Khalil wept, "After all this time..."

Kathy cried harder, "I did...I had a private investigator check on you years later. It must've been around the time you moved in with your friend, because when I noticed your address changed and made Darryl take me by the house. I was prepared to risk it all to see you, but then I *saw* you. You were all dressed up in your Sunday's best, apparently headed to church. There was a little boy with you and a girl who looked a few years older, and y'all were getting into a car with an older couple. You looked so happy that I couldn't bring myself to disrupt your life, just to fulfil my own selfish desires. I'd already put you through enough."

"I *was* happy...for the first time in years, since you left me. But I still wished that you'd come for me. I'd spend my nights imagining what it'd be like to not have to borrow somebody else's mama...to have my own family. People with the same blood." Khalil sniffled.

"Khalil, baby, I'm so sorry for everything I put you through. I'll never be able to make up for what I've done. I just wanted you to know the whole story; that you weren't just thrown away. I've never stopped loving you or thinking about you. I've prayed for you, through it all, that my mistakes wouldn't keep you from everything God had instore for you." Kathy professed wearily.

"I need to go and try to process this shit, alone." Khalil wiped his eyes with the back of his hand.

"Uh…okay. I'll be here, for the next week. But I'm willing to extend my stay however long you need."

Khalil shook his head, "Don't change your plans for me."

"You are my only plan and priority right now. *You*, Khalil."

"Alright, I've got to go." Khalil fought to maintain his composure.

"Okay…I'll be here. Call me when you're ready." Kathy slowly opened the passenger door.

"Alright." Khalil nodded.

Kathy paused then suddenly threw her arms around him, squeezing him tight. When she let go, she turned his face toward hers and looked him in the eyes, "I love you, son. With all my heart. Nothing will ever change that."

Khalil couldn't fight the tears from falling as he stared into Kathy's eyes. As angry as he was, her embrace and the warmth of her gaze made him feel safe in a way he'd never felt.

"I…I love you too…Ma."

Those words echoing back into his ears nearly broke him. Khalil quickly wiped his face, and Kathy released a soft sigh before stepping out of the car.

Chapter Sixteen

Maleah looked up from her computer at the sound of a knock at her door and to her welcomed surprise it was Xavier, accompanied by his sister Jhana and her twin daughters.

"Oh my God! Hey!"

"Hey, girl!" Jhana smiled as she walked over and met Maleah at the side of her desk.

The two women embraced and then Xavier walked over, kissing Maleah sweetly.

"Baby, these are my nieces I was telling you about; Anaya and Anahj." Xavier pointed toward the girls who smiled awkwardly.

Anaya and Anahj were identical in every way except their personalities and style of dress. Anaya was a girlie girl, dressed in a bubble gum pink velour sweatsuit with white Nike air forces. Anahj, being the polar opposite, wore a cropped denim jacket, black graphic tee and leggings, with combat boots on her feet. Even their choice of hairstyle differed, Anaya's hair was braided up into two buns atop her head and Anahj's hair was braided in several small cornrows, pulled back into a bun.

"Hi, nice to meet you." Maleah waved.

Jhana pushed Xavier aside and grabbed Maleah's left hand, "Okay! You did good. I didn't want to have to kick your ass twice."

"I am so sorry, Jhana, I had no idea that he hadn't told you."

"You don't have to apologize girl, he's the one who waited days after to call me." Jhana punch Xavier in the arm.

"Damn, I said I was sorry." Xavier turned to the twins, "I told y'all you should've left her on the ship."

Anaya giggled and Jhana punched him again.

"Alright, Jay. Damn, you hit like a nigga!"

She poked him in the cheek with her stiletto nail, "And I'll kick your ass like one, if you pull some shit like that again."

Xavier chuckled, "I won't. Promise. Anyway, we're about to take the girls to have lunch with a special guest, you have time to join us?"

"Special guest? I hope it's Daleesha!" Anaya blurted.

Anahj sucked her teeth, "I hope it's Typhoon...he's fine."

Xavier turned around with his face frowned up, "What you know about *fine*?"

Anahj shrugged and smirked, "I know Typhoon is it."

"Aye, Watch it! Don't make me tell your father." Jhana warned.

"Tell him what? That I think a guy is cute? Would you rather I think Daleesha was cute?" Anahj sneered sarcastically.

"Hey! Watch how you talk to you mother, or you can go back to the house and miss out on everything we're doing today." Xavier scolded.

She mumbled under her breath, "I don't care."

"Excuse me?" He walked over to Anahj, towering over her.

"Nothing."

"That's what I thought. You better check that attitude, young lady."

Anahj folded her arms and turned her head, mumbling something inaudible.

"Nana, just be quiet before you ruin the whole day." Anaya whined.

"You better listen to your sister. Cause I'm two seconds from snatching you up." Jhana threatened.

"How about this, you all head down and I'll give Anahj the tour of the office. I know a fashionable girl like her would appreciate seeing all the racks of designer shoes and clothes. Not to mention the handbags. What do you say, Anahj? Would you like that?" Maleah interjected, trying to play peacemaker.

Anahj shrugged, "I guess."

Maleah smiled and nodded, "Then it's settled, we'll meet you down there. Let me just text my assistant and let her know I'll be out of my office."

Jhana sighed and whispered, "Thank you."

"It's no problem. We're family."

"Alright, well y'all have fun. Come on Naya, let's go." Xavier smiled holding out his hand.

"Okay!" She exclaimed grabbing his hand giddily and the walked out the office.

Jhana stopped at the door, "Nana."

She sighed, "Yes?"

"I Love you. Behave yourself."

Anahj nodded, "Okay."

Jhana waited a moment longer then exited the office.

"Alright, where would you like to start? You wanna see the boardroom, the wardrobe department or the studio where we shoot some of the magazine covers and ad campaigns?"

"Doesn't matter." Anahj shrugged.

"Okay…how about we just walk the office and visit each place as we get to them." Maleah suggested.

Anahj nodded and followed Maleah out the office. They walked to the left and headed down the hall, ending up at a huge boardroom that had a panoramic view of the city. Anahj walked up to the glass and stared out at the city.

"Beautiful, isn't it?" Maleah broke the silence.

Anahj sighed, "I wish I could live here."

"Maybe we can arrange with your parents for you to come stay with us for a little while. Maybe during the summer."

"They'll never let me." She shook her head and walked away toward the door.

"Why do you say that?" Maleah pried.

"Because, every time I ask to come here, they say no and never give a reason. I was surprised when my mom said we were coming here, after the cruise." Anahj shared.

"Well, maybe this is a sign that things will change."

Anahj sucked her teeth, "If you say so."

"Have a little hope." Maleah playfully nudged Anahj on her way out of the boardroom.

They made their way down the hall toward the wardrobe department, which covered the rest of that end of the office. When they walked inside Anahj's eyes grew wide at the beautifully lit space that was filled from floor to ceiling with garments, shoe racks, purses, accessories and fabric.

"Better than the skyline?" Maleah whispered.

Anahj tried to stifle a smile, "Definitely."

Maleah chuckled as they walked up to Gene the resident tailor and preserver of all the rare and priceless garments lent to the agency.

"And who's this fashionable little diva?" Gene smiled, stitching the hem of a chiffon dress.

"Gene, this is Anahj, my newest fashion consultant. She's here to help me pick a few pieces for an upcoming shoot." Maleah stated boldly.

"I'm what?" Anahj looked up at her in confusion.

"Yup. We're gonna put your design eye to work and see what you come up with. If it's good, it'll be in the shoot."

Anahj gasped, "You're serious?"

"Yup. Come on." Maleah smiled.

"You've got this!" Gene winked.

Maleah took her by the hand and led her through the massive 12,000 square foot space. Anahj was enamored by the variety of well-organized garments, sorted by fabric, color, style and season.

"I want my closet to look like this when I grow up." She stated, dragging her fingers along a row of blazers.

"Careful, some garments don't respond well to the natural oils on our hands." Maleah advised.

Anahj quickly retracted her hand, "Sorry!"

"It's okay, just a little tip for my newest consultant. So, here's what we're going to be selecting from. These are all pieces that tie into the theme of the shoot." Maleah pointed to a section of clothing and shoes.

"What's the theme, rainbows and lollypops? Naya would've loved this." Anahj rolled her eyes.

Maleah chuckled, "Not exactly. But close. It's an ad campaign for a cosmetic company that has a new array of pink blushes."

"Oh yea, Naya would definitely love this."

"Well, maybe I'll talk to your uncle, and we can try to convince your parents to let you both come to set when we shoot it."

Anahj slowly turned around and looked at her with a confused expression, "You would do that?"

"Of course! Once you pick out a bomb outfit for my models, I'm gonna definitely need you there to help style it."

"Are you just being nice to me, to get on uncle X's good side?"

Maleah stifled a chuckle, "Honey, I *am* your uncle's good side. So, no I am not being nice because of him. I'm doing this because I see some of me in you. I had a little edge and attitude to me too when I was your age. And while it wasn't cool, at all, I had my reasons. But once I found something that brought me joy; picking out my outfits and styling my friends from their closets, I had less reason to be angry at the world."

"How'd you know I liked fashion?" Anahj quizzed.

"Baby girl, I'm Maleah motha-lovin' Jones. You better ask about me! I know a well styled look when I see it. You clearly take after your mama." Maleah winked.

Anahj giggled and quickly looked away.

"Was that a laugh? A smile and a laugh in the last twenty minutes...my God, she's cured!" Maleah teased.

Anahj burst into laughter and Maleah joined in.

"What's so funny, I want to hear the joke."

Maleah turned to see who was talking and her smiling face immediately turned into a stone stare at the sight of Eric. He was holding a garment bag with an obnoxious grin on his face.

"Can I help you with something *work related*, Mr. Yeboah?"

He chuckled, "Yea, actually can you show me where to hang these suits?"

"You could've just given them to Gene."

Eric shrugged, "He wasn't up front when I came in."

"Gene!" Maleah shouted.

"Yea?" Gene shouted back.

"Looks like he's back. He can help you." She gave a fake smile.

Eric smiled then turned his attention to Anahj, "Aren't you going to introduce me to your little friend here?"

"No."

253

"I like your t-shirt. What do you know about *Public Enemy*?" Eric spoke to Anahj disregarding Maleah's visible disinterest in his presence.

"I know you're probably the same age as them." Anahj quipped.

Eric placed his hand on his chest, "Ouch, that's hurtful. Do I really look that old?"

"You don't look that young." She shrugged.

Maleah chuckled to herself.

"Cute. You're a real spitfire. But I like it. What's your name love?"

Anahj frowned her face, "I'm not supposed to talk to strange old men."

"Well, you already failed at that, now, haven't you?"

"Alright, that's enough, Eric. Goodbye." Maleah waved him off as her cellphone started to vibrate.

"Is that lover-boy?" Eric grinned mischievously.

"Bye, Eric!" She flagged him, answering her phone, "Hey, baby. We're almost done up here, we'll be done in a few."

"Wow…I remember when you used to call me baby."

Maleah rolled her eyes, "Can you go, please."

Eric walked past the two of them, toward another section designated for men's and unisex apparel.

"Lying ass…" Maleah muttered, "Huh? Oh, nothing babe. Like I said we're almost done…no one babe, I was talking to myself. I'll see you in a bit. Alright, love you too."

She hung up and was met by the skeptical expression on Anahj's face.

"That guy is your ex-boyfriend?" She questioned.

Maleah sighed, "Unfortunately, yes."

"She didn't always feel that way." Eric chimed in, walking back over to them.

"Can you please go do whatever it is you do here?" Maleah scoffed.

"Your auntie Leah and I used to be madly in love. But we had a disagreement, and she chose to run away to America, leaving me heartbroken."

"Well, I would've left too because you're not a good listener and my mom says a good man listens and pays attention. And she's told you to leave more than once and you're still here." Anahj rebutted boldly.

Her candor caught both Eric and Maleah off guard.

"Aren't you a smart one." Eric chuckled.

Anahj rolled her eyes, "Smart enough to know when someone doesn't like me anymore."

Maleah covered her mouth, preventing the involuntary laugh from escaping, "Pay him no mind. Let's get back to what we were doing."

She pulled Anahj by the shoulder and led her over to an accessories rack.

"We'll talk later, Mal."

"The British schooling system in Peckham must be shit, because your comprehension skills are clearly non-existent." Xavier spoke calmly as he walked up.

"If it isn't Mr. Label man himself. Ready for that fitting?" Eric's demeanor made it clear that he wasn't fazed by Xavier's presence.

"Shit." Maleah huffed to herself.

Anahj stepped over near Maleah, "Ooooo, you're in trouble now."

"Do I look worried, Love?" Eric quizzed amusedly.

"Don't talk to her." Xavier spoke through clenched teeth.

Maleah walked over, pulling Anahj with her, "Come on, babe. Not here. Let's just go."

"Take her and go meet Jhana in my office." Xavier instructed, never breaking eye contact with Eric.

Maleah placed her hand on his chest, "Xavier, this isn't the place."

He placed his hand on hers and then looked into her eyes, "Take her."

"X, please. Just come with us." Maleah whispered.

Eric laughed, "Relax, bruv. It's not that deep."

"Shut the fuck up!" Xavier barked.

Anahj gasped, staring between the two men in shock.

"Alright, let's go." She pushed Xavier's chest, but he didn't budge, like a sturdy oak tree.

Eric started clapping, "Bravo! Didn't know you had that in you?"

Xavier rubbed his hand over his beard and shook his head as he chuckled to himself, "Come on."

He took Maleah by the hand, and they walked out with Anahj in toe.

"How did it go?" Gene shouted toward their backs as they exited.

Anahj just shrugged as Maleah pulled her, led by Xavier whose long-legged strides and hasty pace caused her to speed walk in order to keep up.

∞∞∞∞

Paul slapped Monique on the ass as she placed a pan of macaroni and cheese on the dining room table.

She laughed, "Cut it out, you know T.Y. is here."

"He's old enough to know his mother's a woman first and has needs." He kissed her on the neck, wrapping his arms around her waist.

"Paul!"

"Ooooo, I like it when you yell my name."

She slapped his arm, "Seriously, cut it out before he comes downstairs."

The sound of footsteps coming down the stairs cause Monique to push Paul back and turn to greet her son. Tyree stared at her with his eyebrow raised.

"Hey, son."

"What's up, ma." He responded, looking the two of them over in suspicion.

"Your brother and sisters should be here soon." She smiled.

"Mhmm." Tyree nodded and headed for the front door.

"Where're you going? You're not staying for dinner?"

Tyree spoke over his shoulder, "Yea, I'll be back."

"Aye, let me holla at you really quick, Tyree." Paul asserted.

Tyree stopped at the front door and both he and Monique looked at Paul with a confused expression.

"T.Y." Tyree corrected.

"My bad, T.Y." Paul walked over, "I won't hold you up. We can talk on your way to your car."

Tyree stared at him for a moment then nodded. Paul followed him out of the house and Monique rushed over to watch them through the glass of the front door.

"So, I'm having a bit of a problem, and I was wondering if you'd be willing to help me out." Paul finally shared.

"What makes you think I can or would help you, with anything?" Tyree asked dryly.

"Because I believe this problem may become a problem for you too, very soon."

Tyree stared at him blankly, "I'm listening."

Paul pulled out his phone and showed a picture of Niecy to Tyree, who stared at it emotionlessly.

"Am I supposed to know who that is?" Tyree quizzed.

"I was hoping you did, because it seems she knows either you or one of your siblings, and I think she's plotting some shady shit." Paul spoke just above a whisper.

"And you know that, how?"

"Because she broke into my office, making demands and offering to handle the people who murdered my son, so I didn't have to look my woman in the face with a guilty conscience."

Tyree shrugged, "Who's your son?"

"His name was Charles, but you might've known him as Chuck."

"Never heard of him."

"That's surprising since y'all would've been running the streets around the same time." Paul rebutted.

"Who said I ran the streets?" Tyree questioned.

Paul threw his hands up, "You're right. My bad, I ain't mean to dry snitch."

"Ain't shit to snitch on. Anyway, I don't know anything about what happened to your son, nor do I know her."

"Well, either way I believe she's plotting something, and I know it'd kill your mother if something happened to you or one of your siblings. I know firsthand what losing a child can do to you."

"Condolences. But you don't have to worry about my mother or my siblings. I've got them." Tyree responded nonchalantly.

"You sure? This chick is certifiably off her rocker. The mothafucka shook me down for a couple hundred racks." Paul huffed.

"A couple hundred? Y'all bringing in money like that at Lou's?" Tyree quizzed.

Paul smiled, "Let's just say, I've been saving since the eighties and have a healthy retirement fund."

Tyree nodded, "Well, like I said, we're good. She'll find out the hard way the mistake she made, threatening my family."

"Alright. I just figured I'd alert you, before saying anything to your mother." Paul informed.

"Don't say shit to my mother. This ain't nothing she needs to be concerned with, like I said we're good." Tyree gritted.

Paul took a step back, "Alright, relax. It'll be between us. I trust you'll handle your business."

Tyree opened the drivers' side door of his car and ducked inside. He started the engine and rolled the window down.

"Aye!" He called out to Paul who was halfway up the steps.

Paul turned, "What's up?"

"You didn't believe her when she insinuated that one of us did it?" Tyree asked.

"Nah." Paul shook his head.

"Why not?"

"Because I actually know who did."

Tyree nodded, "I trust you'll handle your business."

"Without a doubt."

Tyree rolled up his window and Paul opened the front door, met by Monique with a concerned look on her face. Tyree waited until they closed the front door and then sped off.

∞∞∞∞

Sky stepped out of a black town car and tightened the belt of her coat as she stepped under the awning of *Uncle Eddie's*, a newly Michelin-rated and black owned restaurant in Harlem. The warm lighting that was dim lit set the mood and complimented the brown and deep olive-green décor. There were abstract and Avant guard paintings on the walls outfitted in copper frames. And exposed pipe and brick that added a rustic, industrial essence to the ambience. The overall vibe was cross between elegant and gritty, while the food could be described as elevated Caribbean cuisine with a twist.

"Good evening, ma'am." The valet nodded at her.

"Hello." Sky smiled.

She made her way inside the entrance, met by the sounds of *Bob Marley's "Turn your lights down low (ft. Lauryn Hill)"*.

She stopped at the host station, looking around at what appeared to be a practically empty establishment from where she was standing. After waiting a few minutes, she walked through the short hallway and looked out onto the restaurant floor to see it was empty and the middle of the floor was cleared except for one table, with two chairs and a floral arrangement of her favorite flowers: Lilies.

"May I take your coat?" A server walked up to her with a smile.

Sky slowly took off her wool coat, revealing the pink silk dress she wore. The dress clung to her modelesque frame like a glove and came just about her knees. On her feet she wore her favorite pair of metallic gold John'Clair heels from Tequia'Charde's newest collection. As she walked over to the table, her phone started to vibrate in her purse. She opened her purse and checked it then quickly hit the *decline* button.

"Hey, beautiful."

She turned around and was greeted by Chris's charming smile.

"You know, a gentleman meets you at the car." She quipped.

Chris placed his hand on his heart, "You're right and that's my bad. I was in the back making sure the chef knew you were allergic to avocados."

"Hmm…I'll forgive you, this time." She smirked.

Chris took her by the hand, "Come on."

They walked over to the table, and he helped her into her seat before taking a seat across from her.

Sky picked up the bouquet of lilies and inhaled deep, "I Love lilies. I can't remember the last time I got flowers."

"Say no more. You'll have a fresh arrangement every week."

Caught off guard by his response, Sky just stared down at the flowers.

"You don't have to do that." She finally looked up to see him texting someone.

"It's already done." He stated as he placed his phone down on the table.

"You know, when I said I always wanted to try this restaurant I didn't think I get to experience it like this."

"I wanted to make your first time special."

Sky blushed, "Well…mission accomplished."

"Nah…I haven't even come close to accomplishing what I've set out to do."

The perfectly timed server came over to the table pushing a wine cart. The woman placed down two glasses before them and explained in great detail the various wine options. After some thought, Sky yielded to Chris' choice of an imported Venetian Amarone wine. And after the first sip, Sky was even more impressed with the man across from her.

"I knew you'd Love it."

"Who said I *loved* it?"

"The moan you released the moment it hit your tongue." Chris spoke in a tone that almost made her choke on the sip she'd just taken.

"Whew, okay. I need to use the powder room. I'll be right back."

"You need help finding it?" Chris got up from his chair and walked around to help her from her seat.

Sky nervously moved around him, "Uh, no I think I'll be okay."

"Alright." He laughed to himself.

She quickly looked around and spotted the signage for the restrooms and made her way across the restaurant. When she turned the corner, she noticed Chris still standing, staring at her. Once she was in the bathroom, she checked herself out and took a deep breath, trying to calm her nerves.

"Relax, Sky. It's just dinner with a fine man. A fine man who remembered your favorite flower after only mentioning it once and wants to send them every week. Who also closed down a Michelin star restaurant for you and has great taste in wine. Omg, this is a terrible peptalk." She sighed hard.

The sound of someone knocking at the bathroom door startled her and turned to see Chris standing the doorway.

"You're not supposed to be in here, this is the ladies room sir." She quipped with a nervous smile.

"There's no one here but us…minus the chef and serving staff." Chris leaned against the doorway, undressing Sky with his eyes.

"Why're you looking at me like that?"

"Cause I'm fighting the urge to fuck you, right there on the edge of that sink."

His directness was startling yet exciting and honestly had her considering turning his thoughts into reality. But she couldn't do that, because they were just supposed to be two friends having dinner. That's the story she told Jared when he asked what she was doing tonight; she was going to dinner with a friend.

"I'll be out in a second." She smiled nervously.

Chris nodded and smiled, "You want me to fuck you, right here, right now. Don't you?"

Sky inhaled deep as he walked over to her, bracing herself against the sink. Chris slid his hands around her ass and lifted her up, gently plopping her down onto the counter.

"We really shouldn't do this." Sky exhaled, placing her hands on his chest.

"Cool. Tell me you don't want me to fuck you, and we'll go back out there and have a nice platonic dinner."

Sky stared into his eyes, her heart rate increasing and hormones screaming at her. She ran her hands over his chin and sighed.

"I really shouldn't."

"Say less. Come on." He patted her on the thigh.

Chris backed up from the sink and Sky snatched him by his shirt, pulling him into a passionate kiss. After a moment of passion, Chris broke away from the kiss leaving Sky with a confused expression. He walked over to the door and locked it then returned to her, pulling her to the edge of the sink. She wrapped her long legs around him and the two proceeded to kiss passionately as he reached under her dress and slipped off her thong.

"Put your legs on my shoulders." He instructed sternly.

Sky immediately obliged his command and before she knew it, Chris had pulled on a condom and was so deep in her, she felt pressure in her abdomen.

"Ooooh fuck!" She gasped experiencing a beautiful mix of pain and pleasure.

"Mm…I knew this pussy was platinum." Chris grunted, "Put your arms around my neck."

As soon as she did, he lifted her off the sink and stepped back then proceeded to hoist her up and thrust her down on his shaft.

Sky gasped and held onto tightly as her eyes rolled in the back of her head, "Oh shit…that's my spot. Please don't stop."

"You gonna cum for me?"

Sky bit her bottom lip and threw her head back as she felt the orgasm slowly creeping up. Chris kept a steady pace but shortened the length of his thrust, steadily beating against her g-spot. In minutes, her walls tightened around him, pulling him in as she succumbed to the body shaking orgasm.

∞∞∞∞

"Hey, Ma! Where's everybody?" Korena hugged Monique.

"Hell, if I know. I told everybody dinner was at eight, figuring that y'all would at least get here by eight-thirty." Monique huffed.

Korena took off her jacket and laid it on the banister, then plopped down on the sofa, "Well, I'm ready to eat whenever you are."

"Where's Khalil?" Monique asked, surprised to see her daughter roaming without her *bodyguard*.

She shrugged, "He said he hand something to handle, so he dropped me off and said for me to call when I'm ready to go."

DING! DONG!

Korena scooted to the edge of the couch and slowly got up as Monique rushed past her.

"Girl, sit yo pregnant ass down. I've got it."

"I'm not an invalid, you know." Korena huff.

Monique ignored her as she opened the front door to see Tyson and Brielle with her grandson, Tyson jr.

262

"Is that my T.J.? Gimme my grandbaby!" Monique reached out, pulling him from Tyson's arms.

"Hey, ma." Tyson greeted, holding the door open for Brielle to enter before him.

"Hey, son." Monique responded quickly, giving baby T.J. all of her attention as she walked him into the kitchen.

Brielle mumbled under her breath, "Went from not claiming the baby, to *hand me my grandson.*"

"Ay, chill out." Tyson scolded, hearing what she'd said, "Hey, sis."

Tyson reached down, pulling his sister up from the sofa into a hug. Brielle just stood off to the side with her arms folded.

"Hey, Brielle." Korena attempted to be cordial.

"Hey." She responded dryly.

Korena chuckled to herself, "See, this what I get for trying to be nice."

"Ree, please don't start."

"What? What did she say?" Brielle cocked her neck to the side.

Tyson put his hand out to stop her, "Yo, what did I just tell you in the car."

"Fuck that! I told you I wasn't about to sit around and let your family disrespect me. I didn't even wanna come to this funky ass, fake ass family dinner with people who accused T.J. of not being yours. Your mother didn't even have the decency to come to my baby shower." Brielle ranted.

"Whoa, whoa! What's going on." Paul came walking through the door with a bag of ice, "I stepped out for two minutes, what happened?"

"I don't know what's going on but I'm not tolerating no disrespect in my house." Monique came walking back into the living room.

"Man, I don't have to be here. Like I said, I didn't want to come in the first fuckin' place!" Brielle spat.

"Watch your damn mouth around my grandbaby!" Monique shouted.

Brielle sucked her teeth, "Give me my baby. Tyson you can either come with me or stay at your mother's tonight. Your choice."

"Come on, Elle. You're blowing shit out of proportion. Just calm down, it's not that deep." Tyson rebutted.

"No, I'm not about to stand here and be disrespected and disregarded by this bitter old drunkard nor this bitch who's just jealous that my nigga actually gives a fuck about me!" Brielle shouted.

Korena stepped forward, "What?"

"Yo, watch how you talk to my mom!" Tyson barked.

"It's alright son, I ain't worried about her. She's lucky she's holding my grandbaby, or this bitter drunk bitch would whoop her ass." Monique quipped.

"The baby ain't always gonna be with me!" Brielle challenged.

Korena stepped closer, "Hoe, are you threatening my mother?"

"Hoe? Bitch, if it wasn't for that baby in your stomach, I'd drag yo ass!" Brielle spat.

"That ain't gotta stop you. Try it, let's see what happens." Korena quipped.

Tyson stepped in front of Brielle, "Ain't nobody doin' shit to anybody. You're gonna calm down and apologize so we can have dinner like we planned."

"Fuck this!" Brielle huffed and headed for the front door.

Just as she reached for the doorknob it swung open and she jumped back, to avoid her or T.J. being hit.

"Why y'all look like y'all about to jump somebody?" Myeesha chuckled, stepping inside the doorway.

"Please, Eesh, don't." Tyson huffed.

Myeesha threw her hands up, "My bad…and here I thought I'd be late enough to *miss* the drama."

Brielle stormed out of the house and Tyson chased after her.

"What the hell happened?" Myeesha quizzed.

Korena shook her head, "I'm not in the mood. I'll tell you later. Honestly, I'm ready to go home."

"So, y'all just gonna fuck up my family dinner, huh?" Monique turned on her heels and stormed into the kitchen.

Paul followed behind her with the bag of ice leaving a trail of water along the way.

"How're you gonna leave when you're the one who convinced me to come. I was sort of looking forward to the possibility of getting one of Monique's famous half-assed apologies." Myeesha smiled.

"I know but I'm not in the mood anymore. I'mma just call and tell Khalil to come get me." Korena sighed, pulling out her cellphone.

"Hang up, I'll take you home. It'll be my excuse to leave, so I don't have to hear your mother's mouth."

Korena shrugged and grabbed her coat off the banister then they headed out the front door.

Mook walked up to the driver side of a parked car and tapped on the window.

The tinted window rolled down, revealing Tyree, "Get in."

Mook walked around to the passenger side and got inside the car. Tyree took a long pull of his blunt and then extended it toward him.

"Nah, I'm good. That's not my preferred vice."

Tyree shrugged and took another puff, "I need you on standby, ready to go when I send the signal."

"You know I can't guarantee I'll be available. I'm already on payroll which means I'm on-call for the organization first."

"So, you're telling me no?"

"No, nigga. I'm telling you I can't guarantee that I'll be available. But if you hit my line and I am, I've got you."

"Yea, whatever. If I call and you ain't available, you and me gonna have a real problem." Tyree warned.

Mook chuckled, "Is that supposed to scare me?"

"I don't give a fuck what it does to you, as long as you understand."

"Nigga, you've clearly been locked down too long."

"Just make sure you're ready to rid my house of two very big rodents." Tyree instructed, disregarding his insults.

Mook shrugged, "Just two? Fuck you need my help for? Why you ain't ask that nigga Mike to help you?"

"Because I'm asking *you*."

Mook burst out laughing, "Let me get the fuck out this car before you piss me off."

He opened the passenger door and stepped out the car.

"Answer when I call, nigga." Tyree shouted out his window.

Mook shook his head as he walked down the street, back to his truck. Once he got inside, he quickly pulled off while dialing someone on his burner phone.

"Yo, C. I know you don't want to hear this shit, but I think this nigga T.Y. about to become a problem"

"The nigga *you* vouched for?" Chris asked dryly.

"Man, I know I pitched the nigga, that's why I'm bringing it to you, now, before things get out of hand. I don't need you thinking I'm apart of whatever rampage this nigga is planning to go on. I ain't about to fuck up my bag." Mook huffed.

"Yea, whatever. He's your responsibility, so I suggest you stick close and keep an eye on him. If any of his plans fuck with my shit, you know what to do. But just know, you'll be held responsible for his territory in the event of his absence." Chris spoke sternly before ending the call before Mook could respond.

"Fuck. That's what I get for helping niggas out." Mook gritted, slamming his fist against the steering wheel as he sped through a red light.

Chapter Seventeen

Brynn James, Esq walked like a lion on the prowl in front of the courtroom, giving his closing statements to the judge and jury. He sported a well-tailored olive green *Yeboah Bespoke* suit, with traditional lapels to tone down his look for relatability.

"Esteemed members of the Jury, in the last few weeks you've heard and read countless testimony from not only experts in the field of policing and forensics but also the in-camera testimony of those who must remain anonymous due to finding themselves in such a threat of danger, due to the unscrupulous deeds of those delagated to protect and serve, under sworn Fraternal oath. During these proceedings you've not only witnessed the revelation of police safe houses found with copious amounts of drug paraphernalia and more money than many could hope to attain in a lifetime, given the income disparities in our great nation, but I digress. The evidence is insurmountable, proving that the prosecution is defending a broken system that's quite frankly operating the way it was designed; to capitalize off of those below the poverty line, those who've face oppression on all sides and to come out on top by any means necessary. Even if those means are murder, deceit, corruption or falsely accusing someone whose only crime appears to be being born dark-skinned, black and woman, not to mention queer. The duplicitousness runs so deep that it's only right a reckoning comes by way of the most disrespected demographic in America. And as you've witnessed with the dismissal of Count II: Murder in the first degree of Officer Shaw, another black body used as a pawn by this corrupt system, the evils defended by the prosecution can no longer prevail. But to make to bring this reckoning to full fruition, it will require the grit and bravery of those who make of the very backbone and foundation of this great democracy: You! I implore you to find my client Brenda Hanson, Not Guilty of Count I: Murder in the first degree. For, she was simply a victim of the very system you and your loved ones could be faced with at any given moment, and I'd pray that your decision today impacts their outcome in a positive way. That they do not find themselves cornered having to resort to self-defense or worse, losing their life to further the protection of a wicked system. So, again, we ask you for a verdict of Not Guilty on the count of murder in the first degree of Detective Johnson. Let us see the scales of Justice tip fairly in the direction of the real victims. Thank you, your Honor, the defense rests." Brynn exhaled, feeling accomplished in doing everything he could and now hopeful that it would be enough for the jury to return the verdict they desired.

He walked back over to the defenses table and sat down beside Brenda whose expression was a mix of hope and worry. He placed his hand over hers and for the first time she didn't retract it.

Judge St. Claire faced the jury, "Ladies and gentlemen of the jury, you've listened to testimony, reviewed evidence and heard closing remarks from both the defense and prosecution. It is now time for you to deliberate to deliver a verdict based on evidence provided and the law as I've explained it to you. You'll be dismissed to the jury room; you must select a foreperson then proceed with deliberations. Any questions or concerns should be written and sent through the Bailiff. You may begin."

Once the jury cleared the room, she addressed the courtroom, "Court is now in recess. Counsel, please remain close by in the event that issues arise, or the jury presents a question. Court is adjourned, pending the jury's verdict." She struck the gavel and then rose from the bench and exited to her chambers.

∞∞∞∞

"Korena, where do you want me to put these?" Tyson asked, holding a case of water.

She pointed, "You can put them in the kitchen, beside the cooler."

"Ma'am you're supposed to be upstairs getting ready." Maleah playfully chastised as she came walking in the house, carrying the cake.

"Hey, Korena." Xavier walked in behind her, carrying foil pans of food into the kitchen.

"Hey, X."

"Go upstairs, get ready and let us handle set-up." Maleah instructed.

"This was supposed to just be something small and intimate. We could've order pizza and wings." Korena retorted.

"Ew, no. There's no way in hell I'm letting my sister/friend celebrate her baby with pizza and wings from some hit or miss neighborhood spot."

Korena smiled and fought the joyful tears at the sound of Maleah claiming her as sister and friend, something she wasn't sure would ever happen again months ago.

"Yea, take your ass back upstairs and sit down until the party starts. You're still technically on punishment." Khalil shouted from the kitchen.

"Punishment?", Maleah sat the cake down on the dining room table.

"Mhmm…I'll tell you later." Korena whispered.

Maleah giggled, "Uhn, uhn I wanna hear the tea now."

Xavier walked up to them, "Once we bring all the food in, where do you want to set it up?"

"Set up the heating trays on the island countertop, so the hot food can be placed on them. Then, you can put the cold food in the refrigerator and crudité pans on the dining room table with the cake." Maleah instructed.

"Yes, ma'am. I love when you go into boss mode." Xavier smiled and leaned in, stealing a kiss.

"Ew, please. I'm nauseous enough these days." Korena joked as she frowned up her face.

Maleah laughed, "Alright go ahead. Once you bring the balloons and stuff in, we can start hanging stuff."

"Alright." Xavier nodded.

"Tyson, can you help him?" Maleah asked.

"Yea, I've got you." He came walking out the kitchen, eating a bag of chips.

"How're you in the kitchen eating, and you're supposed to be helping?" Korena questioned playfully.

"Man, look, after that shit between you, mommy and Elle I ain't had a home cooked meal. Mommy pissed and Elle be doing petty shit like just cooking for herself and buying shit I don't eat." Tyson huffed.

"Oop, what happened?" Maleah turned to Korena.

She shook her head, "Girl, I'll tell you later."

"Yea, tell her how y'all got me jammed between a rock and a hard place, because no one wants to act like an adult." He huffed.

"I said I was sorry, Ty. Jeez, I'm pregnant, the hormones be taking the wheel."

Xavier chuckled, "Come on, man. Let's go get this food."

Tyson sighed and followed Xavier out the house, and Korena made her way back upstairs.

"If you're coming up, kick them shoes off downstairs." Korena instructed, hearing Maleah behind her.

"Oh snap, I almost forgot." Maleah quickly stepped out of her sneakers and placed them at the bottom of the stairs.

When they got inside her bedroom, Korena sat at her vanity and proceeded to do a light face of make-up.

Maleah sat down on the ottoman at the foot of her bed, "Ok, so what the hell happened?"

Korena sighed hard, "I almost got into a fight with Brielle's bitter ass."

"What? Like a fist fight?" Maleah gasped.

"Yup. I called myself being nice and she gave me her ass to kiss. Then she went on a rant about how she didn't want to be there in the first place, calling my mom a drunk and talking shit about me." Korena shared trying not to re-anger herself.

"Oh uhn, uhn! What did she say about you?"

Korena sucked her teeth, "Some bullshit about Khalil not giving a shit about me."

"What that hell does she mean by that?"

"I don't fuckin know, but that shit set me off and I was ready to snatch her bald. She's lucky TJ was in her arms, because me and my mama was about to jump her ass." Korena sneered.

"I see why your ass is on punishment, now." Maleah laughed, "Your pregnant ass can't be out here fighting, like you're used to."

Korena sighed, "I know...I said it was the hormones."

"Khalil is going to lock your ass in the house."

"Trust me, he's trying to."

∞◌◇◌∞

It was early afternoon when Tone stepped in the side entrance of *Lou's* to find only a few patrons sitting at the bar, being served by a barmaid who was definitely *'Baller bait'* and another who resembled an older version of *Ronnie* from *The Player's Club*.

A light film of smoke filled the bar and the sounds of *Frankie Beverly's "Can't let go"* played at a low volume.

"What can I get you, sweetheart." The older one cooed.

Tone smirked at her audacious flirty tone, "Nothing. I'm good. I'm here to meet someone."

"Alright, well, let me know if you change your mind."

Tone adjusted the baseball cap on his head as he walked over to a table beside the front door which allowed him to see the entire room. After a few minutes, in walked Paul, headed toward the *staff only* doors. Going unnoticed, Tone was able to get up and follow behind him. But feeling someone behind him, Paul turned and was face to face with Tone. Once he removed the dark sunglasses he was wearing, Paul realized he was looking at the man he'd been plotting to kill for months.

"Just relax, I only came here to talk. Let's not make this a scene." Tone grinned, covertly flashing the gun in the front of his waistband.

"You know you fucked up, right?" Paul smirked.

"Let's go have a talk in your office."

Paul shook his head and pushed through the doors, leading toward his office. Once they were inside, he sat behind his desk and Tone stood by the door.

"Aht, aht. Keep your hands above the desk." Tone pulled the gun from his waist.

Paul threw his hands up, "Nigga, whether I shoot you now or later, your days above ground are limited."

"But why though?" Tone questioned.

"Mothafucka, what? Are you serious? You killed not only one but both of my fuckin' sons!" Paul spat.

"False."

"False?"

Tone nodded, "I only killed one."

"That's bullshit! I know Geno gave you the order to kill Rich."

"Says who? Your other son who was also on a rampage based on false information?" Tone challenged.

"Bullshit! The streets were talking; everybody knew you did it. The way he was found had you written all over it!" Paul barked.

"Nigga, do you hear what you just said? The fact that he was *found* should tell you it wasn't me. Shit, the only reason Chuck was found, is because circumstances weren't a hundred percent in my favor." Tone stated boldly.

"I don't believe you! Niggas knew that whenever y'all wanted to send a message to the streets, y'all would leave mangled bodies. Snitches without tongues and thieves missing fuckin' fingers; the way Rich was found." Paul refuted.

"Mothafucka, *you* were the thief! If Geno wanted to send a message, your dope fiend ass would've been the one found mangled in a fuckin' dumpster."

Paul clenched his jaw, irritated at the reference to his past struggles with getting high on his own supply. And the memory of how his actions led to the death of his son Rich also added to his internal agony.

"Maybe you didn't kill Rich, but I know for sure you killed Charles. And for that, you still gotta die." Paul gritted.

Tone smiled, shaking his head, "Now, Pauly you know damn well that's not how this shit works. The street code we live by states that it's *an eye for an eye*. If you come for me, it's going to restart the whole cycle, and I know you don't want that. Especially with your new lil' family you started."

"Mothafucka, you go anywhere near her, and I swear..."

"Relax, P. I have no intentions of harming your lady. I'm just asking that you reconsider your decisions regarding me. The facts are your son sent the order to have my son executed and I repaid that *eye* for an *eye*. Shit is settled now, no need to keep this going. I know it's painful, you lost both your boys, but you can't hold anyone responsible for that except yourself. Us street niggas must take responsibility for the karma we create for our families and hope that God will show them the mercy we don't deserve."

Paul sat silently ingesting his words, grinding his teeth in extreme frustration, "I can't let you live."

"Is that your final answer?" Tone asked, raising the gun and pulling out a silencer.

"You might as well, because as long as there is breath in my body, you'll never be safe."

Tone screwed the silencer onto the gun, shaking his head, "It didn't have to be this way, Pauly."

"Charge it to the game." Paul shrug coldly.

Tone stepped closer to the desk, "Any final words?"

"Just one question; if you didn't kill Rich, do you know who did?"

"That's not my truth to share. Not even with the dead."

TAP! TAP!

Tone quickly tucked his gun as the office door opened.

"Boss man, I'm headed out for the rest of the day." The young barmaid peeked in.

Tone stepped back behind the door, out of sight. Paul stood up from his desk and walked over to the door.

"I'mma walk you out, I need to talk to you about something."

"Uhm, okay. Is it something serious?" She asked.

Paul ushered her out of the room, "No, no it's nothing serious."

Tone huffed and slammed his fist against the door. He put his sunglasses back on and secured the gun in his waistband before sneaking out the office, in search of a back door.

BEEP! BEEP!

Xavier turned around from the trunk of Maleah's truck, holding a bag of decorations he'd forgotten to take inside. He looked and saw a familiar face in the passenger seat of a car, waving for him to come over. Looking around to see who else was outside, he quickly walked down Korena's driveway.

"Porsha, what the hell are you doing here?"

"Damn, hello to you too X." She sneered.

"You need to leave, this ain't the time or place for this shit."

"Just go tell Khalil to come outside, we ain't here for your lectures, nigga!" The woman in the drivers' seat shouted.

"Look, I don't even know you so you can chill out, talkin' crazy to me." He rebutted.

"X, I ain't leaving until I talk to Khalil."

The driver put the car in park and turned on the hazards. Xavier huffed, clenching his jaw, "Fine, just pull up a little bit, away from the driveway."

Porsha rolled her eyes, "Move up."

"Whatever." The driver reluctantly pulled forward in front of the house next door.

Xavier quickly rushed into the house, handing the decorations to Maleah, who was preoccupied putting together party favors.

"Kha, let me holla at you really quick."

"What's up?" Khalil asked, halfway up the stairs.

"Right now, man. Before we have a situation." He tried to whisper.

Noticing the concern on his face, Khalil walked back down the steps and stepped into his slides. He followed Xavier outside and down the driveway to the curb.

"Alright, what's going on?"

Xavier pointed toward the car, "That. That's what's going on. Nigga, you need to handle it before this baby shower turns into a baby mama brawl."

"Baby mama brawl? Don't fuckin tell me that's…"

"Yes. Go handle that. I'll try to keep the women occupied."

Xavier walked back inside, and Khalil walked over to the car trying to maintain his cool, despite the anger rising in him.

"What the fuck are you doing here?" He spat.

"We came to speak to the woman of the house!" The woman shouted from the driver's side.

"Porsha, didn't I tell you if you came anywhere near Korena, it'd be a problem?" Khalil gritted.

"I don't care! My child deserves everything you plan on giving hers!" Porsha shouted hysterically.

"Who the fuck told you that?"

Porsha rolled her eyes, "What? That your bitch is pregnant? It ain't like she been hiding it. Not like how you've been hiding *me* and this baby. But that ends now."

"Ain't nobody fuckin' hiding you! That ain't my baby." Khalil spat.

The woman in the driver seat started laughing, "I knew you were a piece of shit! I tried to tell Tyson but he's just so sure you're a solid nigga who's good for his sister. Wait til I tell T.Y. what you're out here doin' behind his sister's back!"

The wheels in Khalil's head began to spin, connecting dots at the speed of light and he immediately walked around to the driver's side of the car.

TAP! TAP!

He knocked on the window, "Roll your window down."

The lightly tinted window slowly rolled down and Brielle stared out with an attitude plastered across her face, "What, you're about to threaten *me* too?"

"I don't make threats."

"Yea, yea, whatever nigga. Call it what you want, but if you think you're about to scare me into being quiet like you did my cousin, you're sadly mistaken." Brielle bucked.

Khalil smiled devilishly, "I highly suggest y'all take your hoodrat theatrics and get the fuck on."

"Or what? You gonna make us disappear like my cousin Chelle? Yea, I know all about that. And as a precaution, I told my sister where we'd be, in case anything happens to either of us. Plus, I know Tyson is inside and if I call him, you know what that means...you're gonna have to deal with T.Y., 'cause ain't no way he's letting you press his baby brother. And based on what Ms. Mo's messy ass said when T.Y. came home, he had yo ass on mute."

Khalil took a deep breath and leaned into her window, "You don't know me well enough to feel comfortable making those kinds of threats."

"What's that supposed to mean?" Brielle leaned back from the window.

Khalil just smiled, "Y'all get home safe."

"Whatever, nigga! I could just come tell Korena myself or maybe I'll call and tell Tyson to do it." Brielle shouted.

Khalil stepped onto the sidewalk then stopped and turned to face Porsha. The smile on his face sent chills through her body. He winked and then turned back around, headed up the driveway.

"Khalil, wait. Wait! If I agree to let the shit with my sister go, will you at least take the DNA test?" Porsha pleaded.

He stopped in his tracks and sighed heavily then turned around, "Fine. But after that shit confirms what I already know, you better stay the fuck away from me and mine."

Porsha wiped tears from her eyes, "Okay..."

"I'll be in touch." Khalil nodded then walked back to the house.

"What the fuck, Porsha? Are you crazy?" Brielle barked.

"Just take me home."

Brielle put the car in drive, "You're really gonna let him get away with what he did to your sister?"

Porsha leaned against the window, tears streaming down her face, "I don't have any real evidence to prove he did it and...I've honestly been thinking it over for a while...if I have to sacrifice knowing what really happened to Rochelle, to secure my child's future, I will."

Brielle scoffed, "Wow..."

"I can't do anything about Rochelle, but I still have a chance to do something about my child's life! It's not about me anymore! It's about him." Porsha belted, rubbing her belly, "You should understand that as a mother."

Brielle sighed, "I guess..."

"Even if you don't, just please respect my wishes. And that means not involving Tyson and his family. I don't want anyone else to get hurt, I just want Khalil to do right by our child."

Brielle huffed, "Fine."

"Promise me."

"Yea...but if that nigga tries anything, I'm reneging on my word." Brielle pulled off.

∞∞∞∞

"Has the jury reached a verdict?" Judge St. Claire asked the woman who was appointed jury Foreperson.

She nodded, "Yes, Your Honor."

Brenda and Brynn held hands as the courtroom sat silent waiting for the verdict to be read.

"Please hand it to the Bailiff." Judge St. Claire instructed.

The woman passed a slip of paper to the Bailiff who then handed it to the judge.

"Will the defendant please rise." She instructed.

Brenda slowly stood, feeling like her knees were made of Jello.

"In the matter of the State versus Hanson, on the charge of murder in the first degree by firearm, we the jury finds…"

All of a sudden Brenda's ears started ringing and all she saw was the judge's lips moving as she fainted.

"Help, we need a medic!" Brynn shouted, knelt to the ground beside her.

"Bailiff clear the room. Let's get a paramedic in here immediately. Court is in recess until further notice. Stay nearby in the event we resume today." Judge St. Claire shouted.

Everyone filed out of the courtroom as Brynn knelt beside Brenda, shaking her.

"Faking a medical emergency won't change the verdict. But I guess, if she dies, you'll at least have a new martyr for your Black Lives Matter movement." Leonard sneered.

"Fuck you, Leonard!" Brynn spat.

"Counselors! Enough, before I hold you both in contempt. A woman has collapsed, and this is how you act? Shame on you, Leonard."

Leonard shuffled his stout frame out of the courtroom just as the paramedics were entering. They had Brynn step aside as they worked on Brenda and after a few minutes of checking her vitals and providing oxygen, she regained consciousness.

"There we go. Take your time." The paramedic slowly helped Brenda sit up.

"What happened?" She spoke through the oxygen mask.

"You passed out. But we checked your vitals, and it appears it was just stress related. However, I've advised that you receive a follow up check-up to assure nothing else is going on."

Brenda nodded, "Thank you."

"You're welcome. We're rooting for you." He winked.

The paramedics helped her up to her seat then packed up and informed the judge that it was safe to proceed before exiting the courtroom.

"Bailiff, tell the clerk to call everyone back, so we can resume." Judge St. Claire instructed.

After about thirty minutes the courtroom was full again and everyone had returned to their respective places.

Judge St. Claire struck her gavel, "We are now back on record following the unexpected medical emergency involving the defendant. After being given immediate medical attention and thorough evaluation, we are prepared to proceed."

Leonard stood, "Your honor, if I may. I would just like to say that the Prosecution is glad that the defendant is okay."

Brynn sucked his teeth and mumbled under his breath, "Conveniently when we're back on the record."

"Thank you, Counselor. That's kind of you." Judge St. Claire acknowledge dryly, "Will the defense please rise."

Brynn helped Brenda slowly rise to her feet and stood with her as Judge St. Claire pulled out the jury's verdict slip.

"In the matter of the State versus Hanson, on the charge of murder in the first degree by firearm, the jury finds the defendant...Guilty."

∞∞∞∞

Khalil and Korena stood in the backyard of her townhouse, holding a knife together as they prepared to cut into their cake.

Everyone shouted in unison, "Five, Four, Three, Two, One!"

"Oh my God!" Maleah squealed as they sliced.

Korena stood frozen as tears formed in her eyes and looked over at Khalil who also had a tear in his eye. He smiled and turned to her then kissed her sweetly.

Maleah rushed over, "Ahh! It's a Girl!"

Everyone shouted in excitement as the women rushed over to hug Korena. Xavier and Chris walked over to dap up Khalil.

"Yup, it's a girl. Told you this womanizer would have a daughter as karma." Chris teased, talking to Isaiah on facetime.

He turned the phone to face Khalil, revealing him and Keira holding their newborn baby.

"Well, at least our little Kyra will have someone to play with." Isaiah laughed.

"Congratulations, Khalil!" Keira smiled.

"Thank you! Congrats to y'all too. She's beautiful."

"You're up next, big dawg. You ready?" Isaiah asked.

Khalil sighed, "Ask me in a couple months."

"Don't worry, you'll be okay. And Zay is here if you have any questions." Keira chimed in.

"I appreciate it."

"Alright, we're gonna let you both go enjoy your celebration. Just wanted to say congrats, since we couldn't be there in person." Isaiah informed.

"Oh, and he'll be by to bring your gift sometime next week." Keira interjected.

"Alright, y'all go enjoy your newest edition." Chris turned the phone back to himself and they ended the call.

Across the yard, Khalil noticed Tyson coming out the house followed by two women.

"Aye, Khalil. They said they were family, so I let them in." Tyson walked over.

Khalil nodded, "It's cool, they are."

"Who're they?" Xavier asked.

As Kathy and DeeDee walked out on the grass, Monique walked over to them.

"You must be related to the dad; the genetics are strong." She pried.

Kathy smiled and nodded, "Yup. And you are?"

"I'm the grandmother of the baby. Or the *Mimi*, I haven't decided what I want to be called yet." Monique shared.

"Nice. Congratulations."

Khalil walked over with a look of concern, "Hey, everything good?"

"Of course. Why wouldn't it be?" Monique raised her eyebrow.

"No reason. Just a question."

Monique twisted her lips in disbelief, "Anyway, nice meeting you, what did you say your name was?"

"Kathy."

"Nice, meeting you, Kathy. Let me get back to my daughter." She sauntered away, "Ree! Cut me a piece of that cake!"

"Sorry we're late, I had to wait for De'Shaye to get off work and then we got a little lost." Kathy explained.

"It's cool. I'm glad y'all made it."

"Oh, um, this is De'Shaye. Your sister." Kathy moved aside.

DeeDee smiled awkwardly, "Hey."

"What's up." Khalil nodded.

"Y'all, uh, want to me Korena?" Khalil asked nervously.

Kathy nodded, "Of course."

"Sure." DeeDee agreed.

Khalil walked over and they followed as Korena and the women looked in confusion.

"Hey, can we have a second?"

"Why?" Monique questioned.

"Ma, just give us a sec. You've got your cake."

Monique rolled her eyes and walked back inside the house.

Maleah nodded, sensing the vibe, "Come on Eesha, we can cut the cake inside and plate it for everyone. Sky and Lisa can you check the food trays and make sure there's still water in the bottom pans, so nothing burns?"

The women all dispersed and Khalil took Korena by the hand, turning to face Kathy and DeeDee.

"Korena, this is Kathy and De'Shaye. My mom and sister."

She clasped her hand over her mouth in shock, "Oh my God. Khalil, you…"

"Congratulations. You look beautiful." Kathy smiled.

Korena dabbed the tears in her eyes, "Thank you."

"This is for you." DeeDee extended the gift bag in her hand.

"Thank you." Korena smiled.

"Who knew that night, I was talking to the mother of my future grandbaby." Kathy smiled as tears formed in her eyes.

Korena handed the gift bag to Khalil and pulled Kathy into a hug and the two women rocked side to side for a moment.

Khalil smiled, "Alright, alright. Come on, crybaby. Let them go grab something to eat and get comfortable. All the hot food is in the kitchen, you passed by it on your way out and the drinks are in the cooler."

DeeDee nodded, "Ok, thanks."

"Congratulations, Khalil...I'm really happy for you." Kathy placed her hand on his cheek as more tears formed in her eyes.

Khalil gently took her hand, "Thank you."

He looked away, fighting the urge to cry as she caressed his cheek with her thumb.

"Alright, come on DeeDee. Let's go see what they have to eat. I'm starving." Kathy smiled.

They both walked back into the house and Korena grabbed his hand, "I'm proud of you, Khalil. You make me more and more sure that I wouldn't want another man to share this with. You're gonna make a great dad."

Her words were the final straw, and the tears instantly began to flow. Korena reached up and gently swiped them from his face as he turned to hide his face from the party goers.

"Thank you, for loving me." He whispered.

She caressed his ear, "It's not as hard as you think."

"Ayo, Kha! Come here!" Chris shouted from across the yard.

He and Xavier were standing together watching with curious expressions on their face.

"Go ahead, I'm gonna go inside and check on the girls and make sure Monique isn't harassing your mom and sister."

"I love you." He stared into her eyes sincerely.

"I know." She winked.

He tapped her thigh and pulled her close, causing her to giggle.

"I love you too, Mr. Anderson." Korena kissed him sweetly.

They lingered for a moment the separate and Khalil watched her until she was inside before heading over to the fellas.

"What's up?"

"*What's up?* Nigga, who was that?" Chris questioned.

Khalil chuckled, "Nosey ass."

"Was that…your mom?" Xavier asked.

Khalil nodded, "My mom and sister."

"Oh, shit! You have a sister." Xavier smiled big.

"Nigga, how'd she go from *level three fucked up* to an invite to the baby shower?" Chris quizzed.

"Long story for another day."

"Man, I'm proud of you." Xavier dapped him up.

"Yea, man. Now, you just need to handle your other baby mama problem and you're home free." Chris quipped.

"Nigga, what's wrong with you?" Khalil looked around to see who was within earshot.

Chris chuckled, "Man, nobody heard me. And you're lucky nobody caught that close call earlier. You need to handle that before it blows up on you."

Khalil turned to Xavier, "Really, nigga? You told him?"

"He already knows what's going on, I ain't think it mattered."

Khalil huffed, "Yea, whatever. Anyway, that wasn't the biggest issue."

"What else happened?" Xavier asked concerned.

"Did you see who was driving?"

Xavier shook his head, "Not really, why who was it?"

"Tyson's baby mom." Khalil spoke in a low voice.

Chris chuckled, "Oh yea, this shit finna implode."

"This shit ain't funny, man!"

Xavier shook his head, "How the hell do they know each other?"

Khalil shrugged, "Fuck if I know!"

"So, what you gonna do? Because if Korena here's it from Tyson's girl instead of you…shit's not gonna go well."

"He's right, Kha. What're you gonna do?" Chris agreed.

Khalil clenched his jaw, "I'mma get the fuckin DNA test. Clear this shit up once and for all."

"And if it's yours…" Chris asked.

"I'll cross that bridge *if* I get to it."

"Alright…well I hope you ain't the pappy, 'cause if you think you and T.Y. got beef now, it won't be nothing compared to when his little sister comes crying." Chris added.

"Really? What happened to *you ain't gotta worry about T.Y. let me handle it?*" Khalil quipped.

"First of all, nigga that's not exactly what I said, and I don't sound like that. Second, relax. I promise I won't let the big bad T.Y. get you." Chris teased.

Khalil shook his head, "You're just full of jokes today, huh? What, you a comedian, now?"

"No, you're just a sensitive angry yellow man." Chris grinned.

Khalil sucked his teeth, "Fuck you."

"You two niggas are fools." Xavier shook his head, "Let me go check on my woman."

"You know what, that's a good idea. I'mma join you." Chris smiled.

"To check on *my* woman?" Xavier frowned.

"No, nigga. You ain't the only one with something to check on." Chris rebutted.

"Nigga, don't tell me you and her homegirl…"

"Gentlemen don't kiss and tell." Chris chuckled, walking away toward the house.

Xavier laughed, "That nigga is lowkey a menace."

"If that's what you wanna call it."

∞∞∞∞

Brandon checked his gun then carefully checked his surroundings before getting out of the car. He cautiously walked toward the warehouse and entered through the open side door, as he was instructed. Earlier that evening, he received a message stating that he was greenlit to work and that T.Y. had something he needed delivered. So, he was instructed to meet at the warehouse they'd met at before, to collect the package.

"Ayo!" He called out as he made his way inside the warehouse, which appeared to be empty.

Hearing footsteps but seeing no one, Brandon quickly pulled out his gun and surveyed his surroundings nervously. He walked out to the open floor and froze at the site of clear tarp covering the floor and a large cart on wheels, that you'd find in a post office.

"Drop that shit before I put two in your skull." A voice whispered.

Brandon quickly tossed his gun once he felt the pressing of something cold and metal against the side of his head.

"Yo, what the fuck? Is this supposed to be another test?" Brandon blurted.

"Shut the fuck up and walk to the chair."

The person pushed him in the back, and he reluctantly walked toward the chair in the middle of the room. Once he took a seat, he was blindsided by the butt of a gun being slammed into his head. When he finally regained consciousness, his vision was blurred, and he was tied to the chair.

"Wha…what the fuck?" He muttered.

"Finally, he's awake."

Brandon squinted as he tried to make out the face across the poorly lit room.

"T.Y.?"

"I'd ask you who's idea it was to try and set me up, but it's painfully obvious you're not the fuckin' brains of the operation." Tyree chuckled.

"Look, I don't know what you're talking about. You've got it wrong." Brandon pleaded.

"Oh really, do I?" Tyree walked over sporting a devilish grin.

"Yes. Man, look, I don't know what shit Niecy did, but I wasn't apart of none of it." Brandon professed.

"Hmm…even if I did believe you, you're still guilty by association and in T.Y.'s world, that's a punishable offense. And can you guess what the punishment is?" Tyree circled him like a shark.

"You'd really kill me for some shit I had nothing to do with?"

"But you do. You have everything to do with it. You and *Niecy*, if that's her real name, are a packaged deal." Tyree explained.

"If we're a packaged deal, then why am I the only one tied to a fuckin share with my head cracked? Why am I here and she isn't?" Brandon questioned desperately.

"Yet. She isn't here, yet. That's where you come in...you're gonna reach out to her on your burner; text, call, however you usually do and tell her you need to meet asap. That it's an emergency."

"She'll never believe that." Brandon huffed.

"Well, you better make it believable. Because if I have to go searching for her, I'm going inflict the same torture I have planned for you, on someone you love." Tyree threatened coldly.

"Why can't you just kill *her*? Why do *I* have to die?"

"Are you slow, dumb or deaf?" Tyree asked callously.

Brandon sighed hard, "Fuck it, if I gotta die at least she's going with me."

"That's the spirit." Tyree grinned.

He put on a pair of gloves then grabbed the burner phone from the floor beside Brandon's chair.

"I'm assuming this is her, since it's the only number you have saved."

"I don't usually reach out first, she usually just texts me a location when we need to meet up." Brandon shared.

Tyree shrugged, "Maybe that'll make the emergency more believable."

He got up and cut one of Brandon's hands loose, "Try anything stupid and I'll make your death slow and painful."

Brandon nodded in agreement then took the phone, "I don't know what to say."

"You better get creative, 'cause the clock is ticking." Tyree gritted.

Brandon paused for a moment then began to type quickly. Once he was done, he sat the phone on his knee, "I texted her *Emergency, call ASAP.*"

"Alright, now we wait."

After almost two minutes, the phone started ringing, and Brandon nervously picked it up.

"Answer it." Tyree instructed.

"Hello. Yea, I need your help. I was contacted saying that I was finally greenlit to work and that I needed to pick up some shit from the spot we met at before and deliver it somewhere but when I got here the nigga who's supposed to give it to me said he doesn't trust me and ain't giving me shit. I don't know if this is another one of y'all tests but if I don't deliver this shit, T.Y. says I'm dead."

He listened to the response, which was brief then ended the call.

"So?" Tyree stared, waiting for an update.

"She's on her way."

Tyree laughed, "See. Told you it'd work. Now, it's night-night for you."

He pointed the gun at Brandon's head, the red beam landing at the center of his forehead.

"Wait, wait! Can I call my family first?"

"Mothafucka this ain't death row, you don't get last wishes." Tyree sneered.

"No, it's not like that. You said it yourself, I'm not the brains, she is. And she's maniacal with her shit, collecting leverage on anyone she deals with. So, I need to warn my brother to get to my niece, in case she really didn't believe me." Brandon shared anxiously.

Tyree thought about it for a second, "I'm feeling generous today, so I'll give you 60 seconds."

Brandon quickly dialed his brothers' number, grateful that he'd memorized it while in jail, "Hey, hello! It's me B. Look, I don't have long to talk, where's Addie? What do you mean why? Just answer the question! She's with you? Okay, good!"

Tyree snatched the phone and ended the call, "Times up. It was nice not doing business with you."

BANG!

He shot Brandon in the side, clearly puncturing his lung because he began to choke on blood, gasping for air.

"Don't worry, I won't let you suffer long." He smiled.

Tyree waited another minute and then shot Brandon in the head. His body fell over, slumped in the chair and blood poured from the holes in his body onto the tarp.

"Dissolve his ass before she gets here." Tyree instructed.

Mook walked out from the shadows, wearing a white disposable biohazard suit. He proceeded to cut Brandon from the chair and then hoisted his lifeless body into the cart, dropping him inside.

"Damn, good thing the nigga already dead, because you definitely broke his neck." Tyree chuckled.

Mook shrugged, "The nigga is heavy and it ain't like you helped me lift him."

"Touché, my nigga." Tyree nodded, "I'mma go watch by the door for ole' girl Handle your business."

He walked away and Mook proceeded to push the cart with Brandon's lifeless body toward the back where the industrial incinerator was. After about thirty minutes, Tyree grew impatient and sent a text on the burner phone: *ETA?*

He went back inside to find the bloody tarp replaced and Mook nowhere to be found.

"So impatient."

He turned around to see Niecy's grinning face holding an AR-15. She was dressed in all black, wearing a tactical bullet proof vest. Letting off a few rounds, she caused Tyree to run toward the back of the warehouse, out of sight.

"Aw, don't run baby. I thought you wanted to see me." She taunted, firing more shots in the direction he'd ran.

Tyree fired back from the shadows, and she ducked down behind a steel beam.

"Come on, T.Y. you're way too gangsta to be hiding. That's for bitch ass niggas, like Brandon." She laughed, crouching down and firing more shots.

All of a sudden Tyree stepped out of the shadows and started shooting in her direction non-stop. Niecy ducked down behind the beam as low as she could, while bullets ricocheted all around her.

"What's that you were saying, bitch?" Tyree spat.

Niecy peeked around the beam and saw Tyree's shadow on the ground a few feet away. She carefully checked her gun then shifted to get a good shot when she felt something pressed against her neck.

"Aht, aht."

Niecy huffed and slowly raised her hands in surrender.

"Nice try." Tyree walked over with a devilish smile, causing her to try and see who was behind her.

Tyree removed the AR-15 from her with a wicked grin plastered across his face, "This'll be a nice addition to my collection."

Niecy's top lip twitched as she stared at him with pure vitriol and hate in her eyes.

"I guess crazy bitches really do give the best head." He chuckled.

Enraged by his arrogance Niecy swiftly leaned left and elbowed Mook in the eye, then forced the gun out of his hand. She took it and aimed it at T.Y. and he shot her with the AR-15, puncturing her neck and arm.

"How you let the bitch get to drop on you?" Tyree quizzed.

"Nigga, how was I supposed to know the bitch was G.I. Jane?" Mook huffed.

"Take her ass to the incinerator but remove the vest first." Tyree instructed.

Mook sucked his teeth, "Nigga, I ain't stupid."

"Could've fooled me."

"Yea, whatever."

Mook knelt down to grab Niecy, and she whipped out the tactical knife she'd covertly hidden and stabbed him in the shoulder.

"Ah, fuck!" He shouted, leaping back to his feet.

Mook pulled the knife from his shoulder then snatched the AR-15 from Tyree and proceeded to empty the clip into Niecy's body.

"Alright, nigga. She's dead! She's not a fuckin' zombie, relax." Tyree shouted.

Mook huffed and proceeded to snatch Niecy by her ankles and dragged her toward the back, where the incinerator was.

"Hurry up, nigga. All this gun play put a timer on us. Drop her in and let's bounce." Tyree shouted.

Chapter Eighteen

THE FOUR SEASONS HOTEL - MIAMI, FL
APRIL 5th

Korena, Maleah, Sky and Myeesha posed as Xavier took their picture on multiple phones. They were all dressed in bathing suits and beachwear, headed for brunch then the spa and planned to reconvene with the fellas, later at the hotel's pool.

"Alright, I got some good ones." He smiled and handed everyone back their phones.

"Thank you, baby." Maleah cooed.

He wrapped his arms around her waist and palmed her ass, "You're welcome, Mrs. Smith."

"Uhn, uhn it's my weekend. Save all that for y'all wedding. Which better not be until I drop this baby and this baby weight." Korena quipped, pulling her away from his embrace.

Maleah laughed as Korena pulled her toward the door.

"Hol'up, where is the rest of your bathing suit?" Khalil barked.

Korena sucked her teeth, "Puh-lease, Khalil. You're just now noticing what I'm wearing?"

"Hell yea! If I noticed it when you were getting dressed, I would've made you change." He rebutted.

She shrugged, "Well, it's too late now."

Korena was wearing a white, one-piece swimsuit with a cut out in the front exposing her baby bump, and the back was completely exposed. But that wasn't what had Khalil upset, it was the fact that it barely covered her ass.

"Uhn, uhn, nope. I saw you pack like fifty bathing suits. Go change." He demanded.

"I'm wearing a cover up." She huffed.

"And it's fuckin' see-through!"

"Khalil…" She whined.

"Korena."

Korena stormed toward the bedroom of their suite, "Ugh! You just want me to be an old, frumpy, humpty-dumpty looking bitch. First, I can't wear heels over two inches, now I can't show my ass. Mind you, this ass is how I pulled you."

"I love you too."

"Kiss my ass, Khalil!" She shouted from the room.

Myeesha chuckled, "Let me go help her, before she hurts herself."

Maleah went and sat on Xavier's lap, kissing and cooing flirtatiously while Sky took a seat on the sofa beside Chris and Khalil.

"You look beautiful." Chris whispered.

Sky smiled, "Thank you. You look handsome yourself."

After a few minutes and the sound of Korena fussing from the bedroom, she and Myeesha finally returned. She was now wearing a red two-piece swimsuit with a knee-length matching sarong tied around her waist and mesh white crop-top that said *MILF*.

"Happy now?" She rolled her eyes.

"Turn around."

She obliged and flipped the sarong up, flashing her ass to Sky, Chris and Khalil.

"Aye! Your ass ain't about to go nowhere, keep on playing with me."

"Come on, y'all!" She waved the girls over as she headed for the door.

Once they were out of the room, Khalil released a sigh, "She loves trying me."

"Nigga, why you ain't tell me Korena's sister had ass like that?" Chris blurted.

"Nigga, what?" Khalil turned to look at him with a confused expression.

The expression on Chris's face caused both Khalil and Xavier to bust out laughing.

"Nigga, why would that be something I share with anyone? I'm not lookin' at her ass." Khalil laughed.

"So, you're telling me you ain't notice that wagon she's draggin'?" Chris twisted his lips in disbelief.

Khalil shook his head, "Yo, you're sick."

"So, I'm sick, because I noticed her sister's ass is fatter than a Mississippi chick fed on cornbread and grits?" Chris asked with a straight face.

Xavier fell over laughing, "Yo, what the hell is wrong with you? Have you already started drinking, nigga?"

"I may have had a little *hair of the dog* to shake a hangover. I'm on vacation, first one in a while, cut a nigga some slack." Chris smiled and shrugged.

"Don't you drink nothin' else until after five, cause you wildin' nigga." Khalil laughed.

"How am I wildin'?"

"Cause you over here plotting on my girl's sister like you ain't fuckin' her friend."

Chris shrugged, "So! I make it very clear to any woman I deal with what my stance is on monogamy. Plus, Sky is engaged, she knows we're just having fun."

"That sounds good in theory, but we all know that fuckin' with women who know each other can be a recipe for disaster." Xavier chimed in.

"Can y'all niggas relax, I just said her ass was fat. Y'all the ones talkin' about me fuckin' her." Chris huffed, "I'm about to hit the bar, you two niggas are killing my buzz."

Chris got up and headed for the door leaving Xavier and Khalil shaking their heads.

"He doesn't need to drink." Xavier chuckled.

"Really doesn't. But yo I need you to do something for me."

"What's up?"

Khalil pulled out his phone and extended it to Xavier, "I need you to open that email and read the results. But don't blurt it out, just read it."

"Is this the DNA results?"

Khalil nodded, "Yea…"

"Damn, that took long."

"I know, they said some bullshit about the lab being backed up and things being tested in order of importance." Khalil explained.

"Alright…well, here it goes." Xavier tapped the phone.

"Wait, wait…just hold on." Khalil took a deep breath then exhaled, "Alright, go ahead."

"You're sure you wanna do this here? You don't want to wait until you get back?" Xavier asked.

"Nah, this shit gonna fuck with my head until I know. You know I don't do well with waiting; I just need to rip the Band-Aid off so I can white knuckle this shit."

"Alright…well, it says…" Xavier read the email in silence.

"What? What does it say?"

"Kha, that's yo baby, man."

Khalil leaned over and dropped his face into his hands, "Fuck!"

"We're gonna figure this shit out man, let's just enjoy this weekend and then when we get back, we'll make a game plan."

Khalil didn't respond, he just sat with his head in his hands.

∞◊◊∞

Tone put the truck in park in front of Jhana's childhood home. After a spending the whole morning and afternoon at *American Dream* mall's waterpark, they planned to have dinner with Jhana's grandparents. The girls had slept the whole ride back to the city and Jhana was in and out of sleep herself.

"Alright, come on sleepy heads. We're here." He announced.

"Come on, girls." Jhana tapped them.

Anaya and Anahj slowly sat up and stretched as Tone got out the car and opened the back to door to help them out. All of a sudden, a black sedan came skidding down the street and out jumped two white men.

"NYPD! Anthony Waters, we have a warrant for your arrest." One of the men shouted as he walked over with his hand on his gun.

"Warrant for my arrest? For what?" He challenged.

"For the forced entry of an establishment and intimidation with a firearm." The other officer informed.

"Oh my God, daddy!" Anaya squealed.

"Where's the warrant? Let me see it!" Tone barked.

"And while you're at it, show us your badge!" Jhana chimed in from the other side of the truck.

"Ma'am stay where you are." The man on her side of the truck unholstered his firearm.

"Oh my God, daddy he's got a gun!" Anahj shouted.

"Girls, stay in the car." Jhana instructed.

"You came for me, right? Point that gun this way. Take me wherever just get that fuckin' gun off my wife." Tone gritted.

The man reluctantly turned and aimed at Tone while the other pulled out cuffs and put them on his wrists.

"What precinct are you taking him to?" Jhana shouted as they walked him toward the sedan.

"You'll be notified once he's processed."

"That's not how this fuckin' works, you have to tell me something! You can't just take him!" She exclaimed.

"Ma'am." The trigger-happy man placed his hand back on his gun.

"Jay, take the girls inside." Tone instructed sternly.

Tears began to form in her eyes seeing the expression on his face. It felt like he was telling her this was it; the moment they'd planned for.

"No!"

"Jay! Go inside...I love you." Tone spoke maintaining his demeanor, unwilling to let the two men see him break.

"I love you too." She cried.

They shoved him into the back of the car as Jhana stepped onto the curb. When they pulled away, the girls jumped out of the truck and ran over to her.

"Where are they taking him?" Anahj asked.

"Is daddy gonna die?" Anaya cried.

"No, no...daddy's gonna be fine. Mommy's gonna take care of it." Jhana tried her best to keep her composure.

She took the girls by the hands and quickly led them up the steps of the house and rung the doorbell. After a moment, Mrs. Smith, her grandmother came to the door.

"Hey, baby. Wait, what's going on? Why's everyone crying?" Mrs. Smith questioned.

"I can't explain right now, Ma. I need you to take the girls and watch them until I get back." Jhana informed.

"Jhana, what's going on? Talk to me."

"Ma, I can't. I've got to go." Jhana left out the house, closing the door behind her.

She rushed to the truck and realized that Tone had the keys in his pocket when they took him. So, she ran back into the house.

"Ma, I need to borrow your car. Where's your keys?"

"On the hook, by the door." She shouted from the kitchen.

Jhana snatched the keys and ran back out the house and stopped at the truck, checking the armrest. She sighed, happy to see Tone hadn't listened to her and had indeed brought his gun. She pulled it out and put it in her purse then closed the doors of the truck. Once she was inside her grandmothers 2009 *Camry* she pulled out her phone.

"Please work, please work." She muttered to herself as she checked the GPS app on her phone.

Ever since their previous trip to New York, Jhana made a point to sew mini-GPS tags into the hem of his jackets, so she'd always know where to find him and she was happy to see the one in his jacket was active and reporting. Jhana started the car and quickly pulled out, holding up the GPS map as she drove.

"I'm coming, baby."

"Ramirez, Cap wants to see you in his office." One of the rookies shouted into the locker room.

Sean buttoned his shirt and made his way out the locker room to the captains' office. When he got there, he found Capt. Howard sitting with the head of Internal Affairs.

"Have a seat, Officer Ramirez." Capt. Howard instructed.

Sean took a seat, "What's this about?"

"It's been brought to my attention that you've been seeking assistance from one of my I.A. agents." The head of I.A. shared.

"Is that a problem?" Sean asked.

"Yes, when it is used to bypass proper protocol and roadblocks intended to assure sensitive materials are only accessed by those with authority and clearance."

"I thought as long as I had them notate who the information was for and the case it applied to; it was okay." Sean rebutted.

"Well, that's why we have handbooks filled with that very information, so you don't have to rely on your assumptions."

"You're right, I checked first. But the information accessed was necessary for the case you told me I could consult on, Cap." Sean challenged.

"A case that now has an additional homicide attached to it, since you joined. And not just any homicide, the murder of a witness whose identity was legally mandated to be concealed. Coincidence? I think not." Capt. Howard rebutted.

"Cap, you really think I had something to do with that leak?"

"The honest answer is, we don't know. And won't know until the investigation is concluded. So, for now Officer Ramirez you're suspended from duty. Hand over your gun and badge and clear out your locker. Your access to any NYPD system is suspended until further notice, as well as access to this building." The head of I.A. spoke mechanically, as if reciting from a script.

"Cap…"

"Now, Ramirez."

Sean huffed and removed his badge, placing it on the desk. Then he unholstered his gun and placed it on the table.

∞∞∞∞

Khalil and Xavier stepped off the elevator, into the hotel's lobby greeted by the unexpected sight of the ladies standing in the seating area. They were hovering over somebody, and Korena appeared to be cussing someone out, from what they could hear.

"What the fuck?" Khalil muttered to himself.

Xavier extended his arm to block him, "Let's not jump to conclusion and cause a scene. Let's just go see what's going on."

Khalil sucked his teeth, "Man, move."

Xavier sighed as he took long strides to keep up with Khalil. Sky turned around and spotted them with a look of terror on her face. All of a sudden, the women all turned around revealing Eric Yeboah's smiling face.

"What's going on?" Khalil grilled.

Korena huffed, "Nothing, we're fine. *Mr. Beans and Toast* here can't take a damn hint. My girl doesn't want you!"

"Baby, I'm fine." Maleah walked up to meet Xavier, placing her hand on his chest.

Xavier swiped her hand away and proceeded to snatch Eric from his seat by the collar of his shirt and slammed him into the ground. The women screamed as other guest in the lobby exclaimed at the sight of blood spewing from Eric's face as Xavier's fist repeatedly rammed into his face.

"I fuckin' told you I wasn't talkin' anymore, nigga!" Xavier gritted.

"Baby, please! You're going to kill him. X!" Maleah shouted trying to pull him by his shirt.

"Khalil stop him!"

He sucked his teeth then moved Maleah out the way and tried to pull Xavier from Eric but had no luck. All of a sudden Chris came running over and started helping. When they finally got Xavier off of him, Eric was lying in a puddle of blood, face mangled and a tooth missing from his bloody mouth.

"Oh my God!" Sky exclaimed at the sight.

"Leah, step over here. Let them handle it." Myeesha whispered, gently pulling her by the arm.

"Oh my God. What if he's dead?" She cried, "He's going to jail."

"Fuck! Let me call my lawyer." Chris huffed, pulling out his phone.

Cops came rushing into the lobby and immediately handcuffed Xavier then checked Eric's vitals.

"He's alive. I've got a pulse." One of the officers stated.

Maleah dropped to her knees and cried, "Thank you God."

Xavier looked over at her with shame in his eyes, "I'm sorry."

She nodded, "It's okay."

"Come on, Leah. Let's go change so we can meet them at the station to bail him out." Myeesha grabbed her by the arm, helping her up.

The ladies all walked toward the elevator as Khalil followed the officers with Xavier out the hotel and Chris talked on the phone, not far behind them.

∞∞∞∞

"Wake yo bitch ass up!"

Tone was startled awake by what felt and smelled like dirty mop water. He'd been unconscious since the *so-called* officers, who picked him up, pulled over to beat the shit out him while he was handcuffed.

"I knew them bitch ass niggas weren't cops." Tone spat as the water seeped into his eyes caused them to burn.

"You should've shot me when you had the chance, instead of trying to negotiate a cease fire." Paul stepped into view with a smug grin on his face.

"Hmm...so this was you, Pauly?"

Paul threw a left hook, cracking him in the jaw, "That's not my fuckin' name, nigga!"

"My bad, it's Paula. I forgot you used to turn a trick for yo *treats* back in your dope fiend days." Tone laughed flashing a bloody smile.

"Fuck you!" Paul threw another left, "I ain't never did no foul shit for my fix. I might've had a habit, but I had the money to maintain it."

Tone chuckled and shrugged, "You ain't gotta prove shit to me. That's none of my business."

"We'll see who's laughing when I blow ya' shit off." Paul threatened.

"Whoa, whoa! Pause. You're really not helping your case, Pauly."

Paul became enraged, throwing one punch after the other until Tone's nose started leaking as well.

"You hit like a bitch!" Tone spat a wad of bloody mucus in his direction.

"Mothafucka!" Paul pulled his gun and shot him in the thigh.

"Ah, fuck!" Tone gritted.

Paul chuckled, "Yea, not so tough now, huh? Where'd all the laughter go?"

"Fuck you, nigga. Just go ahead and do what you came to do." Tone barked.

"Oh, nah. You're gonna suffer the same way my son did. See, the M.E. report says he was shot in the thigh a few days before you killed him. So, I'mma let you rot down here for a few days in your own blood, piss and shit. Oh, and don't bother yelling, I've insulated the room so no noise can escape." Paul smiled maniacally.

"You better kill me now." Tone warned.

"Or what, you're gonna break free like the hulk? Nigga your ass is chained to a steel pipe and I've got the keys." Paul jiggled his pocket and laughed.

"Okay..." Tone spoke coldly.

Paul chuckled to himself as he walked up the steps of the basement. Moments later, Tone could hear the sound of locks being placed on the doors.

∞∞∞∞

As soon as Sean turned off his car, his phone started to vibrate. He pulled it out and huffed at the sight of the familiar number.

"It hasn't even been a full hour since my suspension, what the hell?" Sean sighed, letting the call go to voicemail.

He sat in silence for a while then reluctantly got out of the car and trudged up the front steps of his home. He slowly turned the key then pushed open the front door and walked into the living room to find his wife Amber sitting on the sofa with the house phone to her ear and tears in her eyes.

"Babe, what's wrong."

"It's your brother...he's dead."

It felt like the room started to spin as her words echoed on repeat in his head.

"He what?"

She jumped up from the sofa and walked over to him, "I'm so sorry baby."

"Nah, nah that's not true. He's just doing his usual shit, going ghost, posted up at some chick's house because he doesn't like the rules here. But he'll be back." Sean reasoned delusionally, trying to avoid the resurfacing memory of Brandon's cryptic call, the last time they spoke.

"Sean, no…one of the detectives from the precinct called. He said he'd been trying to reach you before the news released the story. Apparently, there was an anonymous tip about drug activity in a warehouse and they found…bone fragments and…teeth in an incinerator. And the DNA for some of it matched Brandons'."

He quickly opened his phone and played the voicemail, "Hey, Ramirez. It's Abrams. Look, I'm sorry to leave this on your voicemail but I wanted you to hear it before the news released the story and revealed the victims' names to the public. Apparently, they're going to try and make a big spectacle of this, connecting it to your mother's murder. Anyway, I'll cut to the chase… genetic material from your brother was found in an incinerator at the scene of an alleged drug den. Again, sorry you had to hear it this way but the jackass detective who was supposed to tell you waited too late and you were already gone. Oh, and I heard about the suspension…that's rough. But yea, my condolences. I'll also try you on the other number we have on file."

The voicemail ended and Sean stood frozen, staring straight ahead.

"Baby?" Amber moved closer to him, placing her hand on his arm.

Sean instantly fell to his knees and began to weep, "What the fuck man? First, mi madré now B!"

"I knew he was into some shit…all the coming and going, two phones and that fuckin' car he said his homie gave to him!"

"Really?" Sean looked up at her, "My brother's teeth were found in an incinerator, and you choose right now to bitch about him? He's fuckin' dead, Amber!"

"Don't frickin cuss at me! You knew your brother refused to stay out of trouble. Now, you're mad at me for telling the truth?"

"Jesu Christo, Amber!" Sean shouted.

"Fine, make me the bad guy." Amber leapt up from his side and stomped up the stairs like a toddler throwing a tantrum.

"Qué cojones!" He slammed his fist into the floor as he cried harder. "Válgame Dios…"

∞∞∞∞

Jhana pulled up at the last location Tone's GPS tag pinged. It literally stopped in the middle of the street. She looked left then right and saw a Bodega, Chinese store, Dry Cleaners and a bar. She quickly pulled over on the side of the bar and checked the gun's clip. Then she stepped out the car and walked across the street to the Dry Cleaners.

"Hi, I just came by to ask if you've seen this man?" Jhana showed a pictured of Tone on her phone to the Asian woman behind the plexiglass.

The woman shook her head *no*.

"You're sure?" Jhana asked, dropping the phone back into her purse and resting her hand on the gun.

"Ma'am my grandmother doesn't speak English well." A young boy came from behind a rack.

"Oh ok, well, have you seen him?" She pulled the phone back out and showed him the picture.

The boy squinted, "Hmm…not today. But some time ago, I think I saw a man who looks like him."

Jhana returned the phone to her bag and her hand to the gun, "Where at? Did he come him here?"

"No, he was headed over there." The boy pointed to the left.

"To where? The bodega or the bar?" Jhana asked growing anxious.

"The bar."

Jhana nodded, "Thanks."

She quickly exited the dry cleaners and made her way across the street cautiously, watching her surroundings like Tone had always told her to do. When she walked up to the bar, she pulled the purse up onto her shoulder and smiled at the security standing outside smoking a cigarette.

"You know those are bad for you." She flirted.

He chuckled, "I know, my mama been saying it since I started twelve years ago."

"You should listen to her." Jhana laughed, making her way inside the bar.

The security rushed behind her, "You just gonna walk in like I ain't right here?"

"Boy, you just trying to find an excuse to touch me." She quipped.

"Nah, it ain't even like that. It's just my job."

"You really think I came here to start trouble?" She smiled.

He blushed, "Alright, man. Go head. It's early anyway, ain't nobody really in there."

Jhana winked and walked inside. She locked the door behind her then turned to face the open bar where only a handful of patrons drank, served by one barmaid.

"Everyone, out! Through that side door, now!" She commanded.

The patrons and the barmaid looked at her like she was crazy, so she pulled the gun from her purse and fired a shot into the ceiling. People froze out of fear.

"Everybody, get the fuck out! Now!"

Immediately people leapt up from their seats and filed out of the side door, including the barmaid and cook from the kitchen. And Jhana followed behind them, locking the side door as the security man tapped at the front door.

"Who the fuck locked the door?" He shouted.

"Don't make me shoot you, nigga!" Jhana shouted back.

"This some bullshit. I don't get paid enough for this shit." She heard him complain, sounding like he was moving further away.

Jhana cautiously checked the kitchen then made her way through the staff only doors, listening to see if she heard anyone. Suddenly she heard the sound of a door opening, so she stepped back inside one of the open doors which was to the staff bathroom. She peeked out and saw a man coming out a door.

"Is my husband down there?"

"I told them they should've shot yo ass." The man sneered.

Jhana fired a shot, hitting him in the shoulder, "Where the fuck is my husband?"

"Ah, fuck! You crazy bitch!" He shouted, reaching for the gun in his waistband.

BANG! BANG! BANG!

Jhana shot him twice in the chest and once in the head. The man fell backward and she stood frozen for a moment, as her heart beat increased. She quickly shook her trance and then carefully stepped down the basement steps and squinted to see in the dark.

"Tone." She whispered.

"Jay?" He shouted.

"Oh my God, baby!" She squealed fumbling to get her phone out of her purse while holding the gun.

She shined the light from her phone and finally found him, in the corner chained to a steel pipe. He was bloody and smelled of urine.

"You came for me?"

"Of course I came for you! I told you I'd burn this fuckin' city down for you." She cried.

"Where's that nigga Paul?"

"The old nigga with the Kango hat?"

"Yea, where is he? You put him down?"

"Yea…"

"That's my girl. Did you get the keys?"

"No…"

"Go get the keys, baby. They're in his pocket. It's the only way to get me out these chains."

Jhana quickly crept back up the stairs and crawled over to Paul's lifeless body, sticking her hands in his pockets. She pulled out the keys and tipped back down the basement steps.

"Good girl, now get me the fuck out these chains so we can roll."

Jhana proceeded to feel for the padlock then unlocked the chains, and Tone began to unravel his arms.

"Alright, give me the gun." He instructed.

Jhana passed him the gun and he stuff it into his waistband.

Once he was free, she helped him up and he released a growl.

"Fuck! The nigga shot me in the leg."

"He what? Oh my God." Jhana gasped.

"It's alright baby, it's not the first time I've been shot. You know that. Come on, let's get out of here."

Tone put his arm on her shoulder, and they quickly made their way out the basement, carefully stepping over Paul and heading for the rear side door.

Once outside, Tone grimaced and used his hand to shield his eyes from the sunlight. Jhana hit the button on her keys to unlock the car then opened the back door and helped Tone inside.

"Freeze!"

Jhana huffed, "Not these fuckin' fake ass rent-a-cops again."

She turned to find real officers dressed in uniforms with guns pointed at her. She threw her hands up immediately and one of the officers mistook her phone for a gun and opened fire, shooting her twice in the stomach.

"No!" Tone screamed.

"Fuck, I thought it was a gun." The officer shouted in shock.

Tone crawled over to Jhana as she coughed up blood and convulsed.

"Call a fuckin' ambulance!" Tone shouted.

One officer immediately got on his radio and called for immediate medical assistance while the other kept his gun drawn, pointed at Tone.

"Fuck...I'm so sorry, Jay. I love you so much, please don't do this to me." Tone pleaded as tears fell from his eyes.

"I...love." Jhana struggled to speak between coughs.

"Shh...don't talk. Save your energy. You're gonna be okay. This ain't goodbye. I've been shot plenty times and look at me. I'mma stay by your side and nurse you back to health just like you did for me, every time." Tone professed as more tears fell from his eyes.

Tears flooded Jhana's eyes as she touched his cheek.

"I love you too." He whispered.

"Sir, we need you to step back so we can provide medical assistance." One of the paramedics interjected.

Tone kissed Jhana's hand then scooted back, so they could begin to work on her.

"Put your hands behind your back, sir." One of the officers instructed.

He followed their orders and one cuffed him as the other patted him down.

"Gun. We've got a gun." The officer announced.

The other officer pressed his radio and proceeded to update dispatch on the scene's details.

Chapter Nineteen

Judge Alana St. Claire struck her gavel, "Ms. Hanson, you have been found guilty of murder in the first degree by a jury of your peers. Pre-sentencing reports have been reviewed, counsel has been heard and the court has considered the statements provided here today, including your own."

Brenda nodded sorrowfully, fighting back her tears, while Leonard released a joyous grunt but quickly composed himself. Brynn just stared stoically and sighed in irritation.

"The crime committed was not only a violation of the law but a betrayal of the oath you swore, to protect and serve. Taking all factors into account, it is the judgement of this court that you be sentenced to 25 years to life."

Brenda's knees immediately became weak, and she braced herself on the table.

"Counselor, does the defendant require medical attention?" Judge St. Claire inquired.

"No...I'm okay, your Honor." Brenda spoke weakly.

"As I was saying, it is the courts judgement that you be sentenced to 25 years to life. However, given the defendants mental health evaluations and law enforcement background, it is the courts recommendation to the department of corrections that placement in a facility with appropriate psychiatric care and protective housing be considered. With that, sentencing in this matter is concluded and the defendant is remanded to the custody of the department of corrections to begin serving the sentence, as imposed. Court is adjourned."

Judge St. Claire struck the gavel.

"Don't worry, with the judge's recommendation I'll have you in a nice minimum security, private prison. I have a friend in the department of corrections who owes me a favor and a buddy I golf with who owns shares in a private prison in Connecticut. And once you're settled, where gonna continue to fight this." Brynn whispered.

The bailiff stepped around the table and placed cuffs on Brenda's wrists.

"I'm done fighting. I'm tired. If you can swing the private prison thing, that'd be cool. But as far as this goes, I'm done. Just let it go, Brynn. You did your best. I'm just part of your twenty percent." Brenda shrugged, emotionally numb as the Bailiff walked her through the secure doors to her holding cell, to await transport.

Brynn was stuck. Completely at a loss for words and unable to move from his spot; a rare instance for him. For the first time since law school, he was personally affected by the loss of a case. Somehow, Brenda managed to creep her way past his steel gate of professionalism. He felt like he'd failed her, and it choked him up.

"Good game." Leonard extended his hand in front of Brynn.

WHAM!

Brynn threw a right hook, sending Attorney Eisenschmitt flying like Jazz from the *Fresh Prince*.

"Bailiff! Restrain Attorney James." Judge St. Claire shouted.

The Bailiff quickly rushed over.

Brynn held out his hand to stop him, "Relax, big man. I ain't gonna hit him again."

"Bailiff, call for medical assistance. And to you, Mr. James, I am holding you in contempt and will be making the proper notifications to the bar. Now, remove yourself from my courtroom."

"Understandable, your Honor." Brynn smirked, satisfied with the sight of Leonard sprawled across the courtroom floor with one of his shoes missing.

"Leonard, Leonard!" Judge St. Claire shouted.

Brynn chuckled as he pushed through the courtroom doors, "Knocked that nigga out his penny loafers."

After sitting all night and half the morning in a Miami PD precinct, Chris's lawyer finally arrived and got Xavier released from jail on grounds of stalking and harassment allegations against Eric.

"Don't worry about this, I'll make a few calls and *Mr. Tea and Crumpets* will be glad to drop the charges versus facing the potential revocation of his visa." She smiled confidently.

Xavier nodded, "Thank you. I didn't get your name."

"Stephanie DeSoto. Here's my card. Any friend of Chris is a friend of mine." She winked.

Stephanie walked him out the precinct, where Maleah stood waiting with Chris.

"Oh my God! Baby!" She threw her arms around his neck and kissed him.

"Hey, baby."

She punched him in the chest, "Don't you ever do no stupid shit like that, again! You wait til you see that nigga on the street, not in the middle of a fuckin' hotel lobby with cameras!"

Maleah continued to punch and slap him in the arm and chest until her grabbed her arms and pulled he into him, kissing her passionately.

"I'm sorry I scared you." He whispered.

She sniffled, "You really did."

"I know, come here." Xavier wrapped his arms around her and hugged her tight.

"Nigga, you ain't even do a full twenty-four hours." Chris teased.

Xavier laughed, "Thank you, man. For real."

He stepped back from Maleah and the two men dapped each other up.

"You know I got you, nigga. You're my brother."

Stephanie waved, "Alright, my flight leaves in an hour and a half, I've got to get back to the airport.

"Thank you, Steph. Send the bill to my office and add your flight cost." Chris quickly hugged her, and she scurried off to her rental car.

"Where is everybody else?" Xavier asked, "I was expecting a larger welcome home party."

"After a twenty-hour bid? Nigga, please." Chris laughed.

"Khalil took Korena back to the hotel last night, so she could eat, rest and take her prenatals. Sky and Eesha left maybe one o'clock this morning. But it's a good thing Khalil and Ree went back early, because the hotel packed all our shit and put it at the front desk." Maleah informed.

"Damn, they did?"

Chris nodded, "Yup, but I got us a condo on the beach. That's where everyone is now."

"Alright, well, let's roll. I need a shower, a nap and something to eat." Xavier rubbed his stomach.

"Hol'up, this that nigga Kha calling me now." Chris answered his cell, "Relax, he wasn't in there long enough to become nobody's girlfriend. We on our way there."

Chris' smile was quickly wiped from his face as he looked over at Xavier.

"What's going on?" Xavier asked concerned.

"Alright. We'll be there soon. I'll call and see how soon we can be wheels up." Chris hung up then quickly dialed someone else, "Hey, Carl. How soon can we fly out. I need the soonest availability you got. Alright, hit me back as soon as you know."

"Chris, what's going on?" Maleah asked nervously.

"Yea, why we need a flight?"

Chris stared off in the distance, biting his bottom lip.

"Ay, man. You're scaring me. What the fuck is going on?" Xavier pressed.

Chris rubbed his hand over his face, "It's...Jay."

"Jay? Jay who? My sister, Jay?" Xavier questioned intensely.

Chris nodded his head, unable to make eye contact.

Maleah gasped.

Xavier walked over to him, "Look me in my eyes, Chris. What's wrong with Jay? What happened?"

Chris reluctantly turned his head and looked him in the eyes, "She was shot..."

"Oh my God!" Maleah screamed, as tears formed in her eyes.

"You're lying!" Xavier shouted.

"Nah man, that's what Khalil called to tell me. He said your grandmother has been trying to call you, so she called him to find you. To tell you that Jay's in the hospital in critical condition." Chris shared, hurt by the pain in Xavier's eyes.

"What the fuck? How? That nigga Tone assured me my sister wasn't in danger!" Xavier belted, as his chest heaved turning into a guttural cry.

He braced himself against the truck and wept. Maleah rubbed his back, as she cried with him.

Chris walked over to Xavier and grabbed him by the collar, "Your sister ain't fuckin' dead. Jay is alive! So, there's still a chance she could pull through. We just need to get back to New York and make sure them doctors know failure ain't a fuckin' option."

Xavier wiped his eyes and composed himself the best he could, "Alright."

The all hopped in the truck and Chris sped through the streets of Miami.

∞∞∞∞

DeeDee walked up to *Lou's,* just to see it with her own eyes. And there it was, a blood stain on the pavement and there was yellow crime scene tape on the entrances.

"Welp, it was fun while it lasted. On to the next." She sighed.

BEEP! BEEP!

She turned around and saw the passenger side window of a black Tahoe roll down, revealing Tyree's smiling face.

"What do you want, Smiley?" She rolled her eyes.

"You still mad at me?"

DeeDee sucked her teeth, "What? Mad at you? Nigga, you're the one who walked out on me and been ghost for over a month."

"That wasn't personal, baby. I ain't petty like that. I was handling business." Tyree grinned.

"Yea, whatever. Well, wherever you been, stay there. I'm better off." She turned her back to him.

"Really?"

"Really!"

"You know you miss me."

DeeDee looked over her shoulder, "You're still here?"

"De'Shaye!"

The base in his voice startled her but she played it cool. She quickly started making her way to her car when she heard tires screeching and Tyree stopped just inches from ramming into the drivers' side of her car.

"What the fuck is wrong with you, you lunatic!" She shouted.

Tyree hopped out the truck and walked around the front of her car, charging straight toward her. DeeDee stepped back nervously as he walked up on her, gripping her by the collar of her jean jacket.

"Why you got me out here acting crazy?" He whispered; his lips so close to hers his breath tickled her lips.

"I don't have you doin' shit." DeeDee quipped.

He chuckled, "I missed you."

"Whatever!" She pushed him and he released her jacket.

"You really ain't miss me?" Tyree walked up on her, packing her into a parked car.

"No." She turned her head.

He gently grabbed her chin and turned her face back toward his, "Yes you did. This little fake attitude proves it."

"Whatever, Tyree. You can't just ghost me then come back whenever you please. This ain't a fucking revolving door!" DeeDee quipped.

"Alright, fine. I apologize for walkin' away. While I *was* handling business, I can't lie, I was a little mad when you chose your cousin over me." He admitted.

"But I didn't choose! I told you I just wanted to remain neutral." She fussed.

"I know, I know…and after much consideration I realized I was wrong. So, if you're willing to forgive me, we can leave that shit in the past and focus on our future." He spoke lovingly.

"Our future? What future, T.Y.? We barely have a present."

"Then let's change that." Tyree pulled out a *D* initial keychain with a set of car keys and what looked like house keys.

"What's this?"

"The keys to our future. I've got a new house that I want you to move into with me and I bought you that Jeep you were telling me you wanted."

DeeDee stared into his eyes then looked away, "If you pull anymore disappearing acts, it's a wrap. I don't do third and fourth chances."

"I ain't goin' nowhere. You and me are locked the fuck in. *Welcome to Death Row Records,* baby." He grabbed her chin and pulled her toward him, kissing her with a rough passion.

DeeDee threw her arms around his neck, and he lifted her off the ground, carrying her over to his truck.

When Xavier and the group arrived at the hospital, they were informed that Jhana had been rushed back into surgery due to complications that arose while in the ICU. They also found out from the officer who came by, that Tone had been arrested and was being held without bail. Once Jhana was finally out of her second surgery, they allowed Xavier to visit her in the ICU and Maleah went with him.

"Jay, you gotta fight. I can't lose you..." Xavier knelt at her bedside as the tears flowed down his cheeks.

Maleah rubbed his back and prayed silently as she silently cried. The sound of his crying broke her heart in a way she'd never experienced. She wished she could take the pain from him but there was nothing she could do but be there for him in that moment.

"Are you the husband?" A doctor walked over to them, speaking gently.

Xavier wiped his eyes and stood, "No. But I'm her brother."

"Will her husband be arriving soon?"

"I highly doubt he'll be coming at all. So, whatever you need to say, just say it to me." He tried to suppress his frustration.

"Ok...well, I'm Doctor Mallory and I was a part of your sister's surgical team. I just wanted to inform the family of what we found during surgery. It's not easy to say, but did you know your sister was pregnant?"

Xavier shook his head, "No..."

"It turns out she was, but it's possible she didn't know yet given the size of the fetus. It appeared to be just about twelve weeks old, so just about three months."

"Oh, my goodness." Maleah placed her hand over her mouth.

"So, what happened to it?"

Dr. Mallory cleared her throat, "Unfortunately due to the severe trauma and blood loss, as well as the fragility of the fetus at this stage, the pregnancy wasn't viable."

"So, the fetus is dead?" He asked dryly.

"Unfortunately, yes. You have my sincerest condolences. I know loss of life at any stage can be devastating." Dr. Mallory spoke remorsefully.

"You could've kept that shit to yourself."

Dr. Mallory gasped, "Excuse me."

"X, baby…" Maleah rubbed his arm.

"No! Fuck that. My sister's hanging onto her life by a fuckin' thread and you came in here to talk to me about a dead fetus that was probably more like a blob of skin cells and underdeveloped tissue. You could've kept that shit to your fuckin' self!" Xavier barked.

"Sir, look, I absolutely empathize with you and understand your dealing with a great deal of distress, but I have to ask that you keep your voice down and refrain from that language. There are many people fighting for their lives in this ICU and they deserve respect." Dr. Mallory chastised.

"I need some fuckin' air."

Xavier walked past her and out the room, leaving Maleah standing awkwardly with Dr. Mallory.

"I apologize. This is a lot for him. His sister basically raised him." She shared.

Dr. Mallory nodded, "I get it…I've learned not to take much personal in my line of work. Grief and pain can be vicious beasts."

Maleah nodded and Dr. Mallory made her way to check on another patient across the way. After standing at Jhana's beside for a moment, Maleah peeked out into the hall but saw no sign of Xavier. Instead, she saw Khalil with a concerned look on his face.

"What the hell happened?" He asked.

"Go check on him, please."

Khalil nodded then made his way toward the elevators. When he arrived on the first floor, he walked out the main entrance to find Xavier pacing.

"Yo, X, talk to me. What happened in there? What did the doctor say?"

Xavier stopped and huffed, "Some unnecessary bullshit."

"About Jay?"

"Yea…she came to tell us that apparently Jay was pregnant but because of the bullets them bitch ass, trigger happy cops put in her stomach, it died." Xavier shared angrily.

"Oh shit…"

"Why the fuck did she have to tell us that shit? Who gives a fuck about a mass of tissue and cells? I'm worried about my fuckin' sister and the two kids she already has! Man, what the fuck am I gonna tell the girls, if she doesn't make it?" Xavier's rant unraveled into weeping.

Khalil pulled him into a hug, "Don't talk like that. Jay is strong, she's gonna make it."

He pushed back from the embrace and went to sit on a bench, "You don't know that, Kha. They said they had to cut out some of her intestines, trying to save her!"

"Key word, *save her*. Chris made calls and assured she had the best doctors tending to her, getting mothafuckas to come from other hospitals since she couldn't be transported." Khalil reassured.

"I don't know man…the shit looks bad, bro." Xavier rubbed his forehead, trying to massage away the migraine throbbing in his head.

"Look man, all we can do is wait and have faith like Zay be saying. A lot of people swear by prayer during these moments."

Xavier looked over at him with a confused expression, "Who the fuck are you?"

Khalil shrugged, "Niggas can't grow?"

"Yea, I guess."

"Why don't we grab something to eat. You ain't ate shit in over twenty-four hours." Khalil suggested.

"Man, I ain't hungry."

"You at least need to drink some water, before you pass out from dehydration."

Xavier sighed, "Alright, man."

313

They both stood up from the bench and walked back inside the hospital. Khalil grabbed five bottles of water and several snacks from the gift shop for Korena, who refused to go home until Maleah did.

When they arrived back at the visitor's room for family members waiting to visit, Khalil passed two bottles of water and some chips to Xavier. He reluctantly took them and headed back to Jhana's room while Khalil walked back into the visitors' room where Korena was sprawled out on the sofa and Sky sat across from her on her phone.

"Where'd Chris go?" He asked Sky.

"He literally just left out before you came, you must've just missed him. I think he had to take a private call or something."

Khalil nodded and sat down beside Korena, he lifted her head onto his lap, "You should've gone home with Eesha if you wanted to sleep."

Korena turned over and made herself comfortable, "Yea, yea…if you're gonna be my pillow you're gonna have to hush. My pillows don't talk."

Khalil chuckled and shook his head, "And to think I brought your ass some water and snacks."

Korena sat up quickly, "Gimme."

"Ask nicely." He teased.

She poked out her bottom lip and he leaned forward to kiss it then handed her the water and a soft pretzel.

She moaned, "Oh my God, I haven't had a soft pretzel in forever."

"Did you bring me anything?" Sky looked over.

"Of course, what kind of gentlemen would I be if I didn't?" Khalil smiled.

Sky walked over and he handed her a water and let her search the bag for whatever she wanted.

"Thanks!" She smiled.

"No problem."

Khalil watched in amusement as Korena dance around in her seat as she ate the soft pretzel and scrolled through social media.

PING!

A notification popped up showing she had a direct message from someone who wasn't her friend on social media. She nosily clicked on the profile and rolled her eyes when she realized it was Brielle. Swiping back the message, she was tempted to delete but the preview said *image,* so she opened the message.

"What the hell?" She mumbled to herself.

"You good?" Khalil asked.

"Mhmm…" She responded as she tapped on the image to enlarge it.

Korena gasped and immediately spun around, shoving the phone into Khalil's face.

"What the hell are you doin'?" He pushed her arm away.

She shoved it back, "What the fuck is this Khalil?"

"What is what?" He grabbed the phone and reviewed the image.

It was a picture of the paternity results from the DNA test he and Porsha took.

"You got that bitch pregnant!" Korena screamed in a rage, snatching the phone out of his hand.

"You are ninety-nine point nine, nine percent a DNA match! You see this shit, Sky?" She walked over, showing the image to her.

Sky gasped and looked over at Khalil with her hand over her mouth, "Oh my God. Ree."

"Let me get that back, really quick. Thank you." Korena grabbed the phone from Sky and hurled it at Khalil, hitting him I the shoulder as he tried to dodge it.

"Korena, calm down and let me explain."

She charged toward him, "Explain what? How you've fuckin' around on me?"

"I haven't been fuckin' around."

"You're a fuckin' liar!"

Khalil ducked and dodged her swinging fists, but some of the punches landed. Finally having enough, he grabbed hold of her wrist and pulled her down onto the couch with him.

"Korena! Calm the fuck down, before you make yourself sick!"

She struggled to pull away, "Fuck you! I'm already sick! Sick of you and your fuckin' lies!"

"I didn't lie to you! I haven't been fuckin' around."

"Then what do you call getting another bitch pregnant, while I'm pregnant?" She screamed in his face.

"Calm Down!" He barked.

The bass in his voice bounced off the walls and startled Sky, who was watching unsure of what to do.

"You said you loved me…why would you do this to me?" Korena wept.

"I do love you. And I'm not lying. I haven't been fuckin' around on you, she's almost seven months pregnant, Korena. The shit happened before we got together." He explained sincerely.

"What?"

"Yes…" He sighed, releasing her arms.

Korena sat in silence, processing his words, "How long have you known?"

"I just found out that baby's mine a few days ago. I didn't want to tell you on your birthday trip, but I was going to tell you." Khalil professed sincerely.

"No…how long have you known she was pregnant? I saw the date of the results in the photo." Korena rebutted.

Khalil looked away and sighed, "I didn't think the baby was mine, so I didn't think it was necessary to get you worked up over nothing."

"How long, Khalil!" She shouted.

He huffed, "Since January."

"You've known for months, and you never said shit?"

"Korena, you weren't in the best head space when I found out and like I said, I didn't believe it was mine."

"Was there no moment in the last month where you thought it might be okay to finally tell me or was I just going to meet your fuckin' bastard child one day at your got'damn funeral?" Korena shouted hysterically.

"Korena! Calm. Down."

Korena tried to steady her breathing as tears poured from her eyes, "This is so fuckin' embarrassing."

She stood up from the seat and Khalil grabbed her arm.

"Where are you going?"

She snatched away, "To the bathroom, if that's okay!"

"I'mma come with you." He asserted.

"No! I need a fuckin' second, Khalil. Damn." Korena headed for the door.

"You want me to come with you, Ree?" Sky asked.

"No. I need to be by myself for a second. I'd like some time to process my humiliation without an audience."

Korena left out of the room and walked down the hall where the bathroom and elevators were.

"I'm going to go...I'll call and check in with everyone later." Sky awkwardly stood up and left out the room.

Khalil leaned over with his face in his hand, overcome with emotion from everything happening. He let a few tears fall just as he heard the door open, and Chris walked in.

"What the hell happened in here? Something happened with Jay while I was gone?" He asked concerned.

"Nah, no new update since you left."

"Then why the fuck you look like that?"

Khalil shook his head, "She knows..."

"Huh? She knows? Oh...oh shit! You told her?"

"No. That bitch baby mama of Tyson sent her a picture of the results in a fuckin' DM!" Khalil gritted.

"Daaaamn...that's fucked up. She must really hate you or your girl." Chris grimaced.

Khalil clenched his teeth so tight he could crack a molar. In a spontaneous fit of rage he slammed his fist into the wall beside him, leaving a dent.

"Fuck!"

"Nigga, come on man. You can't be fuckin' up the property. I just got one of y'all out of jail less than twenty-four hours ago."

"Why does every fucked-up thing have to happened at the exact same time? Can a nigga catch a fuckin' break?" Khalil shouted at the ceiling.

"Nigga, who you talkin' to? Thought you don't bang with God." Chris quipped.

"Man, fuck you..." Khalil huffed.

317

Chris shrugged, "I'm just sayin', you were really disrespectful a couple of months ago to the Big Man and shit been rolling downhill ever since."

Khalil sucked his teeth, "That's not how that shit works."

"How would you know?"

"Because…I've been talkin to Zay since the baby shower, getting advice about dad shit and he's been making some solid points about…God."

"Oh wow…like what?" Chris quizzed.

"I'm not about to share if you're going to be an asshole the whole time."

"Look at the resident asshole asking for empathy. You really have been talking to Zay." Chris chuckled.

"Man, whatever. Never mind."

"Nah, go ahead. For real, I wanna hear what you've learned. Enlighten me."

Khalil exhaled hard, "He just started putting shit in perspective for me…I also thought God was punishing me for the shit I said back at the hospital, but he helped me see how God will use the fucked-up stuff to be a bridge to good, if we let it."

"I don't think you're supposed to cuss while referencing God but continue."

"Man, whatever. I'm new to this shit. But anyway, it had me looking at my life different. Realizing how I wouldn't be who I am without the bad…stuff. I wouldn't have the hustle I do, know how to handle myself in the streets, know what kind of father not to be and most importantly I wouldn't have met y'all niggas. My brothers." Khalil shared sincerely.

"Damn. That's deep. I guess Zay's lil Menstruation Ministries ain't half-bad." Chris smirked.

Khalil laughed, "You stay bringing up old shit."

"Nah, I'm just the grio of the group. I hold all the history so y'all niggas never forget where you come from or when you owe me money."

Khalil sucked his teeth, "Yea, whatever. You'll get your money for that game, even though the refs cheated."

"I ain't worry. You'll be getting an invoice very soon."

"Whatever. Let me go check on my girl in the bathroom." Khalil stood up.

"Bathroom? When I saw her, she was getting on the elevator." Chris shared.

"She left?"

"I guess, unless she was headed to the gift shop."

Kahlil huffed, pulling out his phone and dialing her, "Fuck, it's going straight to voicemail."

"Either her phone is dead or she blocked you."

"Fuck! I don't need her hormonal pregnant ass doing something crazy." Khalil paced.

"Go see where she's at, I'll let X know you stepped out if he asks and I'll hit you up if anything changes with Jay."

"Alright, good looking out." Khalil dapped him up then hurried out the room.

"And this is exactly why I don't do relationships. Too much fuckin' drama."

<u>EPILOGUE</u>

Brenda leaned against the window of the prison bus and each bump in the road caused her head to collide with the metal gate covering it. She was on her way to *Attica*, having been let down yet again by the infamous Brynn James, esq.

All of a sudden, the bus came to a screeching halt, throwing her into the seat in front of her. The sound of a gun went off and a bullet hole appeared in the bullet-proof glass of the front window. The driver fell over, and the guards drew their weapons.

"Everyone, stay seated and don't fuckin' move." One of the shouted.

Another guard at the front of the bus stood up and turned toward the other and shot him in the head.

"Oh fuck." Brenda gasped, sliding down in her seat.

"Alright, everybody off. This is the last stop!" The guard yelled.

Some of the prisoners cheered while others were terrified as the guard walked to the front of the bus, opening the door. Brenda remained ducked down as she heard the sound of inmates running off the bus.

"Get the fuck off the bus!"

Brenda looked up to see the guard towering over her. He grabbed her by the collar and dragged her off the bus.

"Y'all are all free." One of the inmates announced, she appeared to be in on the escape, "Except her, she helped her pedophile boyfriend lure little girls."

One of the masked men in black turned and shot the woman in the head.

"Alright, now you're free to go." She waved.

320

The inmates had all been uncuffed were all running in different directions, while one woman sat on the ground beside the bus and Brenda stood beside her.

"You didn't hear me?" The ringleader inmate walked over to the woman.

"I have nowhere to go." The woman shrugged.

"Well, you can either find somewhere or die here. But there will be no witnesses when the cops arrive."

The woman shrugged, "Then I guess I die."

"I like a woman who stands her ground. Omega, Gimme the Glock."

One of the masked men handed her the gun and she shot the woman in the head.

Brenda stood composed despite her heart beating out her chest.

"You're the cop, right?"

"Look, I won't say shit. I just want to do my time in peace." Brenda stated calmly.

"Didn't you hear the options?"

Brenda shrugged, "I did, but I didn't like them."

"Badass Lawwoman til the end. I respect that."

"So, what, you're going to shoot me now? I've got twenty-five to life, you'd be doing me a favor." Brenda quipped.

"Lady, I gave you the chance to run free."

"So, you can pick me off for sport? I heard you say there will be no witnesses, yet you just let a ton go and judging by your military bravado, I'd say you've seen war and never really came back. I've met plenty sociopaths like you, who treat killing like a game. Joining the military or law enforcement to exercise your trigger finger without consequence. That is until you're dishonorably discharged and get sent back to civilian life, where there *are* consequences."

The woman tucked the gun under her arm and proceeded to clap, "I like you. I'm not going to kill you, like the others. Charlie, Alpha, put her in the truck and let's roll out."

Two of the masked men grabbed her and carried her to their black SUV, tossing her inside before sitting on either side of her. The third masked man started the engine as the ringleader hopped in the passenger seat.

321

Brenda huffed, "Where the fuck are we going?"

"Mexico, my darling!"

"From New York? We'll be caught before we make it to Pennsylvania."

The woman turned around in her seat and smiled at Brenda, "Who said we're driving?"

∞◇∞◇∞

Chris sat down at the visitor's window and picked up the phone. Tone picked up the phone as well, on his side.

"How was the funeral?" Tone asked.

"It was nice."

"It's fucked up they ain't let me attend."

Chris sighed, "I really tried to make that shit happen, but the warden is a racist son of a bitch."

"Aye, chill. They listen in on some of the calls and I don't need them fuckin' with me."

"My bad. How're you holdin' up?"

Tone shrugged, "Fuckin' rotten away mentally…every time I close my eyes, I see her body on the ground.

Chris sighed, "Man, why the fuck you ain't just leave shit alone, like I told you."

"Cause I'm a man, nigga. And a man handles his responsibilities and protects his family." Tone gritted.

"Doesn't look like you accomplished that."

"Man, fuck you! You don't know shit! I did what I thought was necessary so my kids would be safe. They were begging me to come to New York and every time I told them no, I saw their love for me fading." Tone explained sorrowfully.

"Don't put this on them…you decided to do what Tone wanted to do, despite wise counsel."

"Fuck it, you're right. I fucked up and now I have to live with that."

"And your kids have to live without their parents."

Tone swiped tears from his eyes, "Maybe they'll be better off with X and his girl. They can have a normal life instead of the façade I tried to create."

"Maybe." He stared at Tone for a moment then sighed, "Keep your head up, OG. Watch your body and don't trust anyone. I'll make sure your books and commissary stay stacked. See you in Ten."

Chris hung up then stood up from his seat. Tone hung up his phone as well and wiped his face then straightened up his demeanor.

"Korena, where the fuck are you?" Khalil shouted into the car phone.

It'd been over a month, and no one would tell him where she was. Her mother, Myeesha and Tyson all said they didn't know where she was, but they said they'd spoken to her briefly, when she'd call to check in. Myeesha advised that he give her time, which was the same thing Isaiah said but he was losing his patience. Between her disappearance and Jhana's death, it was starting to affect his ability to execute at work. And with Xavier taking a sabbatical to tend to his nieces, Khalil was spiraling trying to hold things down while worrying about his almost seven-month pregnant, missing woman.

VRRRRRB!

He quickly pressed *answer* on the CarPlay screen, "Korena?"

"No, it's me, Porsha. You know, your other baby's mother? I just thought you'd like to know that I'm in active labor!" Porsha spat.

The call quickly ended just as Porsha was screaming her way through a contraction.

"What the fuck!"

Khalil made a hard right, speeding toward the hospital she'd told him she planned to give birth at, while trying to call her back.

"One, two, three…" Xavier counted as he and the girls held an Urn of Jhana's ashes and poured them over the side of the yacht.

Some of the ashes fell to the ocean below while the rest blew away with the breeze, as they sailed the crystal blue waters of Antigua and Barbuda.

Anaya clung to his left side as Anahj stood to his right, holding onto Maleah's hand.

"I'm gonna miss her." Anaya cried as she buried her face into his side.

"Me too, Naya. But she's always with us, watching over us from heaven." Xavier pulled her in tight.

"And we get to hold her tight in our memories and in our hearts." Maleah added.

"It's not fair!" Anahj cried out.

"I know, sweetheart…" Maleah pulled Anahj into her arms.

Xavier and Maleah spent every day since Jhana's death, consoling the girls through the ebbs and flows of their grief. Answering questions as best they could and really making a team effort to support them and one another.

Despite the unfortunate and undesirable circumstances, Xavier had to admit that Maleah's presence during one of the worst moments of his life, solidified his decision to marry her. While he was sure before, he found himself reassured, beyond the shadow of a doubt.

Once the twins were finally in bed, rocked to sleep by the ocean's natural lullabies and the gentle rock of the yacht, Maleah and Xavier laid out on the day bed at the port of the ship, staring out at the beautiful Caribbean sunset.

"You're sure about this?" Maleah asked him.

"Yea…she doesn't use a cellphone, and I can't tell my mother that her only daughter is gone, in a post-card."

"I feel you…just checking to see where your heads at."

"I appreciate that, baby." Xavier kissed her on the forehead.

Maleah sighed, "And look at the bright side, we finally get to take that cruise we've been talking about."

∞∞◇◇∞

"These fuckin' black American bastards think they can punk me? They think they're fuckin' gangsta but mans don't know nothin' about real gangsta shit. Take them through our fuckin' ends, through the estates and they'd be shaking in their fuckin' boots!" Eric Yeboah shouted angrily into his phone.

He sat behind his large Acacia wood desk sipping from a crystal glass of scotch. Majority of his face had healed, visibly, despite the fractures below the surface. However, he was still without a replacement tooth, distorting his once alluring grin. And to make matters worse, the place where his forehead was split open, healed poorly, leaving him with a nasty scar above his left eyebrow.

"What time do you land?" He inquired calmly.

"Flight lands around seven, tomorrow evening." The man on the other end of the phone responded.

"And you've sent for Osmond and Bohannan?" Eric smiled devilishly, revealing his missing tooth.

"Their flight out of Ghana is tomorrow evening, so they'll arrive a day after us."

"Perfect."

THE END...

(for now)

SATIN & STONE II

SATIN & STONE II

SATIN & STONE II

COMING
SOON!

audible

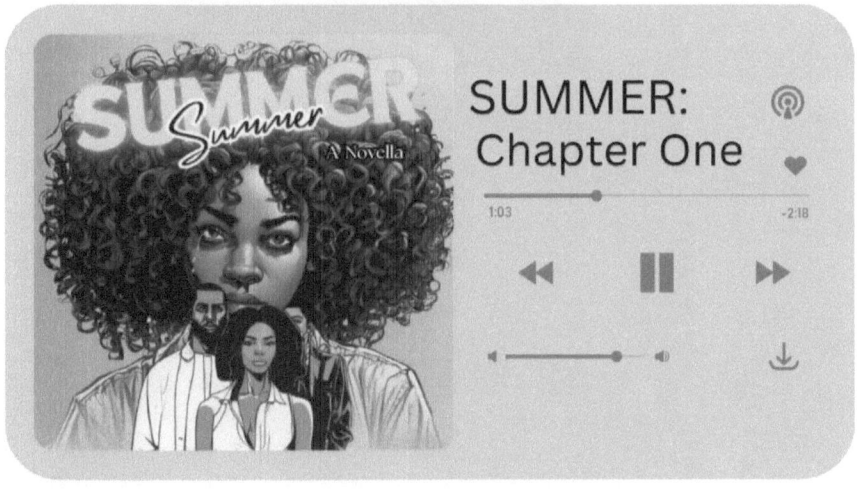

SUMMER:
Chapter One

1:03   -2:18